HELL AW

Then those shutters crashed inward and something was outlined horrifically against the stars.

An oath was torn from the sell-sword's lips—"*Yod and Vrooman!*"

Crouched there at the window was something unmistakably evil. Where it clung, talons scrabbled, leaving deep gauges in the thick wood. Gunthar had a fleeting glimpse of burning eyes and dark leathery wings sprouting from naked ebon skin hard as iron before it launched itself into the room. Then he was battling desperately for his life.

Paralysed with fear, any ordinary man would have died right there under those steely, slashing talons. But Gunthar was no ordinary man. He had been raised on the bitter escarpments of Tatukura where every moment was a bleak struggle for existence against inhospitable odds. Not for nothing had the steppe riders named him the Black Wolf. Now, as the demon grappled with him in the darkness, he braced the whole strength of his iron corded body against its ravening attack. Snarling in fury, his sword wove a defiant web of steel around him as giant wings beat terrifically in the dark. Talons clawed agonizingly down the length of his back and blood ran in scarlet rivulets over his torn flesh. But he struggled on, his indomitable will refusing to break before this summoned creature of the outer hells...

From – 'The Devil from Beyond.'

GUNTHAR
Warrior of the Lost World

STEVE DILKS.

A Carnelian Press publication.

This book is dedicated to-
Steve 'Macky' McAlinden.

'Prietess of the Fire-Gods' originally appeared under the title-
GUNTHAR: THE PURPLE PRIESTESS OF ASSHTAR (2013).
'The City of the Black Flame' originally appeared under the title-
GUNTHAR AND THE JAGUAR QUEEN (2013).

Gunthar: Warrior of the Lost World.
© Steve Dilks 2019.
Cover art © by Régis Moulun.
Interior art © by Steve Lines.
Carnelian Press.
All rights reserved.
This edition © 2020.

CONTENTS

Priestess of the Fire-Gods *(w/Glen Usher)* 9

The City of the Black Flame 51

The Devil from Beyond 117

Lord of the Black Throne 209

PRIESTESS OF THE FIRE-GODS *

* with Glen Usher.

I - THE THEFT OF THE IDOL.

It was midnight when a young acolyte of the deathless god Yorm noticed the sacred idol was missing. The gong sounded furiously throughout the temple, bringing a swarm of yellow-robed priests spilling into the grounds, scimitars clenched in swarthy fists.

They came charging up the winding staircase of the main tower until, at last, they reached the sanctum of the idol itself.

It was an elder priest who pointed to the effigy of the monstrous statue. The others, turning to where he indicated, gaped in amazement. The space beneath the statue's grossly carved belly, where usually resided the figurine of Yorm's blasphemous offspring, was empty.

The long tapers in the chamber cast only murky shadows but there was no doubting that sacrilegious theft.

There was a stunned silence. Then a priest cried out and they all turned, blades reflecting what moonlight filtered through the tower's open apertures.

They saw, standing on the jade floor behind them, a tall figure. He was dark, not swarthy like the priests or the squat men of the granite wastes, but bronzed; as from the light of fierce suns. Beneath a tangled shock of yellow hair, eyes danced like blazing emeralds, mocking and devilish. He was naked but for a pair of high strapped sandals and a red silk breechclout. Over one shoulder a leather satchel was slung and in his right hand he held a curved sword, such as the riders of the steppes carried into battle.

He was frozen in the act of padding across the floor to the stairway behind. Now a score of voices were raised in outrage and the yellow robed priests of Yorm rushed him, scimitars thirsting for his lifeblood.

The tall figure of the man hesitated a moment, then, with a cat-like bound, was among them. Swords slashed and robes whirled; shouts echoing furiously throughout the tower chamber. Then the half naked figure was through them, his own curved blade flashing and trailing crimson, his strong white teeth bared in a fighting smile. Three corpses fell to the floor but the rest surged on, their blades crying out an angry song of vengeance as they surrounded him. Seeing a gap in the press he bounded out from among them, weaving his sword in a glittering arc to avoid the cold touch of death.

He backed into a corner, severing the tops of the tall candles as he passed. The tower was plunged into darkness.

Priests stumbled over themselves, and each other, as they reached the spot where he had just been. Their blades cleaved only empty air and they fell back, cursing the darkness.

A low laugh echoed throughout the tower. They whirled to see him standing high up on an aperture, his lean figure outlined against the stars. As they rushed forward he turned, leaping far out into the night. Reaching the sill they craned over and, looking down, saw him sprinting through the gardens below.

An elder priest curled his lips in a sinister smile. "Fool!" he whispered and there was a note of finality in his tone, "You may have lifted the sacred idol from its resting place—but none have escaped the death gardens of Yorm!"

II - THE INN OF THE SLEEPING DRAGON.

Gunthar ran along the gravel pathway that wound through all three tiers of the magnificent gardens. The pathway was bordered by columns and plinths, each one representing a loathsome deity from the pantheon of Yorm's obscene kindred gods. It seemed to him, as he passed, that each misshapen visage was more loathsome than the last.

The gardens were ornate and gorgeous; every inch tended to perfection by the Order. Each tier was marked by the boundary of a low brick wall descending to the next level.

Gunthar's powerful legs carried him over the first wall down into the next, some ten feet below. His upbringing in a land of mountainous terrain made him no stranger to feats of cat-like agility.

He had seen no sign of pursuit, but was wily enough to stick to the gravel path and not seek cover of the shadowy fronds. He knew the reputation of the priests in their creation, through thaumaturgy, of deadly traps and assassins.

At last Gunthar reached the high granite wall marking the final barrier between himself and the road to the port of Shumzun.

Crouching down, he looked around as the moon cast its incandescence over the scene. It had been deceptively easy. He had stolen the idol at the behest of Seruya, priestess of the goddess Ishanna. She had provided him with ample expenses for the deed; half now and half upon delivery. The allowance had been more than generous—he still had the majority of the proffered gold coins in his purse.

He unfurled his rope. The grappling hook caught on top of the wall and he pulled back, finding a steady hold.

In that instant some of the shrubbery, along the verge, rippled with motion. Thorny, venom laden tendrils grasped at his bare legs above the high strapped sandals. Other tendrils lashed about his body. Gritting his teeth, he fell back as those vines tightened agonizingly into his flesh. Most snapped easily in his hands, but others dug in, injecting their stinging venom. A floral head rose. Its segments parted and a gust of powder blew into his face. He coughed as the narcotic substance began overpowering his senses. Reaching swiftly across, he jerked out his sword and decapitated the member with a single shearing sweep. Green ichor splashed and, with a tremor, the tendrils relaxed. As the plant fell back, he managed to untangle himself before mounting the last few feet of the barrier and falling heavily to the ground on the other side.

Dazed by the narcotic effects, but still in control of his senses, he slumped against the wall, breathing deeply. He checked his satchel. Satisfied he still held the idol in his possession; he staggered into the shadows and made his way, in all haste, down the road to the port of Shumzun.

* * *

"Holy Warden, he has escaped out onto the main road. He is most likely heading to the port of Shumzun. He… has the sacred idol, my lord," declared Sartton, chief eunuch to Bulbara, high priest of Yorm.

Bulbara rose from his dais. He came slowly down the steps and, with a vicious swipe, struck Sartton full in the face. The underling fell to the floor and groveled, nursing a bleeding nose.

"What of the guardians, fool? How did he surpass them?"

"Holy Warden, the *diskardrox* plant was found beheaded. But it had discharged its pollen and venom beforehand!" whined the eunuch, holding his face with one hand.

Bulbara thought. This was no casual theft. Of that he was certain. Only a handful of people in the world knew of the idol's true value. Reaching on to a table, he threw Sartton a cloth. "Clean yourself up, fool, and see to it my laboratory is made ready. Stop snivelling, you worm. Set a good example!" he added with a sneer.

Soon Bulbara was seated alone in his laboratory. All the instruments of his pursuits adorned the room; charts and tomes of thaumaturgy, ancient scrolls and rites in runic characters, impossible to read by all but the most esoteric elite. In jars were obscenely preserved specimens of huge spiders and insects, as well as weird hybrids of man and reptile. Bulbara pulled the velvet cover from a crystal globe resting on a marble plinth and, sitting cross-legged before it, stared into its emerald depths.

"Very well, *diskardrox*, you have dosed him with your poison. Thus it shall be easy for me to trace this miscreant in the astral realm."

Closing his eyes, he fell into a deep trance…

* * *

Stalking swiftly, Gunthar made his way through the shadows that played along the wharf front of Shumzun. A copper coin had purchased him a concealing cloak from a merchant and, from the confines of the drawn up hood, his eyes scanned the harbour. He came down cautiously, for the port often swarmed with soldiers and men-at-arms of the coastal guard.

It was muggy this time of year. Fishing boats came in; alley cats and gulls fought over the remains of the cast-off catch. Ships, laden with cargoes of timber, came in from the great tropic continents of the south. Others, laden with cargoes of grain, made sail to ports along the Kilbarz Sea of the civilized north.

The sun began to rise across the low mountains to the east, casting its rays upon the waters of the straits of Kaxar. Through the haze one could vaguely make out the coast of Tharmaggar, the great western continent, some ten miles over. To the south, those straits broadened out massively into the ocean of Cheb; huge and barely navigable, for even the most fool-hardy of sea captains hugged the shoreline in fear of its stormy depths. To the east, many hundreds of leagues distant, that shoreline became a skeletal desert, gradually changing to verdant swampland and impassable forest. To venture there was death in the form of hostile natives and venomous reptiles. Nonetheless, some hardy settlers had established outposts along these routes and maintained a thriving timber trade.

Gunthar saw an inn, the hanging sign inscribed with the appellation, 'The Inn of the Sleeping Dragon.' It seemed nondescript enough for his purposes, so he ventured within. It was busy at the entrance. Shouldering through a press of assorted ruffians and hangers on, he threw back his hood and, shaking out his unshorn mane, slammed a fist on the desk. A portly red haired man in an apron appeared.

"Innkeeper, I require a night's lodgings. Be quick about it, man!"

The innkeeper, looking him dubiously up and down, fiddled among some papers on the desk. Then, sniffing haughtily, he said; "I regret, sir, we are packed to the rafters. Can't accommodate you I'm afraid."

Gunthar was in no mood for this. Reaching quickly across, he grabbed the front of his tunic with one hand and dragged him over the counter.

"Ilkara!" the man gasped out.

From the back kitchen, a red haired wench appeared in the doorway. In one hand she held a crossbow. Seeing the altercation, she swung it up, leveling it in both hands. An arrowhead was aimed directly at Gunthar's heart. Beside her stood a pot boy with a meat cleaver and a coarse-faced kitchen drudge with a sharp knife.

"Release my father, knave!" cried the redheaded girl. She was rather comely, long of limb with bright green eyes.

More in surprise than actual fear, Gunthar released his hold and the innkeeper fell back, coughing and massaging his throat.

"My apologies," said Gunthar in gruff fashion. He opened a small bag of coins and the contents thumped heavily on the boards. Examining them, the innkeeper licked his lips.

"It would appear there has been a cancellation, Ilkara. Prepare a pallet for that Niall fellow out by the stables, if you would be so kind!"

He reached up to a hook, from which hung a series of room keys, and handed one to Gunthar.

"That's room ten with a harbour view," he said, smiling.

"Very well. I will have some roasted boar and a flagon of ale. I'll sit in the corner out of everyone's way."

He flipped another coin. "Keep the ale coming," he growled. As he walked past Ilkara, he jerked a thumb in her direction.

"Have this one bring it to me."

Ilkara, lowering the crossbow, was taken aback by the swaggering yellow maned warrior. Her lips pouted defiantly. "Get about your business, girl!" her father shouted, snapping her out of her reverie. "Niall needs a pallet and this fine gentleman is awaiting his meal!"

III - FEVER DREAM.

Gunthar sighed and, stretching his rangy frame, began working studiously on the ale mug before him. Presently Ilkara, the serving wench, came and slammed a heavy platter down on the boards. The smell of steaming juices assailed his nostrils. Gunthar smacked his lips with relish. About to tuck in, he noted the girl still hovering at the table. Seeing his diamond hard eyes upon her, she tossed her flaming hair back haughtily and stared at him.

"I see they breed the wenches for insolence around here," grunted the warrior, tearing at a roasted leg and cramming it into his mouth. His frank eyes never left hers as he reached across for a handful of bread.

"You have the manners and smell of the boar you eat," came the reply and, with that, she turned on her heel and, in a flourish of ragged skirts, was gone.

Wiping his greasy hands on his cloak, Gunthar grinned and drained his mug. He scratched absently at his arm. Looking down he saw a thorn embedded under the skin and, with a grunt, pulled it out. It was large, the size of a rodent's tooth. At one end, near the root, was a small empty sac.

All of a sudden his head began to swim and he lurched up from the table.

"Too much ale..." he muttered then staggered forward. He passed a hand over his brow and suddenly, weary as with a great fatigue, his legs gave way and he crashed headlong to the floor...

Gunthar's dreams were fraught with strangeness. He thought to be lying on his back, on the deck of a ship, in a storm-wracked sea. Through nebulous mists he glimpsed faces peering down and heard indistinct voices calling out to him. He saw terrible shapes, lurking and shambling, just beyond the edge of his reason…

"Gunthar…" A musical voice swam out to him across that heaving ocean, "Gunthar…"

Dimly, through soft veiled mists, he thought to see the features of a woman. A beautiful woman. She had a heart shaped face and dangerous eyes. On her brow was the sacred stone of the goddess, Ishanna. He recognized the priestess Seruya and wondered at the strangeness of it all.

"You have been poisoned by the thaumaturgy of Yorm… even now, on the astral plane, Bulbara, the high priest of that dread cult, searches for you. His necromancies are strong, Gunthar. You must fight if you are to win through. You must fight the poison that seeks to drag you down… I can only hold him at bay for so long. I cannot… do this… unaided."

Her form faded. It seemed to Gunthar that he reached out for her, but she was gone. Then he heard other sounds. Forms rose up before him, vile slinking shapes of madness and nightmare. For what seemed like an eternity there was confusion and disorder.

Then, quite suddenly, there was calm and he saw again the cragged faces of his childhood adopters, the wild riders of the Tatukura steppes. Once more he laughed with them into the cold eastern winds as they rode their swift legged mounts over the desolate wastes, under an open sky… Then those visions faded too and he found himself staring down the long dark road of oblivion…

Then, suddenly, a light flared, banishing the darkness.

Gunthar looked to see Seruya's head hanging gigantically above him. From the tiara, fixed over her brows, the gem blazed an outpouring of cosmic luminescence. A soft aura played around her.

She spoke; "The sacred stone of Ishanna has marked you, Gunthar- chosen you as her vassal! Come to me… awaken!"

IV - GUNTHAR AND ILKARA.

Gunthar awoke with a startled jerk, his eyes swiftly drinking in the unfamiliar surroundings. His gaze was met by the startled faces of the portly innkeeper and his comely daughter, Ilkara. He was in a rudely furnished room whose wide shuttered windows looked down on the tall masts of the ships in the bustling harbour below.

"What happened to me? Where is this place?"

"You're in your room, above the Inn of the Sleeping Dragon," Ilkara replied. "You collapsed and fell into a fever, doubtless brought on by the scratches you bear all over your torso. Some terrible poison had worked its way into your system. You've been crying out in your sleep."

At this point the Innkeeper interrupted her; "You look like trouble, outlander. I was all for throwing you out into the streets. I confess to feeling less than charitable after your efforts to choke the life from me. Lucky for you, Ilkara convinced me not to do so. That and the idol in your satchel. Ilkara has nursed you these last three days whilst you shouted and babbled in your delirium. It seems it has passed."

Gunthar sat up straight in the bed. "My satchel."

"Do not worry; I have it safely stowed away for you."

Gunthar relaxed slightly at this improved news.

"We now find ourselves facing another problem," he continued, "Word around the harbour is, the tower of the priory of Yorm was robbed of some such idol as you carry, three nights ago. Bulbara, the high priest, is appealing to King Thelmso to have every inch of the old town turned over until the missing object is recovered and the offending thief brought to justice. Thelmso, the coward, fears the priesthood. He lets Bulbara interfere in the kingdom's affairs too much for my liking."

Gunthar rose from the bed. With scant regard for his modest displays before Ilkara, he started gathering up his belongings. He threw on a sleeveless leather waist jacket and, tightening his belt, gathered up his sword in its lacquered wooden scabbard.

"My advice to you lad, is to find passage on a ship heading north. There are many carrying settlers, and fighting men, to the logging outposts. Men are sick of the unemployment and corruption in this city. I believe Captain Sandroz sails to Uhremon this afternoon. You may find passage with him. Seek after his ship the *Zephyr*."

Gunthar made ready to leave, gathering his meager belongings about him. He extended his hand and the innkeeper made a motion to shake it. Gunthar withdrew it. "My satchel if you please, Innkeep!" came his curt reply. The innkeeper grunted and, taking the leather satchel from below his stool, threw it to him. Catching it deftly, Gunthar replied, "North is where I intend to go. It is well. For what it's worth, innkeeper, I do appreciate what you have done." He fumbled around in the satchel and produced his bag of coins. Taking some out he laced the rest up and dropped it on the bed stand.

"Stop calling me Innkeep, or whatever, lad! I have a name, they call me Jolmo! Once my body was strong as yours. I was a foot soldier in Queen Feya's campaign. I'm a veteran. I brought Ilkara's mother back as a prize, may her shade rest in the serenity of the Blessed Goddess. Bah! Queen Feya would turn in her crypt, seeing the simpering weakling her son has become under the influence of that swine, Bulbara! "

Gunthar turned to depart from the chamber, his meager belongings swinging in the satchel at his side. "Wait!" cried Jolmo the Innkeep, standing. "Take Ilkara with you…" He reached down and, picking up the bag of coins, handed it back to him. "She deserves better than this."

* * *

Gunthar, a thief from the wild plains of Tatukura, and Ilkara, the serving girl, strolled along the walkway beside the wharves.

"Up ahead is the *Zephyr*," said Ilkara, pointing. "I'm known to Captain Sandroz and his crew. They are frequent guests of ours."

Truly, the *Zephyr* looked to be a magnificent ship, two hundred feet or so in length with three masts. She was ready for sea, carrying a cargo of, amongst other things, preserved barrels of salted beef, barrels of strong liquor, and a plethora of other luxuries and essentials that northern colonists tended to miss about their civilized lives.

"Captain Sandroz!" Ilkara cried out. The man supervising the loading of the ship, a slim and handsome captain, looked up from his work. "Aye! Who's asking?"

V - FLIGHT FROM SHUMZUN.

"Ilkara!" Sandroz exclaimed from the deck. With a wide smile he stood on the rail and, grabbing a cordage line, swung down onto the pier. Ilkara received him in an embrace.

"Did I forget to pay the bill again, lass?" he laughed. Looking over her shoulder, he added; "I see you've brought company." He nodded to where Gunthar stood to one side, arms folded over his chest.

Ilkara nodded; "Captain Sandroz, this is Gunthar. He needs help to escape the city."

Sandroz looked him over with an appraising eye. "It won't be the first time I've had a warrior with a debt of blood on board... If you have gold, warrior, my ship is yours."

"I can buy passage," replied Gunthar, hefting a small weighted bag in one palm. "The price for the wench's help seems to extend to paying for her also."

Sandroz raised an eyebrow. "Oh? What's this, lass?"

"My father fears for me now that the king is in the pocket of the brotherhood of Yorm. Gunthar, here, finally woke him up to the man he once was... I know how hard it must have been for him to send me away. But I've always yearned for a better life. Here's my chance."

Sandroz sighed. Rubbing a hand across his stubbled jaw, he looked uncertain: "Well, I happen to like the old man. If I thought you were running away with this here young blade, I would send you back forthwith." He cast a wary eye at Gunthar who snorted and hooked his thumbs through his sword belt.

"Believe me," quoth the warrior, "the last thing I need right now is a woman slowing me down with half the city hot on my heels."

Sandroz nodded. "You have the look of an honest man, Gunthar. I know you riders of the steppe take pride in your word being unbreakable as your steel... Well, let's aboard. We sail with the eventide. These winds and tides wait for no man!"

* * *

Wind snapped through the triple mast sails, thrummed though the taut cordage, as the *Zephyr* swung slowly out of the harbour into the straits of Kaxar. Salt sea spray lashed the deck as her prow cut through the heaving swells.

At the rail, Gunthar watched the port city of Shumzun fade slowly from view. The purple wings of night were fast approaching. Stars began to appear, blinking furiously through fast whipping clouds.

Still weak from the after effects of the poison, Gunthar was busy devouring a basket of fruit as he stood planted at the rail, the frigid wind biting over his tough corded frame. Feeling a presence at his back he turned to see Ilkara, standing by a pile of drawn up netting, watching him.

"Come over and save your eyes, girl," he said gruffly, tossing an apple core overboard into the white tipped waves.

"What makes you think I was staring?" countered Ilkara, as she made her way across the slanting deck. Though little more than a girl, her ample charms were more than enough for any red blooded man. Gunthar looked askance at her.

She came up and leaned with her back to the rail beside him, the wind playing a raging fire through her unshorn tresses.

"Do you have any idea what lies ahead for a young woman like you, alone, in this savage world?" He shook his head. "Bah! Your father must be mad. If he had any sense he'd marry you off to the first drunken nobleman that passed by and reap a nice dowry for himself."

Ilkara swung round to face him, her eyes flashing angrily; "I'm my own woman! What of you? You are barely little more than a boy yourself! If you can find a place for yourself in this world then so can I if that desire be tempered with courage!"

Gunthar grinned; "Those are warrior's words, lass. Maybe there's a little more of your father in you than I at first thought, I admit. But mark me, this is a man's world. Only the strong survive."

There was silence, interrupted only by the creak of timber and the snap of yard cloth in the braces. An occasional order was shouted and lost over the moaning wind. Ilkara shivered, wrapping her cloak closer about her.

Gunthar stood with his leather waist coat open to the salt spray, seemingly oblivious to the cold. The better part of his teenage years, spent on the bitter escarpments and frozen ridges of the Tatukura plains, had inured him to the harsh extremities of wind and snow.

"What is it about this idol that makes it so important?" Ilkara asked presently.

Gunthar shrugged. Reaching into the satchel he drew it forth. "Who knows," he grunted, turning it this way and that. It was intricately carved, of some jade-like substance, the size of two clenched fists held together. The face was an impression of both the mocking and the obscene.

Yet there was a beauty in the craftsmanship, an exotic attention to detail that showed a reverent, almost slavish, devotion by the sculptor.

"The priestess of Ishanna paid me enough to filch it for her. She seems determined enough to fight for it, even against Bulbara's necromancies." He shivered from something other than the frigid wind. "By Yod the Accursed, once I get the rest of my share, I'll be glad enough to be rid of it."

He weighed it in his hand a moment before replacing it back in the satchel.

The journey was nearly at an end. He only had but to deliver the idol to Seruya in her tower at Tarshish and he was a free man once more. He stretched his wolfish frame in the wind and smiled at the girl by his side.

A cry from the crow's nest, cutting knife-like through his reveries, brought him about. Dimly, outlined against the darkening sky, he could see the lookout's arm stretching and pointing back the way they had come. There, in the distance, outlined against the dying embers of the fast sinking sun, was the unmistakable sail of a ship bearing the yellow crested symbol of Yorm.

VI - SEA MAGIC!

Bulbara found it no difficult matter to arrange the services of a pirate ship. King Thelmso's own flotilla was now virtually useless and close to mutiny, following months of no pay. Discipline among that once proud fleet had broken down and inspections, in and out of the port of Shumzun, were virtually non-existent.

Bulbara, and his aid Sartton, laid on the services of Captain Hydrok in one of the seedier inns along the aged wharf front of Shumzun. A ship, the *Osprey*, was theirs for the hiring, along with its cut-throat band of mercenaries. Soon Hydrok and his crew, after some haggling, agreed to sail on Bulbara's terms. Flying the hated yellow crested emblem of Yorm, the *Osprey* was soon riding through the straits of Kaxar, following in the *Zephyr*'s wake. Its trained oar crews swiftly allowed the gap to narrow on the broader and larger ship

Where the Tartukuran thief was headed was easy for the sorcerer priest to ascertain; north to the Kilbarz Sea and the fortress isle of Tarshish, home of the priestess of Ishanna.

The pace of the *Zephyr* picked up as it approached the spectacular limestone cliffs marking the headlands at the end of the straits.

Bulbara and Sartton stood on the raised poop deck with Captain Hydrok, who passed the viewing glass to Bulbara. "Our quarry has noticed our pursuit and quickened their pace. They are almost out of the straits. With a good wind at their backs, once they make the open sea we won't be able to close the gap," he remarked.

Bulbara's powers were at a perilously low ebb. Large dark rings had formed under his eyes and he struggled to stand upright. Meditations on the astral plane always took their toll. But this time had been different. This time he had been blocked and he now knew the source. Sartton's womanish concern was evident as he flapped and tended best he could to his masters travails. Bulbara meekly brushed the eunuch aside as he supported himself on the ships railing.

"By Yorm, they'll be slaves in the lowest tiers of hell this night!" he said and, breaking loose of the effete ministrations of Sartton, raised his pendant medallion, the dreaded symbol of Yorm, to the sky. The resulting evocation, from his incantations, struck with terrifying effectiveness.

Just forward of the *Zephyr*, a vast barnacle encrusted chunk of sea floor rose up. With a thunderous roar of spray, the accompanying wave almost caused the *Zephyr* to roll on her back. Aboard, men and cargo were tossed high, the vast and jagged limestone ridge looming up massively before the prow. Evasive action was futile. A gash was torn deep in her hold and rapidly became flooded. She began to list heavily to port.

Chaos ruled the decks. Men were flung overboard by the impact, some to their deaths on the barnacle encrusted outcrop. Others were being assisted back by their shipmates, shaken but relatively unscathed as they clambered, spluttering, out of the raging sea. Gunthar surveyed the scene. Captain Sandroz barked orders to his men, his experience rapidly bringing the situation under control. Among the smashed flotsam in the water something caught Gunthar's eye; a figure in the tides—*"Ilkara!"*

Diving far out over the railings, he struck the water and, in powerful gliding strokes, swam quickly across to her. Cradling her chin and keeping her head above the choppy surf, he began to swim back in the direction of the *Zephyr*. She had suffered a nasty gash to her temple but still took in breath. She spluttered, expelling salt water from her lungs.

"To arms men!" cried Hydrok, surly cutthroat captain of the *Osprey*. His men readied their weapons. All manner of arms, both blunt and honed to razor sharpness, crowded the rails.

Bulbara, assisted by Sartton, smiled grimly at his handiwork. "It worked, by Yorm! It stopped them in their tracks… Remember, Captain Hydrok, the outlander must be delivered to me. The rest- the accursed sea god, Posiedus, may drown them all!"

He laughed as the *Osprey* closed in rapidly on the stricken *Zephyr*.

VII - FIRE ON THE SEA.

Barely conscious, Ilkara hung limp over Gunthar's straining shoulder. Gripping the rail in one hand he heaved her up onto the listing deck and clambered aboard. He stood panting, legs braced wide on the rocking planks. Sailors, running to and fro, stopped short at sight of him. To them he was Posiedus incarnate; heaving himself up out of the ocean's depths and come to wreak terrible vengeance on the crew.

Seeing their fear filled expressions, Gunthar looked out over the heaving swells. He saw the yellow sailed ship of Yorm bearing down on them like some monstrous centipede, her oars plying in perfect unison, and cursed. Looking to the sailors, he outflung a corded arm and roared; "Alright you scurvy dogs, here's where you make your captain proud! Prepare to repel boarders!"

The sailors, snapping out of their superstitious awe, jumped into action. As they scrambled for position, Gunthar knelt to the girl lying at his feet. He raised her head, turning it to one side as she retched up a brine of salty water. "Easy, girl," he grumbled. Tenderness did not come easily to him.

Over the slippery deck, a figure came reeling toward them. Gunthar looked to see Captain Sandroz, his white laced shirt torn open, a cutlass in his fist. A mixture of anxiety and rage was written on his face.

"Damn you, warrior!" he choked, "If I didn't need every available blade aboard right now, I'd run your bronze hide through myself!"

Gunthar stood slowly. Tossing back his tangled mane, he said; "Time for recriminations later, captain. What cargo are you carrying below? Think quickly."

Confused, Sandroz sputtered; "Food, spices. Oil... Why—?"

Gunthar grabbed him by the shoulder, eyes blazing.

"Oil! What type of oil? Quickly, man!"

"Whale oil, of course. For lamps—"

Gunthar's face split in a grin.

"Have your men bring up every barrel on deck, Captain. By Vrooman's brazen rod, we'll win through this day yet!"

Swinging away, Gunthar leaped to the stern and roared at the helmsman stood at the wheel; "Tack hard to starboard you worthless sea scum!"

Turning, he leaned over the rail, stabbing a finger at the crew bailing furiously in the waist below; "Break out the oars, damn you! One bank to starboard side only! When she comes in, head straight across her bows!"

Dazed, the sailors turned to do his bidding. They accepted his authority without question. Others, at Sandroz's behest, began rolling up heavy barrels of oil from the hold.

Captain Sandroz, mounting the stair to the stern, came up to Gunthar.

Facing each other squarely, the captain raised his sword.

"On any ordinary day I would have you flogged and tossed overboard for assuming command of my vessel!" He looked over the jagged raised outcropping as the *Zephyr* braced hard away from it. "But this is no ordinary day."

Gunthar nodded. "We're floundering, but I've bought us some time."

The captain sheathed his blade and, hands on hips, grinned; "So I see, lad! Now tell me- what's the plan?"

From the poop of the *Osprey*, Bulbara stared intently as they gained on the struggling *Zephyr*. Then suddenly that ship lurched about. As if by some divine intervention she began to swing around. He felt Sartton's long nails drive deep into his arm.

From the main deck below, Captain Hydrok looked to his men, even as he tugged a battered helmet down over his ears.

In silence they watched as the *Zephyr*, still taking water, tacked hard to starboard and, using only that one side of banked set of oars, sweep on straight toward them. "What madness?" muttered the cutthroat captain then, eyes wide in terror; "She's going to ram us!" Whirling, he shouted down to the quarter master below, "Hard to starboard, damn you!"

But it was too late. The *Zephyr*, sweeping across her bows, crunched into the prow of the lighter ship. With her heavier momentum she swung by and men from the *Osprey* screamed as they were sent hurtling and spinning through the air. Wood splintered and beams cracked. Those not affected were nonetheless jarred from head to heel by the impact. Sartton screamed as he fell to the floor, dragging his master with him in a blaze of sulphuric curses. They regained their feet, just in time to see the heavier merchant ship lurch past them. On the stern of that ship Bulbara saw Gunthar, his teeth bared in a fighting smile. They looked directly into each other's eyes before the Tatukuran, bringing his arm down, shouted; "Now!" and, from the main deck, sailors rushed forward to a long line of barrels lashed to the rails. They knelt and Bulbara saw them hacking at the stoves with short handled hatchets. Then the ship had passed them, leaving the *Osprey* rocking in its wake.

On the deck of the *Osprey* men ran frantically to and fro, Captain Hydrok barking blasphemous curses and barely comprehensible orders. All was confusion, yet Bulbara stood calmly staring after the *Zephyr*. He noted the broken barrels flung from her decks and, looking down, saw a long slick trail glistening blackly on the water. It traced all the way back to the *Osprey*, where she listed in the tide. Then, with sudden fear and understanding, he whipped his head up and looked to the aft quarters of the *Zephyr* just in time to see a comet's trail of arrows launching toward them from across the sky.

Bulbara's mouth fell open as the flaming tips struck the blackened waters. With a violent hiss, a gigantic wall of flame sprang into hideous life and came roaring toward them! Sartton had time for one last squeal of fear before the flames, reaching the *Osprey*, engulfed the ship in a blazing inferno. Men screamed, leaping far out into the waters below, little realizing that, they too, were burning with an unquenchable thirst. Timbers crackled and blistered as the fire raged on through the decks. Those that stayed on board to tackle the blaze were boiled alive in their half armour.

Everywhere the stench of burning death.

Captain Hydrok raced for the poop where, above his main quarters, Bulbara stood.

Sarrton, quivering with fear, fell to the floor and gripped his master's knees. "Save us master!" he blubbered, "use your necromancies!"

The flames surged all around them now, the timbers glowing red hot as they smouldered in the searing heat. With a crack, the mast snapped and Hydrok, half way up the stair, turned, a curse dying unborn on his lips as it splintered and came down, crushing him with its full force. Bulbara looked away as the stair beneath it disintegrated. He shuddered, drawing himself up to his full height.

Sartton looked up at him, hope and desperation in his eyes. "Perhaps," he sighed, "I have enough energy for one last spell." He leaned heavily on the aft rail and turned again to the sacred sigil of Yorm. He bent his lips to it, murmuring ancient, eldritch mantras that were old before man ever was. The flames swerved and seemed to bend away. A dark wind began to blow, followed by bleak, ominous clouds that began to descend from on high. Rain began to fall.

Sartton, raising his face, began to laugh. "It's working master—it's working!"

"Yes," intoned the sorcerer priest, "but great sorcery does not come without a price, Sartton. Yorm is a fickle god who must be appeased. I promised the soul of the outlander for my last spell. Now the balance must be redressed." From beneath his robes he whipped out a gleaming curved knife.

Sartton went pale with dread. "M- master?"

"Farewell my servant." The knife plunged down and Sartton's unanswered query died with him in a bubbling welter of gore.

Bulbara opened his arms to the dark clouds rolling in on thunderous wings above him and, with a sorcerous gesture, they enveloped him and he was gone.

From the aft deck of the *Zephyr*, Gunthar and Sandroz saw the strange events being played out on the poop of the *Osprey*. They knew that, with the aid of necromancy, Bulbara had avoided the fate which had overtaken the rest of the crew. They watched in dejected silence as flames devoured the ship, dragging it down. Cheers went up from below when the hated symbol of Yorm at last fell, the prow upending into the lapping waves. A thick cloud of smoke drifted on the flaming sea as it blasted furnace waves of heat toward them.

"Well, you did it, lad," Sandroz said, slapping a hand on

Gunthar's shoulder.

The thief from the wild Tatukura plains said nothing but stood looking at the devastation wallowing before them. He shook his unshorn mane then, placing a hand on the rail, vaulted to the aft deck below. Moving swiftly to the main cabin he wrenched the door open and stood looking in. In the dim light he could make out Ilkara's form on the main draped bed. He moved over, kneeling silently at her side. She slept. As if sensing his presence, her eyelids fluttered open. She smiled wanly. A purple welt above one eye showed the beginnings of a nasty bruise. Gunthar was relieved to see nothing serious. "Good for me you swim like a shark," she said and the warrior grinned. "Get some sleep. I think we'll make it to the next port. Once there you can rest up."

"You think you're getting rid of me? Not a chance. I'm coming with you to deliver that idol and don't you forget it. Besides, how can you leave a poor injured girl all alone in this savage, untamed world?"

Gunthar smiled and, taking her hand, stood. "Rest," he said then, turning, moved to the door. He stopped short, seeing Captain Sandroz leaning against the door frame, a mysterious smile on his lips. "For someone who doesn't need a woman dragging him down, you take a lot of risks for a mere girl."

Gunthar, saying nothing, moved past him onto the deck. He swung about.

"Can we make it to the isle of Tarshish? I have a bargain to uphold that is proving more trouble than its worth. I would see an end to it. If you are willing to join swords with me I will share equal payment with you."

Sandroz looked him over thoughtfully a moment. "Is this payment big?"

Gunthar nodded.

"Well," sighed the captain, "The hold needs bailing... makeshift repairs to the hull may slow us down, but I think we can make it to the fortress isle within the next day. We'll need a row boat from there. Reefs surround the island. What then?"

Gunthar folded his arms over his chest. "We deliver the idol and wait. Something tells me this is far from over."

VIII - WARRIOR WOMEN OF ISHANNA.

In close to no time, repairs to the *Zephyr* had been carried out. Nails, pitch and timber from the cargo had proven useful. With a strong wind at their backs, the *Zephyr* limped its way northwards through the tides of the Kilbarz Sea.

Soon the rugged shoreline of Tarshish came into view. The fortress isle lay just a few miles off the eastern shore, its rugged fastness rising out of the azure depths with monolithic grandeur. On the mainland, a river mouth emptied into the sea directly opposite the island, its desolated location adding to its sense of impregnability.

Sandroz turned to Gunthar and Ilkara, who stood with him on the main deck. "Well lad, there she is—the isle of Tarshish. I dare not come any closer. The reefs will tear our keel and this tub won't take much more of that kind of punishment. We'll take the row boat from here. That way we can navigate our way through the narrow passages and reefs. I will accompany you. Fulbon will serve in command in my absence. I've given him orders to set sail for the port of Uhremon in the event of us not returning."

"I'm coming with you," interjected Ilkara.

"Out of the question, I could never console myself should something befall you, lass!" Sandroz swiftly replied.

"I don't wish to be left here alone with your men."

Sandroz paused a few moments. "Very well," he grinned, "I suppose you're better off under my watchful eye than with these ruffians. Good lads though they are, self control is not among their strengths when it comes to wenches!"

Gunthar stood motionless, gazing out over the isle of the looming fortress, as the setting sun cast strange shadows on its eerily deserted shore.

The row boat made its landing on that shore, close to where a small river tumbled down onto the broad sandy beach forming a narrow strip between the sea and the huge craggy cliffs. Everywhere was in evidence of ruin. Fallen blocks of masonry, spires and minarets among the rocks and boulders all overgrown with clinging vines until it seemed to swallow up the last vestiges of the past. Gunthar made his way towards the cliffs while Sandroz and Ilkara dragged the small boat up past the high water mark to conceal it in some foliage growing along the river's edge.

"What now, Gunthar? Must we make our way into this isle to find this Seruya?" inquired Ilkara.

"We wait here. Set up camp on the beach if need be. My dealings with Seruya have taught me that little escapes her gaze. Have patience."

The group set about making camp by the neck of the small stream. Ilkara, moving off, began gathering firewood.

Gunthar's keen senses, sharpened on the wild plains of the steppe, sprang suddenly into life. He turned, his sword springing into his hand. "Ilkara!" he bellowed.

From the bushes, in front of the serving girl, sprang a throng of figures. They were dressed in armour and battle helmets, all polished to a gleaming luster. Sharpened spear points levelled at her breast. Stepping back and dropping the firewood, she slowly raised her hands. Sandroz and Gunthar rushed to her side, blades gleaming in the last rays of the dying sun. More figures appeared from among the ruins where they had evidently been concealed all along. The three found themselves with their backs to the stream flowing lazily into the sea. Gunthar, crouched like a panther at bay, growled deep in his throat. By this time there were far more than a score of the armoured figures hemming them in.

Slowly, Gunthar rose. Stepping forward he lowered his blade and raised the satchel up in his left hand.

"Tell Seruya that Gunthar has arrived and has what she seeks," he growled to the armoured assembly. A figure moved out from the press and removed their helmet. Long brown braided locks spilled loose, framing the profile of a hardened elfin face- a woman's face!

"You've been expected, Gunthar," she said.

The three looked around them. All the figures were women; lithe and armoured.

"I am Captain Teera, of Seruya's militia. Welcome to the fortress isle."

Seruya's soldiers guided the party into the interior of the island. It was an arduous journey that led through forest paths, over steep embankments and up slimed, rock hewn steps.

At length they came to the central court of Seruya, the purple priestess of Ishanna. The chamber was long and fairly narrow. She waved her hand, dismissing the company of guardswomen. The priestess reclined back on a long couch of exquisite finery, amidst silken pillows. To merely describe her as beautiful would do her great injustice. Her long shimmering hair and lithe figure, combined with alabaster limbs, ample bosom and clear intelligent eyes took the breath of the two men who beheld her, much to the discomfort and annoyance of Ilkara. Serving girls went to and fro, bringing wines and viands that were set before the three visitors. They were seated on pillows at the feet of the priestess.

"So, it is the success of your venture that has brought you here, Gunthar—greatest thief and swiftest sword in all Shumzun."

Gunthar proffered her the leathern satchel. The priestess took it and opening it, examined the idol. A purr of satisfied pleasure escaped her lips.

The three picked at the viands and sipped a little of the wine until, at length, the priestess spoke;

"Allow me to enlighten you as to why I hired your sword. Come, follow me." She rose, gesturing them with a wave of her hand. They were led into an alcove at the rear of the chamber, where they came up a narrow, winding staircase that clung to the ancient stone walls as it spiraled upwards to the top of a huge domed tower. The top of the staircase opened out into a chamber situated in the dome. The structure of the dome itself was partly laid open to the sky; a multitude of stars glowing like fireflies on the backdrop of the endless void. The chamber, it seemed, served as an astronomical observatory. Charts and tomes about stars and heavenly bodies were all about. Looking glasses mounted upon tripods were directed heaven-wards.

Seruya turned to them. "Observe, through this glass, the sun as it sets now over the sea. This device projects the image of the orb onto this screen. To look at the sun itself would damage the eyes, causing blindness."

The three gathered around the enigmatic device that magnified the image of the setting sun as it sank below the ocean

"What do you observe, Captain Sandroz?" asked the priestess.

"Why, there would appear to be a large dark orb on the disc of the sun itself," came Sandroz's bemused reply.

"Mere weeks ago this dark patch was no more than a speck. Now it covers a full quarter of the sun," came her reply. "This is no mere fluke. The alignments are all correct."

Gunthar interrupted gruffly, "Of what do you speak? This is beyond our ken. It is better we be on our way. Instruct your treasury to have my gold ready, priestess. We are ready to depart."

"Wait, Gunthar!" said the priestess, coming over to him. "Know that this structure sits on the ruins of what was the hub in this world of the ancient race, the ones who ruled before the necromantic wars." She indicated one of the tomes lying open on a page of inscriptions, written in the script of some forgotten language.

"Bulbara has set in motion plans to bring back their dark gods. Those of corruption and greed, famine and destruction, so long ago banished into the abyss. His plans are stymied now he no longer has the idol. It is the key to closing and sealing that gate forever." She turned, indicating the idol stood on the desk before her.

"Abyss? What do you mean?"

"The sun," she said. "The dark patch on the orb of the sun is the opening of a portal through which the Elder Ones will arrive. A gateway to their dark universe, their dark realm. Once it is fully open, our world will be theirs and they will flood in. Nothing will stand against them. As in the past, they will corrupt man, twist his soul and rend the earth into their own distorted image."

There was silence in the room as the four figures looked on to the projected image of the sun setting over the Kilbarz Sea.

* * *

Darkness had fallen over the ruinous splendour that was the isle of Tarshish, lying tranquil and forgotten on the timeless tides of the Kilbarz Sea.

The three companions were seated at their table in the dining hall. All around them the other women dined. The younger votaries of the priestess sat apart from the women of the militia who dined at separate tables. Wine, ales and fine viands were brought. There was an atmosphere of merriment. Women milled around on every side. "Now this is more to my liking!" remarked Sandroz playfully, as he looked around. Gunthar grinned. It was evident the wines were beginning to have their effect on the jovial captain.

The captain of the militia, Teera, came and seated herself at the table opposite Gunthar. As more wine was imbibed she was eventually seated on Gunthar's lap. As his garrulous talk became more incoherent he noted that, despite her somewhat hard features, she was indeed far from uncomely.

Sandroz had disappeared to empty his bladder about an hour before and had not returned.

Ilkara found her mind beginning to wander, until Teera, by a motion of her hand, upset an ale flagon that spilled over her. Apologies were made and Ilkara wiped herself clean with cloths brought by serving girls. A little more than ten minutes later the same thing happened again with a goblet of Ishkerrian wine. This was intolerable. Ilkara leaped to her feet, her eyes flashing angrily, her small fists clenched down at her sides. Teera, sprawled drunkenly on Gunthar's lap, only threw back her head and laughed uproariously. Ilkara kicked out and the captain of the militia was sent flying onto a table of her dining subordinates, sending food and drink spilling. The table crashed beneath her and she rolled, sprawling on the floor at the feet of her astounded comrades.

The captain rose slowly and dusted herself off. She stalked up to Ilkara in the midst of a dining hall that had now fallen into a stunned silence. She towered over the redheaded serving girl from Shumzun by a full head of height.

"You behave in a manner not fitting your station, kitchen drudge!" she ground out and, at that, drew a dagger from her belt.

IX - AWAKENING OF THE GODS.

A hand clamped vice-like over her wrist and, turning, Teera found herself staring into the ice hard eyes of Gunthar. He pulled her close and the dagger fell from her grasp.

"Easy, wench," he scowled "I think the wine has gone to your head."

She pulled away and, with one last angry glance at Ilkara, skulked off down the hall.

Gunthar bent and picked up the fallen blade. He saw Seruya approaching, her gown of purple midnight shimmering across the floor. The Tatukuran sell-sword could not but help notice the accentuated curves of her body beneath the clinging material as she moved.

"Is there a problem, my friends?"

Gunthar, with a glance at Ilkara, shook his head. "One of your warriors had a little too much wine is all." He handed her the dagger, hilt first.

"My apologies," she sighed, looking at Ilkara, "The women don't see men very often and are prone to getting a little excitable. I hope this has not spoiled your enjoyment of the feast."

"The food is wonderful, priestess. Thank you."

Seruya smiled, placing a hand on her shoulder. "Thank you. If you wish to clean yourself up there is a wash chamber down through the hallway."

Ilkara nodded and, with one last look at Gunthar, moved off.

"I … was hoping to speak with you alone," the priestess whispered lowly.

Gunthar looked at her.

"There is something I want you to see."

Down a long steel lined corridor, Gunthar followed Seruya. The warrior marvelled at the globes, mounted along the walls, that lighted as they passed them. They came down a spiral staircase, further and further, until he thought they must be deep inside the earth. At last they came before a steel wall and there Seruya turned to face him.

"Beyond here lies the salvation of man from extinction and the chaos of darkness." She motioned with her hand and a heavy riveted door moved across into one side of the wall. Gunthar, impressed with a sense of the unknown, stepped back. The priestess, oblivious to his awe, walked in ahead of him.

Gunthar blinked in amazement as he came over the threshold. A thousand impossible sights met his eyes, sights he could never fully hope to understand. Instruments and banks of machinery throbbed with life. A pulsing red light presided over all, adding to the strangeness.

Seruya whirled and the long purple gown that clung to her body moved with her like a live thing. Gunthar looked. She stood on a raised dais. Behind her, leaning and pointing upward, stood huge monstrous banks of pointed steel.

They gleamed under the red stained glow, etched with archaic symbols.

"Behold," cried the purple priestess of Ishanna, her arms outflung, "The spears of the gods!"

Gunthar stood and looked. An instinctive fear played down his spine.

"With these weapons we will defeat the Old Ones and forever seal the portal against their return! The prophecies of Yorm will come to naught, and peace and harmony shall reign on the world."

"By Yod the Accursed..." Gunthar whispered, "these... these are the weapons of the old wars that the gods wielded to destroy our world in the long ago."

"Yes!" cried Seruya, her face a fanatic's mask, "Where we stand was the heart of what was once a great and powerful city. Those that built and lived in this city were not gods, Gunthar, but men of flesh and blood like you and I! They possessed knowledge of something called science—far more potent, far more deadly, than any magic. And it is with this science that we will rid the world of magic forever! A new golden age will be born."

Gunthar shook his head. "You cannot revive what was broken in the long ago. It is a thing against nature."

Seruya laughed. "Ever the superstitions of the barbarian holding back progress.... Don't you see? This is the return to nature and her ways we have long been waiting for. From here, at Tarshish, we can usher in a new era of prosperity and peace."

"With threats of annihilation?" Gunthar balked.

"With the technology of science. There are many things here we are working on, Gunthar. Many things I, and my women, have learned that can help heal the world..."

Gunthar thought for a moment. "Why did you want me to steal the idol from the monastery of Yorm? What is its real purpose?"

Seruya smiled. Stepping down from the dais, she said; "Follow me."

Brushing by him, she mounted a steel railed platform set in one corner.

Gunthar followed. No sooner had he stepped on it than the

priestess spoke an alien word and the platform, with a hiss, shot upward. The warrior clutched at the rail. Eyes wide, he saw that they were shooting silently toward the top of the vast building. It began to slow, at last, before coming to rest on another level.

Casually, Seruya stepped off and, with one last uneasy look below, Gunthar padded gingerly after her. As she thrust aside a hanging, he saw that they were standing in her observatory. She moved over to where the jade idol of Yorm's offspring had been left sitting on a table with astronomical books and charts. Picking it up, she turned to the thief.

"Many centuries ago the priesthood of Yorm and the matriarchy of Ishanna worked together to help forge a better world. The alliance did not last. Ishanna wanted to rule by understanding, science and order. Yorm saw that chaos, fear and magic were the only ways to control mankind. When the final battle came, the priesthood of Yorm hid the sacred key from us that would unleash the might of the spears of the gods. It was thought forever lost... until I divined its whereabouts on the astral plane."

Then, raising the idol in one hand, she hurled it crashing to the floor. It shattered into a thousand tiny fragments. Gunthar stood in silence; no expression betrayed his thoughts. Seruya knelt and began sifting through the broken shards. When she straightened she held in her hand a silver object. A triangular shape of unknown metal. On one side was a rune etched in red. Her face, as she beheld it, was one of ecstatic awe. "At last..." she breathed, "the silver key is again ours."

She moved over to a panel in the wall where bronze levers, rods and dials were fixed. Staring into the centre of the room she pulled down on a lever. From the floor, a hexagonal shaped slab rose, coming up in the form of a column at waist height. Gunthar looked on as, moving over to it, she took the triangle of metal and fixed it into a corresponding mould imprinted on top of its surface.

The Tatukuran thief from the wild plains knew nothing of electro magnetism. If he did he would have understood that when the triangle was fixed in place it radiated a glowing red pulse that connected with circuits, wired to the monstrous banks of machinery below, and armed them. As it was, the expression on Seruya's face told him all he needed to know.

"Tomorrow, at mid-day," she said, looking up at him, "there will be an eclipse of the sun and moon. As the moon passes across the sun, the gate will be opened and darkness will again seek to reclaim the earth. In that moment- we strike!"

It was a troubled Gunthar who came stalking into the sumptuous quarters the three had been given on the top floor of the west wing. As he came through the doors, Captain Sandroz turned from the window he had been staring through and Ilkara fairly leapt from the stuffed divan where she had been sitting.

"Well, lad, you look no more pleased than we've been, stuck in this gilded prison awaiting your return," said Sandroz in a jovial manner that betrayed his words.

Gunthar grunted and slumped moodily onto a stool. Ilkara came over hesitantly.

"What happened?" she asked.

In a few brief words, Gunthar related what he had witnessed, there in the vaulted depths beneath ancient Tarshish. Sandroz leaned against the window, one hand resting on his hilt as he gazed wistfully at the tossing tides.

"We have to leave this place," murmured Ilkara. "There is a wrongness here... those warrior women are everywhere. They stand stationed at the door and follow our every move."

Sandroz laughed; "Didn't she call you the greatest thief and swiftest sword in all Shumzun, Gunthar? Surely escaping here will be easy for one of your guiles."

Gunthar stood. With a tired yawn he stretched his limbs. "I'm for bed. It's been a long day." With that he moved to one of the bunks at the far end of the chamber and was soon sound asleep.

* * *

With morning, Seruya came to their chambers, flanked by two guards. With them stood Teera who, upon seeing Ilkara, looked at her disdainfully. The three adventurers had already bathed and fed. Refreshed, Gunthar greeted the priestess with a smile.

"Good fortune to you, Seruya," he said.

The priestess nodded. "Good fortune, Gunthar... I trust you have all slept well. Preparations begin. I would be honoured if you would all accompany me to the observatory."

The sun, still low in the morning sky, was a bruised and burning disc. On its surface the dark stain contracted and expanded, forever changing its shape. As they reached the dome, they saw all was, indeed, in readiness. Women moved to and fro, organized and disciplined as a well oiled machine. Charts were readied, telemeters checked, and dials set. Looking around him, Gunthar noted the triangle of unknown metal fitted into position on the plinth column.

Seruya turned to face him. On her brows was the tiara bearing the sacred stone of Ishanna. "Observe, my friends, the awakening of the gods."

She led them over to the magical viewing device that allowed them to see at various points on the island. The finder swept over desolate rocks and shorelines, then on through the vine tangled ruins of an elder civilization. There, amidst the crumbled decay of long forgotten ruins, they beheld an awesome sight. Rearing up from beneath the ground came an incredible bank of machinery. Gleaming chrome tips of steel pointed up into the heavens.

The spears of the gods- lifted from vaults below.

Ilkara gasped. Captain Sandroz drew in a breath.

The sun was rising, climbing steadily into the vaulted blue. It swung over the horizon and they saw clearly for the first time the dark spot on its surface, fluctuating and crawling like some grotesque stain.

Then they beheld the pale, almost translucent, orb of the moon. She came swinging in on her trajectory and, as she did, it seemed the isle of Tarshish held its breath in waiting. As if sensing its time was nigh, the dark stain on the sun began to ripple and grow, straining to break away. Shadows, deep and dark, began falling across the face of the earth. The moon, caught in the edge of the sun's rays, was no longer a pale ghost-like object but a blackened disc. Slowly, in a heavenly bonding old as time, they came together.

There was quiet in the darkness. Quiet and dread. Then the shadows began to lift. Light came creeping back in, banishing the night away. When Gunthar looked he saw Ilkara standing close to Captain Sandroz. They held each other's hands tightly.

Through the finder, focused tightly on the sun, they looked upon a sight of soul-freezing terror. The dark stain had expanded and broken away at last. It flowed in on silent wings of abysmal horror, down toward the earth. As it drew closer it began to take on form and shape. Writhing, indistinct shapes became outlined in bold relief. Gunthar's nape hairs lifted at the sight. Blasphemous, terrible- that which came hurtling on down toward them was all the sum of man's atavistic fears and nightmares. He had a fleeting glimpse of writhing tentacles and cavernous, slobbering maws. Winged bat-like things, with serrated swords, flew all naked against the sky as phantom queens lashed on skeletal steeds from golden chariots whose hooves rang and spurned sparks from the anvils of the stars... An army of the damned come to claim the earth for its own.

Seruya, daring to wait no longer, moved to the column plinth. Her hand hovered hesitantly a moment then she pressed down on the silver triangled key. It sank into the column, the rune glowing scarlet. There was a rumble from far off, growing gradually louder. The observatory shook and, with a thunderous growl, something monstrous launched itself from the ground and into the sky.

They looked to see the first of the spears of the gods arcing out across the skyline, trailing an inferno of blazing fire. It dwindled away, became a sliver of silver against the ominous cloud coming in to devour it.

"By Poseidus," gasped Sandroz, his face sweating, "it won't be enough!"

The observatory was silent, as if held on a single collective breath.

The sliver disappeared; swallowed by the dark cloud.

Suddenly there was a terrible flash, white and blinding; filling the sky from horizon to horizon. Then it was gone and there was a roar as of the deepest doors of hell being slammed. A halo of fire arced across the heavens, pursued by a white hot cloud that purged the skyline.

"By Vrooman's brazen balls!" whispered Gunthar, "never have I beheld such a thing."

X - THE KISS OF A PRIESTESS.

Seruya's face was one of pure triumph. "It worked!" she cried. "Now shall those who rule by necromancy know fear when confronted by the science of the past!"

She whirled back to the plinth and, pressing the silver triangle, it popped up from its housing. She fixed it about her neck onto a long thin chain, the key dangling between the globes of her ivory breasts. Gunthar watched through narrowed eyes. Sandroz and Ilkara stood looking on in astonishment.

"Congratulations, priestess," the thief from Shumzun spoke; "The world will, indeed, be a different place under your hand. No longer will the people need to fear the wrath of the gods when you have their power at your fingertips."

If Seruya noticed the thinly veiled spike of his words she affected not to notice. Moving gracefully over to him, she drew herself up and placed a hand on his shoulder. From her brows, the sacred stone of Ishanna glowed its violet luminescence.

"Truly, Gunthar, you and your friends will be greatly rewarded in the dawn of the new order."

"The gold I was promised is compensation enough, Seruya."

The priestess smiled, a wickedly curving smile, beneath eyes that sparkled with a fanatical gleam. She stepped back, looking up and out and into the clear skies beyond. "Oh, but I have dreams, Gunthar. It is not by chance that the sacred stone of Ishanna chose you to be her champion.... A new era is fast approaching and that era will be a dawn of men! Men of cunning and steel! Have you not wondered why there are only women on this island?

"Hand picked from the four corners of the world for beauty, intelligence and strength, they have been trained to serve Ishanna all their lives. But what are women without the seed to procreate? A new race must be born... to usher in the new order. A god-like race of warriors—a race of supermen!" She swung round, turning to face him.

"You Gunthar, will be the father of that new dynasty. From your seed a new race will bring salvation to the world. What say you?"

She swept up to him and the fire of her passion was such that Gunthar took her into his arms in a hot embrace. He pressed his mouth to hers and she drank deep from the fierceness of his kisses, his corded arms entwining about her. She pulled back with an effort, panting in exertion.

"I say your beauty is like a fire that needs to be quenched," spoke Gunthar huskily, wiping the back of a hand across his mouth.

She laughed and suddenly the lights, mounted along the walls, began to flicker and dim. The warrior women looked about in confusion.

"A power depletion from the main banks on the island, high priestess," said Teera, pointing to a needle graph.

Gunthar, looking across to Ilkara and Sandroz, motioned them over with a quick jerk of his head. They came across quickly as Seruya and her warriors milled about in confusion, checking dials and nodes.

Their attention diverted, Gunthar decided now was the time to strike. He turned to his companions. "Follow my lead and keep close. We're getting out of this madness."

Sandroz raised an eyebrow. "Oh? Looks to me you were just starting to enjoy yourself."

Gunthar, turning, leapt for the back of the chamber. On the far side of the wall was a drape. Flinging it aside he stepped through and stood staring over the rail of the steel platform he and Seruya had used the night before. His companions came close behind. "Hang on," he said and repeated the strange syllable he had heard uttered by the priestess. Instantly the platform began to descend in a steaming whoosh of hydraulics. Ilkara gasped and, clinging to the rail, she threw a pale face up to Sandroz, who stood looking down into the darkness. A howling scream reached down to them and, looking up, Gunthar saw Seruya on the ledge above, her warriors crowding behind her. The warrior grinned and gave a mocking salute.

But then, without warning, the platform began to slow. Pressure dropped and it came to an abrupt stop. They looked into the yawning abyss below as, around them, lights began to waver and dim. Soon the whole building was plunged into darkness. What light there was filtered from above.

Gunthar turned. They had barely made it to another level. Drawing his sword he stepped off the platform and padded silently into the mouth of a long tunnel. Sandroz came close on his heels, his own cutlass bared in one knotted fist. Ilkara, beside them, regretted the lack of a weapon.

There was light ahead and they began to run towards it. It came from a window at the end of the long corridor and they followed a curving set of steps leading down. They met no one on the stairway but knew it was only a matter of time until they ran into troops of Seruya's militia. Quite suddenly, they reached a doorway and stood blinking in the clear sunlight. They stared a moment until Sandroz, getting his bearings, gripped Gunthar by the shoulder. He pointed over to a rocky promontory. "This way! If Vrooman favours us our boat should still be at the shore."

They sprinted across the rocks until at last they came to the waterfall and the fast flowing river leading down to the sea. Plunging deep into the undergrowth they dragged out the rowing boat. With a curse, Gunthar wheeled.

The sound of metal clashing against metal reached their ears as Seruya's warrior women poured out from the fortress toward them.

With a titanic heave, Gunthar braced his feet in the sands and dragged the prow of the boat down to the shoreline. Ilkara jumped in as the two men pushed it out into the crashing waves. Grasping at the oars, Gunthar began to row, the muscles standing out in corded ridges along his shoulders. The warrior women made it down to the shoreline and stood howling curses at them, waving their spears in their silver half armour and gleaming helmets.

Before them Gunthar spied Seruya standing with her feet in the tide. Her face wore no expression, just a weary resignation. The stone of Ishanna glowed from her brows as her gown of purple midnight floated around her on the waves.

Sandroz turned, scanning the horizon. He sighed and, slumping, shook his head. "The *Zephyr* has gone... Well, I told them not to wait. Looks like we're doomed after all."

Suddenly, Ilkara grabbed him by the shoulder and threw out her arm.

"Look!" she cried.

They had barely made it out of the cove surrounding the bay. Reefs up thrust their jagged teeth as breakers crashed against the rocks but, around the corner, a triple-masted ship hove into view.

"The *Zephyr!*" Sandroz exclaimed, his jaw slack with amazement. "How the devil—?"

From the mid-deck a figure waved its arms. "Captain!"

Sandroz cursed then laughed; "Fulbon, you idiot! Are you trying to sink my ship?"

XI - GUNTHAR'S DECEIT.

Three figures stood on the aft deck of the *Zephyr* as it raced away from the fortress isle of Tarshish. A full wind was behind her and it filled the tight braced sails. The spired crag and crumbled decay of Tarshish's once glorious towers fell behind and, with it, all dreams of a new era.

Captain Sandroz sighed and, leaning on the rail, frowned. "No gold and nothing to show for it but our lives." He shrugged; "The mark of all good adventures."

Ilkara, leaning in the curve of his arm, looked slyly across at Gunthar, who stood gazing silently out across the waves, the wind blowing through his tangled locks. "Why so pensive? Regretting not taking up the high priestess on her offer? To think, you could have been the master of a new race."

Gunthar grinned slyly. "Let's just say the kiss of a priestess has its own rewards."

From his belt he took out something that shimmered in the sun when he held it up. Ilkara gasped and Sandroz swore feelingly. Dangling from a thin silver chain was the silver key.

"It just happened in my hand when I drew her in for a kiss."

Sandroz laughed. "Well, she was right after all! The greatest thief in Shumzun you truly are!"

"I don't know about you," said Gunthar, "but I like the world as it is. Science and sorcery... men and gods. What sort of a world would it be, one without the other, I ask you?" He snorted. "Certainly not one I would like to live in."

He drew back his arm and hurled it far out into the sea. It flashed in the sun before it fell and was gone. He turned, leaning with his back to the rail and breathed in deep of the fresh salty air. "And what of you two? I see the dreaded love sickness has struck you both down."

Sandroz looked at Ilkara who blushed. "It's early days for us yet.

But I think we'll be happy," the captain said with a grin. "And you my friend?"

Gunthar shrugged and hitched his sword belt up a notch. "I'm for Uhremon. Drop me off at the next port and I'll see if a good sword arm can't earn a man a fortune there. I hear the wine is good and the pickings easy."

Sandroz nodded and clapped him on the back. "Come! To my quarters then! Before we reach land I want to drink this tub dry!"

XII - THE PRICE OF FAILURE.

In the opulent gardens of Yorm, Bulbara sat wearily on the curb of the fountain that stood resplendent in the main courtyard, beneath the tower of the idols. The day was overcast and a cold wind blew in jaggedly from the straits of the Kilbarz Sea. He shivered in his yellow robes and, turning to stare at the water rippling in the fountain, noticed his reflection.

No longer did he see the cruel featured man that had once brought the kingdom of Shumzun under an iron grip. He saw only a broken man, bent, fragile and old. He bowed his head and sighed.

"Thou hast failed, Bulbara." The voice, like a thousand tombstones being dragged through the vastness of the netherworld, roused him from his reveries.

He jerked his head. Reflected on the water, he saw a gigantic shape standing behind him. It was neither scaled, mottled or hairy but a hideous compound of all. Blazing red eyes bored down on him from a huge tusk-snouted face.

Bulbara cowered. Not daring to look round, he sank to the stones and quivered under that burning gaze.

"Dread lord! Master Yorm! Have mercy..." he gasped.

Behind him a thick taloned hand reached down and Bulbara screamed. At last understanding was borne in on him for the price of failure from a dark and abysmal god.

The shaven headed priests, who were first on the scene at the sound of that soul freezing shriek, stood aghast at what they found. They could not understand what had frightened their sadistic leader so badly that, in death, his face was a mask of pure frozen terror.

THE CITY OF THE BLACK FLAME

I - *The Black Flame of Life.*

"And that," said Gunthar, sitting back and taking a huge swallow from his leathern mug of ale, "is how I stole the sacred idol from the priests of Yorm."

Two young serving girls, transfixed by the tale, leaned forward in his lap, their pert young bosoms heaving with breathless excitement.

Gunthar, wiping a studded wristband over his lips, grinned appreciatively at the view.

"Ooohh," cooed the first girl, running a finger through the hairs of his chest where his leather waist coat lay open; "was there ever a more daring act this side of the Kilbarz?"

Gunthar licked his lips. His voice was low and dry when he replied; "I can think of some daring acts a man and two maids can enjoy... "

They giggled. Gunthar leaned in for a kiss then blinked as he saw that girl jerked from his lap by a fist knotted in her red hair. He stared, even as the other girl was handled roughly aside by calloused hands.

"Well, well—what do we have here?" a voice sneered. Gunthar looked up. He saw three men standing over the table where he sat in the middle of the low beamed tavern. They wore jerkins and studded leathers. Pushing forward their sword hilts, they looked at him through menacing eyes. Gunthar smiled. Scratching his stubbled jaw, he set down his drinking jack.

"Nilus, do you know it's rude to interrupt when a man and a maid are talking?"

The addressed man leaned over the table, his lips writhing back to expose yellow rotted teeth. "Don't play games, Gunthar. You've upset the guild for the last time. Now, where's the loot, dog? You know going out on your own is in direct violation of the code. Give us the gold or face the consequences."

Gunthar leaned back and, taking up his ale, finished it with a swallow. "Afraid I can't do that, Nilus. I've already spent it."

Nilus snorted. "Don't play the fool. You haven't had time."

Gunthar raised an eyebrow. "Oh? Do you know how much your mother is charging these days? I've only enough left over from her greedy loins for this ale. And you really should write to her you know. She misses you—for all that you're a foul smelling *herthrung*."

A howl of impotent rage was torn from Nilus' lips. He hurled the table aside with one hand and dragged out his sword with the other. Gunthar leaped back, his own blade ready in one bronzed fist. He held up his left hand before him as he found himself surrounded by the edges of three thirsty swords. They paused, looking hesitantly at the tall, rangy muscled man before them. They noted the wide sweeping shoulders, corded arms and lean, narrow waist- characteristics of the natural swordsman. Beneath a yellow tousled mane of hair, green eyes danced recklessly. Sensing their uncertainty, he smiled.

"Easy now," he said softly, "there's three of you and only one of me. Scarcely a fair fight... But I'm a sporting man. Do you want me to wait here while you go and get some more men?"

"Why you—" choked Nilus, lunging forward with a wild thrust.

Gunthar parried and, as he did, the air around them constricted, as if charged with some magnetic force. He felt the hairs on his arms standing on end. His sword hand jerked involuntarily and, looking down, saw that it was fighting him—*trying to sheath his weapon!* Across the broken table a similar story was being played out. Nilus backed off, his eyes wide in astonishment as his arm bent round and slammed his sword back into its scabbard. Then, like a drunken man, he spun on his heel and tramped jerkily to the door, his two cohorts in close and bewildered attendance.

"Sorcery!" Gunthar croaked. The veins on his forehead stood out in bold relief as, gritting his teeth, he fought the awful power being exerted upon him. But from where—? With an effort he turned his head. His eyes swept the tavern, coming to rest upon a draped alcove at the back of the room. It was from here, he felt sure, that the waves of that invisible energy were being directed. With a wolfish snarl, he turned. From behind that blank curtain he could feel monstrous waves of energy beating down his will. Step by slow agonizing step, he made his way across, though every muscle screamed out in violent protest.

As he passed, patrons shrank back from him or else made quietly for the door.

Coming to the alcove he reached up and, with one hand, wrenched the curtain aside.

A toad like man, grotesque in every attribute, met his gaze. He squatted on a chair behind a low table. Eyes, like flakes of hypnotic gold, bored deep into his own. Shaking his head, Gunthar leaned across and, grasping the man by his flowing tunic, laid the bare edge of his sword against his throat. Instantly, the invisible bond that held him snapped. The toad like man licked his lips with a pale tongue; "Excellent," he said. "You are undoubtedly the man I seek."

To either side of him, half hidden in the shadows, two steel clad men held crossbows; the wickedly barbed bolts aimed directly at his heart. Looking up, only to note the curious blank masks they wore, Gunthar's eyes narrowed.

"Speak fast, fat man. Who are you and what do you want? I have no love for mutants."

"My name is Zoolath Q'uann. If you will allow me five minutes of your time, I have something in your line of work that may interest you."

"Go on."

The fat man looked down at the steel pressed into the folds of his sagging flesh and, reluctantly, Gunthar eased off. Snapping his sword back into its wooden sheath, he stepped away and stood with bare arms folded across his chest. Zoolath Q'uann raised his hand. Behind him, the steel clad warriors lowered their crossbows.

Rearranging his tunic, the mutant leaned forward. When he spoke, his voice was like the dry rasp of a venomous snake; "Beyond the Burning Wastes lies the rimless sea. Beyond there, the jungles of Dafu. Somewhere, in that vastness, lies the lost city of Tikka Chuanda. I want you to find that city, Gunthar, and bring back from it the black flame of life!"

"By Yod the Accursed! You don't ask much, fat man. And what does a dead man command in way of payment for such a venture? Assuming, that is, the black flame actually exists."

Zoolath Q'uann chuckled. "Oh, it exists. Nor do I expect you to make the journey alone, my impetuous friend… "

Reaching up, he tugged at a brocaded rope that hung from the ceiling. Instinctively, Gunthar's hand snatched for his hilt. To his left, another curtain whipped aside.

Seated there, at a similar low table, were two figures.

The first was a man whom Gunthar recognized at once. He was tall and wore gold plates of armour beneath a winged helmet of northern design. His single eye was bleak, countering the right eye which was covered by a sombre patch. A jagged scar ran down one side of his face above a dark and bristling beard. He was Vorgun, the pirate, and no love was lost between them.

But it was the woman sat across from him that roused Gunthar's interest. She was ebon skinned, with a lean, muscular figure. She wore no armour, only gold accoutrements. About her loins was the hide of a great spotted cat. From the belt at her waist depended a wickedly curved sword. Her face was strongly chiselled. The mystery of the wild burned in the quiet darkness of her eyes and, as he gazed upon her, Gunthar felt his pulse quicken to the throb of unseen drums.

"These will be your companions if you choose to accept my little venture," Zoolath Q'uann said, sitting back and placing misshapen hands on his huge belly. "Each of you has been vetted long before I came into contact with you. Such is the importance of this mission. I am determined it shall not fail."

Gunthar gave a grunt, "You seem pretty damned sure I'll accept."

"I thought and said much the same, warrior. Until I heard what was offered as reward."

It was the black woman who spoke. Rising to her feet she moved sinuously across and, folding her arms, leaned with her hip against the table before him. "I am Niama, from Zelba."

Gunthar appraised her coolly. "Well met, Niama. I am Gunthar. Once I, too, had a land I called my own but… that was long ago. Tell me more of this reward."

A bark of laughter brought their attention to the man still sat at the low table behind them. He quaffed deep of an intricate carved goblet before setting it down. One gauntleted hand rose and slammed a vicious double headed war axe on the table.

"What's this? Gunthar, the man they once called the Black Wolf, panicking over a little trek in the jungle? No wonder you left the high seas, boy, if this is what you've become. A whining, cowardly wreck."

Gunthar straightened. "Vorgun, we meet again. Maybe I will take up the offer so we can fight as comrades. Just like in the old days."

Vorgun cursed. "Comrades, you dog? You turned my crew against me and damned near sank my ship… Aye, partners we'll be. But Skull Smiter here, still hungers for your head. Mark me."

As he spoke he lovingly caressed the axe on the table.

"Just what is this reward?" asked Gunthar, unmoved by the threat.

The mind mutant leaned forward, his fat bulk quivering with excitement.

"Gold! Immortality, everlasting youth… the very secrets of time itself!"

"The devils keep your immortality! I'm no magician."

Zoolath Q'uann looked uncertain. "Then- you refuse?"

Gunthar deliberated. True enough, his purse was nearly empty.

Not only that but he wearied of the guilds in this decadent city, always seeking to deprive an honest fighting man of his livelihood. Once again, the freedom call of the open road beckoned him.

He laughed then, as if at some secret jest only the gods knew.

"No, Zoolath Q'uann... I accept your offer."

He turned to stare at Niama, standing close beside him. "Let's just say, for now, that there are things in life, other than jewels and power that are equally worth fighting for."

II - Secrets of the Burning Wastes.

Under the orb of the waning sun, three swift legged zamas thundered across the rocky plains. Behind them the spired domes of Uhremon receded into the purpling sky.

The zamas—strange slim beasts, distant relatives of the zebra and antelope, seemed to barely touch the ground as they fled into the approaching dusk.

Night fell. A thousand glittering stars lay dusted across the heavens. On a rocky escarpment, before the hollow of an empty cave, the riders settled for the night. Tethering their long legged steeds, they set about and began making fire. Gunthar took first watch. He stood leaning against a tree, looking down into the valley below. Behind him, he felt Vorgun's watchful eye on his back as he lay wrapped in his bear skin cloak near the crackling flames. He did not have to look to know that the haft of his axe, Skull Smiter, was ever near his hand.

Gunthar kept his hand near the hilt of his own curved sword. In the event of a showdown he would not be found unprepared. But the night wore on without incident and soon snores, from where the pirate sprawled closest to the fire, could be heard resounding throughout the valley.

He stood there listening to the wild things of the night as they prowled and played out their lives beyond the distant rim of firelight. He sensed Niama behind him, even before he heard the soft step of her bare foot on the dusty earth. Seeing her, he unlimbered his tall, rangy frame and yawned into a knotted fist.

"All quiet?" she smiled, taking up position beside him.

"Aye. There should be little trouble. Nothing big enough to eat us could make its way up here unseen."

She nodded and Gunthar, unloosening his sword belt, turned for his camp roll.

"Back in the tavern," the warrior woman spoke suddenly, "you said that, once, you had a land you called your own, but no longer… What did you mean?"

Gunthar paused. Looking off into the night, he turned to face her.

"It was not always destined that I should be the man I am now," he said and there was a tinge of sadness in the edge of his words. Niama shifted in the uncomfortable silence that followed.

"It's alright," he grinned; "you just caught me off guard. I come from a distant land, somewhere to the west. The son of a king. Neither land nor king exist now."

Seeing her eyes on him, he ran his hand through his hair and, crouching down beside her, plucked at a blade of grass. There, under the cold light of the stars, he began telling her the tale of his past. He told of a wealthy baron who claimed a trace of royal blood that coveted the throne and, in bitter words, recounted how a mercenary army had sacked the kingdom. The towers were burned to the ground, he said, the royal line executed in cold blood. His mother—

In the shadows of the flickering firelight his face contorted, whether in memory of horrors past or in barely controlled rage, Niama could not tell.

"I alone of my line escaped," he continued, regaining his composure, "I roamed… a broken youth, no more than twelve summers old. I came to the hills bordering the steppes of Tatukura. It was there that the steppe riders found me. Starved and half frozen to death, they took me in and nursed me back to health. Among them I became a man. At fifteen I could ride, shoot a bow and hunt the great *herthrung* of the plains. I had proven myself in combat against the rivals of our clans. I was still an outsider, but every man is expected to lay down his life for his chieftain.

"During a raid, I saved the life of an elder who adopted me as his own.

"It was he who named me Gunthar—the battler, the warrior… the boy from the pinelands of the west. It is a name I earned by blood. The old name I had worn, the life I had known, had been washed away by the cold rains of the steppe, blasted from me by the winds of the mountains…." His eyes clouded with memories. "After so long, I had a name again. Not a title, but a name. And it is one I shall carry with me until the day I die and the wolves howl my death song…"

Lost in the tale, Niama stared at him, her dark eyes glistening like jet in the starlight. Only the sound of the night breeze, whispering up the pass, disturbed the silence. Gunthar stood and, with a backward glance, smiled down at her.

"Goodnight, Niama," he said and moved off to the fire.

* * * *

The next day found them riding hard over the granite plains. A dismal sky roiled over them, dark and foreboding. Occasional flashes of lightning flared, but there was no thunder, only the passage of a shuddering wind blowing in hot from the desert.

The Burning Wastes were a cursed place. Some said that the area was blighted, infected by the necromantic wars of long ago. Men who dwelled there became sickly; poisoned, many believed, by the evil taint of the land. Their offspring grew into twisted forms, some gifted with strange and terrible powers—the curse of the ancient ones that once ruled there.

These thoughts were heavy in their minds as the three

adventurers pushed their striped beasts onward.

Presently they came to the end of the fused plains. Reining up they stared out across the desert. There was no break in the monotony of the red tinted sand before them, unless one counted the bleak wind that sifted that sand into occasional whorls of movement that danced like waves on a blood stained sea.

The sun glared down above them, an oval shield; merciless and unrepentant. They looked to each other in silence, daunted by the prospect of the journey ahead.

Suddenly, Niama laughed and, reining forward, cried; "Why so glum? This reminds me of home!"

Vorgun, looking to Gunthar, grumbled a curse and, spitting in the dust, heeled after her.

The hours passed in slow monotony. The going was hard. A jagged wind blew, hot and sulphurous, as if from the burning lungs of hell. They made slow progress, hunkered down in their saddles, black burnooses wound tightly over their heads. Their mounts fared little better in the heat and they stumbled on occasion, unused to the sighing drifts of the desert sands. Everything became stained with red dust as it blew and whorled around them.

Every now and then one of them would look up, to ease the stinging of grit in their eyes, only to see the furnace eye of the sun glaring back down at them.

The day wore on.

It was Vorgun who saw them first. He cried out hoarsely, even as he lowered the water canteen from his cracked lips. The others, looking to where he pointed, made out the distant silhouettes of riders far off to the left. They were some distance away but, how far, was impossible to tell through the heat waves dancing over the sands. They thought to hear the jingle of harness, the creak of wagons; all borne to them on a vagrant wind. There were snatches of laughter too, and even singing, beautiful and melodic.

"A caravan!" croaked the pirate. "By Poseidus! A caravan!"

Gunthar looked uneasy. One hand fell to the hilt of the sword at his side. He looked across to Niama who sat statue straight in her saddle, a carven figure of exquisite ebony.

"Madness…" muttered the tall plainswoman, "no caravan master in his right mind would dare attempt these wastes. There are no trading posts from here to the rimless sea."

Gunthar said nothing. His eyes slid over to where Vorgun, leaning over his saddlebow, gripped his reins tensely.

"There must be an oasis close by," he said then, stiffening, cried out; "Listen! The women are singing! What beauty—never have I heard such voices!"

As he talked he moved his zama forward. Gunthar heeled after him. "Vorgun, don't be a fool!" The pirate turned sharply, his one good eye blazing. "Listen!" he cried and Gunthar, the hairs lifting on his nape—*heard*.

An eerie dirge, like the timeless song of forgotten places, pulled at him. He found himself yearning; longing for something he knew not. He broke off the feeling with difficulty, shaking his head and muttering a curse. The song swept toward them, alluring and enchanting. Looking, Gunthar saw Vorgun, his face a mask of unholy rapture as it turned to the sky.

Then, from out of the crimson sands, a figure appeared. It came across the dunes, a naked shadowed shape, exquisitely formed; both delicate and light.

It was a woman, her form disguised by the whirling drifts that kept time with her. She danced as a shadow dances, and the tambourine she held in one upraised hand made no sound. They saw the long play of her hair, streaming out behind her on an invisible wind, her finely contoured body spinning in ritual abandonment of its surroundings.

Behind her came other shapes, each more beautiful than the last, and Gunthar, pulling back on his reins, moved away in primitive dread.

An aura of unreality presided over all.

With a howl, Vorgun heeled his mount up the dunes and, with a curse, Gunthar reined after him. He caught up with the pirate and grabbed at his tunic sleeve.

Foaming at the lips Vorgun wheeled, catching him a glancing blow behind the ear that rocked him to his foundations.

More by luck than judgement, Gunthar lashed out, catching the pirate with his own fist on the point of his jaw. His head snapped back and, with a cry, he fell from the saddle, dragging Gunthar with him onto the sand. They rolled straining in the dust, each man grappling for a hold, biting and cursing.

Vorgun's one good eye blazed with volcanic wrath and he snarled incoherently. They gouged and kicked, each man seeking the advantage. The pirate, finding he was no match for the wolfish strength of the youth, groped at his sword belt. Heaving up, he ripped out a knife as the Tartukuran lay beneath him in the dust. The blade glittered in the sun and, as he lifted it on high, Gunthar snarled in hopeless fury as he stared up at it from beneath the hand clamped around his throat.

"Hold!" the order cut across their senses like a dash of icy water.

Gunthar looked beyond the upraised blade to see Niama, astride her mount. Her bow was drawn, the point of the arrow aimed squarely at Vorgun's back.

The pirate froze. Sweat glistened on his brow, dripped darkly from his face.

Slowly, the madness left his one good eye and he blinked, lowering the blade. He looked around him, bewildered. Niama held the bow fixed. Seeing her, he mumbled a curse. Then, rising stiffly to his feet, he turned and stalked off. He mounted his zama and, head lowered, rubbed at his jaw.

"Apologies," he grumbled.

Gunthar, shaking the dust from himself, rose and tramped over to his own mount.

Niama lowered the bow. "We ride," she snapped and heeled forward. They followed. None looked back.

As they mounted a slow rising crest of sand, Niama turned at last in her saddle to stare back the way they had come. Shading her eyes, she pointed back along the trail. "There!" she cried, "There is your caravan of dreams with its rich reward!"

Both men turned in their saddles, looking back across the burning wastes to where she indicated.

There, in the forever sighing drifts, they saw the gleam of bare white bones, the broken wreckage of caravans, heaps of wares lying forgotten in the dust. Among the debris they saw squat, ugly shapes slinking to and fro. They were men but not quite men; hideous deformities. They skulked and lived out their meagre half lives there, preying on travellers and the unwary.

"Mutants…" muttered Gunthar.

Niama nodded. Looking over to Vorgun she said; "Mind vampires. Ghouls. What you saw and heard was no more real than a mirage. Had Gunthar not gone to get you, they would be even now cracking open your bones and feasting on the marrow."

Vorgun said nothing but stared, looking grimly down. Then he turned the head of his mount and pressed on.

Some miles on there was an oasis. They come upon it warily, their weapons close at hand. There were men there but they kept to themselves, shunning the adventurers.

When Gunthar went down to the pool's frond shaded edge he knelt in the sand, drinking and washing his face from a cupped palm. Looking across he saw a crippled hooded shape watching him from a tuft of reeds. It moved off, but not before Gunthar saw yellowed eyes and scaled skin beneath the confines of the hood. A cool breeze whispered through the palms and he shivered. Moving back to his companions, where they sat in the shade of a huge tree, he nodded across the water. "More mutants."

Vorgun glared and moved the handle of his axe nearer his side.

They rested and, soon, stars began to blink out overhead as the night wind rustled the dry grass.

Dawn found them mounted and on their way again. Gradually

they left the desert behind and, by afternoon, they were following the strata of a worn canyon.

Rock lizards basked in the sun as buzzards wheeled in the sky.

Then they had climbed the broken trail to come out on the shore of the rimless sea.

III - Plith.

"We're being followed." Gunthar reined up close to Niama as they cantered through the last of the rocks lying strewn, as if by some giant's careless hand, before the shoreline. The plainswoman nodded. Her eyes registered no surprise.

Gunthar relaxed his reins, allowing himself to fall back behind Vorgun. When they rounded the last of the great outcroppings, only two zamas came out again.

Behind them, a shadowed shape slithered silently over the rocks, pulling itself up and over with frightening speed. Under the confines of a black hooded cloak, yellowed eyes burned. A long tongue flickered out, tasting the air.

Looking down from a precarious perch, it saw the three riders disappear around the curve of the final outcropping. Then, with a grotesque leap, it bounded far out onto the boulders below. Misshapen feet slapped the rocks and it crouched in the shadows, watching as the two riders moved across the pale sands.

A noise made it turn suddenly, to see the figure of a tall man stood leaning in the shadows of the rocks behind. In the right hand of the figure was a long curved sword. Beneath a wild mane of tangled hair, emerald eyes played hard. Startled, the creature moved back and the edge of that sword whipped up, pressing sharply against his throat. Gunthar grinned; "Well, well, the mutant from the oasis. Any more friends lurking around out here- or did you come alone?"

As he spoke he moved forward. The mutant fell back, spreading curiously webbed hands. He hunched down and Gunthar, in his high strapped sandals, stood over him.

The mutant looked up. "I came alone, master... I wish to join you. I can guide you through the jungles of Dafu to the city of Tikka Chuanda."

Gunthar's eyes narrowed. "How do you know of our destination?" he scowled.

The mutant stared. "Why else would the true folk pass over the Burning Wastes, if not to seek the legendary city?"

"You have seen it?"

"Oh yes, my lord. I have been there many times. But the way is not easy. Not for one such as you. You will need a guide. Those of the jungle outpost cannot be trusted."

Gunthar deliberated. He noted the creature's flat features, the yawning frog like mouth and hideous mottled scales. He was a reptiloid, one of those curious branches of genetically mutated beings sometimes seen lurking at the edge of townships scavenging for scraps.

"How are you called?"

"Plith, master."

"Well, Plith," he said, ramming his sword back into its scabbard, "I have no love for mutants. Why should we trust you?"

"Not all mutants hate the true folk for their untainted blood, master. If you have money then I will lead you... we tainted ones also need feeding."

Gunthar looked up. The zamas of his companions came into view, approaching slowly toward them.

"What's the hold up?" bawled Vorgun, "slay the wretch and have done with it!"

Gunthar rubbed a hand over his stubbled jaw. "He wishes to join us. He says he can lead us to Tikka Chuanda," he called back.

"Stab us in the back more's the like!" came the blasting reply.

They reined in close and looked down on Plith who cowered in his tattered cloak before the hooves of their mounts.

Niama frowned. "You know the way to the lost city?"

Plith, not looking up from where he crouched submissively in the dust, nodded.

The warrior woman deliberated. "If he can lead- let him join us."

Vorgun spat in the dust; "He could have friends waiting on the other side. Who's to say he isn't leading us into a trap?"

"Gunthar?" the plainswoman asked, looking round.

Moving to his zama, the Tatukuran warrior shrugged as he swung agilely into the saddle. "Well, what money we give him will be less than hiring a guide at the trading outpost. The danger of being robbed, or worse, is no greater."

Niama nodded. "Then it is agreed. You can come. But play us false and you will die. Be assured of that."

Plith, looked up. His face split open in a wide grin. "Yes mistress! Thank you!"

Vorgun mumbled as the mutant leaped to his feet and began running lizard like in the dust after their mounts as they made their way down to the sea.

IV - Bilus Urquhart.

Their mounts slowed as they came across the soft sands toward the shore. In the distance they could see the skeletal remains of a ship in the surf. Gulls wheeled above it, their cries drifting mournfully on the breeze. Beyond it, the mirrored waters of the sea stretched placidly over the horizon. They carried on down to the water's edge and, as they drew closer, they saw that the gigantic hulk before them was not the remains of a ship at all but, rather, the upturned carcass of a monstrous crab, its armoured legs braced stiffly against the sky. Gulls ripped at the armoured underbelly as they fought over this unexpected feast.

They were not sure just how long the figure had been standing there watching them. He seemed to materialize beside the crab, his back to the sea, staring calmly at their approach. They saw an impossibly tall, inhumanly thin figure, cloaked from head to heel in a flowing mauve robe. A cowl was drawn up, shadowing the features. Niama held up her hand as they came to a halt before the silently lapping waters.

"Greetings," she called. "We are travelers wishing to cross the rimless sea to Dafu. Do you know of any boats that can carry us across?"

The figure did not reply at once. In one hand he held a curious ebon staff that he raised toward them. Then, slowly, he made a motion with it, pointing out across the sea.

"From there is one who will come," he said at last. His voice rasped, as if muffled behind a wad of cloth. Looking up they noticed small stunted shapes clambering over the crab, sawing and cutting at the soft white flesh with serrated blades. They gibbered in frustration as they fought frantically with the gulls for the best parts. Hacking off great white chunks of flesh, they were busily throwing them into baskets strapped to their backs.

"Scavengers," Vorgun muttered in disgust. The tall robed man leaned against his ebon staff. "For a good price we have all you can eat. The meat is still fresh."

"No. Thank you. We have our own supplies," replied Niama, "How long before the boat comes in?"

Turning to the figures swarming over the crab behind him, the man shouted something in a strange tongue. Fending off the darting beak of a gull, a dwarfish mutant with a bulging forehead screeched something in reply. The tall hooded figure nodded. "An hour... maybe more. There is a landing point just across this ridge. You can wait there."

Niama nodded thanks and, jerking their mounts, they reined to where he indicated.

Crossing over the ridge, they soon found the landing platform. Half buried in the sand, it was little more than a walkway of ancient, corroded metal. Dismounting, they sat down beside it and prepared themselves to wait. Presently, they saw something approaching over the horizon. Something that hissed and thumped.

A ship. A curious ship with two great wheels fixed to either side of the hull, constantly turning. Behind it the milky tides churned and frothed.

"What relic is this?" snorted Vorgun.

With a grind and splutter the wheels stopped as the ship drifted silently into shore. They stared in bewilderment as the metal tub of the flat keel came to rest in the shallows. A landing plank was extended. As it thumped out onto the platform with a dull clank, a short, rotund figure, bizarrely dressed, appeared at the top. He bowed extravagantly, doffing a purple top hat.

"Good day, my friends! I hope our scavenger friends have not caused you any alarm. Can't afford to lose custom. They're quite harmless. But enough jabbering from me! Come aboard and be welcome!"

Looking to each other, the companions led their wary mounts up the gangway and entered the confines of the steel hulled boat. They saw a complicated arrangement of decks.

In the main hold their zamas were stabled, taken there by two silent short, burly looking men with bushy brows and stern faces. They wore greasy coveralls that smelt of oil.

They were led up onto the main deck by their host who, after much chattering, introduced himself as Bilus Urquhart. He was the captain of the vessel that, he explained, was not a ship but something called a 'tide trawler.' He wore an ill fitting purple suit with a white frilled shirt underneath. His fat, friendly face, constantly wreathed in smiles, was framed by thick red sideburns and a neatly trimmed beard.

*   *   *   *

"We get a lot of tourists," he said chirpily, sitting on the high end of the raised fore deck, pouring tea. "Tikka Chuanda has become quite the attraction. The outpost people don't mind. Takes their mind off logging. Gives them an opportunity to arrange trips and what not. I see you have your own guide... Plith, is it? Ahh, yes... Well, they don't really mind strangers, so long as they can take a few coins from them."

They sat around the table and watched the placid milky tides churn by. From the aft, the two gigantic wheels chugged deafeningly. Bilus Urquhart seemed not to notice as he sat contentedly looking over the horizon, sipping from his china cup. They had paid a reasonable price for the journey and the passage only took a few hours. Gunthar wondered if he could bear the noise that long.

Vorgun leaned across the table. "You say the settlers take people into the city?" He had to shout to be heard.

"Oh no! Not that far. Dear me, no... You can view from a distance. The views are quite marvellous. To enter the city itself, well... let's just say some tourists have tried. Much against the advice of the settlers. Queen Barastiis still reigns there, you see. She claims direct descent from the ancient Jaguar dynasty. While her subjects have degenerated, the blood of her line is kept pure."

Suddenly, from the aft, there was a crunch, followed by a protesting grind of shrieking metal, and Bilus Urquhart started, spilling his tea. "Curses!" he said, jumping up and wiping himself down with a handkerchief, "what are those two idiots up to now?"

He marched off down to the aft deck from where a thick greasy cloud of smoke was billowing. There was much shouting as the two short, burly men, their faces covered in soot, waved their arms and yelled at each other.

When the captain was out of earshot Vorgun, turning to the others, pulled out a sheaf of papyrus from under his tunic. In ring fingered hands he unrolled it and laid it on the table before them.

It was a map. Gunthar and Niama leaned in close.

"Zoolath Q'uann gave me this map before we left," he growled,

"It's a layout of the city. An explorer drew it when he escaped there, some months ago. It is as our captain says. Visitors are not welcome and the penalty is death. The people of Tikka Chuanda are throwbacks, except for Queen Barastiis who is said to be immortal. Legend is she drinks from the blood of jaguars to sustain her. But we know different. The secret of her eternal youth is, of course, the black flame. Our explorer friend has even seen it."

"So we sneak into her palace and just steal it?" Gunthar asked.

"That's what you were hired for, boy," the pirate replied in a surly tone.

Niama interrupted. "All very well. If the city is run down and the people degenerate as we are led to believe, it should not be difficult. Guards will be lax, walls will be in ruins and there will be lots of jungle overgrowth in which to hide."

Vorgun nodded. "My thoughts exactly." He looked to Gunthar. "You can hide in the bushes and wait for us if you like."

Gunthar choked off an angry reply and clenched his jaw instead. He rose and, moving to the rail, leaned on it, staring off over the horizon into the distant haze beyond. Toward the blunt nosed fore of the trawler he noticed Plith, perched on the rail with both feet. He made his way over to him.

The reptiloid did not move as he came up. He seemed to be basking in the afternoon sun. Gunthar looked at him, at his tattered hooded cloak streaming in the wind. He noticed the hilts of two sabres sheathed and slung cross wise over his back.

"Can you use those swords, Plith?"

The reptiloid turned his head. Gunthar noticed a clear film over his eyes drawing back as he blinked. He stared at the warrior as if noticing his presence for the first time. Plith nodded, drawing the blades out slowly in both hands. They were old, notched and pitted with rust. "These are my prize possessions, master," he said. "They once belonged in the hands of a great swordsman. I found them buried, along with his bones, in the sands. Aahh, what glories these weapons must have witnessed in the long ago." His yellow eyes clouded as he turned the corroded blades this way and that. Gunthar sighed, and leaning on the rail, shook his head.

After much shouting and banging, the tide trawler was soon under way again. Bilus Urquhart, more jovial than before, took great delight in pointing out the various wonders about them. Once, far off in the distance, they saw the translucent coiling hump of a gigantic worm whale as it searched mournfully for a mate. The sound of its melancholic call echoed out in endless reverberations across the sea. Then there were the fabled spires of drowned Saliopolis, rising forever lost into the sky. What mysteries lay below them only the strange denizens gliding silently beneath the waves knew. Vorgun stared hungrily at those spires and dreamed golden dreams of fabulous treasures. He swore to someday return and loot whatever glorious riches lay beneath. Bilus Urquhart smiled and sipped his nettle tea.

Just as the sun was beginning its slow descent into the west, they saw the rugged vastness of the Dafu jungle rising up out of the mist before them. Fishermen, drawing up their catch of blind cullut fish in woven nets, stopped to stare as they came in.

They made landing on a rough wooden pier and saw the settlement of a primitive camp hacked out of the jungle along the shoreline.

"Cheerio!" the captain said, as they bumped up onto the landing platform, "I'm sure we will be seeing each other again, soon."

He bowed and, taking Niama's hand, pressed his lips to it as she led her mount down the gangway. "Don't forget to cover up," he said; "It is not often the men hereabouts see such ravishing beauty!"

Then he stepped back, waving off each of his passengers in turn as they came down.

No sooner had they stepped onto the pier, then the two short, burly crew members drew up the gangway and they were off again, chugging and sputtering out into the sea.

V - *The terror jungle of Dafu.*

The storm came in suddenly, the accompanying wind whipping wildly through the tight packed trees. Dark clouds rolled and lightning forked out over the sea. Thunder cracked. Then the rains came. In cyclonic fury it slanted down, hammering on the sands and drumming on the makeshift shelters of the huts strewn along the shoreline.

Through muddy village streets, people ran for shelter. Even they, who had lived most of their lives there, could not safely predict the wild weather patterns along the Dafu coast.

The companions found themselves drying out in a crudely built tavern. The rain drummed on the ceiling, dripped onto the dirt floor through the densely packed fronds that served to insulate the bamboo lashed rafters.

They sat watching silently as, in the darkness beyond, the storm raged and howled. Occasional flashes of lightning etched their surroundings in bold relief.

"Makes me nostalgic for Bilus' boat," sighed Niama, her chin propped in her hand as she leaned on the rough hewn table, staring past the open decking into the storm wracked night.

Settlers sat calmly ignoring the storm, drinking and playing cards. For the most part, they were a surly, coarse hewn lot, hardened by years of outpost living.

Vorgun looked around him as he swilled back a jug of banana wine. Their ways were not to his liking at all, used as he was, to the uproarious life of sailors and vagabonds. Grumbling drunkenly to himself, he upended yet another foaming jack. He thumped the empty vessel on the boards and, wiping the back of a hand over his lips, blustered; "Let's play cards!"

Gunthar sat back and turned away, sipping of his own watery ale. Niama affected not to notice. Only Plith, from where he sat crouched on the floor, looked up as the pirate spoke. Vorgun, looking around the table, cast his one good eye on the mutant.

"What about you, mutant? Care to lose those rusty old blades in a game of dice? I wager that cloak would serve me well in the winter…" He laughed, looking around him again. Seeing his companions ignoring him, he lurched drunkenly to his feet. "Ignoring me, eh? I know what you all think… filthy pirate, scum o' the sea… pah!"

He swung around, glaring angrily at anyone who might catch his eye. He grumbled. "I get no more respect from you than as if I were a… damned mutant!" He turned and, with a yell, gave Plith a vicious kick in the ribs from where he crouched at the wall nearest the table. The mutant fell back with a hiss, raising his arms protectively as he sought to scramble away.

Laughing, Vorgun staggered after him, drawing back his boot for another kick. Gunthar was on his feet. His arms shot out and Vorgun, shoved from behind, was hurled roughly forward. He hit the dirt, face first. Niama jumped up and the Tatukuran held out his arm, motioning her back.

Slowly, Vorgun rolled over. He sat for an instant, looking up to where Gunthar stood over him, brace legged and ready for trouble.

The pirate laughed uproariously. "You and me, boy! When this is over… it's just you and me."

"I think it's time you went to bed, Vorgun. We have a long trek ahead of us," Niama said.

The pirate rose stiffly to his feet, stretching his back and rolling his shoulders. Without a backward glance he moved over to the front steps and stalked off into the stormy night, making for one of the huts where they had been housed.

Niama stared out into the storm after his retreating figure. "Best we all turn in," she sighed, laying a hand on Gunthar's arm. "Good night." Their eyes met. Then, flinging her cloak round her shoulders, she hunched over and ran out into the rain, splashing through the muddy streets toward her own hut.

Gunthar, looking after her, frowned. He turned, seeing Plith crouched in the shadows.

"Will you be alright? We're turning in."

Plith nodded. "I will find a shelter in the trees, master. These settlers like mutants even less than city folk. Thank you… for what you did."

The warrior nodded. Moving slowly down the wooden steps, he stepped out into the slanting rain.

*   *   *   *

Early next morning found them wading deep into the jungle, following a well worn trail. The going was easier than expected, as it was mostly game trail used by settlers. They followed the path as it wound gradually upward. From the beach they had seen the distant peak of a volcano, smoking and dominating the skyline. Toward it they now toiled. Tikka Chuanda, it was said, lay in its shadow.

They carried machetes. As they forged ahead the need to use them became more frequent. They chopped back the creepers and lianas dangling in their path, hacked at the foliage sprouting unchecked along the overgrown trail.

Ahead of them, Pltih leaped through the jungle. He moved so surely it seemed he slithered and glided like the lizard he so resembled.

Before mid-day they took their fast under a canopy of trees. They sat in a circle. Vorgun, morose, broke a hard packed rice cake over the silver heel of his boot and chewed in silence. The haft if his axe, Skull Smiter, stood up beside him.

Gunthar looked to his clothing. He wore a sleeveless red tunic, leggings and moccasins of supple doe skin. His sword, tied across his back in its lacquered wooden sheath, was carefully oiled and dried against the rising humidity.

Niama's light accoutrements allowed her to move freely and easily through the jungle. Beneath the dark halo of her tightly curled hair she wrapped a strip of red cloth. Her spear was ever at hand. Unlimbering her bow, she replaced the string with a tougher cord against the dampness and checked her arrows.

Above them, in the branches of a nearby tree, Plith sat with a small blunt knife, hunched over and carving on a piece of wood.

Afternoon came. They had made good progress, forging on through the dense foliage, their machetes working tirelessly. As the way became more tangled so too the slope became more treacherous. Sweat filmed them and they gasped in the sweltering heat. From far off they heard the sound of a distant rumbling. Birds took flight from the trees. The ground beneath their feet trembled slightly then was still.

Stopping in her tracks, Niama turned. "Did you feel that?"

The others had also stopped. Vorgun, crouching low, looked around him. Plith came racing back through the trees. "It is the voice of the volcano. It speaks often. Do not worry."

He pointed. In the distance they could see a thick pluming black cloud rising into the sky.

Gunthar wiped the back of a wrist over his dripping brow. "How much further, Plith?"

"Not far now," the reptiloid grinned, hopping off back through the bush. He alone among them seemed to thrive in the equatorial heat.

Gunthar moved after him, slashing right to left as the brush fell back. Suddenly he jerked his head. A shadow fell across him and he saw Plith diving for him, hands outstretched, mouth yawning wide. He barely had time to raise his blade before the reptiloid had leaped over his head and went crashing into the foliage beyond. He turned in time to see the mutant rolling and thrashing in the grass.

Niama stood frozen, her spear arm drawn back for the killing cast as Plith rolled over and over. They saw thick black coils looping about him. There was a hiss, a crack, then silence. They saw him crouched low in the bush, his tattered cloak falling over him. Then the glistening coils relaxed, falling limp. He rose, holding a dead snake in his webbed hand.

"Can I feed? I have not eaten since before the last rains."

Gunthar moved over to him. He looked at the mutant incredulously. Slowly, Niama lowered her spear. Vorgun laughed and moved off through the trees, his machete swinging before him.

"You're lucky, Plith," the Tatukuran said, shaking his head. "Niama very nearly killed you."

The mutant looked at him and shrugged. "I saw the snake reaching through the branches above you, master. What was I to do?"

Gunthar grinned, putting a hand on his shoulder. "Apologies, Plith. And thank you... You saved my life. Of course you can eat."

It was late afternoon when they came upon the first of the vine tangled ruins of the outer city. Statues, eroded by time, lay sunken in the soft loam. Here and there were broken columns and walls, evidence of a once much larger metropolis. Then, climbing a steep rise, they found themselves looking down on the lost city of Tikka Chuanda itself.

In wreathing mists lay a wide curving valley, cut from the heart of the equatorial jungle. Dimly, through those mists, they could see the decayed splendour of a once powerful city. Vine tangled streets lay empty. Temples and domes, cracked and decayed, stood silent as, between crumbled columns and trees, many coloured birds rose gaily into the sky.

Across the valley basin reared the volcano; dominating over the skyline like some grim grey god.

They stood looking down in awed silence, panting from their exertions.

Squatting by a broken column, Plith swept his arm over the valley.

"Here is as far as visitors go."

Vorgun looked on. "But you know a safe way in, right?"

The reptiloid nodded. "I know a way in, master, but safety is your concern."

"Then lead on," the pirate growled.

They came down the steep cliff face leading to the valley basin. From the thick shrouded shrubbery birds took flight, startled by their approach. Broken remnants of columns stood here and there. Occasionally, beneath their feet, they felt worn paving and steps.

The sun was a bloody orb sinking slowly to the west when, at last, they reached the valley floor. Here the way became easier, the jungle shrubbery cut back and kept in check by unknown hands. Plith, squatting on the cracked paving, turned to his companions. He parted some fronds with one hand and pointed through.

They found themselves staring down a broad avenue. Vine tangled columns flanked either side. They caught a distant glimpse of firelight and heard snatches of a hide drum, borne to them through the stifling heat.

"Queen Barastiis holds court," the reptiloid hissed, quietly, "It is said that no man has glimpsed her revels and come away sane."

Niama stepped back with a shudder and rose to her full height. "Then it is best we camp here until we get our bearings. We'll begin reconnaissance in the early hours. No fires -"

The rest of her sentence was never uttered. From the trees above, forms dropped crashing down through the branches and, as she wheeled, the very thickets about them exploded with life as dim shapes rushed toward them from the shadows.

Gunthar, reaching over his shoulder, ripped out his sword with a deadly hum.

Then—*madness!*

VI - *In the Lair of the Jaguar Queen.*

From all sides, dim shapes surged around them, weapons gripped in shaggy fists.

Vorgun, swinging Skull Smiter, grunted as a hairy form fell back beneath a wheeling stroke, its face a crumpled red ruin. He leaned aside as an outthrust spear grazed over his leather mail. On the back swing he severed the gnarly arm that held it and snarled in triumph as the resulting howl filled the night.

Niama, ducking beneath a swung blade, up-thrust her spear through a shaggy neck. Wrenching her spear back, she drew out her sword. Feet planted wide, spear dripping in one hand, curved tulwar in the other, she looked wildly about her; "Make for the trees!" she yelled, "They have us out here in the open!"

Indeed, the small clearing worked to their disadvantage, hemmed in, as they were, by grotesque, hairy figures.

Gunthar looked up as a woven net came hurtling down from the trees above him. He dived and, rolling, came up at the edge of the clearing. A hairy form loped toward him and he caught a glimpse of an apish head atop a bull like neck before ducking beneath the heavy blade it wielded. He slashed back with his own curved steel, feeling it rip across the thing's leather harness. Then the heavier form crashed into him and he was fighting desperately for his life, rolling with it through the tall grass into the thickets beyond.

Plith, leaping high up into the air, came down again with both swords in his hands. His first slash ripped open a snarling face and, landing in a crouch, he sprang from the broken paving, the rusty sabre in his right hand running through a thick set body with a powerful thrust. The figure barked out its life and collapsed, thudding to the ground.

"Alive!" a stentorian voice bellowed, "Take them alive, you curs!"

They pressed in and soon, by sheer weight of numbers, Vorgun was dragged down, cursing as he was trussed and bound by brutish hands.

A circle of spear points jabbed at Niama's throat. Seeing resistance was futile she stood proudly and lowered her weapons at her sides.

Only Plith stood at bay, his sabres dripping darkly in his hands. He crouched low as the squat forms moved in warily around him.

One eye looked to the trees and, for a moment, he hesitated. Then, as if making up his mind about something, he lowered his blades to the ground and raised his hands. The hairy figures moved in. Wrenching his arms behind him, they tied him swiftly with ropes of woven grass.

A dark, hairy figure, broader and uglier than the rest, moved on bowed legs into the centre of the clearing. He was harnessed in black leathers and wore a bronze helm. In one hand he held a double bladed war axe. He ground his teeth in the semblance of a smile.

"I am Gulla, captain of the Queen's guard." He thumped his chest resoundingly as he spoke, looking round at his captives through small piggy eyes. "You are now my captives and property of the Jaguar Queen of Tikka Chuanda."

He stepped back and motioned with his axe. The three were pushed through the trees. As they emerged into the dusky light of the streets they saw, for the first time, their captors. Niama noticed their simian appearance, both brutish and shaggy. They walked with a rolling gait, their heavy bodies thick with corded muscle beneath coats of matted fur. Beneath ridges of low set brows, small red eyes stared out above flaring, flat nosed faces.

They were garbed in the studded leathers of warriors, harnessed and helmeted. In their hands were weapons of old, fantastic, design. Swords and axes, shields and spears. Emblazoned on those shields was the crested symbol of the Jaguar. Beneath leather kilts they went bare footed, their apish feet slapping over the rough shod ground. But she had little time with which to ruminate on the devolution of these near men.

Up ahead they were approaching a wide spaced square. Torches, mounted on long poles, burned against a darkening sky. The hollow sound of drums throbbed incessantly; beating like the heart of some savage jungle god.

They came down a wide set of steps, emerging out into a broad plaza. Before them, at the end of that plaza, was a crumbled dais.

Upon it stood an ebon throne. On that throne sat Barastiis, the queen of Tikka Chuanda.

Torches, mounted on long poles, guttered to either side.

Great spotted cats prowled among the dense shadows, their eyes burning feral in the darkness. Toward her the prisoners were now escorted and, at the obsidian steps, Captain Gulla fell to his knee and bowed his head. Around him, other warriors did the same. It seemed to Niama that they trembled with fearful expectancy.

The Jaguar Queen rose languorously to her feet. She was tall, dark and powerfully built. The torches, glistening from her naked skin, highlighted her voluptuous figure. Beneath long, straight midnight hair were almond slanted eyes. A wicked smile played on her lips and, as those eyes swept the captives below, she came slowly down the steps. A belt made from silver coins jingled, striking from the sway of her hips as she walked.

Thrust in the backs from behind, the three companions fell to their knees.

She looked down on them with mocking indifference. The two great spotted cats, following lazily behind, snarled in the gathering dusk.

She raised a bangled arm and, suddenly, the drums ceased to throb. All that could be heard was the sound of torches burning in the wind. She stood insolently, flaunting nothing but a spotted hide slung about her loins. Lifting her head she spoke;

"Transgressors! Do you know the penalty for entering the sacred city of Tikka Chuanda?" The words, spoken in the common tongue, yet sounded with a barbarous accent.

Vorgun, staring through his one good eye, swallowed thickly.

"Your majesty, forgive us. We are explorers who have become lost."

Queen Barastiis threw back her head and laughed; a soft, rich musical laugh, full of scorn.

"Fool!" she said and the word was spat with venomous fury.

Her eyes blazed with anger as she stared at them.

"You are outsiders who have come seeking the sacred treasures of the Jaguar Dynasty. None that enter here return again to the lands that birthed them. But you shall see the treasures you have become so greedily desirous of. Aye—and you shall pray to your weakling gods that you had not!" She raised her arm, pointing to a massive columned structure beyond the plaza.

"Take them to the palace dungeons!" They were hauled roughly to their feet. As they were it seemed the queen's gaze lingered on Niama a moment before they were dragged off across the main square. The drums began to throb again. Primitive howls shook the night as figures leaped and capered. Women, only slightly less hideous than the men, danced with wild abandon.

The prisoners were marched up into the mouth of the building. Down a wide sweeping hall they came, their feet echoing in the dusky silence. Fires, lit in huge copper bowls, could not fully dissipate the shadows playing above. They came down a winding staircase to find themselves in a subterranean lair. Here the walls were clammy and damp, the spaces dimly lit. Their weapons, the guards slung unceremoniously in a heap in one corner before they were pushed into a cell. An iron door slammed shut behind them.

A huge simian, dressed in leathers, emerged out of the shadows, a long barbed whip coiled at his belt. A grunted conversation took place and he took up a stool at a rough hewn table before the door.

The troop of guards departed, tramping up the worn stair.

Vorgun, gripping the bars of the cell, snarled. Swinging round, he threw himself down in the straw.

"Well, Gunthar got away. He always had a streak of luck attached to him that boy." He cursed then spat. A rat squealed before scuttling off into the shadows.

Niama crouched beside him "I wouldn't write him off just yet, Vorgun. If I know him, he wouldn't abandon a comrade."

Vorgun smiled. "Aye, maybe…" then added, "If he lives!"

VII - *Priests of the Volcano God.*

Gunthar, rising from the tangled undergrowth, dropped the rock he held in both bloodied hands, and shook his head dizzily. He looked on the still form lying lifeless at his feet, its head caved in by a single mighty blow, and wiped a shaking wrist over his brow.

Of his battle with the huge simian warrior he recalled little; a frantic whirl of thrashing limbs, blows hard struck and hands that had sought to crush out his life before he groped dimly around him for something, anything, with which to fight back with.

Now he stood in the dusky light, panting and drinking in of the stifling humid air. Staggering away, he made off through the undergrowth before melting into the shadows of the fronds. Over in the clearing, he heard apish voices and knew that his companions had been captured. Unarmed he waited there, expecting at any moment for a detachment of those hideous beastmen to come crashing through the bush in search of him. But the sounds of their voices turned away and headed back toward the city. Gunthar listened. When he was certain they had gone, he crept back through the tall grass.

Moving past the still form of his vanquished foe, he retrieved his fallen sword. Sheathing it slowly, he knelt in the trampled glade and considered his next move.

That his friends had been captured, and no search for him was immediately forth coming, led him to assume that the ambush had been a surprise for both parties.

He looked up, squinting through the over lapping branches of the trees. He saw a makeshift platform there, a lookout post no doubt. The guards had not seen them until they had stood virtually underneath them. Without waiting to access the situation they had dropped down on them. Very likely, Gunthar thought, they did not know he was even there.

Moving quietly into the clearing, he stared through the foliage.

The street beyond lay deserted. The sun was fast sinking as night began drawing down over the valley. In the distance he could see the guttering fires and heard the drums as they fell strangely silent. The sound of a woman's voice carried, echoing through the streets, though he could not make out the words.

He squatted, listening and thinking for a long while before deciding on his next course of action. Then, in an uncoiling of rangy limbs, he was moving. He headed straight for the nearest tree and hauled himself up, climbing swiftly into the branches. He swung into the leafy fastness of another bole overhanging the outskirts of the city.

From tree to tree he made his way, going swiftly and silently, until he came into the heart of the city itself. He stared through the foliage, into the cracks of a domed building below.

Padding silently across it, he leapt agilely into the coverage of another tree. From there he crouched at the end of a great branch and sat looking down into the square.

He gazed upon the revels of the Jaguar Queen and wondered at the degeneracy of her people as they gorged and feasted. In the shadows, he had a glimpse of strange practises and averted his eyes. He saw Queen Barastiis, heard her peal of laughter, as she lounged seductively on the ebon throne. She sat back, stroking the pelts of her great spotted cats as they purred contentedly at her side.

She looked on those revels with great interest, her eyes burning with fevered lust.

How long he crouched there in the leafy shadows, observing those obscene rites, Gunthar never knew. He only became aware that is was time to move when a red moon rose, bloody and full, over the jungle. Rousing himself, he turned when a noise from below him made him freeze. He heard the sound of voices.

Peering down he saw two brutish warriors lounging in the doorway of the crumbled domed building over which his branch hung. They stood smoking on fat rolled up brown leaves. The noxious smell wafted up to Gunthar, where he crouched above them in the tree. His nose wrinkled in disgust. He saw that they leaned on pikes and that they were sentries. Their lax attitude seemed to indicate Tikka Chuanda was not usually prone to attack or alarm.

Stretching out across the branch at full length, he leaned down to catch their words.

"Maybe later we can steal a jug of banana wine," growled one.

The other grunted. "We deserve it. We lost five warriors tonight taking those prisoners. I won't be surprised if their deaths are long and painful."

The other laughed and, coughing, threw the stump of his rolled up leaf into the street.

"All except the black skinned woman, of course."

"Aye. Barastiis will have need of her."

"By Kor, the hairy one, do you have any dice?"

The other snorted. "You know rolling dice is forbidden on duty. Or have you forgotten what happened to Kiggar, already?"

Gunthar drew himself back up silently through the branches, his brow furrowed in wonder. What dark purpose could the Jaguar Queen have in mind for Niama?

As he crept back through the branches he began deliberating on a course of action to free his companions.

Padding back over the dome of the great building, he came into the trees over looking the boulevard. There were houses here, run down and dilapidated, but still habited. Presently a door opened in one. He watched as a large squat shape moved out into the avenue. The figure ambled in the opposite direction before turning off at another branch leading down a side street.

Something in the furtive way that figure moved, carrying no torch in the darkness, piqued Gunthar's curiosity.

Looking over, he leaped, catching the coping of a tall building across the way. He hauled himself up onto the roof and began making his way silently across in pursuit. He ran along the edge of the buildings until he reached a narrow place where, in the street below, it overlapped with shadows.

Here Gunthar dropped down on his quarry, his full weight landing on his back.

With an astonished grunt, the beast-man went to the ground beneath him and, whipping his corded arm around its throat, he held the point of a long dagger before his eyes with the other hand.

"As you value your life, make no sound!" he snarled.

Gunthar was surprised by the resulting squeal of fear. He smelt the faint odour of perfume and noticed his captive was decoratively garbed. On his head was a floral wreath, his body wound up in a rich toga. Gold bands were on his upper arms. He had obviously caught a rare prize; a beast-man of the upper nobility. Gunthar tightened his grip, pressing the point of his blade under the jaw line.

"Who are you and where do you go at this hour, while Barastiis holds court?"

"M-my name is Hrun... a priest of the volcano god, Vangar. Are you going to kill me?" he gasped in a high pitched voice.

"Why should I do that?" Gunthar asked, genuinely confused.

The beast-man swallowed. "Are you not, then, a demon summoned by Barastiis? She who would kill the priests and drive out the worship of Vangar, for good?"

"Nay, beast-man. I have only come in search of my friends who were captured... Why would Barastiis do such a thing?"

"If it pleases you... It is known that she hates us for not allowing her reverence as the true divinity. For all that her sorcery gives her eternal life she must still make obeisance to the volcano god. As have all the descendants of the Jaguar Dynasty, since time immemorial."

"Where are my friends being held?" he asked impatiently.

"In the dungeons of the main palace."

Thoughts turned over rapidly in Gunthar's mind.

"Tell me, Hrun, where were you headed in such haste and

stealth before I accosted you?"

The beast-man turned his head stiffly against the blade held at his throat.

"To a conclave... Queen Barastiis would see the worship of Vangar wiped out, so we have to meet in secret when she is at her debaucheries. Her militia have made it difficult for us to worship. Spies and assassins are at every turn."

"So there is no love lost between you and the Jaguar Queen?" Gunthar mused.

Releasing his hold on the priest he stepped back and, sheathing his dagger, stood with arms folded. "It seems I must meet with these fellow priests of yours, Hrun. I think we can work things to our mutual advantage."

* * * *

The priests huddled silently in the dim lit chamber were roused by the sound of rapped knuckles on the heavy door. When the coded signal ended, a votary, Gruk, moved to the panel and drawing it aside, peered out. A word was hissed and, with a grunt, he drew back the bolt and opened the door. They all started frightfully to their feet when, not one but two, figures emerged out of the shadows into the room. Standing before them, Hrun raised a hairy arm and motioned for quiet. Behind him, the lean shadow of a stranger, who had caused the upset, silently closed the door. They saw a hairless man; a stranger from the world beyond, and wondered.

"My Brothers, do not be alarmed. Here is one who hails from the world outside Vangar's shadow. His name is Gunthar and he has come in search of his companions. As some of you already know, they were captured by Queen Barastiis' soldiers near the valley wall some hours past."

"Art mad, Brother Hrun? Dost thy neck yearn so readily for the executioners axe?" exclaimed a hump backed elder with stringy hair, bounding to his feet and leaning on a gnarly knobbed staff. A murmur of assent went around the room.

Hrun, moving into the centre of the chamber, spread his hands wide. "Brothers! Harken, harken! Truth to tell I was given little choice. But after hearing the manling's words I think he has much to offer. Aye, he could help us in banishing the Jaguar Queen from Tikka Chuanda for good!"

The elder stared at Gunthar, looking at him through rheumy eyes. "You wear the look of violence about you like a cloak, outlander. Speak!"

Gunthar moved toward the priests and they shrank back from him in awe.

"If you will aid me in getting into the palace dungeons, I will take from Barastiis her source of power and end her reign once and for all."

A gasp went around the chamber. "You mean to destroy the black flame?" a voice grunted in astonishment. The elder, stumping over, thrust his head forward and stared into Gunthar's face. "Pah! Destroy it? He has come here, like so many before him, to steal it!"

The warrior shrugged. "Destroy, steal—what's the difference? So long as she no longer wields the power to enslave you."

Another votary shook his head. "Many have come searching. None have succeeded manling."

"This is heresy!" cried another and many were the voices raised in agreement.

Hrun raised his arms. "So long have the teachings of our glorious ancestry kept us in check, brothers! The Jaguar Dynasty, as we once revered it, is no longer. Barastiis has corrupted the teachings and values we upheld and used them to her own ends. Look ye upon her wicked ways, the depths of depravity to which she has sunk, and tell me she needs not be overthrown!"

Silence met these words as the gathered priests mulled over his speech. For each knew, in their heart, that Hrun spoke truth.

After some muttered deliberation the old timer stepped forward.

"If you seek to capture Barastiis, outlander, then we can guide you to the palace dungeons. But beware! Many such visitors as yourself have fallen under her spell. Her appetite for you manlings is insatiable, as is her capacity for cruelty and lust. Many have found themselves captive to her desires, only to be locked up and chained as her plaything."

Hrun nodded. "My brother speaks truth. Only one man has ever escaped from the city. The rest are kept prisoner until they go mad, die, or both."

Gunthar thought of the escaped explorer who had drawn the map and asked;

"What is her interest in one of my companions, a woman?"

Hrun looked at him uneasily. "Get her away from here outlander, and quickly. The woman's youth is crucial to the rites of the black flame. She is the key to Barastiis' immortality. I, myself, have heard the shrieks of young maids as their souls have been torn screaming from their bodies to feed her desire. For the Jaguar Queen is old, outlander—aye!—old as drowned Saliopolis itself!"

"Once I have the black flame," said Gunthar, "I will need to get word to you quickly. If you have men, you will need to overpower the militia and seize control of the city. Can it be done?"

Hrun looked around uneasily. "We have supporters…"

"I will rally the resistance," growled the elder, "When you have the black flame, make your way to the Crimson Tower. It is the largest building over looking the city. We will await your signal to strike."

Hrun nodded. "Young Gruk will guide you by the abandoned sewers into the dungeons beneath the palace. There are no doors in this city we, of the priesthood of Vangar, cannot unlock. From there, outlander, you are on your own."

Gunthar nodded. "So be it."

* * * *

Presently Gunthar, concealed in a dark hooded cloak, made his way down a shadow darkened alley leading toward the main palace. At his side skulked Gruk, a larger shadow striding beside him. They came to a bend and there the votary upheld a thick hairy arm and pointed across the way. Looking to where he indicated, the Tatukuran warrior saw a red bricked tower looming up and etched against the star flecked night; staring gigantically down over the vine tangled ruins of that once mighty city.

"The Crimson Tower," he grunted, "It was built many lifetimes ago by King Ekhor IV, Barastiis' first husband. That was in the long ago days before the black flame warped and corrupted them both. King Ekhor was a manling. A great scientist. The tower holds many of his greatest inventions and discoveries."

"What happened to him?"

"Only a strong mind can withstand the corrupting influence of the black flame. It is said he went mad and poisoned himself. Barastiis grieved mightily. She ordered the citadel locked and sealed. His mouldering bones still reside there among the treasures of his creations. From that day she changed… The black flame has long since driven her mad."

Gunthar stared up at the brooding tower a moment and then they were padding across a small square into the shadows beyond. Gruk bent down and, with a grunt, lifted up a large and rusted grill. They looked down into the blackness of a dark well.

"The abandoned sewers. This passage will take you up directly into the palace dungeons."

He handed Gunthar a cloth wrapped branch, some flint and steel. He laid a hairy hand on the warrior's shoulder. "Vangar be with you, outlander."

Gunthar nodded and, grabbing the torch, lowered himself into the well.

VIII - *Swords in the shadows.*

Time passed slowly in the dungeons. The slow drip of water, the steady glare of the torch bracketed on the wall behind the jailer's head- these were the prisoners only companions.

Presently they saw a large shadow move across the wall. There was a clink of armour as a detachment of guards made their way down the worn stair. The jailer stood. Words passed between them and he moved to the door, the keys jangling in his hand. It swung open and the three companions turned their faces as a torch was thrust toward them.

"One eye! You are summoned before the Jaguar Queen!" said Captain Gulla from the doorway.

Vorgun stood. Niama and Plith looked as he was taken from the cell. The heavy door slammed shut behind him.

He was led down the dank corridor and up the winding stair. His hands were not bound but he knew resistance was futile against those armoured hairy mountains of muscle.

They came into the great hall then padded across to a carven set of steps. Up these they went before coming down a lush carpeted hallway. At the far end two armoured sentries stood before a huge double set of doors. At their approach, those great doors swung silently inward and Vorgun was led within.

The pirate was little prepared for that which met his gaze. A lifetime of roving had impressed upon him the importance of untold riches. The sight that met his eye caught his breath and brought all the inner greed rising up within him. But even the accumulated wealth of an empire, a thousand years dead, could not compare to the beauty of her queen.

Rising from an ermine couch, Barastiis got to her feet. The splendour of her sun bronzed body was wrapped in tight fitting red silks, her upper arms adorned with circlets of hammered gold. She moved across to Vorgun and in her tread was the grace of the primordial wild. As he gazed upon her, the pirate felt the stirrings of a passion he thought long buried.

Coming within arms length, she stood before him and her eyes smouldered with untamed passions.

"You stare... Am I so beautiful, or perhaps, so terrifying?"

Vorgun swallowed hard and a bead of sweat formed on his brow.

"I have sailed the oceans of the Kilbarz, plundered the coasts of Tharmaggar... yet never, in all my years, have I beheld a woman so beautiful," he said thickly.

Barastiis laughed. "You are bold, outlander."

The pirate shrugged. "A man, with nothing to lose, has little but boldness left... my queen."

She moved back, indicating the ermine couch. "Come, then. Let us be seated."

As they sat down she offered him a crystal goblet. He drank from it, marvelling at the thick cut glass even as the wine stung his palate. Incense, burning from copper dishes, drifted lazily in the air. She stretched out beside him and the scent of her nearness made his senses reel.

"You came seeking the black flame," she said and Vorgun hesitated, the goblet frozen at his lips. She smiled. "Do not lie, you are not the first. The gift of eternal life is a precious thing. But it is a lonely existence. Centuries have I ruled here, watching this city wax and wane. I have seen the tides, of what is now the rimless sea, shrink and withdraw into the distance. I have witnessed the jungle grow as the heat rises; seen our once splendid nation fall into ruin and despair... I have watched as my people degenerate into little more than beasts. Only tradition keeps them from sliding into the murk of barbarism. My power over them slips daily, as they regress further down the chain of evolution."

The pirate set the goblet down. "You are the last of the Jaguar line?"

Barastiis nodded slowly. Her eyes, when she spoke, were

strange as if haunted with long remembering, "I have lived over a thousand years. Yet, to this day, I have conceived no child to continue the line. No man has produced for me a future queen and, without her, the dynasty dies. The Jaguar Dynasty is regenerated and kept alive in the sacred fires of the flame. My powers need rejuvenating by the youth of females of my own kind. The women of Tikka Chuanda have regressed so far that they no longer sustain me."

She turned to him and her eyes blazed hotly through the narcotic haze of the chamber. "Stay here and rule with me—every desire, every treasure of this kingdom shall be yours! I weary of these degenerate beast-men. I yearn to be held in the arms of a real man. Your woman companion will be delivered up to me. In the sacred rite of the black flame, I will give you knowledge and power—*the very secrets of immortality!*"

Vorgun recoiled, his mind dazed by the images conjured up by her words. He hesitated. She leaned in, gripping his arm with an inhuman strength.

"Is it the woman? What is she to you? I offer you the riches of a forgotten and sacred world!"

The pirate shook his head. "Nay. She is nothing to me… " He stared in wonder at the face of the Jaguar Queen. Yet his thoughts were of those he called his comrades. He remembered that they were chained in the dungeons below. Then he thought back down the long trail of a bitter career that had led him here, to this very moment, into the quarters of an immortal queen. His decision was made.

*   *   *   *

Lifting her head, from where it rested on her drawn up knees, Niama stared through the barred grill at the torches approaching their cell. Again the iron key fumbled in the lock. As the door swung open, she was surprised to see Queen Barastiis standing in the doorway, hands on hips, her eyes burning with unfathomable desires.

Outlined in the torches behind, Captain Gulla stood with a handful of guards.

"You came seeking the secrets of the Black Flame," the Jaguar Queen declared, "Tonight, as promised, you shall learn its secrets!"

The guards moved into the cell. Levelling their spears, they motioned for the prisoners to rise. Getting stiffly to their feet, Niama and Plith were led into the corridor. As they stepped over the threshold, Niama saw Vorgun standing next to Captain Gulla. The pirate averted his gaze. Behind them the jailer swung the prison door shut. They turned and mounted the stair.

Suddenly, a faint noise from behind made the rearmost guard turn, his torch held high in the subterranean gloom.

Something had detached itself from the shadows. There was a flashing blur and the guard half spun, gurgling as his life blood splashed from a severed throat. The torch fell from his hand and went out beneath the weight of his fallen body. Bedlam ensued in the tight confines of the narrow corridor and on the winding stair.

There was the sound of grunts and hard driven blows. Torches, tossing wildly, made out struggling figures and dimly seen shadows on the slimy walls. There was the sound of clashing steel, ending in a yell, cut violently short, and then silence.

A torch flared up again. Shading her eyes, Niama saw Gunthar, sword dripping darkly in one bloodied fist, a torch held high in the other. At his feet were a trail of dead guards. Striking from the shadows, he had picked them off with the unerring accuracy of the seasoned warrior. But even he could not manage such a feat alone.

At the top of the stair, by the heavy oak door, Plith rose from the mangled remains of Captain Gulla. The mutant, guided by eyes that could see in the dark, had killed the captain, as he sought to escape. The brutish captain's neck was broken, his head staring back over one shoulder. One lifeless hand flopped from the bar he had tried to raise before death had struck him down. The companions wondered at the superhuman strength of the reptiloid, who could break the neck of a full grown beast-man as if it were no more than a dry twig.

They looked to Barastiis. Her eyes were wide in the flickering glare of the torchlight. She stood with her back pressed against the slimy wall, her bosom rising and falling in breathless fear and excitement.

"You dare steal the black flame... *from me?*" she whispered, her voice quivering with outrage.

Gunthar, mounting the stair to where she stood, placed a hand on the wall above her head. "Aye, your majesty, I do," he replied. Raising his blade in one bloodied fist, he smiled; "Now lead on."

IX - *Betrayal!*

Gunthar, standing behind Barastiis, moved out slowly into the great hall. Vorgun, hefting Skull Smiter, came next, his one eye gleaming as he raised his beloved axe. All their weapons had been recovered from where they had been stacked behind the jailer's table. Niama held her tulwar once more, her bow and quiver slung over her back. Likewise, Plith lifted his rusted blades in scaled hands.

They stole out across the ebon floor now, coming up to the steps of a carven throne at the far end of the hall. Here the Jaguar Queen halted and, raising her arm, indicated the hewn blocks of the wall behind it.

"Behind here is a passage," she said. Moving forward, she pressed a hand on various sections of the blocks and stepped back. A section of the wall swung silently inward, revealing a dark passage way. A red smudged glow could be seen in the distance.

Thrusting the end of his doused torch into a burning brazier, the swordsman from the wilds of Tatukura motioned her on with a nod of his head.

Once inside, he pulled the disguised door shut. They came down a sloped incline, the torch casting fantastic shadows over the chiselled walls.

As they walked, the heat rose oppressively. Sweat glistened on their brows. At length the corridor ended, widening out into a great cavern. The red glow revealed itself to be a river of molten lava that flowed below. As they craned their heads over the edge, furnace waves of heat blasted toward them. The stench of sulphur hung heavy in the air.

A stone bridge, hewn from the porous rock, arched out over the burning magma. At the other end of that bridge they saw a double set of ivory doors, carved with ancient inscriptions.

Vorgun spoke suddenly; "Wait," he growled and they all turned. "Lest this little minx betrays us by some trick, best we bind her."

He grasped Barastiis and, drawing her hands behind her back, tied them with a cord from his belt. She turned her head. For a moment, it seemed, she whispered something close in his ear. Then, with a grunt, the pirate finished the binding and pushed her forward again.

The bridge was wide enough for three men to walk abreast. Shaking out his torch, Gunthar stepped onto it. The rest came behind, Plith bringing up the rear. Below, in the flickering shadows, monolithic rocks reared up jaggedly on either hand. The thick river of magma ran slowly between them.

As the great ivory doors loomed up, Niama moved forward, staring at the inscriptions thereon. She passed Gunthar and, as she did, Vorgun struck. The pirate, moving from behind, slammed Gunthar between the shoulder blades with the full force of his weight behind the blow. With a grunt, the warrior was hurled from the walkway. He twisted in mid-air before plummeting into the shadows below.

Seeing Gunthar fall, Plith shouted wildly and dived over to save him. Vorgun wheeled. Skull Smiter licked out and the mutant was dashed to his knees beneath a wheeling stroke that caved in his head. Despite this, the reptiloid sought to rise and, staggering forward, climbed stoically to his feet. With a laugh that was half snarl, the pirate stepped back. A booted foot lashed out, catching the mutant under the chin. Dazed and bloodied, Plith dropped silently from the bridge.

Too late, Niama spun. Eyes wide, she stood with her back to the inscribed doors. "Dog! What betrayal is this?" she ground out, her blade quivering in her fist.

Vorgun, hefting Skull Smiter, shrugged. "Sorry lass. The Queen of Tikka Chuanda made me a better offer."

Snatching at the cord that bound her wrists, he freed the Jaguar Queen with a single wrench. Shaking back her long midnight tresses, Barastiis stared at the plainswoman and laughed. Niama sheathed her sword. Reaching over her shoulder she grasped her bow.

"The trail ends here, Vorgun," she said calmly.

The pirate frowned. Stepping to one side, Barastiis reached up to a gold band encircling her arm. Flinging out her hand, she cast something from it that flashed like frosted fire. Recoiling with a gasp, Niama looked down to see a tiny dart standing out from her breast. Suddenly her whole arm felt numb. Her bow dropped clattering to the stones and, as consciousness left her, she pitched headlong to the walkway.

"Well struck," grunted the pirate, incredulously.

"Bind her, quickly!" the Jaguar Queen cried, walking over to where she lay sprawled before the ivory doors.

Looping Skull Smiter through his belt, Vorgun tramped over and began tying the plainswoman's wrists. Kneeling beside him, Barastiis, ran a hand delicately over Niama's shoulder and down the sleek curves of her back. She shivered with ecstatic expectancy. Then she rose, thrusting a hand against the ivory carven doors.

She stood there, eyes closed, head bowed, deep in concentration. Then those great doors swung silently inward and she stepped through. "Bring her," she said.

Stooping, the pirate slung the tall, dark form over his shoulder and stalked through to find himself in a chamber more fantastic and wondrous than any he had ever known.

The room was huge, carved seemingly from a single block of obsidian that shone like a black polished mirror.

Weird machinery sprouted all around, pronged instruments from a by-gone era. There were huge glass domes, full of bubbling liquids, vats and cables. At the far end of the chamber was a raised dais. Toward it now Vorgun carried the inert form of Niama and, at the Jaguar Queen's direction, he laid her there. "Strap her down," she ordered, pointing to leather wrist and ankle straps at each corner of the dais.

Grunting, the pirate began strapping her down, so that she lay tightly spread eagled, then stepped back.

Barastiis, leaning across, moved a metallic dome, attached to wires, over her head. From the wall behind she pulled up a huge rusted lever. Wired banks of machinery hummed into life. Vats and glass globes began to bubble and seethe. From pole to pole, electric currents cracked and fizzled with energy, across the length and breadth of the room.

Vorgun looked around uneasily.

"Soon," breathed Barastiis, and her voice was a husky whisper, "the black flame of life will be ready."

She moved to a metal chair bolted to the floor, close to where the plainswoman lay. Attached to the top of that chair was another domed metal helmet. Sitting down, she lifted it and placed it down slowly over her head. The currrents crackled above the room in frenetic waves of motion. Barastiis pointed at them.

"When those currents of energy turn from white to black, pull down on that lever," she indicated the switch she had lifted on the wall behind the dais. "Then the woman's life force shall be transferred to my own, leaving her nothing but a dry, withered, empty husk!"

Vorgun looked across to Niama, at her healthy young body, so vibrant with life and, moving across to the lever, placed his hand on it. He swallowed, apprehensive with a strange excitement. He watched as the crackling flames danced wildly from pole to pole across the obsidian domed ceiling. They started to change colour now from a searing white hot heat to a deep, angry red.

Barastiis looked up and laughed. Licking his lips, Vorgun's hand tightened on the lever.

X - *Into the pit.*

When Gunthar fell he twisted toward the jagged outcroppings that lay wreathed in shadow far below. Better the risk of a few broken bones than a certain fiery death. Even as he struck the incline of a rocky escarpment he cursed himself for a fool for turning his back on the pirate. Then he had bounced outward again with rib bruising force, and his sword was sent spinning from his hand.

He landed abruptly. Not with the bone jarring impact he had expected, but softly and in a thick sticky mesh that gave under his weight before springing back tautly. Twisting his head, he saw dimly above him the shadows of monstrous rocks. Above those he saw the bottom of the walkway and was amazed at how far he had fallen. Over to his left, the molten river flowed past, barely yards from where he lay enmeshed.

He tried to move. To his growing horror, he realized that he was caught in a monstrous web, spanning from the shadows of the rock above and out across to the rocky floor below. In the darkness of that rocky floor, he saw the great spider that had weaved those massive strands. But it would trouble him no more.

Blinking, he saw that it lay stiffly on its back, a huge monstrous hairy thing with long spindly legs. It was the size of a large dog and, though dead, it still made the hackles on his nape stand on end. Its underbelly was torn open, its guts oozing out wetly over the jagged rocks. Even as Gunthar wondered what monstrosity could kill such a beast, something stirred in the shadows behind it.

His blood froze. He gazed in morbid fascination as something came slinking out of the shadows, its twin eyes burning in the darkness. A sleek, long tailed form emerged padding over an outcropping of rock.

Gunthar saw that it was a huge jaguar, its ears laid back against the flat base of its skull, its long tail lashing from side to side as it crawled slowly toward him. It growled and the great fangs showed as it hissed at the unwelcome intruder in its domain.

Straining his arm, he sought to tear free but succeeded only in moving the strand of the web where his tunic clung. He looked down, seeing his other hand only inches away from the hilt of his long knife. He groped for it, knowing that the jaguar would be on him and ripping him to pieces long before he could extricate himself. But to die without trying, without a weapon in his hand, was more horrifying a fate to Gunthar than any amount of fangs and talons could otherwise be.

Sweat dripped from his brow. He saw the jaguar settle back on its haunches as it tensed its hind quarters for the death spring. With one last frantic effort he stretched straining fingers for the pommel of his knife but failed. With a wild snarl, the jaguar sprang.

Suddenly, from behind, something dropped and landed squarely on the beast's back. The cat twisted in surprise and rolled, its claws ripping at the thing that had fastened itself there. In a thrashing whirl, Gunthar recognized the tattered clothing of Plith. One arm was locked around the creature's throat, as the other swung a rusted sabre in a knotted fist. The blade hacked wildly, then dropping the sword, the mutant clung desperately as the cat sought to scrape him off by rolling over on the hard granite floor and rubbing him along the outcroppings.

With tenacious strength, Plith fastened himself around the

barrel of the beast's torso. Both hands locked and clamped powerfully behind the jaguar's thick muscled neck. The curved fangs glistened as the head bent forward, its eyes blazing with terrible wrath. They reared up and stood frozen, two powerful images locked in a terrific battle of wills to the death. Then there was a cracking snap and the beast fell limp.

Plith released his hold. He reeled back and fell with a slump to the dark granite floor without moving. The jaguar lay still beside him. Even in death its face was a stiffened mask of bestial rage.

Straining forward, Gunthar tore partly free from the web, leaving most of his tunic behind. Half dangling, he drew his knife and, after an eternity of hacking, came free, at last, onto the rocks. He staggered over to where Plith lay and fell to his knees before the blood spattered body. He looked down on the reptiloid, both appalled and amazed at the mutant's incredible vitality. His wounds would have killed three strong men. He bent down now, lifting the scaled head from the folds of his hooded cloak. The yellow eyes flickered and stared up with recognition. Blood started from the thin lips as they twisted into a smile.

"Easy, Plith," murmured Gunthar.

"I tried to stop him, master," the mutant whispered and the warrior nodded.

"You did well. I was a fool to trust him."

"I made you something. When we were in the jungle... I want you to have it... to remember me." He looked up at Gunthar through filming eyes. Reaching into his cloak he held up something from a clenched fist. He opened it and Gunthar took what was there.

The mutant grimaced, his eyes clouding.

"Quick," he gasped. "My time approaches. Give me my swords so that I may enter the afterlife as a warrior... not as this broken, pitiful thing."

Looking around, Gunthar picked up the fallen swords and placed the hilts in his webbed hands. Sighing, Plith drew them close to his chest. A slow puddle of crimson was forming steadily behind his head from the wound inflicted by Vorgun's axe.

He stiffened suddenly and, with a dry rasp, Plith sank back to the rocks.

Gunthar rose slowly to his feet, his eyes grim in the flickering light. He looked to the small wooden carving in his hand. It was an intricately carved replica of his curved Tatukuran sword. A thin cord was threaded through the pommel and, lifting it over his head, he slung it about his neck. He turned. In the shadows he spied his sword lying some way off near the magma river's edge. Climbing across, he picked it up and sheathed it over his back. He looked up at the jagged rock wall rising sheer above him. Casting one last glance at Plith's still form lying in the shadows behind, he bowed his head in solemn salute and began climbing the wall.

Death was in his eyes.

XI - *A reckoning in steel.*

Beneath the metal dome on her head, Barastiis lifted her eyes to the flames flickering above as they painted her face in a mask of unholy ecstasy.

Niama stirred fitfully against the leather bonds, her head turning from side to side as the effects from the dart began to wear off. She moaned, her limbs straining against the straps that bound her to the black dais. Before her, the Jaguar Queen squirmed on the black metal chair, her hands gripping its arms, her long shapely legs moving from side to side in slow orgasmic anticipation of her death.

Vorgun's heart thudded in his chest. His palm was slick with sweat as it tightened on the lever that would send the ebon skinned beauty to her doom and revitalize Barastiis in an act of mind ripping, orgiastic lust.

Across the obsidian domed ceiling the crawling flames began to darken as they snapped and crackled with polarity reversing energy. Deep shades of red gave way to black.

Slowly, Vorgun began to pull down on the lever and, as he did, from the doorway behind came the sound of a mocking laugh. He jerked his head. He stared at the figure framed there and the blood froze in his veins. Then, as that figure stalked boldly into the chamber, he curled his lip in a sneer.

"The black wolf of Tatukura!" he snarled. "Vrooman's balls! What must a man do to make you stay dead?"

"Come and find out," said Gunthar, padding slowly into the laboartory.

He approached the dais, ignoring the strange marvels about him, with sword in hand. At the foot of that dais he stopped. He glared up at Vorgun where he stood on the platform, his hand frozen on the metal lever.

Beside him sat Barastiis. She twisted in her chair, her eyes blazing with anger. "Complete the rite, you fool!" she cried.

Ignoring her, Vorgun stepped forward. Reaching for Skull Smiter he ripped the axe from his belt and hefted it in his right hand. "Sorry, your highness," he growled, "a lackey I may be, but some things in life take precedence—even over you."

Then, with a howl, the pirate leaped over the dais in a mighty bound, his axe swinging back for the death blow. Crouching low, Gunthar sprang to meet him. They came together with a crash and sparks flew from the grind of steel on steel.

Vorgun's face was a snarling mask of hate. Gunthar's blade played like a web of lightning and on his lips was a sinister smile, his eyes cold as the blue steel dancing before him. The pirate pressed him close, driving the leaner man before him with whistling sweeps of his axe. The cold edge reached out, yet the warrior avoided those hungry strokes with lean twists and countered with his own curved steel, the blade striking like a rending talon.

Around the obsidian chamber they fought, as ozone crackled

from the energy of the black flame above them.

Vorgun lunged in and Gunthar ducked as the axe, following through, shattered a huge cylinder behind him.

Gunthar rammed his shoulder under the pirate's upraised arm, slamming him back onto the edge of a metal table bolted to the floor. With his free hand Vorgun grasped Gunthar's throat as the youth, seeking to press home his advantage, sought to break his back over the edge of the table.

Then began a desperate struggle. Gunthar braced the palm of his own left hand under the pirate's chin, forcing his head back. He lifted his sword but, before he could strike, the pirate coiled his legs under him and booted out with both feet.

Gunthar catapulted away, landing on his back some yards distant. Vorgun rushed in for the kill. With a roar, he swung up Skull Smiter in both hands and brought it down in a vicious sweeping arc. Quick as he was, the warrior from the wild Tatukuran steppe was faster. Rolling, he came up, his sword sweeping out from where he crouched on the floor. There was a silver blur and the pirate's roar of triumph turned to a desperate howl of agony as his arm was torn from the elbow in a crimson spurting fountain. His one eye widening in disbelief, he stared at the gushing stump before Gunthar, striking again, slashed downward with a stroke that ripped him from right shoulder to left hip.

Vorgun swayed a moment and Gunthar lunged in, ripping up murderously with the curve of his Tatukuran steel.

"For Plith," he growled as he pulled the pirate in close, the blade standing out and dripping darkly from his back. "Who died a better man than you ever lived."

Then he wrenched back and Vorgun collapsed to the floor in an ever widening pool of blood.

Shaking scarlet drops from his sword, Gunthar turned. He saw Barastiis standing before the dais, the flames crackling above and around her. There was an eerie silence as she stood there, raising herself up to her full sensuous height before him. Then suddenly a huge tremor shook the room. The black flames fizzed and one of the poles exploded in a shower of sparks.

Gunthar shielded his gaze. Barastiis staggered but otherwise seemed unmoved. A crack appeared down one length of the wall and chips of obsidian showered down. The Jaguar Queen raised her arm, pointing accusingly at the swordsman before her. "Vangar has awakened! Doom is upon the city! Doom is upon us all!" she shrieked.

There was a rumble, as of boulders grinding deep in the bowels of the earth, and then the whole floor split open, with a tumultuous crack, beneath their feet. Gunthar leaped back with a curse. From behind Barastiis, a hand reached out and spun her round. "Go embrace eternity, witch!" Niama snarled, and swung a fist that crashed hard against her jaw. The Jaguar Queen's head snapped back. Her knees gave way and she fell, dropping down through that widening crack, into the molten flames far below.

Looking over to a foreboding piece of angular machinery, Niama crossed toward it and, when she whirled back, she held something in her hand. A cylindrical black object made of some glassy substance. Gunthar slid down the tilting floor toward her as the crack widened between them. Niama reeled back from the edge, her eyes wide as she swayed for balance. "Quickly!" the warrior cried over the tumult, "Jump!" He outstretched his arm. Tucking the cylinder under one arm, the tall plainswoman from the savannah of Zelba leaped.

She fell short and Gunthar, leaning out, caught her outflung arm in one hand. With a straining heave he held onto her a moment before her bare arm, slippery with sweat, began to slip slowly from his grasp. Grimly, he held on. Looking down, he saw her swinging out over the molten abyss. His other hand shot out, clamping around the support of one of the upright poles behind him.

"Give me your other hand!" he gasped, the sweat starting out on his brow. Niama hesitated. In her other hand was the black cylinder. Gunthar held her by her wrist now. His other hand was gripped vice like around the upright and, legs braced, he strained to keep balance as the floor tilted crazily beneath him.

"Damn it, Niama! Let the cylinder go!" he yelled as he felt her slipping. At the last moment her left hand shot up. The black cylinder disappeared, spinning into the lava flames below.

Gritting his teeth, Gunthar heaved her upright, the muscles standing out in iron bands along his shoulders.

Niama gasped. Rolling onto the obsidian floor she turned and knelt at the edge, looking into the fires raging below. "The black flame, lost... " she panted.

Gunthar wiped a wrist over his brow.

"You're welcome," he grunted and then, "Come on. We're not out of this yet. We have to get to the Crimson Tower."

Another tremor shook the chamber as they stumbled over to the ivory doors. They stood on the ledge before the bridge as rocks, tumbling from the ceiling, began shaking loose and plummeting around them. Lowering their heads, they sprinted across. Then they were groping their way along in the blackness of the corridor before coming, at length, to the secret panel that led into the throne room. Fumbling in the dark, Gunthar lifted the lock and pushed open the heavy door. They stepped out and, coming down the steps of the throne, made their way across the hall.

Reaching the entrance, they stopped short. Flames lit the dark and, from the shadows, they stared out at a city gripped in panic and despair.

XII - *The doom of a city.*

Struggling knots of figures were etched against a city in flames. It took a moment for Gunthar to realize those fires were not the result of the volcano, but had been started deliberately. Women ran shrieking through the streets as tremors shook the earth. Masonry, long crumbled, began to shower down.

Beast-men leaped from the shadows, axes and spears in their hands. They crashed against the upturned shields of the bewildered militia and blood was spilt. Outlined against the backdrop of a burning cart, Gunthar recognized Gruk as he rammed his spear past the shield of a harnessed ape man and into his chest. Then he was over him and moving into the square. At his back were a howling mob of armoured beast-men, their eyes burning with hate as they gripped notched weapons in their hairy fists. They swept on past the palace. A thin line of guards reared up from the plaza to meet them. Caught off guard and befuddled with wine, they were no match for the blood mad votaries of the volcano god.

They glutted their vengeance in a whirlwind of splintering spears and crashing axes. The stars looked down on a grim scene of butchery as the earth trembled. Over the valley, the night was illuminated by an orange glow. Looking up, they saw the dark ridge of the volcano sprouting a geyser of erupting fire, lighting the sky like a beacon of doom.

Through the aftermath of that swirling chaos, Gunthar spied Hrun, stumbling into the streets behind the sweeping onslaught of his warriors. One hand gripped his toga. The other held a block of masonry for support while the tremors subsided. At his side was the bent figure of the elder, leaning on his staff.

Gunthar staggered down the palace steps toward them. Niama followed. On the way she paused to pick up a spear and a short sword from the hands of a fallen beast-man.

Seeing their approach, Hrun stepped up to them through the dust. "Praise Vangar, you are safe!... Barastiis?"

Gunthar shook his head. "Dead. The black flame has been destroyed."

The elder nodded sagely. "It is Vangar's will."

"What happened here?" asked Gunthar, looking at the turmoil of the fighting.

Hrun sighed. "The youths became impatient. When Vangar erupted they saw it as a sign and began attacking. But, at least, under cover, I can guide you to the Crimson Tower. From there we can get you out of the city."

Gunthar stared at him. "What do you mean?"

Turning, Hrun spoke to the elder and ordered him to gather what priests he could find and head for the hills. As he shuffled away, he turned back to Gunthar. Laying a hand on his shoulder, he said; "Tikka Chuanda is fallen. But all is not lost… As I told you, there are no doors we priests of the volcano god cannot unlock. The doors of the Crimson Tower are no exception. Come!"

* * * *

Then, with the priest leading the way, the three were hurrying through the side streets, avoiding clumps of battling figures that crossed their path.

Presently they came to the clearing before the Crimson Tower and stood staring up at it from the mouth of a darkened alley. The courtyard was clear, the tower looming grimly against the sky. They stole out and, as they did, a detachment of warriors came staggering from the shadows of an alley across the way. A shout was raised and they began loping toward them. Hrun, holding up the hem of his toga in one hand, quickened his pace. "Hurry!" he gasped.

"Go!" Niama cried. Splitting from Gunthar's side, she veered out into the path of the oncoming beast-men. As she ran, she drew back her arm and cast her spear. The javelin arced through the night. The near most warrior fell, the spear driven through his harness and standing out from his back. Then she was sprinting behind her companions as they made it to the tower.

Gunthar whirled and, with sword upraised, stood facing outward as Hrun fumbled at the sealed metallic arch of the door. As Niama made it up to them, that door opened with a groan and they piled within. The priest heaved the door shut and, as he did, he turned a huge spindle that shot iron locks into the wall. With a sigh of relief, he slumped back; "An army could not batter its way in here now. Not that they will try. This tower is shunned—even by Barastiis' most trusted."

They were in a wide chamber, bare of any ordainments. A stair wound its way upward and Hrun bade them follow. Together they climbed, coming at length, into the innermost recesses of the tower.

"Gods of my ancestors," whispered Niama as she padded slowly into the room. All around them were ancient books and scrolls, lined on shelves or stacked in heaps on desks that groaned beneath their weight. Instruments of unfathomable design stood in the shadowed corners, covered in dust and latticed with cobwebs. Wide paned windows looked out over the city and the sweeping fauna of the jungle beyond. But their eyes were drawn to the centre of the room.

Standing there was a high backed chair. As they drew closer they saw that in that chair was a figure—the mummified skeleton of a man. He lay slumped; his head bowed, his empty eyes staring out as if in shadowed remorse at some long forgotten tragedy. The dust of centuries lay heavy upon him. His strange garments were faded and falling apart. From where he stood, Gunthar could feel the melancholy of this long dead man as an almost tangible thing. For a moment a great pity for the passing of the city of Tikka Chuanda seized him then, shaking his head, he looked to see Hrun standing in the doorway.

"King Ekhor IV," the ape-man muttered, treading carefully over the dusty carpet into the room. "A great ruler... wise and just. His inventions were many. With the secrets of the old ages he created new technologies he hoped would some day bring us salvation. Alas... his thirst for knowledge led him to the discovery of the black flame. The price for that life was a costly one. Loneliness and eventual insanity." He moved over to the chair. Staring sadly at the mute skeleton, he turned to face the two companions.

"Before he died, Ekhor perfected something... something, I hope, will be of great assistance to you." He moved to one side of the chamber and, reaching up onto the wall, pressed a hand there. A huge section slid noiselessly aside to reveal a hidden compartment.

Hanging on the wall, in that concealment, were two silver harnesses. As Gunthar and Niama drew closer, they saw that those harnesses were attached to silver armoured wings, spread and pinned back against the wall to where they were fixed.

Gunthar looked to Hrun who moved toward them.

"King Ekhor discovered the secrets of weightless metal and flight through secret advanced engineering. His plan was to send out an army of winged men across the earth. But, as he became wrapped in the madness of the black flame, his passions became less devoted to the wonders of science and given more to debauchery. These prototypes are all that remain."

He looked at the two adventurers. "They are yours now, my friends. By them is your only means of escaping the doom of Tikka Chuanda."

"What of you, Hrun?" asked Gunthar.

The beast-man looked out wearily as flames etched the dark beyond. Again, rumblings in the earth set the tower to trembling.

"I may yet make it into the hills with the rest of my brethren. But we are done as a race. I know that. We have regressed too far. Without our broken walls and our petty traditions we are just beasts. No more, no less."

Gunthar, moving over to him, placed a hand on his shoulder. "Then we are all of us beasts, Hrun, with some possessing a dignity and compassion far nobler than others."

With the priest's aid, the two were strapped into the light weight harnesses. They discovered that the wings were intricately made, with thousands of individual copper like feathers. Their arms were sheathed into sleeves at the top of the wings, their hands gloved in gauntlets at the tips. Every movement of their arms allowed the wings to flex and spread as they saw fit. The metal was of a lightweight compound, durable and tough as steel, yet easy to manage and light as paper.

Turning to a table, Hrun opened a book before them. On the page were intricately drawn diagrams of every working component. He pointed to a picture of a red jewel accoutrement that was clasped to their chests by the harness.

"This is the source of the wings power," he explained. "The movements of your arms and body make it possible for you to fly. But activating this jewel enables the metal to become energized by the gravity's reverse polarity. Thus, you will be able to glide and soar through the skies using techniques of your own body—as if you were swimming through air."

His sword sheathed comfortably over his back, Gunthar stood brace legged in the centre of the chamber, unfurling the sweep of his wings. At Hrun's direction, he looked down and pressed the studded jewel clasped at his chest. Niama followed suit and, as they did, there was a vibrant hum that slowly subsided. There was no visible change, yet they felt somehow energized, ready and poised for flight against a beckoning sky.

Snapping the book shut, Hrun nodded. "Now you are ready... Good fortune, my friends."

The priest led them, by a smaller stair, to the roof of the tower. The three stood braced against the wind, looking out over the flame filled night. Across the valley, the volcano continued to spew forth clouds of black smoke. Molten lava began to pour down from the rocks. In the streets below, the chaos of the fighting had swept over as men and women began fleeing into the hills. Soon the valley would be flooded and Tikka Chuanda, and all that remained, would be naught but a dim memory.

Gunthar looked to Niama. "Are you ready?"

The tall plainswoman faced him, her eyes dancing in the reflected firelight. With a smile she shook out her wings and they unfurled in a dazzling display of liquid silver. Gunthar paused. He turned to Hrun. "Thank you, my friend. I hope you can build a new life and, perhaps, find a new way."

The priest nodded. "It is the will of Vangar that we start again. Now begone! I would leave this valley and be with my people. There is much work to be done."

Gunthar turned and stepped to the edge of the tower. Looking down, he swallowed. He felt the wind howling about him, lifting the thin copper leaves of his feathers. As they did he felt a strange impulse. The pulse of the jewel clasped to his chest seemed finely tuned to him now—singing to a vibrant pitch. Almost without his own volition, he spread his wings in an arc of silver. A fierce joy surged through him. Then, suddenly, he was free! A gusting passage of wind tore about him and he realized, in that fierce moment of exultation, that he was swooping downward. He flexed his arms straight at his sides and he tore upward again, the wind howling into his face. He laughed in sheer exhilaration. As he tested his new found wings, he looked to Niama. He saw her behind him, swooping and soaring in wild abandonment about the tower. Together, they swept through the night sky with unimaginable force, the silver play of their wings etched against the cold stars.

They circled the valley once, seeing clusters of beast-men climbing up slowly over the cliff trails and heading into the hills. At the opposite end of the valley a molten river of fire swept down, gathering momentum as it obliterated everything in its wake.

Then, with a sweep of their magnificent wings, they were soaring away from that grim spectacle and heading out over the jungle in the direction of the rimless sea and the long voyage back to Uhremon.

XIII - Masks.

The sun was a pale shield in an otherwise featureless sky. Dimly, in the distance, the spires of Uhremon thrust up their jade towers into the steel grey morning.

Rising stiffly to her feet, Niama wiped the chalky dust from her arms and stretched her aching limbs. Beside her, on the ground, was her winged harness.

Even as she looked at it she winced and rolled her shoulders from the tired knots in her neck. Then, shielding her gaze with one hand, she scanned the dusty crags.

Gunthar had risen early. His boot marks led away from the remains of the fire, his discarded harness lying on the rocks near the dying embers.

Presently she saw him as he came clambering back down the broken cliff side. He stopped, some way off, and pointed over to the west. "There's a fresh water stream just beyond this ridge," he said. Sighing with relief, she began climbing toward him. As she passed him, she froze. Gunthar had turned and his sword was in his hand, the point nicking her throat.

For a moment nothing was said. Only a drab wind blew between them.

"Who are you really, Niama?" he asked.

She stared at him, unmoving. A slow smile curved her full lips. "How did you know?"

Gunthar stood unmoving. "I've been in the company of a thousand warriors on a thousand different causes. I know when something is not right. You took the lead in that fight against the beast-men in the glade, showing a head for tactics and jungle warfare you could not have learned on the savannahs of Zelba. True, you could have had previous training in an army... But that could not account for how you escaped from the altar of the Jaguar Queen, after being tied securely. Nor how you knew the whereabouts of the black flame and what it looked like, or how to secure it… "

Niama raised an eyebrow. "Leading you to assume?"

Before he could reply a voice, boomed out over the crags and gave answer.

"That you are an agent working for someone else."

Startled, they whirled.

Down a long narrow pass, a retinue was approaching slowly toward them. In a high sedan chair, borne by his blank visored armoured men of steel, came Zoolath Q'uann. His guards tramped in measured strides on either side as slave girls, dressed in gossamer wisps and tiny tinkling bells, ran to keep pace, fawning and throwing petals before him. Seeing the two companions, a wide smile split his toad like features. He gestured imperiously. The retinue came to a halt.

"Aaahh, my friends… You made it. Though something tells me you do not have that which I sent you to find."

Gunthar lowered his sword. "And something tells me it is not by chance that you happened on our trail… Zoolath Q'uann."

The mutant shifted beneath his finery and sat back with a protesting creak into his chair. "I admit, my impatience does get the better of me. I employed certain powers at my command to find you."

Niama lifted her head. "We have failed. The black flame has been destroyed. What is your will, Zoolath Q'uann?"

A tension played in the air and Gunthar prepared to sell his life dearly as he might in one last savage burst of fury against the mind mutant and his strange visored minions. But, to his surprise, Zoolath Q'uann, laughed. He threw back his head and his fat jowls wobbled as he roared with mirth. Beneath his toga, his huge belly shook obscenely. He dabbed the hem of his robe against a teary eye and looked at the two companions who stood facing him in bewilderment.

"Such a good play, my friends! A jest fit for kings and gods! A-hah! 'tis the thrill you see that is what I seek in life. Bound, as I am, by physical restraints, those thrills I must live through others, such as yourselves. The black flame is lost. Well, that is unfortunate. With it I could have achieved great power... but its destruction also pleases me, for now it can never be used against me."

"A fool's errand," growled Gunthar.

The mutant looked up. "Ahh, but think on what you have learned. Never trust a pretty face, for one. Even one pretty as Niama here," he said, turning his gaze to the tall plainswoman, who stared boldly back.

Gunthar, resting his sword up on one shoulder, looked at her. "Aye. Just what is your story, Niama?"

The plainswoman sighed but, before she could reply, Zoolath Q'uann answered for her.

"She is an agent of Khumrala. Those you are working for, young lady did a thorough job perfecting those psychic dampers to fool my mind probes. They worked—for a while. But you must realize that I am a mutant. Your scientists and magicians have little inkling of the true powers of the mind."

Niama turned to Gunthar. "My mission is to track down ancient artefacts. The black flame and all scientific evidence of the old world must never be allowed to fall into the wrong hands. It is my job, wherever possible, to retrieve or destroy them."

Zoolath Q'uann considered. "And you believe that Khumrala destroys these artefacts once they have them in their possession?"

Niama shrugged. "I am not paid to dwell on such matters, Zoolath Q'uann."

The mutant nodded. "Of course. Yet, for your endeavours, you shall be paid again."

He snapped his fingers. Two blank visored guards tramped forward and, passing the two companions, returned back bearing in their arms the two winged harnesses. Zoolath Q'uann looked them over. "I will take these in lieu of our previous arrangement," he said, "The power of flight both fascinate and excite me... " He indicated the companions casually and the two guards, turning as one, marched toward them, placing at their feet two cloth sacks that thumped weightily on the ground.

Then, with a reverent incline of his head, Zoolath Q'uann bade them farewell. The retinue turned. They watched as the high back of his sedan chair was lifted and carried once more to be lost to view behind the outcroppings of the dusty crags, heading back toward the distant spires of Uhremon.

Shaking his head, Gunthar rammed his sword back into its scabbard. He sighed. Hands on hips, he turned to Niama. "Well, he was right about one thing. I did learn a lot on that journey. Never judge a man until you have walked with him. I was a fool to think Vorgun wouldn't try something and an even bigger fool for misjudging Plith, who died a hero's death."

Niama slapped a hand on his shoulder. Moving over to the two sacks, she untied one and peered within. A small cry escaped her lips.

"He paid us well enough for our troubles at least," she said, flipping a coin through the air. Snatching it deftly, Gunthar weighed it in his palm. A shrewd look came into his eye.

"Khumrala is a long way off," he said at length. "The nearest port is Uhremon... How about a flagon or two before you set sail?"

Niama rose and stood looking him over a moment. "It's a long walk. If you can keep up- maybe I'll let you buy the first round," she said, hoisting a sack up onto her shoulder. Then, with an insolent sway of her hips, she turned and started off up the long dusty trail.

Grinning, Gunthar hoisted his own sack and bent his steps after her.

THE DEVIL FROM BEYOND

"...it shall come to pass that man will smite the earth and, in the calamity of darkness, history shall be written upon him in blood and fire."

- The Book of Dzyan.

- I -

Pashuvia, that little port city on the edge of the Naverian sea, was no place for strangers to go about their business by night. No one knew this better than Rahnya, the courts most favoured dancing-girl, but dire necessity prompted her into those grim narrow streets by the wharf side.

She paused in mid-flight now to throw herself against a white plastered wall and stare back the way she had come. As her hands gripped the stone building behind her she panted from her exertions. Her eyes were wide in the gloom, her strong white teeth bared in the brown oval of her face.

The sounds of pursuit drew nearer and, beneath the torch guttering above her on the wall, she swore feelingly. Then she was off again, strong brown legs pumping hard beneath the silk kirtle that was like a crimson slash in the surrounding darkness.

She made for the city outskirts. From behind she could hear the metallic clank of arms, the shouts of men. The cobbled streets widened around her as she headed up toward the tavern quarter.

She came round the corner of a building and, looking fearfully behind, ran straight into the figure of a tall man coming down the other side. She had a fleeting glimpse of him before she crashed hard into his chest. Staggering, she fell to the stones at his feet.

With a startled oath, the man stepped back. Reaching down, he clamped a hand over her wrist and she winced at his strength, even as he pulled her up. All she saw was the tangled mane of his hair against the stars.

"Vrooman's favours!" grunted the man in a strange accent. "What's the hurry, wench?" Even as he spoke, his other arm slid around her and she found herself gazing into eyes rough as uncut diamonds.

He was well built with wide sweeping shoulders and rangy arms. Under worn furs she glimpsed the links of a steel mail shirt. A curved sword hung from his hip and, beneath a bear skin breech clout, long sturdy legs were encased in ermine trimmed war boots.

Squirming in his grasp, she threw a desperate glance behind her. "Let go, damn you!" she gasped. The tall man grunted in surprise but did not relinquish his grip. He was about to reply when a commotion down the street made him jerk his head up. He saw a group of figures approaching toward them. Some were mounted on the backs of *sampas*, vicious hunting lizards, while others came on foot, carrying torches. All wore scale mail bearing the king's insignia. Seeing them, the party moved slowly in their direction. The tall man, growling deep in his throat, moved a hand over his sword hilt.

"Those are the king's own men. What kind of trouble are you in, girl?"

Her dark eyes flashed at him angrily. "Dolt!"

The sell-sword scowled at her even as he turned to face the retinue making its way toward them. The mounted two legged lizards hissed and stamped in the dust as they came up. The foot soldiers fanned out around them. Some carried crossbows.

"Step aside, outlander. This girl belongs to the courts of Pashuvia and is the property of his most glorious magnificence, King Shunga," a voice called out from the back of a *sampa.*

In the glare of the torches, the outlander saw that he had been addressed by a lean, dark man wearing hauberk and mail. He sat stiffly in the saddle, one gloved hand resting lightly on the hilt of a scimitar. Seeing he was being observed, he raised his chin arrogantly. The swordsman lifted his lip in a sneer.

"Is it common practise in Pashuvia for soldiers to chase women through the streets like mangy curs on heat?"

"Our court affairs are none of your concern. Now move along, lest you provoke my ire."

Throwing back his mane, the outlander laughed uproariously. One corded arm still encircled the waist of the dancing-girl. He swayed slightly and Rahnya thought to catch the smell of wine on his breath.

The mounted man nodded to the foot soldiers and, as one, they moved cautiously forward. In their hands were nets and long billed pikes. Some carried the flexed handles of voltage whips. Instantly, the sell-sword sobered. Lowering his head, he glowered at the advancing soldiers through narrowed eyes. "This isn't going to end well," he said then, turning, snatched a quick kiss from the lips of the girl at his side. Before she had a chance to protest he had swung her away and was moving forward, his curved blade leaping into his hand. He crouched low. The foremost soldiers hesitated.

"If you have somewhere else to be," he growled over his shoulder, "now would be the time to get going."

Rahnya started. Then, turning, she fled up the long winding street. Behind, she heard a blood freezing yell as the outlander leaped into the fray. The near most soldiers fell back before his sword as it slashed left to right in a blue blinding blur. There was a rending shriek and, looking down, the soldiers saw the heads of their halberds lying neatly severed on the stones at their feet. Stepping back, the outlander lowered his blade and gave a drunken, mocking salute. As he turned, a voltage whip lashed out in a crackling hiss of blue flame. It coiled around his right forearm. Before he had a chance to move, another whip snaked out and lashed around his left ankle. He gave a startled grunt. With a jerk, he was yanked off his feet to land heavily on his back. The soldiers came in at a run. He had a brief glimpse of tossing torches before a net was hurled over him and a sword hilt was brought crashing down hard against his skull. Then there was only darkness.

"Drunken dog!" laughed a soldier, stepping back and snapping off his whip with a hiss.

The mounted man in the spiked helmet reined his reptile over. Pushing through the soldiers, he drew his scimitar and pointed with it up the avenue.

"The girl! Don't let her get away you fools!" he rasped. Behind him two men, mounted on lizards, bolted forward—one to either side of the street. They easily outdistanced the fleeing shape of the dancing-girl and, whirling their nets, brought her down. Rahnya sobbed in anguish as the heavy weights dragged her to the ground, her arms fighting desperately against the thick woven strands.

"She is secured Captain Jamal!" cried a soldier from the back of his mount.

"Aye! But she fights like a wild cat!" snarled the other.

From the back of his impatiently hissing *sampa,* the captain ran a gloved hand over his thin moustache. He looked up the street through stony eyes; "She is secured, that is all that matters. As for this drunken lout," he looked disdainfully on the unconscious form below him—"have him chained and thrown into a cell."

- II -

It was the sound of a loud clanging door that roused the outlander from his stupor. He felt consciousness returning feebly and, opening his eyes, was blinded by a searing light. He cursed through a parched throat. Footsteps tramped toward him and he clamped his teeth against the sounds of sandaled feet slapping over rough hewn flags.

"Come on outlander, rise and shine," a voice grunted. The

contents of a bucket were hurled unceremoniously into his face. Sputtering, he rose stiffly and found that he was lying on a bench in a small cell. Shaking out his yellow tangled mane, he looked down to see that he was naked save for the bear skin breech clout tied about his waist. A soldier grasped his wrists. Still numb from the throbbing ache in his skull, he watched as heavy manacles were snapped onto them. "Come on," a second guard growled, pulling on a length of chain and hauling him to his feet; "The magistrate is waiting. Even the cockroaches need a break from your sorry carcass."

He was taken down a rough walled passage way. Torches, bracketed in sconces, stood on every turn. From there he was led up a narrow set of stone steps. At the top, he waited while an iron studded door was unlocked and he was pushed into the room beyond.

He found himself in an ornate chamber, the short looped chain of his manacles dangling before him as the guards took up positions beside the door.

Behind a varnished desk sat a heavy man in sequined robes. From beneath the folds of a white turban, he regarded the prisoner sombrely. One hand held a feathered quill over an outstretched scroll of vellum.

"Name?"

"Gunthar."

The feather described a quick flurry.

"Occupation?"

He hesitated. "Guardsman."

The magistrate looked up at him questioningly.

"I was a guard on the last caravan that came in from Ishkeristan."

The magistrate scrawled.

"Gunthar. You are charged with three counts of criminal activity against the sovereign state of Pashuvia. One—that you obstructed licensed officers during the course of their duties.

Two—that you attacked said officers in an act of aggression and, three—that you criminally damaged weapons and equipment belonging to the state. Your plea?"

Gunthar shrugged brawny shoulders. "I was drunk."

Behind him the two guardsmen sniggered. The magistrate sighed.

"That is a statement. Not a plea. How do you plea to the charges made against you?"

"By Yod the Accursed! What sort of land is this where a man is mocked, shackled and interrogated before he has eaten?" He raised his voice hotly as the guardsman looked hesitantly to their weapons.

The magistrate frowned. "I do not think you understand the severity of your situation. This must go before the governor. Who is your employer?"

"Nesek, a merchant from Khumrala," answered Gunthar sullenly.

The magistrate pondered. "The silk merchant? Does he owe you any money?"

Gunthar nodded sheepishly. "Aye. He owes me a full months back pay. He gives his guards a minimum to live on lest they get drunk in the towns and cause trouble. As luck would have it I had a win at the gaming tables last night..."

Sitting back, the magistrate rested his hands on his round belly. Looking over, he conferred briefly with a scrawny looking clerk who was busy recording everything on a ledger in one corner of the room. They sat whispering for some time. At length, the magistrate leaned forward again.

"These charges will be brought to the attention of the state governor who will decide your fate." He looked to the guards. "Take him to a holding cell. Have him fed and, for the love of Risha, give him something to bathe with."

*

After a closely guarded wash, he was given a stale hunk of bread and a pitcher of water before being led to another row of cells. As the door shut behind him, Gunthar scanned his surroundings. Straw lay in dishevelled heaps on the floor and rodents squealed in the shadows. He made for a bench running along one side of the wall and saw a man already seated there, with legs drawn up, in the far corner. Seating himself in silence he began chewing on the tough bread.

After a while the man in the corner spoke. "Poor fare for one of your stature."

Gunthar grunted nonchalantly and, without looking, gulped down the brackish water with a grimace.

"My name is Tullus Vantio. What are you in for?"

Gunthar, chewing stoically, turned to face him. "What concern is it of yours?"

Leaning into the dirty grey light, the man raised a finger. "We are rogues together. Brothers in chains against the feudal regime. I am a troubadour. A wandering poet. You may have heard of me..."

At Gunthar's profound silence, he continued, "I came to Pashuvia barely a month ago. You?"

"Yesterday."

The poet chuckled.

"No offence, friend! Alas, there is nothing like another's misfortune to make your own ills seem trivial."

Chewing silently, Gunthar glanced over at his cell companion. He saw a slimly built man with a pale complexion and straight black hair cut squarely at the nape. Above an aquiline nose, dark eyes sparkled mischievously.

"You are a traveller, like myself," he observed.

"Aye," the troubadour sighed, leaning back against the clammy wall. "My own story is easily told. Having heard of Pashuvia's love for the arts, I scraped together enough money in Philegarok to buy passage on the caravans to cross to the Naverian sea. I thought that, for one with my theatrical background, here was a city ripe for the picking..." He paused to wipe the back of a grimy sleeve across his nose. "It was not to be."

It was Gunthar's turn to laugh. "I've travelled the length and breadth of this continent, poet, seeking fame and glory with the edge of my sword. Yet here I am, no richer than when I started. Count your wealth in knowledge and wisdom. Aye, and if you are truly lucky, the handful of friends you made along the way."

The poet nodded. "Sage counsel. When I get out of here I will compose a verse on my lute to such effect."

"The name is Gunthar. How did you end up in here?" Gunthar's curiosity was piqued now.

Tullus Vantio shrugged. "There was a festival at the Street of Many Gods. Seizing the opportunity to make a good wage, I hastened there with lute in hand and joy in my heart. How was I to know that the festival of Gorshu coincided with the passover of Lami and that there was trouble brewing? I was seen as a foreign dissenter. There was a scene and some ugly words. Before I knew it, the city watch came and took me away. In order to keep the peace it was easier to arrest me than deal with a horde of blood crazed worshippers. What of you?"

Gunthar's thoughts turned back to the events of the previous night. He remembered a full figure, wrapped in scarlet that squirmed delightfully in his arms and shifted uncomfortably.

"There was a girl..." he said, frowning at the memory, "Dark and soft, with a passion that burned like flame. She had run afoul of the king's guard. I intervened."

Tullus Vantio sucked in a breath and whistled. "Beware the king's men, my friend. Strange times are afoot in Pashuvia. It is whispered the king is not himself and has the mind sickness."

The sound of keys grating in the lock brought them about. The door opened and a yellow light spilled into the cell.

"Troubadour? You're free. Pay the fine but stay away from the Street of Many Gods," a guard growled, jerking a thumb behind him.

Tullus Vantio leapt nimbly to his feet. Straightening his tight fitting coat, he squared his lean shoulders and made for the door. At he reached it, he pirouetted round, turning to face Gunthar. He bowed extravagantly and placed a small fitting cap at a jaunty angle on his head. "When you get out, come see me at The Raja's jewel, a tavern by the fruit sellers market. I am there most nights. We will share a flagon."

Gunthar nodded noncommittally. Then the door had slammed shut again and he was left alone with his thoughts.

*

"Three hundred gold rupulas!" moaned Nesek, the silk merchant, as he waddled down the courthouse steps into the light of the morning sun. Beside him, Gunthar stretched his limbs and girt his curved Tatukuran war-sword about him. Grinning hugely, he breathed deep of the fresh air and lifted his kit roll.

"I would have gladly given double to be out of that forsaken pit," he said, scratching at a flea bite under his arm.

As they made their way across the dust choked street, Nesek turned to face him, his colourful robes billowing out over a robust frame. "Well, it is more than I can afford at the moment. Trade in Pashuvia is not what it was and we have yet to reach Huramin. I have barely sold my quota here. I expect such drunken antics from Kothryk and Brach—even Shukru. But not you, Gunthar." He shook his head in exasperation.

As they conversed they walked over to where a huge, sluggish *gulamgi* lizard lay basking in the sun. The mud coloured beast lay contently in the dust. They were docile creatures, used to carrying the heavy burdens of caravans in long treks across the desert. Beside it stood a guard with spear and shield. The shaded howdah on the back of this one was large enough to accommodate a small party of people. They mounted it now and, with a bellow, the lizard rose and began its slow slithering stomp through the city, its long powerful tail swishing behind.

Sitting back, Nesek pulled the curtains against the rising heat and swatted at the flies buzzing over him. He was a large man, his face drawn in perpetual lines of worry. Yet in his eyes was the whetted shrewdness of a well turned blade. The trade routes were his home. His life was one of constant business, crisscrossing the desert wastes from the walls of Ishkeristan to the minarets of Huramin.

The rest of the journey was carried out in silence as the great lumbering lizard pulled itself through the markets and bazaars. All about them rose the closely packed white walled buildings of the city. Voices, raised in prayer and song, carried to them as Pashuvia prepared itself for another day.

The caravanserai at the edge of the city consisted of little more than a few rude stone dwellings, a run down well and some scattered palms. Lizards complained in the dust as loaders, cooks and guardsmen went about their duties. As the huge *gulamgi* bearing Gunthar and Nesek lumbered through the wooden gates of the enclosure, men jerked their heads up and looked to one another with knowing grins. Through the curtain of the howdah, Nesek saw these grins and frowned. His humour had not improved during the journey. They dismounted and Gunthar, ignoring the attention he was drawing to himself, swaggered over to the well at the centre of the courtyard and drew up a bucket. The sun beat down over his naked bronzed shoulders as he guzzled deep. Then, throwing back his head, he shook out his mane and looked around.

"Ho, dog brother! A good night spent in the hospitality of Pashuvia's finest?" a voice bellowed.

He saw a heavily muscled black man striding toward him, a blanketed load carried on one mighty shoulder. His upper torso was bare, the muscles standing out in great ebon bands along his chest. A gigantic scimitar hung from his belt and wide red silk pantaloons billowed out from his thighs. His head was cleanly shaven, a gold hoop dangling from the lobe of his right ear.

"Shukru! Where are the other dogs? Still loafing on their pallets?"

Shukru shook his head. "Nay. This place has been buzzing since the guards came in last night looking for Nesek... He is not pleased." As he approached, his voice lowered and took on a serious tone. Reaching Gunthar, he clapped a hand on the sell-sword's shoulder. Gunthar grunted. "Aye. The best way to upset Nesek is through his purse strings. What news?"

"That wench you ran into was no ordinary tavern girl. There is more to this than meets the eye." He looked around, "We'll talk later, Nesek is coming. He's desperate to reach Huramin before the rains hit us. Looks like we'll be pulling out early."

Gunthar nodded and made his way over to the crude dwelling that served as the guardsman's quarters. Ducking in, he threw down his kit roll and moved to the wash stand. After a shave and change of clothes he came out and stood leaning in the doorway. He wore his familiar beaten leather waist coat and a red silk breech clout. High strapped sandals replaced his mail linked war-boots and his sword, in its lacquered wooden scabbard, hung at his side.

He saw Nesek approaching toward him, a sheaf of papers and a leather purse in his hand. He slapped the rolled papers into Gunthar's chest and handed him the purse. "Here are your dismissal papers along with the rest of your pay. I can't afford to keep you on any longer, Gunthar... sorry. I have to stay in favour with the state governor."

The sell-sword from the wild Tatukura plains took the items without comment. He opened the purse and peered in. "There's barely 200 rupulas here."

The merchant shrugged. "It's the rest of what you are owed.

Maybe, if you show yourself round the bazaars, a rich sultan might take you on as a bodyguard. I will provide good words of recommendation on your behalf."

Gunthar snorted and jammed the purse into his belt. Without further comment, he turned and tramped back into the guard quarters. Gathering up his kit roll, he slung it over his shoulder and swung for the door. Coming out, he barged through the camp and stomped on down toward the gate. On his way he passed Shukru, busily tying a load onto the back of a *gulamgi.*

"Gunthar?"

"I've been relieved," the sell-sword growled over his shoulder as he passed him. Shukru cursed. "Where are you going?" he called out.

"To see if there are any guilds in this forsaken city that need a blade for hiring. You'll find me at the Raja's jewel."

- III -

Leaning on the balcony of his personal palace quarters, King Shunga II sighed wearily and took another sip from the goblet he held in a jewel ringed hand. He looked through rheumy eyes over the winding breadth of the city, lying, as it did, like a great curving crescent below. Just beyond the rim of the palace walls he could see the golden domes of the temples, the spires striking like fire in the light of the newly risen moon. Over to his right were the low flat roofs of the tenements and, beyond them, the harbour leading down to the sea.

A cool wind rustled the silk hangings, bringing with it distant sounds of prayer. Shunga tilted his head, listening to the voice as it rose and fell. It seemed that he remembered something then or, rather—*felt* something. Something that had slept too long and was, even now, stirring to wakefulness inside him. He closed his eyes, breathing deeply as the soft lilting strains carried toward him through the night. He let the voice move him. There was something he could not remember. Something that racked his brain with fire each time he tried to recall it... But what was it? He screwed his eyes shut and massaged his darkened brow with one hand.

Suddenly a great pain split his turbaned head and he cried out, his knees buckling beneath him. The goblet slipped from his fingers to ring hollowly on the marbled floor.

There was the sound of slippered feet. A hand caught at his arm, steadying him.

"My lord! Are you unwell?"

The aged king allowed himself to be moved over to a nearby divan.

"Is it the headaches again?"

The concerned voice came from Hajina, his youngest concubine, little more than seventeen summers old. Shunga looked at the wide eyed, innocent face before him and smiled wanly. "Yes... the physicians cannot help it seems." He coughed before sitting back with a sigh. "It has passed. You need concern yourself no longer my little dove." He patted her gently on the hand.

She frowned, her eyebrows knitting closely together. She bit her lip and seemed about to say something when a voice from behind made her start.

Standing behind her was a bent and hooded shape dressed in a long dark robe. She recoiled instinctively, as if a foul shadow had entered the room.

"Ahh, Kabir!" the king cried, "Welcome, welcome! I trust you have come to lose another game of chess?"

The addressed man bowed. "Your humble servant serves only to please, your magnificence."

When he spoke, Hajina's skin crawled. Of all the dignitaries she had met during her time at court, never had she met one as so utterly loathsome than the king's personal astrologer, Kabir

Kaaliya. Something about the sibilant echo of his words and the bent crippled shape of his figure turned her blood to ice. As if sensing her thoughts, he turned his attention to her now and bowed stiffly. "My lady."

The words, softly spoken, yet crawled with venomous innuendo. She bent her head and stammered a greeting. As if sensing her unease, which he mistook for shyness, the king said; "You may leave us now, my love."

Gratefully, the young concubine turned and fairly fled from the room.

"Have a seat, my friend. Wine?" The king reached for a beaker on the small table beside him. In a dry rustle of cloth, Kabir Kaaliya seated himself.

"How are the headaches, my lord?"

Pouring into two gold beaten goblets, Shunga waved a hand dismissively through the air. "They come and go. It is almost as if your very presence dispels them, Kabir. I don't mind saying that I feel like a young man when you are near... Good health!" He raised a goblet. Reaching for the other cup, Kabir raised a silk gloved hand and drank to the toast.

"I came to find what news you had regarding the woman," the astrologer said, setting the goblet down on the inlaid table beside him. Shunga looked up, his brow creased in confusion.

"Woman?"

"Yes, my lord. The dancing-girl, Rahnya." He leaned forward, his words dripping sibilantly. His eyes seemed to gigantically fill the room. The king massaged his brow. "Yes—yes, of course! Rahnya... Captain Jamal has her secured."

"Good. I trust the good captain had little trouble with her." Kabir drew back in on himself, his body relaxing visibly beneath the folds of his robes. One black silk gloved hand toyed absently with an ivory chess piece on the table.

"Oh, there was a minor disturbance... something about a drunken outlander that got in the way."

The astrologer started. The chess piece froze in his fingers. "Outlander?"

"Yes, some foreign born sell-sword. He was arrested and taken in."

Kabir Kaaliya digested this information as the king sipped his wine.

"Where is he now, this... outlander?"

"I believe that he was released this morning with a fine. Is he a concern? I have to say Kabir Kaaliya—this whole affair... Are you certain that the girl is a spy? Rahnya... I would never have believed—"

The astrologer regained his composure. "You have heard her wild claims and accusations, my lord. We were still in the process of our enquires when she escaped. She is spreading dissention and fear throughout the palace. There are rumours that she is involved in witchery. Or it may be that she, herself, is tormented by demons. If that should be the case, then they must be expelled in the temple of the Old Gods. I have the requisite skill to perform such a ritual. I have consulted certain charts. What is written in the stars and foretold in the great books cannot be denied. They are the words of a purpose higher than our own. We are but pawns in the grand design of the gods. We ignore them at our peril."

King Shunga lowered the goblet with a frail hand. He nodded but his brow was troubled. "Yes, Kabir. I suppose you are right," he sighed. "These are strange times. A man cannot know his friend from his enemy."

The astrologer placed the chess piece back on the table.

"Come. Let us not dwell on such matters. A game, sire?" he asked.

*

It was a relieved but faintly troubled Hajinna that left the raja's chambers. As she made her way down the lush carpeted hallway, she saw Captain Jamal striding toward her, bound, no doubt, for an audience with the king. To either side of him were two half naked ebon guards, their wide flaring scimitars held against their chests, their great muscles glistening in the oily light. Shrinking aside, Hajinna watched them pass.

"Capain Jamal," she called softly. Hearing his name, the captain turned.

"My lady... Is all well?"

Behind him, the two brawny armed guardsmen looked on with stony expressions.

Standing there before their inscrutable gaze, the young concubine felt suddenly small and stupid. Then, clearing her throat, she raised herself up to her full height. "I am concerned for the king," she said, moving forward. "As you know, he has been unwell of late. I think it might not be wise to tax him too much. Certain people—"

"Forgive me," the captain interjected. "But there are important matters of state that require his attention. I trust you understand. If you would be of service to him and Pashuvia, I would be grateful if you could see that the dancing-girl, Rahnya, is looked after. She is locked in a palace holding cell."

The young concubine started. "Rahnya? Why—?"

Looking around him, Captain Jamal leaned forward; "Do not breathe a word of this," he whispered: "But it could be that the girl is possessed! Demonic forces assail her. Through her, outside forces may be seeking to make an attempt on the king's life. She is under guard and will need constant care. Now, if you will excuse me, I must see his magnificence."

Stepping back and straightening, he gave a stiff bow before sweeping past her, his cloak swirling around him. As the two hulking guardsmen followed at his heels, Hajinna stared silently after them. She stood undecided for a moment, her mind in a daze. Then, in a whirl of silks, she made her way swiftly down the hallway. She did not follow her original destination but came, instead, down a winding set of stone steps that led to the palace kitchens.

*

Turning from the bars in the window of her chamber suite, Rahnya flung herself on the divan at the centre of the room. Clenching her small fists in the hides there, she lowered her head and sobbed in barely controlled rage.

The room was hung with rich woven tapestries. Incense burned in a gold dish on the table and threaded rugs from Ishkeristan decorated the floor. All the opulence of the east was in this chamber but to Rahnya, who had grown up a peasant in a mud village bordering the territorial region of Kulamir, it was still a prison. The walls beneath those tapestries were still of unyielding stone and the stout door at the end of the room was still locked with an iron key. From outside that door now voices murmured and she tensed, looking around for an object, anything with which she could hurl at her captors. A key scraped in the lock and, quickly, she launched herself from the couch and padded silently forward on naked feet. As the heavy door swung open she halted, surprised to see Hajinna framed in the doorway. Behind her, a guard glared suspiciously into the room. As the two girls looked to one other, Hajinna, turned. "Leave us," she snapped haughtily.

"But—" began the man-at-arms. The concubine's eyes flashed angrily. "Do you dare disobey the word of the raja's most favoured?"

For a moment the guard hesitated. Then, shaking his head, he growled; "Alright. Five minutes. That's all."

As Hajinna stepped into the room, the door slammed shut again. Satisfied that he could no longer hear them, she moved across, setting down a tray of food and refreshments onto a nearby table.

"Hajinna!" sobbed the dancing-girl in relief.

The two women embraced.

"Oh, Rahnya! What is happening? Is... is it true what I have heard? I have just spoken to Captain Jamal."

At the mention of his name, the dancing-girl stepped back and turned to the window. Staring out into the night beyond, she hugged her arms tightly about her and shivered. "I am being tormented, Hajinna. Darkness follows me and haunts my dreams... I am being driven insane!" She whirled and Hajinna shrank back from the look of fear on her face.

"How? What is this madness?" Crossing over slowly toward her, the young concubine took the dancing-girl's hand and led her back to the divan. For a while they sat in silence. Then, looking dejectedly at the floor, Rahnya gave a slight shudder.

"I scarcely know where to begin," she murmured. "It started some months ago. At first it was just images in my dreams. Then came the whisperings. One night I awoke to find a shadow looming across my chamber wall. As it spread over me in the dark, it spoke of terrible things. It told me that I was promised to him and that I would be soon joining him as his bride in the underworld. He calls himself Shimunu. Oh, Hajinna!" She looked up and clutched at the young concubine's hand. "It was worse than any nightmare. As he reached for me I saw his eyes burning in the dark. I could not move. A shadowy hand touched my flesh and I felt a chill reach deep down inside me. I screamed. The next I knew, I was being held fast by guards of the court. Without knowing it, I had fled my room and was running naked through the palace gardens. I was taken to a physician. He could find nothing wrong and passed it off as nothing more than a fevered dream. But it did not stop there. Not less than two nights later he returned- his intentions made even clearer than before. For a solid week he came, wearing me down, driving me to the very brink of insanity."

Hajinna sat listening to these revelations in stunned silence. At last she leaned forward.

"Then we must do something... does the king know of this? I will go to him."

As she made to rise, Rahnya grasped her hand. "There is more, Hajinna. Kabir Kaaliya has already been to see me. It is he who ordered me locked away for my own protection. He accuses me of being a spy. The next he accuses me of being involved in witchcraft and that it is affecting the king's health. For, as you know, the raja is ill. The astrologer has announced to all who will listen that he has the mind sickness. But I think he lies. Then, not two nights ago, I had a dream unlike any other..." Her eyes took on a haunted look. As she spoke it was as if she were staring into spaces that only she could see. Her voice lowered to barely above a whisper. Captivated, Hajinna hung on her every word.

"I dreamed that our city was shadowed in darkness. I saw a dragon writhing in blood against the night sky as it devoured the moon. More, I witnessed the down fall of Pashuvia—drowning in fire, our people fed to the maws of dark and abysmal gods— screaming as they were cast into the infernal flames. In that madness I saw a black skull on a bloody altar, the great kings of the east kneeling before it in chains..." Her voice trailed off and blinking, she shook herself. A semblance of normality returned to her eyes and she turned to the young concubine beside her.

"I was granted a vision, Hajinna. A vision of what is to pass. There is evil in Pashuvia and it is working through the palace. The kingdom is in terrible danger. You must trust no one!"

Hajinna's hand flew to her breast, her eyes widening in horror as the gravity of the dancing-girl's words bore down on her. "Th-then, what to do? Where to go?"

Rahnya shook her head wearily. "There is one. A man I met who could possibly stand up to this madness, but—" She frowned to herself and gave a small sigh. Leaning over, Hajinna gripped her by the shoulders. "Tell me, Rahnya! Who? There must be a way."

She looked up. "A man who wears a curved sword," she murmured. "A tall man from the west. Last night I fled the palace. As I was hunted down by Captain Jamal and his soldiers, an outlander defended me. He must have come in on the silk caravans. He is coarse and heathen, yet... strange, his courage was like a ray of light in the darkness. Perhaps, if you can find him and offer him enough gold, he will help us."

For a moment, Hajinna deliberated. Then, slowly, she rose to her feet. In her eyes the fires of determination were fanned.

"I shall find this man." Her words were spoken fiercely. "If there is a hope to free us, I will find a way."

*

In the early hours of dawn a slim figure slipped out of a little used gate in the palace wall. Wrapped in a shawl, tiny slippers padded out over the rough stones of the still dusky streets. Then, as prayer lifted from tower and minaret, that figure made its way furtively toward the market quarter and the caravanserai beyond.

- IV -

Gunthar sat hunched over a rough hewn table in the Raja's jewel watching distractedly as a dancing-girl gyrated to the twangs of a sitar in the centre of the room.

The only other inhabitants were four rogues crowded over a large table, laughing and cursing as a small ivory cube skittered between them. At the back of the tavern the barkeep slouched on the counter, his eyes bleary with boredom.

Lifting his drinking jack, Gunthar drank deep as the slant eyed woman began weaving sinuously toward him. Through the torn rent in her skirt, she turned a well oiled thigh in his direction before looking down at him through kohl hooded eyes. Then, seeing the flat leanness of his purse, she moved away again. The memory of a woman in scarlet rose unbidden to his mind and he scowled, his tankard thumping heavily to the boards. The gamblers turned. Noticing the feral gleam in his eye, they shrugged and resumed their game.

"Only ill comes from a man who drinks alone."

Gunthar looked to see Tullus Vantio standing in the shadows of a column behind him. A worn cloak was slung over one shoulder and, as he regarded the sell-sword through cynically sparkling eyes, he plucked a despondent chord with his lute. Gunthar gave a smile and kicked out the stool opposite him.

"Then grab a drink, 'ere misfortune befalls us both."

Returning the smile, the minstrel did as he was bade.

"Ho, barkeep! An ale for my street parched throat!" he called.

Gunthar grinned. "A good day?"

Tullus Vantio shrugged. "Aye, not bad. I can afford lodgings in this hovel another night. Too, I learned an eastern tuning from a passing street musician. What of you? I pray the court was not too harsh."

Gunthar told him of his dismissal. The musician shook his head sympathetically.

"It could have been worse. Alcohol consumption is at least tolerated in Pashuvia. They see themselves as the gateway to the west and so are not so strict on in it as in other eastern kingdoms. Your punishment could have been a lot more severe otherwise. Pray, what will you do now?"

"A carpet seller gave word of a wealthy merchant looking for a man with a good sword arm. He just had his old bodyguard removed from service for dallying with his wife. I start tomorrow."

A tankard of ale slammed on the table at Tullus Vantio's elbow and, without looking, he handed the barkeep a few grimy coppers. He raised an eyebrow. "Fortuitous luck. Work is not usually so easy to come by. Who is this merchant?"

"Flasio. A dealer in exotics and rare imports, so I am told."

The minstrel, raising his flagon to his lips, sprayed foam all over the table. When he had finished coughing, he choked; "Apologies, my friend! Flasio? The man they call the flayer? The butcher of Pashuvia? *That* Flasio?"

Embarrassed, Gunthar rumbled a curse. "Is there another?"

"His old bodyguard was removed from service, alright! They found him hanging from the city gate with his nether regions missing!" He shivered from some imaginary chill and drew his cloak closer about him. "Surely there is something else you can do? With those shoulders you would make a fine litter bearer for some rich man's wife."

Gunthar snorted derisively. "What do you take me for? Nay. I'll see the colour of this Flasio's gold."

"Best grow eyes in the back of your head then. He has many enemies, that one."

Frowning, Gunthar swept up his tankard and, draining it to the dregs, slammed it down on the table with a hollow thump. "I thought you were here to improve my humour, not worsen it," he said, wiping the back of a wrist over his lips.

Tullus Vantio laughed. Slamming his jack into Gunthar's, he called out: "More ale, barkeep! For tomorrow we may all well be dead!" As an after thought, he added with a chuckle, "Aye, and some sooner than others!"

*

Flasio's villa stood in one of the most affluent parts of the upper city. It had two storeys, the upper level housing artefacts from the world over. A high wall surrounded the grounds and, after being admitted through the iron wrought front gate, Gunthar was led into the main hall. A mailed guardsman accompanied him over to where a large, powerful looking man reclined on an onyx carved seat.

The hall was ornately decorated. Marble friezes with bas-reliefs adorned the walls and rose vines twisted about the thick set columns. Through frescoed arches, the morning sun dappled the flowers in the gardens beyond.

At a glance from the seated man, the guard bowed and departed.

The two men regarded each other in silence. The merchant ran an appraising eye over Gunthar and the sell-sword returned his gaze.

He saw a man of late middle years, hardened by tough living. Here was no high born merchant who idled his days among the soft fineries of his wealth. There was a hardness in the eyes that brooded on him from beneath the square cut of his oiled hair. Beneath the purple trim of his toga lurked a body large and powerful. True, the muscles had started to sag and the fine cut of his clothing could not quite conceal the paunch that threatened to burst the seams, but the hand that gripped the brass goblet on the arm of his chair was still strong. He raised that goblet at arms length now and, from somewhere, a small bird flitted down onto his arm.

The plumage of that bird was quite unlike anything Gunthar had ever seen. It bent its small head and a long needle thin beak thrust deep into the liquid. Its eyes were like tiny jewels.

"A honey sappler. One of the rarest birds in the world... Once they were plentiful in the eastern kingdoms. Their habitats have all but gone now. Swallowed up by the desert."

Gunthar said nothing. He stood like a statue, arms hanging loosely at his sides. The bird flitted away again, up into the shadowed cornices of a rose vined column where it was lost to view.

Flasio leaned back. "So... I hear you are looking for work. I am always on the lookout for a good man who can use a sword." He eyed the long curved blade at Gunthar's side. "You are a westerner, yet you wear the blade of a steppe rider."

Gunthar hooked a thumb through his belt. "I spent time among the peoples of Tatukura. I consider myself one of them," he answered. The merchant nodded. "Intriguing. I am from Uhremon. Truth be known, I can't stand this hell hole. The dry desert heat with ever a spiteful sting in the wind. Not like the clean air that whispers through the vineyards of my own land. Alas, I came here to build my fortune. The taxes are reasonable and the guilds do not interfere with me—so long as I know which palms to cross. But I have enemies. The foundations of this villa are built on the backs of those who stood in my way."

He took a sip from the brass goblet and his eyes were shadowed over the rim. There was a darkness in those eyes that made Gunthar's skin crawl.

"If I choose to accept your services, I will expect you to train as my personal bodyguard. You will have to find your own lodgings with a mind to eventually being housed here on the grounds. The wage is five hundred gold rupulas a month."

Gunthar considered. "How and when will I know if I have been accepted?"

Flasio smiled thinly. "I will let you know personally."

He leaned across to where a small copper gong stood on a table beside him and, picking up the mallet, gave it a tap. A crescendo of sound filled the chamber.

From down the hall, the doors opened and sandals slapped steadily over the marbled floor. The merchant, leaning forward, cleared his throat. "I am told you came in on the silk caravan from Ishkeristan. Was the trail not to your liking? Strange that a penniless swordsman should choose such a place as this to find his fortune."

It was Gunthar's turn to smile. He had to gamble all now on his own honesty. "There was an altercation the first night I was here. My employer decided it was best if we parted ways." He shrugged. "The life of a caravan guard was not for me anyhow. The endless desert, the smell of *gulamgi* dung. There was little in the way of action. The bandits know the silk caravans by reputation and leave well enough alone."

Flasio nodded slowly as the sound of sandaled feet drew closer. From an alcove, just to the right of the merchant, a silk hanging was brushed aside. A stocky man stepped out, dressed in a grey belted tunic and high strapped sandals. He came forward and, as he did, Gunthar noticed that he held something in his right hand.

A black-jack.

Gunthar turned his head sharply. The man approaching down the hall toward them was similarly garbed and in his hand was also a short leather bound club.

Flasio leaned forward, his eyes bright with a sly expectancy.

"Men who wish to enter my service leave this hall in one of two ways, man of the steppe. Either with head held high or thrown into the gutter by my servants... Which is it to be?" He leaned back and nodded. "Begin!"

Crouching low, the sell-sword from the wilds of Tatukura spread his arms wide, his eyes blazing dangerously. He moved back slowly across the floor, trying to keep both men in his line of vision. The first man came from behind at a run, seeking to catch him off guard, his black-jack swinging in a knotted fist. With an oath, Gunthar wheeled and launched himself across the intervening space like a charging wolf. He hit the man hard in the mid-riff and, as the breath whooshed from his lungs, they went to the ground in a knotted tangle of limbs. They rolled and Gunthar, hauling himself on top of his antagonist, drew back a hammered fist. He drove it down and with a crunch, splintered his opponent's teeth. Releasing hold of his tunic he let the man fall to the bloodied marble and rose to his feet. Hooking a thumb through his sword belt he let the scabbarded blade fall to the floor and rolled his shoulders.

"Only two men, Flasio? We men of the steppe feast on the arts of war. This is just play to me."

From his onyx chair, the merchant laughed mercilessly. "Excellent! I commend your style." He clapped his hands and picked absently at a bunch of red grapes on the table beside him. "Now prove it."

Gunthar flexed his hands as the second assailant came toward him. His eyes narrowed. They circled one another warily, each gauging the other's measure. From out of the corner of his eye, Gunthar thought to see the silk hanging behind Flasio's head ripple. He had a fleeting glimpse of a face peering out, green eyes wide with breathless excitement above a thin gossamer veil.

Then his antagonist had come in at a run, his sandals scuffing over the marbled floor. Gunthar braced himself. At the last possible moment, he moved. The club whistled over him, fanning his hair, and then he twisted as it flashed past his face on the return swing. He moved back a step, eyes locked firmly, not on the weapon, but into the eyes of the man wielding it. There was a deadly pause. Then suddenly his fist lashed out in a single straight arm punch. It crashed hard against the man's jaw and he went down like a felled tree to lie outstretched on the marble at his feet. Standing over his motionless form, Gunthar placed a sandaled foot on the man's wrist and kneeling, snatched the black-jack from his grasp. Straightening with it in his hand, he moved like a stalking panther back toward the onyx chair and the powerful man sat there.

The merchant, chewing on a bunch of grapes, lifted his head distractedly as he approached. "What is on your mind, warrior?"

Gunthar stood stock still before him, his legs braced, the black-jack hanging down in one hand at his side. Then, swinging it up, he held it out before him in both hands. His ice pale eyes stared hard into Flasio's as, with a heave of straining muscles, he bent the small club in half. Muscles writhed along his shoulders and chest beneath the sleeveless beaten jacket he wore but his lips were set grimly. There was a pop as the leather stitching came apart then a grinding crack as the wood beneath began to break. With a final wrench he ripped the wood from its thick leather casing and flung the remains at Flasio's feet. Folding his arms casually across his chest, Gunthar stood silently. He had not even broken into a sweat. Flasio grinned admiringly.

"I'm disappointed, Flasio. Your men seem to lack the most

basic of martial training."

Two guards came into the hall, armour clanking. They came up and stood to either side of Gunthar.

Flasio indicated the two fallen men sprawled on the floor.

"Pay them and see that they leave by the back gate."

The two guards nodded and began dragging the men away by their tunics over to a side door. The sound of groans and mumbled curses filled the hall.

Getting to his feet, the merchant flipped another grape into his mouth before walking slowly across to the gardens beyond the frescoed arches.

"Those are not my men. Tavern rogues hired for a mornings work. My reasons for hiring them are twofold." He turned, raising a forefinger into the air. "The first is for me to observe your skill in combat. The second... " He raised another finger; "Now those rogues will be going back to the taverns and proclaiming the prowess of Flasio's new champion and bodyguard. The word on the street is very important to me, as it should be for all those in positions of power."

Gunthar, retrieving his sheathed blade and buckling it about his waist, smiled at the merchant's shrewdness. "I see."

"Do not be fooled into thinking you have taken on an easy task should I choose to accept you. The weapon men of my rivals are not so easily beaten and are highly trained."

Gunthar nodded silently.

Flasio came up and stood before him.

"Very well," he said; "Report back here tomorrow... I have a job for you."

- V -

Flasio, borne on a sedan chair, sat with unconcealed boredom as his carriers forged their way through the market quarter. As they followed its narrowed, winding ways, masses of humanity closed in around them. Two house guards cleared the way with their bills, shoving at the backs of sweating traders and oncoming hawkers.

To Gunthar, striding beside the chair, it was an all to familiar sight, one he had long since gotten used to in the long months he had spent on the caravan trail crossing the great desert. His tangled mane was swept back now, bound at the nape by a copper ring. His uniform was a sleeveless red tunic. Clasped at the left shoulder was a broach stamped with the seal of the house of Flasio. Men who saw that seal stepped quickly aside and averted their gaze. At his waist, one hand rested lightly on a single handed short sword. A simple cut and thrust gladius, he was forbidden any other armament. Gunthar had left his own curved sabre, with its black wolf's head pommel, behind at the Raja's jewel tavern. The merchant's resolve to uphold the traditions of his western homeland refused to let anything foreign contaminate his household. As he shouldered through the sweating throngs of housewives and traders, Flasio leaned down to speak with him.

"This will be a simple task," he shouted above the clamour. "One that will help strengthen your resolve in future days."

Not understanding, Gunthar looked up. He was about to ask more when the merchant, leaning forward, raised his arm.

"Ah, here we are... Harus! Parlu!" he called to the two guards at the front of the sedan, "Clear this rabble away and stand guard at the door."

As the two guards swept aside the throngs with muttered oaths and threats, Gunthar saw that they had come to a narrow street. It was little more than a branched off alleyway. Built into its walls were long rows of shops, their wares spilling out onto the dusty pavement. Weathered men with scraps of cloth twisted about their loins, crouched before baskets and bales of cloth in the afternoon heat.

At a gesture from Flasio, the carriers lowered his chair. Four tribesmen from Zelba, they stood silently at each corner, motionless as ebon statues. Gathering his loose flowing toga about him, the merchant stepped down. He looked around him a moment before nodding to Gunthar. "Come," he said and the sell-sword followed him over to a large shop where the guards had taken up positions beside the entrance way. Striding past them, Flasio flung the silk hanging aside and, ducking in behind, Gunthar found himself in a cool but cramped dwelling. Spicy aromas assailed his nostrils. Plush rugs were on the floor and, as he came inside, his sandaled feet sank into the thick piles. Along the walls, shelves were lined with all manner of trinkets and gewgaws.

At the far end of the cove sat an elderly woman. Her hair was a wild bushy mess. As Flasio stepped up to her she rose stiffly from behind the counter.

"Do you know why I am here?"

The old woman flinched and narrowed her eyes. "You are Flasio," she said simply. The merchant planted his legs wide and lifted his head imperiously. "That's right. I am here to see your son. Fetch him. We have matters of business."

Turning, the old lady shouted in a quavering voice through a beaded curtain behind her. Presently, a slender man dressed in a long flowing cotton shirt emerged from the back of the shop. Seeing Flasio, he trembled and folded his hands before him. Shaking her head, the old woman muttered and hobbled out through the curtain.

"Sunjida!" cried Flasio, moving forward, his arms outstretched in greeting.

Dipping his head, the small shop keeper stepped back. He smiled but did not seem to share in the enthusiasm of the greeting.

Planting a fist down on the counter, the merchant leaned over him.

"Some months ago, Sunjida, I sold you something from my collection. An antique necklace from Ishkeristan. If you recall it was one you specifically desired. Despite my attempts to sway you into buying something cheaper, you said you wanted this more expensive one as a dowry for your cousin's wedding. You were so determined that I was impressed enough to let you take it. That wedding was some months ago now, Sunjida, and I have not seen or heard from you since. What concerns me is the other half of the payment you still owe me. So, I am going to ask—do you have the rest of my money?"

Before he spoke, Sunjida swallowed thickly.

"Most gracious, Flasio," he said, palming his hands together, "First, let me say, that it is an honour that you come to visit my shop and my home. I have spoken to my cousin. He has financial difficulties at present but I assure you - "

"Not good enough, Sunjida," whispered Flasio. Suddenly, reaching over the counter, he grasped the shopkeeper's collar and dragged him over toward him. He cried out in surprise and fear as the merchant leaned down into his face.

"We shook hands, Sunjida! A sign of honour and trust among men! It is what separates us from the mutant filth and the beasts... where I come from it is what makes us civilized. I see you men of the east need reminding of those values. Where are you from originally, Sunjida?"

The shopkeeper's face contorted as the merchant's grip tightened.

"Wha—? Kulamir. I come from Kulamir!"

"Kulamir! And what do they do to thieves in Kulamir, eh, Sunjida?"

The shopkeeper shook his head. "Please, Flasio, I swear—"

"Aye, you brown dog, you swear!" Flasio turned. With his free hand, he indicated the sell-sword standing behind him. "Gunthar!"

Hesitantly, the sell-sword stepped forward. Grasping the shopkeeper's wrist, Flasio pushed his face away with his other hand and indicated the arm braced straining across the counter. "Cut off his arm, Gunthar. At the elbow. Quickly."

Gunthar stood uncertainly. He looked up. "Are you serious?"

The merchant's eyes flashed back at him. His teeth were bared. "Of course, I'm serious! Do it!" he hissed.

As the shopkeeper cried out in terror, Gunthar looked past him into the alcove beyond. Standing there in the shadows behind the curtain he saw a young face. A boy of no more than two or three years of age. His eyes moved back to the contorted features of the man lying face down against the counter and the heavy man holding him there.

"Well? What are you waiting for?" Flasio's face was reddened with effort now as he held down the weight struggling beneath him. Reaching down with one hand, Gunthar mechanically drew his sword. Leaving the scabbard with an oiled hiss, it slid slowly into his hand. He held it there for a second, feeling the weight of it in his palm. Then, as Flasio looked on in tense excitement, he took a single step toward the counter. For an instant he paused there. Then, quickly, he reversed the hilt and, drawing himself up to his full height, struck forcefully downward. The blade slammed point first through the counter, ripping through the hard wood and exiting underneath. Releasing the hilt, he stepped back. The blade, standing upright, still juddered from the force of the blow.

Flasio's eyes widened in outrage. Lifting his head, he stared at the sell-sword.

"What is the meaning of this?"

"You talk of honour and civility. By Yod, I see little of that here. I'll take part no part in this madness." Stepping back, he snatched the broach from his tunic and, flinging it onto the counter, turned to the entrance.

"Gunthar!" barked Flasio. "Get back here and finish this! Or I swear you will never work in this city again. Every house and guild will be barred to you."

At the threshold, Gunthar paused. Slowly, he turned his head to look back over his shoulder. His eyes locked hard into Flasio's.

"Do your own chores," he snarled. Then flinging open the curtain, he barged through the two guards standing there and stepped out into the street.

Flasio's voice howled after him. "Coward! Dog! I will show you how a man handles his affairs." There was a wrenching noise as the sword was ripped out of the table. It was followed by a sweeping sound, a thud then a shriek of agony. Gunthar did not look back but, gritting his teeth, kept on walking. Behind him, the guards watched as he made his way down the dusty street and out into the crowded market place beyond.

As he walked to clear the red rage of mist from his mind, he was scarcely aware of where he his feet took him until, at length, came to the edge of the market square. Here the crowds had thinned and he found himself standing next to a fruit stall. Aware that he had not eaten in a while, he snatched up an apple and threw the seller a copper piece. As he bit into the barely ripened fruit, he leaned against the stall and contemplated his circumstances. His rent in the Raja's jewel was paid up until the end of the week. After that his future was not so certain. His funds could stretch beyond another couple of days or so, but no more. He knew that, as a foreigner without employment, he was fair game in this strange land. He shrugged. Thrusting a thumb through his belt, he looked up to see a rising wall of sand dust moving just beyond the city walls. Squinting into the heat waves, he made out a long train of beasts heading into the drifts. For a while he stood there eating his apple as he watched Nesek's silk caravan disappearing slowly over the horizon, bound on the long trail to Huramin. Then, turning from the awning of the stall he sighed and tossed the half eaten core into the dust. Wiping a studded wristband over his lips, he made back for the tavern quarter.

As he walked he did not see the red hooded figure standing in the shade of a nearby tenement building. A figure with hollow eyes that melted slowly into the jostling throngs then followed him when he passed.

Shadows were lengthening steadily into evening when Gunthar came at last to the Raja's jewel. Pushing open the door, he shouldered through the heaving tables, ignoring the admiring glances of the working girls and the scowls of the toughs as he did so. In the centre of the room he heard a boisterous racket and saw Tullus Vantio standing on top of a table. A crowd was gathered about him. The laces on his shirt were undone, his cap perched awkwardly on top of his head. Judging by his reddened face and the empty flagons cluttering the table beneath him, he was already half way to being drunk. He was running his fingers over the long neck of his lute now and roaring an obscene ballad. Those crowded nearest him cheered and raised their foaming jacks on high. Fists hammered on the tables as slurring voices shouted their encouragement. Tavern wenches giggled as they squirmed their way into the laps of drunken revellers. Catching his eye, the troubadour shouted over to him;

"Ho, Gunthar! Come join us, my friend... there's ale a-plenty over here."

"Not tonight," answered Gunthar sullenly. He moved on to the back of the tavern, thrusting people aside in his efforts to reach the bar. Ordering a platter from the tavern master's cook, he climbed the stairs and headed up to his room.

Outside in the street, a tall red robed figure paused to stare up at the sign hanging above the tavern door. With a satisfied hiss, it stalked slowly away again before melting into the shadows of a nearby alley.

- VI -

The highest tower of the main palace rose like a pale flame into the night. Locked in a small chamber, Kabir Kaaliya leaned on an ebon table, poring over a long yellowed parchment that he held in clawed hands. As he read the hieroglyphs on the page his thin lips moved in silent invocation. Before him a pentagram was drawn on the floor. Outlined with a chalk mixed from the bones of strangled virgins, it was a symbol old as man's most primal nightmares—a portal of daemonic summoning.

The citation completed, he lifted his head and stared at the runes marked so blasphemously before him.

Only a single window was open to the night. There was no breeze. Yet the air pervaded with a clammy chill. The astrologer's eyes were expectant now and, as he leaned forward, his face was a sallow mask stretched over a weathered skull. Suddenly there was a wind, a freezing wind that rushed about the confines of the small chamber. A wind that blew—*from beyond.*

The flames of the tall black candles wavered in their sockets and the tallow that dripped from them fell to the flags in sputtering hisses.

A shadow began to form inside the pentagram and, as it did, the lines of the symbol sprang up and were shrouded in blue fire. Something was manifesting there, something other worldly and deeply monstrous. Two eyes, burning like the molten slag heaps of hell, stared into the room. It was with a sense of vertigo that the astrologer looked on them. For he could not say if they stared up at him or down at him from some great unfathomable height. Nor could he say for certain that they existed in this realm of human existence at all. Indeed, it seemed that they were staring from beyond the great veil that separates the world from the gulfs of time and space. He knew fear at that moment and his blood congealed in his veins. Then, steeling himself, he rose to his full hunched height. One taloned hand grasped at a smoking candelabra beside him and, as he limped around the table, he swung it so that the incense drifted about the chamber. All the while he recited, from memory, the long dead words of the prophet Mazzuhma in an unholy litany. He finished the recital with the words of conjuring; "Rehsu-Nelg, Senil Evets, Cinab

Nivek- I invoke thee, Shimunu- demon of the underworld! Come, dread lord of the abyss... *Stand before me now!"*

A long, shuddering howl split the chamber. The blue flames on the pentagram flared up in a blinding flash and were gone. In its wake, a stench of brimstone filled the air.

Blinking through a pall of black smoke, Kabir Kaaliya lowered the chalice and stood trembling before the huge hulking figure that had materialized in the centre of the room.

"Shimunu!" he gasped, falling back a shuffling step, "Know me as your master!"

The inhumanly tall figure raised its head. Baleful eyes, like piercing orbs of hellfire, scanned their surroundings. The coldly beautiful features were expressionless—stamped with a god like demonic intelligence.

"For what reason hast thou summoned me? Has the girl been found?" The voice rumbled throughout the chamber like a soft reverberation of thunder.

The astrologer swallowed hard and his vulture like shoulders shook beneath his dark gown.

"I have secured the girl as agreed in our previous bargain."

"Good. But it is not yet the day at the appointed hour of the moon. Why am I here?"

"There is a further task I require of you. I have consulted the star charts and the oracle of the black skull. Both tell of an outlander. One who may come between me and my rightful return to the throne of Pashuvia. I have reason to believe that he is here in the city. I want you to find and slay him."

Shimunu's gigantic, hairless naked torso gleamed in the candlelight. No emotion betrayed his pointed features; features marked with the taint of evil.

"It shall be done. How will I know him?"

"Reports obtained through the court say he is a tall heathen from the west. A sell-sword that came in on the silk caravans. A spy I sent into the caravanserai reports that he is no longer in its employ but has taken up residence at the Raja's jewel tavern. You will find him there. His name is Gunthar."

"Your bidding is my will. Is the king still under your influence?"

"Aye. He continues to see this glamour you have cast on me- that of the crippled astrologer, Kabir Kaaliya. The fat fool does not realize that I am in truth his cousin, Jukur Kazim, banished from the throne a score of years past. That, along with my mesmerism, keeps him suggestible. He knows me not."

"It is well. Have the girl brought to the temple at the appointed hour when the dragon devours the moon. At its zenith, she will become my bride in the underworld. Then shall you be given your heart's desire."

The eyes of the astrologer known as Kabir Kaaliya blazed fanatically. He clenched his fist. "At last!" he whispered, "I will have my rightful place and my fool cousin shall see me for who I am. At that moment I will kill Shunga and assume his throne. After a score of years spent plotting in the wilderness... the kingdoms of the east shall bow before me!" He outflung a drape sleeved arm and pointed to the star flecked night beyond the open aperture. "Go then Shimunu!" he cried; "Find this outlander and tear him limb from limb! As reward, a hundred virgins shall die screaming on your altars!"

The inhuman figure bent its head. There was a booming sound, as of giant, leathery wings beating in the darkness, and for a moment the stars were blotted out by a strange shadowed shape. Then the candles sprang up again and the pentagram stood empty.

- VII -

Gunthar awoke from a fitful slumber. At first he thought that he still dreamed. Then, shaking his head, his eyes swept the darkness. The threadbare attic room of the Raja's jewel lay silent yet, despite the sultry night, his wilderness trained senses were fully alert. He was filled with an uncanny premonition.

Then those noises that had first roused him sounded again—a soft scratching followed by a strangely whispered chittering. The hairs on his nape lifted. Silently, he raised himself up on one elbow. The noises seemed to be coming from just outside the room. Twisting his head, he saw a shadowed shape stealing along behind the slats of the window. Then, suddenly, that shadow stopped moving. The sweat froze on his skin as two piercing eyes flamed in at him from the darkness. One hand strayed to the hilt of the sword lying at his side. A wailing howl split the night as something began to exert incredible pressure against the shutters. As they began to buckle and splinter, Gunthar rolled from his bunk, the blue curve of his steel gleaming naked in his hand. Then those shutters crashed inward and something was outlined horrifically against the stars. An oath was torn from the sellsword's lips—"*Yod and Vrooman!*"

Crouched there at the window was something unmistakably evil. Where it clung, talons scrabbled, leaving deep gauges in the thick wood. Gunthar had a fleeting glimpse of burning eyes and dark leathery wings sprouting from naked ebon skin hard as iron before it launched itself into the room. Then he was battling desperately for his life.

Paralysed with fear, any ordinary man would have died right there under those steely, slashing talons. But Gunthar was no ordinary man. He had been raised on the bitter escarpments of Tatukura where every moment was a bleak struggle for existence against inhospitable odds. Not for nothing had the steppe riders named him the Black Wolf. Now, as the demon grappled with him in the darkness, he braced the whole strength of his iron corded body against its ravening attack. Snarling in fury, his sword wove a defiant web of steel around him as giant wings beat terrifically in the dark. Talons clawed agonizingly down the length of his back and blood ran in scarlet rivulets over his torn flesh. But he struggled on, his indomitable will refusing to break before this summoned creature of the outer hells.

   They staggered about the small chamber and, as great wings buffeted furiously about him in the shadows, there were snatches of panted curses from the man. Together they crashed into a flimsy wall and Gunthar was hurled across the room, upsetting a chair into splintered ruins. He rebounded from the floor and launched into the attack, snarling as he slammed the whole might of his thews against the demon's superior strength. The thing towered over him now and, as it sought to bend him back, it was all he could do to stand with legs planted wide on the wooden floor. One hand clamped up against the demon's throat as madly slashing fangs sought to rend him. His other hand wielded his great sword in blind whistling strokes that clove only empty air, the blade almost useless at such close quarters.

   The thing crouched over him, forcing him down. Though the muscles stood out in bold relief, Gunthar's legs began to slowly buckle under the pressure. Black taloned hands clamped about his throat. An incredible, almost supernatural, weight was exerted and his face purpled with effort. Like red burning coals, the things blazing eyes drew nearer and bestial fangs slavered as the jaws opened wide. Inexorably, Gunthar was being forced onto his knees. Dropping his sword, his hand reached back to the bed stand. One hand still locked against the demon's throat as the other groped desperately behind him. Scattering a jug and candle onto the floor, his fingers found and closed on the pommel of his dagger. Swift as a striking cobra he lashed out and the long blade found its mark, burying itself deep in a burning eye socket. Red ichor splashed as the blade sank to the hilt but the demon seemed not to feel the pain. Instead, the hilt burned in his fist and, wrenching the knife back, he saw that the blade was glowing red hot in his hand, the steel melting and dripping onto the floor. He flung it from him with a strangled curse and swung a balled fist into the angled features instead. Blow after hammered blow he delivered but the ebon ridged face seemed cast from iron. Blackness fogged his mind and he felt death stealing in like a dark shroud over his senses.

Suddenly, there were shouts, the scuffle of feet on the landing beyond. Then the door burst in and Tullus Vantio stood framed in the dusky light, a rapier in his hand. At the sight that confronted him he reeled back even as the faces craning over his shoulder paled with fright. The demon snapped its head round and glared at the figures crowding the doorway. There was a shocked silence. Then a terrified scream rent the night. Behind the troubadour, those faces vanished and there was the sound of feet drumming in frantic haste back down the stairway.

For a heart beat, Tullus Vantio stood. Then narrowing his eyes, he swept into the room. As he came forward his left hand reached down slowly to a pouch hanging at his belt. He swallowed yet, as he faced the nightmare thing before him, he was filled with a strange calmness.

The creature, crouching low in the centre of the chamber, growled ominously.

The minstrel's left hand shot out and a grainy reddish dust was flung from his fingers. The demon's eyes flamed with wrath. One arm jerked out, as if to ward off that strange powdered dust and, as it struck him, it snarled in affronted rage. Leaning forward it snapped its wings and hissed a dire warning in a spray of venomous spittle.

"Avaunt, foul demon of the netherworld!" Tullus Vantio cried; "By the sacred seals of Vashim and Senhdu, I banish thee back to the seven hells from whence you came!"

As he spoke, he stepped boldly forward and his hand made a curious gesture in the air. In the wake of that gesture, Gunthar thought to see a fiery afterglow light the room. But, being only half conscious from the taloned hand clamped about his throat, he could not be certain. Then the demon released its grip and the sell-sword fell back with a choking gasp. With a frustrated howl, the demon seemed to shrink in on itself. Slowly, it retreated backwards across the floor; away from the minstrel's advance. Then, incredibly, in a burst of shadowy tatters, it was gone. Only an after image of black titanic wings sweeping along the attic walls could be seen. The very stars seemed to darken before reappearing once more. Under the light of their frosty glare the two men looked around them. But for the broken shutters lying in splinters on the floor, it was as if the demon had never been.

"What in the name of the eleven scarlet hells was that thing?" rasped Gunthar.

"Exactly that," replied Tullus Vantio, moving over to him and offering his hand. Shrugging him aside, Gunthar clambered stiffly to his feet. His rangy muscled torso was streaked with crimson slashes. He reeled dizzily for an instant before passing a shaking wrist over his brow.

"Vrooman's black curses! What mean you, minstrel?"

"That creature was a familiar- a demon summoned from the outer hells." He shuddered; "Congratulations, Gunthar. It seems you have enemies in high places."

The swordsman, staring intently past the broken shutters of the window into the night beyond, fixed the troubadour with an icy stare. "You mean, someone sent that *thing* to attack me?"

The minstrel nodded. "Aye, and our respite is only temporary. I suggest we gather all our personal belongings and make haste from this establishment as quickly as possible. Leave nothing behind. A demon can easily trace you through a single item of clothing or just a strand of hair."

Timid voices from the doorway reached them and, looking round, they saw frightened faces peering in from the hallway.

"Come, let us be away, before the proprietor calls the watch," the troubadour murmured.

Holding his scabbarded blade in one hand and snatching up the bent shape of his melted dagger in the other, Gunthar stalked over to the door. He was a grim sight as he walked, dripping blood at every step. The patrons of the Raja's jewel shrank to either side as he shouldered through them. Hugging the walls, they turned to stare at this grisly apparition as he stepped slowly down the rickety stairs.

Carrying his lute and both their kit rolls, the slender shape of the troubadour followed closely behind.

- VIII -

Two cloaked figures slipped silently through the alleys of the outer city. They crept past the crudely fashioned hovels of the low caste tenements before coming out onto a narrow trail. Worn away in places and nearly forgotten, that trail yet wound its way out of the city proper. There they paused, half hidden in the shadows, glaring suspiciously into the desert night beyond. Only a light breeze stirred and, by the light of the watery moon, they could make out the run down walls of the caravanserai in the distance. Then the tallest of those two figures had detached himself from the city walls. Like a rangy wolf, he loped across the intervening space before leaping high out into the night. Catching the top of the high wooden gate of the caravanserai with both hands, he swung himself up with an agile strength and dropped down into the compound below. Crouched in the shadows, his narrowed gaze swept the moon washed courtyard. Satisfied that it lay deserted, he turned to the gate. He fumbled there briefly and, with a straining heave, pushed it open. As it creaked ajar, the other figure ran across the pale sands to join him inside.

"Nesek's caravan has gone," grunted Gunthar. "The next one will not be in for a few days. We'll spend the night here before deciding what to do." As he spoke, he pulled the gate shut again. Then, throwing back his cloak, he moved to the nearest building.

It was little more than a shack but stacked against the wall was some kindling. He gathered up some bundles and threw them together in a heap on the ground.

Soon a fire was under way and the two hunkered down before it. Gunthar sat cross legged, his sheathed curved blade resting over his knees. His senses were keenly alert, his eyes flickering into the shadows, his head lifting at every nocturnal sound.

Tullus Vantio, spreading his cloak before him, shivered in the night breeze. Laying down his lute, he dragged over his belongings, consisting of a heavy leather satchel, and fumbled inside.

"You took quite a beating back there," he said, sifting through the contents. Finding what he sought, he pulled something out. Carefully unwrapping a soft scrap of silk, he held out a pile of purple stemmed leaves in one hand. Gunthar looked on.

"What's this?"

"Cupona leaves. Cultivated in the mound city of Dingaza. They have magical healing properties. Here, take some."

The swordsman, taking the proffered items in his palm, wrinkled his nose suspiciously. "More of your sorcery?"

The minstrel shrugged. "If you will. A traveller must always be prepared."

"Even against demons?" Gunthar muttered.

Looking up, Tullus Vantio frowned. "I admit, I have not been entirely honest with you."

Leaning over his blade, the swordsman arched an eyebrow. "Pray, tell on, minstrel. If 'minstrel' you truly are."

The troubadour sat back. Then, staring whimsically at the stars, he let out a huge sigh. "Alright. My name is Tullus Vantio. That much is true. And I do come from Philegarok. But that is where the truth of my story ends. Despite my skill with the lute, I am no wandering performer seeking fame and fortune. In fact, quite the opposite. I wish anonymity. Where better than Pashuvia- where every nationality gathers along the trade routes and little notice is given to a lowly troubadour?"

"So! You are on the run! What is it? A gambling debt? Or did you flee the wrath of a jealous husband?" Gunthar asked, stirring the fire with a stick.

Tullus Vantio shook his head.

"Neither. The truth is far more sordid, I fear. I killed a man. A rival sorcerer. One much more powerful than myself. A man of favour and standing. As you have already guessed, I am a student of the arcane arts. I, being but a lowly apprentice, was envious of his position in the secret guild of magicks. Too, he had something I coveted. A book containing the sacred stanzas of Dzyan."

"You sought to steal it?"

"Aye, In my over zealousness, I mixed a fateful compound of sleeping dust. I entered his house on a pretext and, as we conversed, I administered the drug into his wine. I did not have to wait long before the old conjurer fell asleep. Then I left his chambers, thinking to slip undetected through the halls, steal the book and be off into the night before he knew what I was about. Unfortunately, I had underestimated the potency of the dust. The poor fellow suffered a massive seizure. At his death, several of his demonic familiars were called into being with the sole purpose of tearing me apart. Nor could I locate the secret book. I fled the house, empty handed, with only my life to show for it. Alas! The secret guild of magicks fathomed my plot and I had no choice but to flee the country, wearing this minstrel act as a disguise. So I am as you now see me—Tullus Vantio, wandering troubadour and poet."

"That's quite a tale," Gunthar said. He sat with his chin propped on his fist, the flames flickering over his impassive face.

Tullus Vantio spread his hands. "If the authorities ever catch up with me, my fate is sealed. The secret guild of magicks are harsh on crimes against their own, they—" He broke off suddenly and peered across the flames. "You do not so look well, my friend."

Gunthar passed a hand through his hair. His face was haggard and his brow dripped with sweat. "Aye," he panted, "All of a sudden my body burns. I am racked with thirst."

"Take one of those leaves, quickly," Tullus snapped. He leaned forward and there was concern in his eyes. "The scratches from a demon can lead to madness, if not worse."

Climbing stiffly to his feet, the sell-sword reeled into the shadows, making for the well at the centre of the courtyard. He staggered over and half fell against the rim. He leaned there for a moment, breathing heavily in the darkness. Then turning the windlass, he drew up the bucket on creaking hinges. As it reached him he hesitantly placed one of the leaves in his mouth before cupping a palm full of water and swallowing it. Next, he dunked his head deep in the bucket. He came up slowly, leaning there for a moment and shivering as with a fever. Then, with a final shudder, he stood boldly upright and lifted his head. His eyes were bright and clear once more. Already the stinging was subsiding in his veins and his vision was clearing. He breathed deeply and turned back.

Just then a faint sound made his ears prick up. He turned his head sharply and his right hand fell to the pommel of his sword. Squinting, he crept over toward the shacks that served as quarters for the caravan retainers. Out of the corner of his eye, he saw Tullus Vantio stand up and look on curiously from where he waited by the fire. Stealing forward, Gunthar held up his hand, cautioning him to silence.

Before him, the doorways gaped along in silent rows. His nostrils dilated as he paused by the threshold of one. He saw nothing. Then, suddenly, there was the faint whisper of cloth against stone followed by a soft foot fall on the dusty earth. With a growl he catapulted into the nearest doorway and, reaching out, found himself struggling with a wiry figure. Something clawed at his eyes before his hand found and twisted in a mane of tangled hair. Wrenching back, he came out of the shack with a figure struggling desperately in his arms. Twisting them over his hip, he threw the shape down on the ground and drew his sword with a dry rasp. The curved blade flashed under the moonlight and the figure cried out in terror. Gunthar grunted then swore when he saw the lithe shape of the woman cowering before him in the dust. The back of one hand was raised defensively before her even as her eyes gazed up at him in fearful expectancy.

"Who are you? Speak quickly, wench, ere my edge finds your throat!" He crouched over her now and, as he spoke, he grabbed a fistful of her hair. Shaking her head violently, he let the blade play menacingly before her eyes.

"My name is Hajinna!" she gasped; "Please, do not kill me!"

"What are you doing here? Where are there others?" As he spoke he stared suspiciously around him.

"Nay, master! There are no others. I am alone, please!"

"You lie!" he snarled, "I'll soon get the truth out of you—"

"No! No!" she sobbed. "I am alone. I swear it! I came in through the smuggler's tunnel that runs under the wall!"

Gunthar hesitated. "Tunnel?"

"Yes," she wept, "It comes up under the floor into those huts. It is no secret that the marketeers loot the caravans while they stop here."

Grinning wryly, Gunthar straightened before hitching his sword belt up a notch. He lowered his sword. "Well, well. So much for Nesek's standing with the state governor... Vrooman's rod! The bastard's been pilfering his silk caravans and then charging him for the privilege of staying here all along. No wonder his trade has not been so good. Hah!"

Amused, he looked down on the girl at his feet. She was young and lean with slender limbs. As she stared up at him there was a youthful innocence in the wideness of her brown eyes. Her dishevelled hair was a foaming black mass that fell in rippling curls to the small of her back. She wore only green silk garments and slippers. Though her pantaloons were torn, Gunthar noted shrewdly that the bangles about her wrists and ankles were of finest gold. She trembled and he thought that it was not all from fear. He leaned down and, grasping her wrist, pulled her to her feet. "You're half frozen," he grumbled, "What madness led you to hide out here in the dead of night?"

Tullus Vantio came up beside them. "Well! What treasured delights have the night cast up into your lap now, Gunthar?" His eyes danced appreciatively as they travelled up and down the form of the young woman. Under his frank gaze she lowered her own eyes and, despite the coolness of the night, her cheeks flamed.

"Hajinna, meet Tullus Vantio—a poet and a wizard. An amateur at both professions if his luck is anything to go by."

Looking up timidly, Hajinna gasped suddenly. Her hands flew to her breast. The two men started. She was staring in wide eyed wonder at the blade in Gunthar's hand. Her eyes travelled up slowly to meet his. "You- you are the man who came in on the caravans! The man from the west who fights with the curved sword! It is you that I came to find!"

Gunthar stepped back. "What are you talking about, wench? How can you know me?"

"I came here seeking you- but the caravans had already left. I have been hiding out here the past two nights not knowing what to do. I escaped the palace and am afraid to go back. The girl you protected, Rahnya, is in trouble. You are both in dire trouble. You must help us—or the kingdom is lost!"

*

Huddled in a blanket before the fire, Hajinna wolfed down the last of the left over rice cakes and sweet meats from their supplies. In between hastily downed bites, she began telling of the darkened curse that had fallen over Pashuvia. She spoke, in halting words, of the enchantments that tormented Rahnya, as related to her from the lips of the dancing-girl herself.

As he listened to her descriptions of the visitations from the demonic entity known as Shimunu, Tullus Vantio's eyes slid over to the swordsman sitting across the flames from him. Gunthar sat immobile as a statue, wrapped in his dark hooded cloak, the blade of his adopted countrymen resting over his knees. His own face betrayed no emotion.

Then, staring hauntingly into the flames, Hajinna told of the strange illness that had overcome her lord and master, Shunga the second—king of Pashuvia.

"Kabir Kaaliya is behind it all," she whispered, "He has my lord entranced and means the kingdom a great ill."

When she had finished, a weighty silence hung in the air, disturbed only by the snap of wood crackling in the fire.

At last Gunthar raised his head. "All very well. But what do you expect of me? I am one man with a sword. Hardly a match for plots of magic fought in the dark."

Hajinna turned toward him imploringly. A wild desperation was in her eyes that she could not frame into words.

"There is a mystery here," broke in Tullus Vantio. "If Kabir Kaaliya sent this demon, Shimunu, to attack you then there is a reason why he fears you so."

"Aye, courage! And drunken courage at that!" laughed Gunthar, "Nay, Tullus. I am no caster of spells or fighter of demons. By Yod! This sounds more like your line of work than mine."

Tullus Vantio deliberated for a moment. "Aye, maybe." He sat wrapped in contemplation. Then suddenly he slammed a fist into the sand and, with a cry, was on his feet.

"Of course! We banish the demon back! He is the key to this astrologer's power. Without him he has nothing."

"We?" Gunthar looked up.

"How?" Hajinna was on her feet also. She clutched at the troubadour's arm. He turned to look at her. "The temple of Risha.

She is the most revered of all the deities in the kingdoms that surround the Naverian sea. We must call upon her high priests to help us. With just a mixture of salt and iron I managed to fend this devil away. A parlour trick, compared to what can be done with some careful planning and the faith of a goddess behind us. Given the right knowledge and tools, a demon can be trapped and cast back into its own realm. But I'll need the help of a high priest to do it."

He gripped Hajinna's about the upper shoulders with both hands. "Lead us to the temple of Risha. If you are willing to place your faith in one lone swordsman, then I ask only that you honour me the same chance."

He stared at her. For a heartbeat, no words passed between them. Then, drawing herself up to her full height, she gasped out breathlessly; "Yes! I will lead you! May the gods be just!"

- IX -

"There." Huddled next to the wall of a run down hovel, Hajinna pointed across the main square to the wide squat domed temple standing in the distance. Tullus Vantio and Gunthar crouched beside her. Wrapped in their cloaks, they cut incongruous shapes in the jumbled maze of the tenement buildings.

Their progress through the side streets and back alleyways had not been without its dangers. Mailed guards of the city patrol were on full alert now; tramping up and down, thrusting their bearded faces and torches into every nook and cranny. That they were searching for them they had little doubt. Time and again they had narrowly avoided detection as they slipped one step ahead of them through the shadows. Now, at last, they had reached the temple of Risha, standing magnificent in the city square.

Slinking across to it, they made their way up the wide marble steps. The moon was a bent pale shape above them, half hidden behind scudding clouds.

Hajinna came first, the two men padding warily behind. The mouth of the temple stood open. On each side of the entrance stood two heavy braziers of chiselled stone.

As they reached the top a white robed figure materialized from out of the darkness. Gunthar froze, one hand falling to the hilt beneath his cloak.

"Mashim!" Hajinna cried; "Most blessed of the goddess!" She fell to her knees, prostrating herself on the marble.

"Hajinna, my most blessed child. How good to see you." The figure made a gesture over her and she rose swiftly to her feet again.

The two men, conscious that they stood revealed in the soft moonlight, stared on. As if sensing their tension, the robed figure gestured behind him with a long sleeved arm.

"Come, my friends and be received into the temple of Risha."

Stepping quickly inside, they found themselves in a wide sweeping hall.

"Tullus Vantio, this is Mashim, the high priest of Risha," said Hajinna.

She turned to the poet who had thrown back his hood to stand revealed in the soft light of the tapers that burned in the temple. He bowed stiffly. The high priest inclined his head. He folded his hands through the sleeves of his vestments and, as he did, it seemed he peered nervously around him. He was a fat faced man of medium height. Though not old, his hair had receded and was greying at the temples. His eyes bulged and, when he spoke, his voice held a thin, reedy pitch.

"I see that you are in need of refreshments. Come this way and we shall converse."

They followed him down the length of the hall, passing through a thin arched colonnade that upheld the magnificent dome, before reaching a wooden doorway.

There the priest paused, one hand hesitant at the iron ringed handle. He half turned and, licking dry lips, seemed about to speak. Then, shaking his head, he turned and pushed open the door instead. He stepped over and, as they followed him inside, that door suddenly slammed shut behind them. A brazier flared up in the centre of the chamber. There was a wild bark of command and mailed figures sprang out of the gloom, swords brandished in mailed fists.

Gunthar whirled and, ripping out his sword, faced the soldiers lying hidden in wait behind the door. They levelled their halberds at him now and he crouched low, awaiting their attack. Tullus Vantio snatched for the hilt of his rapier. Whipping back his cloak, it sprang into his hand with a silvered flash. He backed to the centre of the room as the mailed ring closed in steadily around them. Hajinna cried out. Under her accusing eyes, Mashim wailed piteously before throwing himself on his knees before the man by the brazier who had shouted the order.

"What is the meaning of this?" demanded Hajinna, her small fists clenched angrily at her sides. When she saw Captian Jamal standing there she gasped. Her hands clutched at her breast. "Captain Jamal!" she whispered. "Surely—"

Pushing the priest casually aside with a booted foot, the captain swaggered forward. He sneered condescendingly as one hand toyed absently with his wide sweeping moustache. "My lady," he purred with mocking civility. "Apologies for the intrusion, but it appears you have fallen in with vagrants wanted for crimes against the crown."

Hajinna recoiled, as if from the hiss of a snake.

"What do you mean? There is dishonour here. The king is in grave danger. I command you—"

"You command nothing, palace strumpet!" yelled Captain Jamal. Crossing over to her, he lashed out with the back of a gloved fist that caught her a glancing blow across the jaw. Tullus Vantio started forward but a ring of steel lifted to hem him in.

Hajinna reeled, half senseless, and the captain pulled her close so that she stared into his cold black eyes.

"Fool! Did you not think I would seek to find you here?" he sneered. "Your petty goddess will avail you naught against the demon that is in our power. The old king is about to be replaced, his throne brought down to ruin. Aye! His weak reign is at an end. For the one true lord, the great Jukur Kazim, has returned. The kingdoms of the east shall again be unified and the world tremble before us!"

Hajinna stared at him uncomprehending. "Wha-what madness is this? Jukur Kazim, alive? It—it cannot be... he is a madman, a traitor bent on oppression and terror."

Jamal threw back his head and laughed. He shook her viciously so that her teeth rattled. "We shall see, strumpet. We shall see." Then, throwing her to the ground, he turned to the soldiers crowding the room; "Take their weapons and bind them," he said, indicating the two men.

There followed a tense silence in which all eyes flickered over to the two fugitives. Tullus Vantio stood, his eyes blazing with conflicting passions, his palm slick with sweat on the hilt of his rapier. With a sigh, Gunthar straightened and lowered his sword. He shrugged and, as he did, the soldiers came in nervously toward him. Then, suddenly, he turned and catapulted into the centre of the room. Caught unaware, the two nearest guards fell beneath his scything steel as it whickered about them in great wheeling strokes. A hideous scream sounded as the first soldier went down, his mail ripped apart from a mighty up curving slash that tore through his ribcage in an arc of spraying crimson. The second guard barely had time to lift his shield before he was driven to his knees beneath a reddened flash that crunched through his shoulder plate and severed his windpipe in a welter of erupting gore. Blood splashed the walls as the Black Wolf ploughed on through the press, his head down like a charging bull.

"Kill him!" shrieked Captain Jamal, pressing desperately into an alcove behind him. "He is just one man!"

"Dog!" roared Gunthar, leaping back from a sea of frantically slashing steel that had risen up to bar his way. He was driven up against the farthest wall, his cloak wrapped over his left forearm. Steel edges caught in the folds as his own sword sang its ghastly song of death. There were sounds of panted curses and yells of torment as, teeth bared in defiance, Gunathar's madly whistling sabre took its toll.

"Tullus Vantio! Grab the girl—I'll hold them off!" Gunthar yelled in broken Philegorian.

The renegade troubadour, his rapier playing like a thread of licking fire before him, jerked his head at the voice. Then, with a wild bound, he broke out of the encircling ring of mailed figures and came to where Hajinna stood pressed against a pillar. Grabbing her by the upper arm, he spun, just in time to parry the slash of a scimitar aimed at his back. His blade bent under the impact before springing back again. Sparks flew and he countered with a wild thrust that drew a sharp cry from his attacker as his blade ripped through the leather cuirass to the heart beneath. Gritting his teeth, he kicked the soldier away and jerked back his blade. For a heartbeat he stood thus, looking in wild desperation around the chamber. Then his eye fell on the burning brazier standing just a few feet away. Reaching to his pouch he flung a handful of dust into it. There was a smoking burst as it flared up in an angry rush of blue flame. For a brief instant there was a complete whiteout and the soldiers nearest him fell back, clawing at their blinded eyes. In that moment Tullus Vantio swept his cloak from about his shoulders and swirled it around himself and the girl beside him. When the flames had died down again, the guards shook their heads and stared in stunned disbelief.

Tullus Vantio and the girl had vanished!

Gunthar, slashing furiously, broke a blade into screaming

shards with a wild sweep of his sword. On the back swing he severed the head of the man wielding it and blood jetted as it spun across the room in a grinning, frozen mask. Uttering a warcry, he pressed out from the wall, cleaving a helmeted skull to the teeth with a single shearing stroke. Brain and matter exploded as the blade crunched home. Then, unfurling his cloak from his arm, he was through them. For a moment the way lay open and he started for the door. Then, a soldier, quicker than the rest, thrust down with his halberd. Tripping over it, the sell-sword crashed to his knees. Before he could rise, a swung shield rim caught him a glancing blow against the base of his skull. He went down with a grunt. Mailed bodies piled on top of him and he disappeared under a mound of pummelling hilts and flying fists.

A guard stepped back and raised his scimitar in both hands.

"Hold!" The order cut across the chamber.

They froze. All eyes turned toward the alcove at the side of the room. Captain Jamal came forward, one hand resting on the hilt of his low slung scimitar. Guardsmen held Gunthar pinned, his arms twisted behind his back as he lay on the bloodied floor. At a gesture, they hauled him to his knees. He was a bruised and battered shape. The soldier with the upraised sword towered over him, like an executioner awaiting the order to strike.

The captain drew himself up to his full height.

"We meet again, outlander. But, I promise, it is for the last time. Now, tell us—before you die—where is your companion and the girl? They used some vile necromantic trick to escape. Tell all and I promise your death will be swift. Otherwise..." He let the word drift into meaningful silence.

Gunthar, twisting his lips in a savage snarl, spat. "There is my answer, dog!" The bloody globule landed with wet plop on Jamal's leathered boot. A soldier cursed and, knotting a hand in the mane of his shaggy hair, wrenched his head back with a vicious jerk. The captain smiled thinly. "You have spirit, infidel. A shame that Jukur Kazim fears you and wants you dead for reasons all his own." Taking off his gloves, he nodded to the handful of guards. They lifted the warrior onto his feet.

One long finger tapping thoughtfully at his chin, the captain looked around the chamber. His eye fell on the burning brazier and, looking up, he spied a wooden beam arched in the shadows above it. "Ah!" he purred, snapping his fingers. "Yes, perfect. The beam and the flame! Oh, we have ways of prolonging your life, warrior! It will be difficult for you, the next few hours. But we will have fine conversation, you and I. Yes, I am sure you will be most cooperative... Bring him over!"

The guards dragged Gunthar over to the brazier. Stripping him of his waistcoat, a long rope was tied about his wrists. Then the other end was thrown over the ceiling beam and, bracing on it, two guardsmen hauled him upward. Gunthar's arms were jerked high above him. Inch by inch he was lifted slowly until his toes left the floor.

In a far corner of the chamber, Mashim looked on with head down. Only an occasional mumble of prayer, interspersed with stiffened sobs, could be heard as he knelt cowering in the shadows. The guards, tying off the tautened rope to the base of a pedestal, moved aside.

Captain Jamal stepped forward. A look of sadistic pleasure was on his face. "A man can take a long time to die," he said softly, as if speaking to a child. Then, looking into the flames of the brazier, he nodded to a soldier beside him.

The guard, a squat hulking shape, moved over to the wall. Reaching up with one hairy paw, he took down an unlighted torch. Waddling back, he thrust the clothed end into the brazier and watched it burst into flame. He looked to Gunthar, grinning crookedly through the open gash of his mouth.

Sweeping back his cape, Captain Jamal settled into a stiff backed chair at the centre of the room. Crossing his legs, he steepled his fingers and relaxed as if he were about to watch a play or a sport at the amphitheatre.

The guard with the torch jabbed out, letting it play against the swordsman's bronzed chest. There was a whooshing sound as the flame swept over him and the smell of singed hair as he yanked it back again. Gunthar stiffened and pulled his head back. He made no sound. Only a bead of sweat formed on his brow as he stared through diamond hard eyes at his tormentor. Again the torch licked out and this time it played across him, moving slowly back and forth against his naked skin. The swordsman clenched his teeth. A small muscle writhed along his jawline but he made no outcry.

The captain, leaning forward, gripped the arms of the chair intently. His eyes blazed with the cruelty of his passions. He laughed lowly. "Ah, what fine sport! Perhaps the added play of a voltage whip, flaying the skin from your back in strips, will help loosen your heathen tongue...." He nodded to another guard. As that man reached for the flexed handle hanging at his belt, the wooden door at the end of the room flew open. More mailed guards stood framed there. A soldier stiffened before saluting. "Apologies for the intrusion, captain, but Kabir Kaaliya requests your presence."

Jamal frowned. Rising to his feet, he looked at the man hanging before him and sighed. "Duty calls, my friend. If you will excuse me." He bowed curtly. Stepping over to the doorway, he snapped over his shoulder; "You three, come with me." The indicated men fell in behind him. At the threshold he paused, turning to look at the two soldiers left remaining in the room. "Clean this mess up and...oh, make sure his death is... pleasantly painful."

The echoing sound of his laughter rang mockingly in Gunthar's ears before the door slammed shut behind him again.

The second guard, pulling out the handle of his voltage whip, wiped a braced wrist guard over his nose. "Well, you heard what the captain said," he growled. He flipped the butt with a practised jerk of his hand and a length of jagged blue flame slithered out across the floor.

The squat guard with the torch stepped to one side as his companion walked slowly around their captive. The swordsman's face betrayed no emotion, his muscles tightening and bunching in his bonds. Then suddenly, from behind, there was the sound of a vehement snap. Pain exploded across Gunthar's back as the coiling flame of the whip writhed about his torso in a knot of excruciating agony. His body arched involuntarily and his face turned in a mute spasm to the ceiling. He screwed his eyes tightly against the welter of pain as it tore like a burning flame through the fibre of his being. For a moment he thought he had blacked out. Then, suddenly, he was hanging limply again, his arms supporting his full weight as he hung there, spent and numb from the aftershock. Then the first guard moved in. Through blurred eyes he saw his hairy, brutish shape as the torch came toward him in a rustling roar. Again, he felt the flame tear in searing waves across his chest.

He wanted to howl but something inside him clamped down like a vice and refused to surrender.

"You are strong, outlander," grunted the guard with the whip, "but no man can long withstand the voltage whip at full power. You will soon be dead."

Slowly, Gunthar raised his head. He knew the guard spoke truth. Yet his eyes blazed with defiance. The soldier laughed. Throwing back his arm, the whip hissed out in a crackle of blue flame as it prepared to strike.

- X -

When Tullus Vantio threw the dust into the brazier, he knew that he had only a fraction of time in which to carry out his desperate plan. Even as the flames erupted in a dazzling flare before the eyes of the guards, he swirled the cloak over himself and Hajinna and was moving back toward the wall. Reaching over to it, he ran a practised eye over the frescoes and crenulations and, finding what he sought, pushed hard against a stone outcropping. Suddenly, that section of the wall gaped open and, without pause, he yanked himself and the girl quickly through. He fumbled briefly in the dark and, on a soft whisper of hidden rollers, the revealing panel slid noiselessly into place again. Then there was only darkness; illuminated by a penetrating beam of light that came in from a thin slot set at shoulder height in the wall behind them. It revealed the narrow dimensions of a small tunnel.

Breathing a sigh of relief, Tullus Vantio slumped back against that wall and threw the cloak aside. Wiping his shirt sleeve over his brow, he looked on down the passage way. "Come on," he panted. Taking the bewildered girl's hand in his own, he lifted his blade. They stole cautiously forward. The air was cold and clammy; every sound echoing into the distance.

Hajinna spoke quietly; "Tullus Vantio, truly you are a skilled magician. What did you do back there? How did you know this passage was here?"

There was something of admiration in her tone as she pressed closer to him in the gloom.

The exiled magician allowed himself a brief smile. "Every temple and palace has a meeting chamber to receive dignitaries. Behind those chambers are hidden rooms, or tunnels like this one, through which they can be spied. This light we are guided by is from a slot in the false panel of the wall. A spy hole. The panel also acts as a door. I just knew where to look, is all. As for throwing that dust into the fire and our cloaked disappearance... A simple illusionist's trick. I was part of a magicks guild before I came east."

The dim light gave way to a murky grey and, presently, the two found themselves standing before a heavy draped curtain. Moving its weight slowly across with one arm, Tullus Vantio peered out into a darkened corridor. He held it aside as Hajinna emerged from the gloom beside him. Then they were making their way stealthily down the corridor until they came to a small set of steps. At the end of them was a bolted door. Padding down to it, the troubadour reached up and silently slipped back the bolt. He pushed it open and breathed a huge sigh of relief when starlight met his gaze.

Stepping out into the night, they kept to the shadows of the temple, creeping through the foliage and hugging the wall as they went. When they came up to the corner at the front of the building, Tullus Vantio jerked back. Hajinna pressed into him and he felt her heart fluttering wildly beneath her silk garments. In the main square, before the marble steps of the temple, stood a regiment of soldiers. Coming down that marble stair now, in long easy strides, was Captain Jamal. Reaching the bottom step he stood conferring with them, his tight fitting black armour gleaming in the moonlight.

"Gods!" the girl breathed. "What of Gunthar?"

"Dead!" Tullus Vantio's eyes held a grim, hardened light. He ground out the word like a knell of doom and, gripping his rapier, would have started forward but for the girl clinging desperately to his arm. "Don't be a fool!" she exclaimed, dragging him back. "They will kill you before you can get within sword's length of him!"

Cursing futilely, he lowered his blade. Then, of a sudden, Hajinna stiffened. The troubadour winced as, beneath the long sleeve of his white laced shirt, he felt her nails digging into his arm. "Look!" she cried. Her eyes were widened pools as she pointed with her free hand into the night sky. "The dragon! Just as Rahnya saw in her dream—the dragon is devouring the moon!" Jerking his head to where she indicated, Tullus Vantio stared into the blue black sky above them.

The clouds had swept away. Stars lay strewn across the firmament like tiny glittering jewels. Staring down was the thin sliver of a pale waxing moon. Coming in beside it was a strange phenomenon. A banked cloud of red mist that swept across the heavens in an undulating formation. Where it passed, the stars were hidden from view. Like a breath from the mouth of a dragon, it seethed ominously and, as it moved, it seemed as if it rolled in upon itself to reveal a gigantic, gaping serpent's mouth ready to devour the moon. What evil portent this foretold, Tullus Vantio could not say but he only knew that, when he gazed on it, he felt a dire sense of foreboding.

"They are moving away," Hajinna observed now. "This is the night that Kabir Kaaliya has been planning! A great evil has come to pass in Pashuvia! All is lost!" She wrung her hands desperately.

As Tullus Vantio stared at her, a great helplessness tore at his heart. All his young life he had schemed and deliberated for gains of wealth and power. Now, as he witnessed the humble love of this girl at his side who had risked and endured so much, he felt only shame for his own vanity and pride. Through smouldering eyes, he turned to look at Captain Jamal, his cloak swirling about him, as the troop moved off toward some unknown destination that would decide the fate of this kingdom once and for all. As he stared at their retreating figures, something hardened like steel within him. Spinning round, he gripped Hajinna tightly about the shoulders. When he spoke, a fierce light was in his eyes.

"I hold by my promise to help you, Hajinna! I will do all I can. Even if it is just to trade sword blows with that damned captain— aye, I will gladly sacrifice my life. By all the gods, I swear it!"

Staring up at him, Hajinna clasped his face in both hands. "Spoken bravely and like a true man! But don't throw your life away on a whim, good Tullus. Nay, let us follow and see what we can do together. Come!"

Before he could protest, she had slipped nimbly past him. Then, gripping his hand in hers, they were racing out across a different part of the square into the tenement quarter beyond.

*

By devious winding ways they followed the regiment of soldiers as they tramped on down the avenues of the main city. They headed east and, above them, the moon was a crimson slash as the strange anomaly of clouds roiled over it. Before long the great white stone washed buildings of the markets fell away and they were heading toward the old district. Here was not only poverty but also the diseased and the shunned; outcasts from a multitude of races. Hajinna shuddered as they crept on down the narrow dirt road under the light of that strangely haunted moon. Strange things shuffled in the darkness of shrouded doorways and, as Tullus Vantio let flash a warning length of steel from underneath his cloak, a tittering laughter followed closely behind them. If not for the tramp of mailed feet that had just passed through here, the troubadour was convinced that they would have been set upon by an amorphous mob. Even now he could feel yellowed eyes staring ravenously at them from the gloom as they passed by.

 Then, soon, even those habitants fell behind them and they were approaching an expanse of broken plain. Tombs of the ancient past lay forgotten in the dust, the paves cracked and fading beneath the stars. Beyond them, cut from the side of a cliff, a vast slab of hill reared into the night. Worn stairs were cut into the rock and squatting at the top of that hill was a black carven temple, decayed and crumbling from the weight of untold centuries. From the shattered dome, obsidian spires clawed at the heavens. Staring up at it, Tullus Vantio knew it intuitively as a place of blasphemy and horror. He paused and, leaning against the trunk of an old tree, turned to look at Hajinna. She stood beside him, her face a pale oval in the gloom.

 "The temple of the Old Gods," she whispered; "Once they held the true power in this land, with their necromancers and their djinn. Worship of them was forbidden centuries ago. It is said that, during his reign, King Shunga's cousin, Jukur Kazim, practised black arts in the crypts beneath the temple. He was a despot who swore to bring down the lands of the unbelievers. Yet it was his own kingdom that he held in a grip of fear. Eventually, the people, led by Shunga, rose up against him and he was overthrown. My lord ordered him banished into the desert to die." She shuddered. "It seems that he was a fool to let him live. In a single moment of weakness, he could not bring himself to kill his own kin. Somehow, he has survived and—" She broke off as something brushed past her face and flew out into the night. Tullus Vantio raised his sword. He lowered it again when he saw a small black winged shape flitting in an out of the mausoleums.

"Just a bat," he snorted, and then, taking her hand, nodded; "Come on." They stole forward, passing through crumbled lines of pillars and tombs.

They came to a column and looking up, saw it was crowned around the top with human skulls.

Hajinna shivered and hugged her arms tightly about her. "This is an evil place," she murmured. "Not even the flow of centuries can hide what was has gone here before."

Suddenly, Tullus Vantio, hissed a warning. Crouching behind a black marble tomb, he jerked the girl down quickly beside him. She stared over to where he was looking.

At the foot of the hill, Captain Jamal had begun stalking slowly up the slate carven steps. Behind him came his retinue of soldiers, carrying torches. But it was the figures stood in the open mouth of the temple that drew their interest. Framed there, under the reddish glow of the moon, stood King Shunga II. Motionless as a statue, his long regal gown glittering from a myriad of uncut gems, he stared out through empty eyes across the broken land. Beside him, leaning on a gnarled staff, was the astrologer, Kabir Kaaliya. His hunched shape turned away now and, as he disappeared within, the king followed, as if at some unspoken command. Even from where they crouched hidden behind the tomb, they could see an unnatural stiffness to his movements. The aged monarch walked as one caught in the midst of a dream. Then the darkened mouth of the ancient temple stood empty again. As the captain and his men began to file up toward it, a bell began to toll. It was an evil sound that bell; a gargantuan peal of thunder rising up from the belly of the underworld. Tullus Vantio gritted his teeth and Hajinna covered her ears as it reverberated in ever increasing waves toward them. Suddenly, on the heels of that tolling, a woman's scream was ripped echoing from the depths of the temple.

   Hajinna started to her feet. "Rahnya! By all the gods... *what are they doing to her in there?*"

   An icy sweat formed on Tullus Vantio's brow. Fear clutched at his heart; fear of the forces, even now, being conjured up in that temple on the hill. For he well knew what dark diabolisms could be unleashed when sorcery was used to summon from the gulfs between the worlds. The shuddering waves of the bell shook the earth, mocking them with its insidious laughter. The air became thick and hard to breathe. Sweeping back his cloak, the troubadour stood and stared up at the temple in trembling fury. He remembered the honour of the girl beside him and the man who had sacrificed his life so that they might live. Then, before the girl knew what he was about, he was striding forward, one hand clutching the pouch at his belt, the other gripping his rapier in a white knuckled grip.

   Hajinna came quickly behind him, keeping close to his back. The slate steps of the hill reared up and Tullus Vantio mounted them now, the silver frost of his sword held low in his hand. Up that carven staircase he went and, close on his heels, came the king's youngest concubine, her heart fluttering fearfully beneath her breast.

   Above them, the red mist twisted about the moon in nebulous coils, writhing across the sky like an old serpent covered in blood. Then they had reached the landing. The bell continued to thunder. In its wake an invocation sounded from the temple, like souls crying in a chorus of the damned. It was a steadily hypnotic chant; rising and falling, like the crash of waves on an eldritch shore.

Tullus Vantio stepped warily inside the entrance way. The hall was vast. Directly above, a cracked rent in the dome was open to the night. But it was what lay before him at the centre of the hall that drew his attention. Etched on the flags was a huge pentagram. At each point, a tall black candle burned with a flame of uncanny light. Beside each candelabra stood a red robed figure. They were tall, those figures, extremely pale and thin, with large dark pupiless eyes and high slanting cheekbones. There was something alien about them, as if they came from some far, distant clime that never knew the sun. It was they that carried out the ritual chant of summoning. Before them, in the centre of the pentagram, knelt a woman. Candlelight glistened from the play of her naked skin and highlighted the full contours of her well rounded body. She held her head down now, the tides of her hair falling in lustrous waves over her globed breasts as she knelt imprisoned in the invisible bonds of the circle.

Standing behind her, his eyes blazing fanatically, was Kabir Kaaliya. It was he that led the ritual chant. In both hands he clutched a skull cut from a single carved piece of black stone that glowed with a green phosphorous aura. The five men at the points of the pentagram were but his vassals. Through them he channelled the words of the ritual to its highest potency. To his right stood King Shunga II, his face an emotionless mask of death.

As they looked fearfully at the scene before them, a lean figure stepped out quietly from the shadows. Hajinna stifled a gasp. Crouching low, the troubadour lifted his blade. It wavered in his fist as he stared over its gleaming edge at Captain Jamal. Behind the captain stood his company of mailed soldiers. They waited in unnatural silence now, heads lowered, with shields braced and swords ready. There was a look of amusement in the captain's eyes. His lips curved in a disarming smile.

"The trickster and the strumpet. How good of you to join us."

Laughter rang out and they looked to see Kabir Kaaliya standing in poised triumph across the pentagram.

There was a dead look in the astrologer's eyes; a look of insanity, as one who has gazed into the depths of a forbidden knowledge too long and has come away forever burned by what he has seen.

"You are just in time to witness the rebirth of our great kingdom," he said, in a hoarse whisper; "Our demon lord will embrace this girl and take her for his own. Then the ritual will be complete..." As he spoke he raised the black skull in one clawed hand. As the sleeve fell away from his arm a smoking mist began to form inside the circle, its lines springing up in a flare of blue flame. The chants of the red robed figures fell to a whispered urgency, like the hissing of serpents slithering through the dark. A shape began to take form inside the circle now, indistinct at first but growing ever larger and more solid with each passing second. Long wings outstretched, beating silently in the void as that something crossed over from the vast cosmic gulfs into this realm of earthly existence.

"O', Shimunu! From the depths of the black abyss, I summon thee! By the unholy fires of Azrul and the enchantments of the black skull, I offer you this offering to take with thee into eternal damnation. Grant me my true guise that I might seize that which is rightfully mine. Come, dread lord, stand before us and be revealed!"

As he spoke, two red flaming eyes stared out from among the billowing mists of the pentagram. Huge black wings swept and a freezing wind filled the temple, chilling the marrow of everyone there. The huge demonic shape of Shimunu stood crouched inside the circle, his eyes burning balefully as they swept the confines of his imprisoning seal.

The tolling of the bell had ceased.

The demon lifted his head. He opened his mouth, displaying double rows of curved, pointed fangs.

"At last. Now, as agreed, I grant you your reward. Stand then... *Jukur Kazim!*" Lifting his arm, the demon indicated the astrologer with a clawed hand. Kabir Kaaliya fell back from the circle with a gasp. His features began to writhe, as if maggots were crawling under the surface of his face. The skin began to seethe; to bubble and blister. Hajinna's eyes widened, the hairs lifting on her nape as something began to claw its way out impossibly from under his skin. She stepped back as the astrologer threw back his head and laughed in horrible insanity. The crippled features of Kabir Kaaliya had sloughed away. Standing in his place now was a well built man with a hooked nose and cruel avaricious features.

Beside him King Shunga II continued to stare into nothingness, his eyes glazed and unseeing. Then, with a leer of contempt, the well built man turned upon him. Seizing the king by the throat, he pressed his face cruelly into his. As if the touch of that hand were a break on the spell that gripped him, Shunga looked dazedly around the hall. The well built man laughed lowly. "At last! The fat fool awakens. What? No welcome home... cousin?"

The aged monarch paled beneath the folds of his plumed turban. "Jukur Kazim! How is this possible? What are you doing here? Where—"

"I have longed for this reunion, cousin! From the first day I arrived at court wearing the guise of that pitiful astrologer, I have been waiting for this moment. You should have killed me while you had the chance. Oh, I came close to death all those years ago when you banished me out into the desert. But you underestimated the powers I held at my command. As I lay there, gasping beneath the sun, I was consumed by an overwhelming hatred for you. With my final words I made a pact with those who dwell in the outer dark.

"A storm blew up and, from out of the wastes, came these five red robed men to watch over me. On black skeletal steeds that spurned the sky they rode and from whence they came, no man may say. They revived me, led me to a forbidden city that lay deep within the heart of the earth. In those catacombs I found the secret crypt of the black skull. As I lay there, grovelling before its altar like a common whore, I bartered my soul for it, craving the dark wisdom it contained. Aye! I have gambled my very soul for this night! Such is my hatred for you, dear cousin. But it is a small price to pay for the vengeance I shall now wreak upon you and this city. Now that vengeance is at hand and your death shall be as no ordinary man's."

All eyes turned to stare at the scene transfixed. Then, from out of his robes, Jukur Kazim lifted a huge knife etched with enigmatic runes. Stretching to his full height, he swung it up in a balled fist. Words of dark incantation dripped sibilantly from his lips. As the blade glittered before the king's fear dilated eyes, it was then that Tullus Vantio decided to act. With a desperate leap, he was moving toward the pentagram, his blade gleaming like silver fire in his hand.

- XI -

Time was a never ending inferno of pain that lacerated Gunthar's senses. He was not aware of himself any more now than he was aware of the voltage whip as it enveloped his torso in burning waves of blue spitting sparks. He hung unmoving, his head slumped forward, his chin resting on his breast. At every stroke, he twisted on the end of the rope and it seemed that he was forever falling; plummeting into a vast abyss.

The guard with the whip stepped back. He stood stripped to the waist now, the oily play of the brazier highlighting the sweat that glistened on his thick set body. Panting, he drew a thick wrist over his brow. "Damn," he growled, "Is the dog dead? He makes no cursed sound. It's thirsty work, this killing of men. Ho, priest! Fetch wine!" He pushed forward his jaw truculently as he shouted over to the huddled figure slumped at the side of the altar. The guard with the torch turned. Waddling on thick bowed legs, he reached down and pulled the priest to his feet. "Wine!" he barked into his face and, pushing him toward the alcove, followed it up with a well aimed kick to his rear. As he staggered away, the guard followed menacingly behind him. The soldier with the whip laughed.

As he stumbled into the alcove, Mashim crossed over to a ceramic jug that stood on a low wooden table. Thrusting his head in from behind, the guard loomed in, blocking out the light. Then, licking dry flabby lips, he stepped inside and bracketed his own torch on the wall. The flickering flames played over artefacts that adorned those walls, silver adornments and strange talismans. But the guard had no eye for these, concerned only with the ceramic jug and the crude wooden cups on the table. "Simple fare, eh, priest?" he remarked, pushing him out of the way, "Hah! I wager the goddess provides you with the season's best vintage."

"Yes—yes, of course," Mashim stammered, bowing and moving back to a small shrine behind him. "The goddess is always happy to provide."

The soldier, swiping up the jug, sniffed at the contents and, with a curious grunt, upended the vessel. Red wine trickled down his jowls as he guzzled deep. Setting it down again with a thump that made the table legs buckle, he smacked his lips with relish. "Aye, is good. Now—"

The rest of his sentence was never finished. Half turning, he looked to see the priest rushing forward, a small knife lifted in his hand. He hesitated, staring incredulously at that knife, and that pausing was his undoing. The blade struck downward in a frenzied motion and the stunned guard slumped back against the table, his lifeblood spraying from a severed artery in his throat. He choked and slipped down to the floor, his eyes widening in the final realization of his own demise. Then, leaning down, the priest silenced him forever with a crosswise slash that slit his throat from ear to ear.

"Aye, the blessed goddess always provides in times of need," Mashim panted. He looked up at the wine jug on the table. Then, wiping the bloodied shaving knife on the dead guard's jerkin, he rose to his feet.

The soldier, leaning idly against a pillar and staring at the man hanging before him, turned when he heard the soft slap of sandals over the inlaid floor. Seeing the priest carrying the heavy pitcher, he straightened and jammed the butt of his voltage whip into his belt. "Where's that oaf hiding now?"

"Apologies. Your companion said he was—hungry. I set him some chicken and bread," Mashim answered, his eyes flitting nervously. Reaching the soldier, he extended the jug. As the guard made to take it, the priest's other hand fell to the end of his sleeve. Then, quick for one of his bulk, he whipped out the small dagger hiding there. Quick as he was, the trained reflexes of the soldier were faster. Jerking back with a curse, he let the wine jug slip from his fingers. As it shattered on the floor, one hand, reached up and clamped over the priest's wrist. The knife wavered in the air above them and, as they swayed there together, Mashim pressed forward, his heavier momentum staggering the leaner man back. Setting his teeth, the soldier tightened his grip and, with a cry, the priest tried to pull away. The blade fell from his numbed fingers. As it did, the soldier reached down with his free hand. Gripping a heavy poniard from his belt, he slashed viciously upward. Mashim gasped. Leaning forward, his eyes started hugely and, with a groan, he sank slowly to the floor.

Looking down on him, the soldier stepped back as the priest knelt in a widening pool of his own blood. "Nice try. But you are no fighting man, priest. Die as you lived. On your knees."

He stepped aside to avoid the slowly widening pool as it mingled with the shattered contents of the jar on the floor. As he did he bumped into something behind him. He turned to see the hanging form of his captive. Lifting his head slowly, Gunthar's glazed eyes sharpened into bright focus. The soldier grinned; "Well, well, back to the land of the living, eh? Enjoy your respite, dog, for it will be your last. We have unfinished business you and I."

"Aye," snarled Gunthar savagely, "We do!" With that his knee swept up and the soldier was lifted onto his toes as his chin snapped up toward the ceiling. There was the sound as of a rotted branch being broken and he dropped in a sagging heap, his spired helmet rolling across the tiles. His legs jerked spasmodically for a moment then were still.

"Priest!" hissed the sell-sword. "Can you reach me? Take this dog's knife and cut me down. I swear, five soldiers shall pay a debt in blood for their sins here."

For a moment there was no answer and, hanging in his bonds, Gunthar fought down a rising surge of panic. Then, slowly, Mashim began to stir. Raising himself up on his hands, he began to crawl over to where the felled guard lay with his neck broken. He fumbled there briefly and, with effort, lifted himself onto his feet. He was a grim sight, swaying in his own blood spattered robes, the poniard dripping darkly in his fist. He stumbled forward and, wheezing painfully, reached, up. He slashed once then twice and, as the rope began to part, he reeled back, sinking wearily to the floor again.

At last the cords parted and Gunthar fell crashing to his knees. His breath came in great racking sobs as he focused against the dark waves of pain that threatened to engulf him. He rose stiffly, freeing his wrists of the chaffing bonds tied about them. Flinging the cords into the brazier, he stumbled over to Mashim and fell to his knees beside him as he lay gasping on the temple tiles. He shook his head. "There's nothing can be done for you, priest and we haven't much time. The man I was with, Tullus Vantio, believed you could aid us against a demon... Can it be done? How can we defeat it?"

"There is only one way," Mashim whispered and Gunthar, reaching down, leaned his head forward. His arm flopped out and he pointed toward the alcove. "The talisman of Rahima. The—the god king... take the necklace..." he sighed and his eyelids fluttered as blood began to well up in his mouth.

Mumbling a heartfelt curse, the sell-sword looked to where he indicated. Setting the priest down gently, he padded into the alcove and stood staring about him in the small confines. Seeing something that gleamed with oddly faceted hues on the wall, he reached up and took it down. Stepping over the corpse of the throat slashed guard, he staggered back into the chamber. He knelt down again, lifting the object before the priest's fast fading eyes. "This? Is this what you mean, priest? Tell me- how can it aid us?"

Reaching up, Mashim brushed his fingers against its broad links and ran his hand over the heavy metallic plates. "Yes... the talisman of the god-king, Rahima... worn in the time when the gods fought the demon lords. A demon's form is made vulnerable in its presence. In the long ago, when men of the old race destroyed the earth with their science, the old gods returned to claim the world. They waged war with the demon lords that had risen to power in the vanquished cities of the fallen. With the aid of talismans such as this, Rahima conquered and banished them..." He started up suddenly and gripped Gunthar high about the shoulders. A weird light blazed in his eyes.

"The temple of the Old Gods. Hurry, before it is too late. Wear the necklace! May it protect and serve you, as it once did our great god-king in the long ago. It is—your only.... hope." With a sigh he sank back down again. His eyes glazed over and he would speak no more.

Looking dubiously at the heavy plates, Gunthar lifted the necklace uncertainly over his shoulders. As it settled about him, the overlapping leaves seemed to mould themselves naturally onto him. It was set with strange glowing gems and etched with indecipherable runes. It was unlike any earthly metal he had ever encountered. He moved across the room and a liquid movement of colour played among the plates in the torchlight as he did so. His sword lay on the floor where it had been left. Picking it up, he slammed the blade back into its scabbard. Fatigued and stiff from his injuries, he moved into the alcove. In his pouch he had found some healing leaves that Tullus Vantio had given him. Cupping a handful of water from a wash trough, he took one in his mouth and swallowed. As the hurts from his various encounters faded, he walked stiffly back across the chamber. Snatching up a discarded cloak he settled it over his shoulders and, opening the door, stepped down the great hall and out into the red misted night beyond.

*

As he came down the wide marble steps, Gunthar was aware of the wreathing cloud of mist as it choked the moon above in a sea of blood. Drawing up his hood, he came slowly across the courtyard. Over by the tenements he saw three figures; late night revellers, straggling in the shadows. They seemed oddly subdued as they huddled close together, looking and pointing up at the moon. He watched as they staggered into the mouth of a nearby alley. As they muttered to one another in hushed tones, Gunthar hailed them from behind. "Ho, friends! Which way to the Temple of the Old Gods?"

Startled, the inebriated trio turned. They looked at him quizzically. "Are you mad?" slurred one, staggering forward. "On a night like this? By Risha, there is evil abroad. Go to your abode and bar your windows, outlander. The kingdom is under a curse."

Frowning, Gunthar made to ask more when a jingle of harness made him turn sharply. Two riders, mounted on lean, long legged *sampas*, were approaching toward him from across the square. Half hidden in the shadows, the sell-sword stood undecided. One hand fell to his pommel even as he looked to the alleyway before him. "You there!" a soldier shouted, "In the name of his majesty, King Shunga the second, stand and be recognized!"

Boldly, and on a whim, Gunthar stepped forward, his hands raising out slowly before him.

The first rider wheeled his mount over. He looked down from his high peaked saddle, a crossbow held slant ways across his thighs. "What do you do there? State your name."

"Are you the king's men? Loyal to the throne of Pashuvia and all she stands for?" countered Gunthar.

The soldier, leaning back, half turned to his companion. "Aye, of course," he snapped. "Now tell us your name."

Stepping forward Gunthar threw back his hood; "I have no time to explain, but—" He broke off suddenly and, reaching up, seized the soldier by his harness. Yanking him swiftly toward him, his left fist swept out and crashed hard against his jaw. As he slumped forward in a heap, Gunthar pulled him from the saddle and, snatching the crossbow from his grasp, swung up onto the reptile's back. Jerking its head around, he levelled the weapon at the man behind.

The soldier froze with sword half drawn.

"Quickly, boy. Which way to the Temple of the Old Gods?"

"Head east," the younger man swallowed, slamming his sword back into its scabbard. "Follow the market town. The tombs of the ancients lay there. The temple stands on the hill."

"Good," grunted Gunthar. "Now dismount. I want you to run to the palace. As fast as you can. Raise the alarm and send every man with a sword to the temple of the Old Gods. There is treachery. Aye, more than swords will be needed this night if your good king is to be still on the throne come the dawn. Now-go!"

As the young soldier did as he was bade, Gunthar wheeled his scaly hissing mount back into the square. Urging the *sampa* forward into long, lopping strides, they passed through the district of the market quarter and were soon racing down the streets of the old city at a reckless gait. At length they came to the broken plain of the mausoleums. Reining up, Gunthar stood in the stirrups, staring up at the twisted spires of the black temple in the distance. From somewhere deep inside, the great bell bellowed its evil wrath and those reverberations sent a shiver down his spine.

   He urged the *sampa* slowly through the abandoned tombs until he came to the stair cut out of the cliff face. Then suddenly, the bell ceased to toll. It rang out into a deathly silence and an almost palpable stillness fell over the land. Discarding his cloak and swinging out of the high peaked saddle, Gunthar padded swiftly up the ancient stairway before him, the crossbow held in both hands. Reaching the landing, he stood in the entrance. As he paused there, framed by the red moonlight behind, he had but the briefest of moments to register the scene before him. Then, raising the crossbow to his shoulder, he pulled the trigger.

- XII -

Tullus Vantio knew that he could never hope to reach Jukur Kazim before the necromancer's rune etched knife killed the king. His was a final futile act of defiance in the face of overwhelming odds. But, though he did not welcome death, nor did he flinch from it. As he sprang forward, his sword whipping before him, a red robed figure nearest his side of the pentagram turned. He ran that figure through the neck. The mouth gaped open silently and he had a fleeting glimpse of gill like slits before he pulled back his blade. Black blood befouled his tip and then he had stepped over the strangely flopping corpse. He paused there at the edge of the circle and, as he did, a plan, born of wild desperation leaped into his mind.

   The pentagram, chalked on the ancient flags, was a seal.

Nothing summoned could escape, unless ordered by a complex spell. By the same token nothing could enter.

But those laws could be reversed... *if the seal was broken.*

For a brief instant he crouched there, staring into the smoking eyes of the demon Shimunu as he stood over the naked figure of Rahnya, a clawed hand knotted in the cascading tides of her hair. Then, leaning down, he rubbed at the chalk of the outer circle with his hand. The tall candles flickered wildly, casting fantastic shadows through the hall. Reaching over, he scrubbed at the inner circle of protecting runes. When he did, a wind sprang up from out of nowhere, sighing across him like a shuddering whisper. Then he was inside the final ring. Before him stood Shimunu, head hunched low beneath the folds of his slowly outspreading wings. A low growl of expectation rose up in the demon's throat and rows of sinister curved teeth exposed in a flesh rending smile. Then, before any could stop him, Tullus Vantio had rubbed away at the final part of the seal. Rising up, he stood within the small gap of the pentagram. Small as that gap was, it was enough. A charnel wind rushed forth and there was a shriek, as of a thousand tortured souls being released from the bonds of hell. Standing there, before the full might of that frigid blast, Tullus Vantio crossed his arms before his face. Something hit him hard and he was hurled back across the hall, to come down with bone jarring force some distance away. He rolled and, shaking his head, lifted himself slowly from the floor. In cyclonic fury, a black wind tore around the temple. The pentagram widened, the chalk marks of the protecting runes evaporating into dust.

Jukur Kazim turned. The words of incantation froze on his lips, the knife raised forgotten in his hand as he stared in dawning realization of the horror about to be unleashed. Then those cyclonic winds smote him and he too, was lifted from his feet, to be buffeted, as if by a giant invisible hand, across the length of the hall. As he came down, the knife fell from his fingers. The ebon skull bounced across the flags, rolling into the shadows. Twisting on his back, he cried out in panic, one hand stretching desperately toward it.

Tullus Vantio forced himself erect. Clenching his teeth, he took an agonizing step forward. Pain, from where he had landed, tore through his right leg. Limping on, he reached into his pouch and raised his rapier.

The winds had formed a vortex about the pentagram. The four red robed priests, caught inside, were hurled and smashed like rag dolls against the crumbled arches and paves. Flagstones were ripped loose and thrown into the air. Then, suddenly as that screaming daemonic vortex formed, it had disappeared.

Shimunu stood triumphant; his great wings outspread before him in unholy rapture. He seemed gigantic now, a fearsome entity revelling in his new found freedom. Clawed hands flexed and his eyes burned with a terrible light. Rahnya lay forgotten at his feet, small and helpless beneath his columned legs. With one hand, he reached out and spoke something in a tongue that had never been designed for human speech. At the far end of the temple, shadows began to twist and form. A howl of frustrated longing echoed as those shadows began to melt slowly down the walls and slide across the floor in oily dripping waves.

Shimunu reached out again, this time at the opposite end of the temple. It seemed he was dragging from the dark all the souls of demons trapped in the ancient stones of the temple. Insubstantial as smoke, more groaned as they ripped themselves from the foundations and came crawling insidiously toward him. For there was an evil in those stones, great and terrible. A thousand demons, drawn there by a thousand unspeakable acts, came clawing out at last into the world of the living.

Scrabbling frantically on all fours, Jukur Kazim reached for the obsidian skull as it rolled into the shadows before him. Just as his fingers reached it, it was swallowed up in a swath of darkness. Lifting his face slowly, an icy terror froze him rooted to the spot. Fear clutched at his heart. Something was forming there on the wall before him. Impossibly it spread, a deep, dense shadow full of cold and hate. Myriad eyes stared at him from vast, unfathomable depths. As he stared at it, a voice whispered his name and echoed sibilantly inside his mind. Slack jawed, he had time for one last chilling scream before those shadows rushed down and closed silently over him. Then, all that remained of the necromancer's former existence was a bright smear of blood splashed across the temple stones.

With fear dilated eyes, Captain Jamal staggered back, his face ashen beneath his spiked helm. Behind him, his soldiers broke rank, gripping their weapons nervously as they backed away from those ominously dripping walls. One soldier, spying Hajinna reached out and grabbed her wrist. Cowering, she looked up into his face. Then, suddenly, that soldier's head jerked back. She blinked as something appeared miraculously from his right eye socket. A thin jet of blood sprouted from a black shaft that had materialized there. She felt his grip slacken as his legs sagged beneath him. Then, tearing herself away in horror, she ran toward the entrance. A figure loomed up before her, silhouetted in the red mist beyond, and she fell to her knees before it in dread. Then that figure moved forward. A hand reached out, lifting her to her feet. Looking up, she stared into the ice hard eyes of Gunthar. Hefting the crossbow against his shoulder he flashed her a quick grin.

"Don't worry, girl," he said; "I'm no ghost. Now get out of here."

"But Tullus—" she gasped, looking behind her.

"Damn it, girl! A battalion of the king's men will be here any moment. I want you to meet them to make sure they don't kill us when they arrive. Now, go!"

Thrusting her behind him with a corded arm, Gunthar watched her flee down the carven stairs of the temple. Turning back, he hurled the crossbow to one side and, crouching low, ripped out his blade with a vicious hum. The soldiers, spilling out toward the entrance, stopped short at the sight of him and lifted their steel.

For a moment the tableau held; the lone swordsman crouching

like a cornered wolf on one side, the soldiers standing with their swords and shields raised uncertainly in the gloom on the other, with only a length of broken pave between them.

Then, from behind, Captain Jamal raised his sword. "What are you waiting for?" he screamed, spittle flying from his lips; "Take him down, you fools!"

Laughing savagely, Gunthar tensed for a spring that would send him launching across the floor into the teeth of his foes.

"Aye, stand forward, dogs! The jaws of hell are gaping wide for you tonight!"

As the nearest soldier levelled his halberd, Gunthar sprang across the intervening space, his curved blade slashing before him. The thick pole arm snapped before his wild stroke and the man was hurled back off his feet by the impetus of his rush. As they crashed to the ground together, Gunthar, rolling, was on his feet before the surprised guards could form a defensive ring around him. He reared up in the middle of them and they fell back before the onslaught of his deadly steel into a disorganized cordon. A half raised shield was rent asunder beneath a furious stroke that broke the arm of the man lifting it. As that guard staggered to his knees, Gunthar wheeled, cleaving another through the torso with a wide arcing slash that left a comet's trail of blood in his blade's wake.

He felt his aura vibrating with positive waves of energy. Whether that energy was synthetic, transmuted to him from the necklace, or whether that necklace amplified his own inner strength into a preternatural almost god-like power, he could not say. He only knew that the bloodlust was upon him. His eyes blazed with volcanic wrath and his teeth were bared in a savage fighting smile. No blade touched him and, as he waded through them, the great gems of the talisman burned with an eldritch light.

Ducking beneath the edge of an over reaching shield rim, his sword swept out, ripping through hauberk and mail in a mighty stroke that lifted his assailant from his feet and sent him crashing back into the arms of his companions in a mangled bloody heap.

Time slowed. Only the sounds of steel on steel and the cries of the vanquished were real. Then the way was clear before him and Gunthar suddenly found himself standing alone among a ring of mail hacked corpses. The remainder of the soldiers fell back, staring at him in wide eyed wonder and fear. Casting down their weapons, they stumbled past him and fled down the stairway. Shaking scarlet drops from his crusted blade, Gunthar moved into the temple.

He looked up, just in time to witness Tullus Vantio hurl the last of his prepared dust into the demon's visage. He saw him rush forward, the sliver of his blade playing before him. This time, however, Shimunu did not flinch away. As that dust sizzled harmlessly from his invulnerable flesh, laughter echoed mockingly throughout the great hall. Titanic wings snapped and the demon crouched forward, his lips drawn back to reveal rows of razor sharp teeth. Clawed hands flexed murderously in anticipation of the kill.

"Worm! Your puny parlour tricks will avail you nothing against me now."

Before the intensity of his gaze, Tullus Vantio staggered back. Reaching out with the fingers of his left hand, he made a fiery sign in the air before him. "By the sacred seals!" he cried; "By silver and flame, I vanquish you into the dark, demon!" Then, gathering himself, he lunged forward, his blade thrusting out before him like a wasp's sting.

Gunthar knew he had to reach the troubadour if he were to save him from the inevitable outcome of that encounter. Snarling an oath, he began to run.

Suddenly, a figure rose up before him and blocked his path. Skidding to a halt, he found himself face to face with Captain Jamal. As the swordsman stared at him through narrowed slits, the captain laughed scornfully.

"Your friend is about to die, heathen, and you will soon be joining him. This time I will make certain." He lowered his head and his features were a waxen mask of hate. Lifting his scimitar, he flung back his cloak so that his close fitting armour gleamed in the dull light.

Scowling darkly, Gunthar was torn by indecision. He lifted his blade, his eyes flitting from Captain Jamal to the scene being enacted behind him. Then, in a flash of inspiration, he reached up to his right shoulder. Grasping a heavy plate with his left hand, he lifted the necklace of Rahima from over his head. Crouching down, he hurled it sliding across the floor, past the captain's feet.

"Tullus Vantio! A gift from the priest of Risha!" he yelled.

Cursing, Captain Jamal came across the pave at a run, both hands knotted on the hilt of his scimitar. He sought to end the fray quickly before his foe had a chance to regain his feet. But Gunthar was already moving. He came up from the floor in a spring of rangy corded muscles, his blade sweeping up before him in a dazzling display. Steel met steel and sparks flared in the dusky gloom as the two men leaped back like startled cats. For an instant they faced each other. Like angry tigers they stood; the age old primal hate of their ancestors rearing up and reflecting wildly in their eyes. Then Captain Jamal rushed forward, his lips curving in a triumphant smile as his blade screamed down in a shearing arc.

As the edge flashed past him, Gunthar twisted to one side, countering with a swift instinctive downward strike that half severed the captain's neck cords in a spray of gushing crimson.

For a moment the captain stood frozen; his eyes widened in surprise as blood sprayed from the neatly executed wound. Then, as his face slowly drained of colour, his mouth sagged open in a vomiting rush of gore and he toppled forward, dead before he hit the ground.

*

As he closed with Shimunu, Tullus Vantio heard his name called in a desperate shout. But then his blade thrust out and he was conscious of nothing but the struggle before him. Dark wings snapped as demonic eyes stared into his. Then that face, twisting in a mask of hate, opened its jaws. Deceptively fast, a colossal arm swept out and lifted the troubadour clear of his feet. He spun away, his sword clashing to the stones as he rolled, half stunned, across the flags. Laughter sounded above him. Face down, Tullus Vantio reached out, groping desperately for his fallen hilt. His fingers closed on something else instead. Something that was metallic and strangely cool to the touch. Blinking, he stared at the gem encrusted necklace of the god-king Rahima. Some blind instinct made him grip that talisman, as a drowning man seizes at a piece of flotsam. When he did, a strange thrill travelled up his arm. His whole body became electrified. Rolling over and coming up onto one knee, he raised his blade in one hand and lifted the heavy talisman slowly in the other. He heard Shimunu's intake of breath.

Tullus Vantio's eyes blazed with the fires of retribution. As they faced each other, the demon's own eyes held the unmistakeable glint of fear. The gems in the necklace burned with a white hot intensity now. Before their light, the shadows crawling toward them from across the floor disappeared like wisps of mist before the rays of a cleansing sun.

"Your brethren have no place here, demon. As they sweep back to the eternal fires that spawned them so, then, I cast you!"

Then, with a wordless yell, Tullus Vantio thrust forward, driving his rapier deep into the demon's chest. As it pierced those ebon ridged bands, black blood oozed out and the temple was shaken by an ear splitting scream. Gritting his teeth, the troubadour pushed his blade ever deeper. Steam hissed from the jagged wound. Still he drove in, his hand knotted on the hilt until the blade bent almost at an angle. Then, at last, it had pierced the black heart beneath.

They stood braced together for an instant; Shimunu with wings outstretched and arms thrown wide, his head thrown back in a wordless roar to the heavens as the exiled magician hunched over him, the slivered length of his rapier driven wholly through his iron body. Then it was as if the demon began to slough away into a shadowy, heaving mass. Clawing hands became insubstantial wisps of smoke, his roar fading out into a time lost echo. Only the eyes, blazing with painful fury, remained. Then, they too, had faded into the darkness of the temple murk. A jewelled flame sprang up from the floor in a blinding flare for a moment and was gone.

Tullus Vantio fell back with a gasp, his sword gleaming hotly in his hand. No blood fouled his blade from the blackened heart. It was as if the demon had never been.

Still clutching the sacred talisman of Rahima in his left hand, he stared at the plated leaves and the glowing gems of the necklace as they slowly began to fade. As he did, Rahnya flung herself at him with a desperate sob. Wrapping her arms about his neck, she began weeping hysterically onto his shoulder. "Easy, girl!" he laughed, staggering back. She stood shivering in the cold night air and, disentangling himself, he managed to whirl his cloak over her naked shoulders.

A little way off, King Shunga climbed unsteadily to his feet. His face reflected the look of a man who had just woken from a deep sleep. Raising tear stained eyes, Rahnya gave a small cry before racing over to help him.

"Oh, my child," the king sighed as she steadied him with both hands. "How can you ever forgive me?"

"You were tricked, my lord... but it is over now."

Patting her gently on the arm, King Shunga looked up at Tullus Vantio.

"And you, my friend. I owe you my life," he said at length. "How came you here—an outlander, with an artefact of the god-kings in your hands, to save my kingdom?"

Tullus Vantio shrugged. "If you should thank anyone, my lord, it is your own concubine, Hajinna. She came seeking help. As for this..." He stared at the heavy plates of the necklace. Then, looking round, he turned to face the entrance. His befuddlement turned to amazement when he saw a bloodstained, half naked figure striding toward them, a curved sword trailing in his fist.

"Ghosts of my ancestors!" he exclaimed. "Gunthar!"

Shaking back his sweat matted mane, the sell-sword from the wild steppes grinned. "Well, poet. Seems that you are the hero of the hour after all."

Sheathing his blade with a resounding clang, Tullus Vantio moved over to embrace him.

"Nay! A true hero is one who would sacrifice his life to save his friends! By the gods, man, how did you escape?" Shrugging brawny shoulders, Gunthar grunted. "It'll take more than a few lackeys to take me down. I'll tell you over a flagon."

Just then a commotion made them turn, The sound of mailed feet tramping up the stairway behind reached their ears and, in the glare of the red misted moon, they watched as a battalion of black mailed soldiers spilled into the entrance way. Swords gleamed in gloved fists as they came to order in regimented formation. Striding to the forefront, a figure pushed back his cape and raised his scimitar.

"Drop your weapons!" he shouted; "In the name of his most glorious magnificence, King Shunga the second, I demand our lord be released at once!"

There was a brief pause. Then a lithe figure in torn green silks struggled out from among them and came running across the temple flags.

"Tullus Vantio!" cried Hajinna breathlessly. Grinning, the troubadour found himself once more the recipient of welcoming arms.

Shaking his head and slamming his bloodied sword back into its scabbard, Gunthar folded his arms over his naked chest. "Vrooman's favours!" he said with a wry smile. "Some men are destined for great things, whether they like it or not."

- XIII -

The sun glared down above the palace, sending heat waves dancing over the tiled roof tops. Leaning on the balustrade of his own personal quarters, Gunthar lifted his head as a light breeze wafted in from the Naverian sea. It whispered through the lush gardens and played against his chest where his white silk shirt was open to the mid-day heat. Scenting the wind, he gazed out over the onion domes of the temples, across the tenements and down to the tall masts of the ships swaying in the harbour. A longing was in his eyes and, as he gripped the balustrade with a corded hand, it was as if he were already standing on the deck of one of those ships as it waited to sail to foreign lands.

His reveries were disturbed by a soft whisper of movement from behind. Turning, he found himself staring into the large brown eyes of Rahnya. She came across to lean beside him against the rail. Standing there in her silks with her arms folded under her ripened breasts, she was very beautiful. For a while nothing was said and only the distant cry of gulls reached up to them from the quay side.

"You remind me of a great cat," she said at last. "One who is at ease in his surroundings but is restless all the same. Are you not comfortable here?"

Gunthar shrugged. Staring into the distance, he remembered another palace in another land and a bitter smile touched his lips.

"King Shunga's hospitality has been more than generous," he replied. "I have more wine than I can drink and more loot than I can carry. But I am a wanderer by nature. Nay, it's time I was away. The walls of a palace are not for me. Besides... there is a debt I must pay."

Moving over, Rahnya laid a hand hesitantly on his forearm. "Court rumour has it that you are no sword for hire at all. They say that you are a nobleman in disguise from some far western land... Is it true?"

Gunthar grinned. Reaching out, he pulled her quickly toward him. She gasped at the suddenness of his action but did not resist.

"By Yod! Does a man ever need a reason to be anything other than he already is? Can he have no secrets to himself?"

"Maybe," she replied with a coy smile, running a finger down the hairs of his chest where his shirt lay open, "But there is yet one mystery I would unravel before you leave..."

There was a brief pause. Then, as their lips met under the eye of the burning sun, two shadows merged before finally becoming one.

*

Night. In the quarters of the upper city, crenulated torches burned along the white stone walls. Watchmen tramped at regular intervals down the paved streets, their mail ringing with every step. Low in the sky, the moon was a pale crescent shard. From somewhere a dog barked and was silent again.

Dominating the corner of the wealthiest of those upper caste streets, Flasio's mansion squatted like a brooding fortress. A foreboding structure, built on the sweat and blood of vanquished men, it was a respected house stood deep in the heart of an alien land.

The hour was late now. What humidity remained in the air had long since given way to a frigid chill blown in straight from the inland sea.

In his second storey quarters, Flasio finished off the last of his wine and, turning from the window, moved for bed. The night found him in ill humour. Earlier in the evening an argument had sent his wife packing, taking all but a skeletal amount of staff with her. Even as he blew out the oil wicker lamp on the mahogany table before him, he looked to the gold hilted sword lying there and cursed her with a vehemence usually reserved for his enemies. Then, with a despondent sigh, he disrobed and threw his naked bulk down on the sheets.

No sooner had he settled back then he was disturbed by the sound of a faint footfall. Instantly, his eyes flew open. He lifted his head to stare at the window he had but moments ago been standing near. Nothing met his gaze save for the curtains stirring in the breeze. He blinked, thinking he had misheard. After all, it seemed incredulous that any could have passed through the guarded grounds and scaled the marble cladding of the house to enter his chambers. Even as those thoughts flashed through his mind, he smiled at his own nervousness. He was about to lay down again when that smile froze on his lips.

For a shadow, deeper than the rest, had detached itself from the wall and was gliding silently through the chamber toward him. A soft bar of moonlight from the window revealed a tall, sun bronzed, rangy muscled man, naked but for a red silk sash upheld by a leather belt. Like a great loping animal he padded and, from under a lion like mane of hair, pale eyes blazed recklessly. The merchant sat bolt upright with a curse. "Gunthar! You dog! What is the meaning of this?"

Even as he spoke, one hand reached for the gold hilted sword lying on the table beside him. Quick as a flash, the intruder snatched a hand down toward his own blade. Leaning half way over the sheets, Flasio froze. His eye fell to where that hand gripped the hilt of that deadly curved blade. He swallowed thickly.

"What do you want?" he growled in a frantic whisper. "Money?"

The intruder shook his head.

"What then?"

Slowly, Gunthar, let go of his hilt. He moved back, his arms hanging down loosely at his sides. He regarded Flasio from under lowered brows. "Go for your sword," he said, lowly.

Sweat beaded Flasio's face. His hand was but a fingers breadth away from the gold decorated hilt. Silence hung heavy in the air. Then, with a wild curse, he heaved himself across the bed. There was the sound of humming steel. A silvered flash of lightning lit the gloom followed by a weighty thud as something dropped in a wet splash to the marble floor. A scream of agony rent the night.

   At the sound of that scream, the night watchman pacing the hall of relics wheeled and came at a sprint down the candle lit hallway. Jerking on a thick braided rope, a bell rang out in a hollow clamour above the house. Coming to the double doors of his employer's bed chambers, he slammed into them with the full force of his mailed might. They crashed open and he crouched inside, lowering his crossbow. Beneath his bronze padded helm his eyes swept the shadows. Was it a trick of the light or did he think to see a lean, dark shape crouching there at the window where the silk curtains blew in the breeze? Even as he blinked it was gone. Directly before him, at the side of the bed, he saw Flasio howling in unrestrained agony at the ceiling. He knelt in a pool of slowly spreading crimson, his left hand clutching desperately at his right elbow. The guard moved hesitantly forward then jerked back again. On the floor, he made out the still twitching fingers of the severed right forearm of his employer. It lay in a slick pool of blood to one side of the mahogany bedside table. On top of that table was a gold hilted sword, its blade still sheathed.

*

The red tint of the sun was just touching the top of the city walls when the lone rider came down the broad dusty avenue. The two guards crouched at the main city gate stiffened when they saw him approaching and, leaving their game of dice in the dust, rose to their feet and reached for their halberds.

   "None may leave or enter the city before sun up," one guard stated, lowering his pole arm.

Behind him, the other guard yawned lazily and scratched at a flea bite under his helm.

Reining his *sampa* up before them, the rider sat silently. They saw an outlander dressed in gleaming mesh mail, a tangled mane of sun bleached hair stirring around a hawkish face. Jammed into the stirrups of his mount, his boots were of finest red leather. He leaned over the saddle pommel now and, as he did, a broad smile played on his lips.

"King Shunga told me I would have trouble with Pashuvia's finest. That's why he gave me this seal."

With one hand he held something up which gleamed in the torchlight. It spun through the air as he flipped it casually toward them. Catching it deftly, the first guard stared at it in the palm of his hand.

"This might pass for a seal where you come from," he grumbled, "but, here, a silver coin is just something we give to beggars."

Shrugging, the rider reached down to a sack weighted at his saddlebow.

"Well, then, that's probably why he gave me these." With a gesture he threw a handful of something that fell in a glittering shower on the pavement around him. Moving over, the second guard craned his head and stared slack jawed at the gold coins lying there in the dust.

The first guard looked up and hastily regained his posture. "Of course, we of the city guard, are always pleased to help those who honour our good king!"

Jerking his head to his companion, they turned back to the gates and, lifting the great wooden bar, began heaving them open. As they slowly parted, the sun's first reddened rays flooded into the city. Stepping aside, the first guard salaamed. Nodding, the rider picked up his reins and urged his mount slowly through.

Just then, a voice rang out and the rider reined around, squinting back into the shadows of the avenue. The guards turned to see a lean, cloak wrapped figure swaggering toward them. Behind him, in the street, stood a *gulamgi*. Peering out from the curtains of the howdah, the heart shaped face of a young woman could be seen.

"Rahnya told us you had urgent business to take care of," said Tullus Vantio, coming up to the rider's stirrup and throwing back his hood. "I trust all has been settled to your satisfaction?"

"Aye," said Gunthar, leaning back in his saddle. "Just some minor details I had to sort out with a former employer before leaving the province. What of you? Looks like you have your hands full."

He looked over to where one of King Shunga's personal soldiers stood guard beside the great lumbering lizard. From the howdah, Hajinna sat staring inquisitively from behind the veiled curtain.

Following his gaze, Tullus Vantio turned back to him with a grin.

"Aye, but not for long. The girl deserves better than a scoundrel like me. Besides, you see before you a reformed man. No longer am I Tullus Vantio, exiled magician, chaser of wealth and power. That man has gone. Now I am just Tullus Vantio—wandering poet and troubadour."

He spread his arms before him and gave a slight bow.

Gunthar leaned over his reins. "You could make a tidy life for yourself here. The girl is obviously quite taken with you. Why not just stay and claim the immunity of the king's court?"

Scratching at the stubble of his pointed jaw, the troubadour shrugged.

"For the same reason you are not staying, my friend. Some men are born with the wanderlust. I have learned a lot on the road since my exile. True, the going is hard, but I would not trade this life for any other. I have learned that freedom is the most precious gift of all."

The sell-sword from the wild steppes of Tatukura nodded.

"Then good fortune to you, my friend. One day, when my

sword arm is weary of the slaughter, I hope to hear your ballads sung in the taverns and around the campfires, wherever good men gather."

Reaching out, he clasped the troubadour's forearm in a steely grip.

Tullus Vantio laughed, his dark eyes glittering like black diamonds.

"Aye! You can be sure of it. I've already been compiling a verse of our adventures. Before I leave here, Pashuvia's inns will be ringing to the rafters with tales of our deeds. Farewell, my friend. May the gods favour and honour you. Mayhap we'll cross paths again some distant day."

"Aye, let that be so," grinned Gunthar and straightening, jerked the head of his impatiently hissing mount back toward the gate.

Then, with a wild shout, he spurred his long legged reptile out into the sifting sands of the desert and was soon lost to view over the ridges beyond.

LORD OF THE BLACK THRONE

- I -

Blood on the wind.

Black were the arrows that darkened in the sky,
Black were the runes that foretold me I would die.
Black were the fortunes I fought through hell to win,
Black were the gates of hell that opened to let me in!

- War-song of the Northern Reaches.

The sun's last rays were touching the cliffs and long shadows lengthened across the face of the earth, drowning the world in darkness and blood. Mail hacked corpses choked the valley and carrion birds drifted on lazy wings like harpies gathering for a feast of the damned.

In the pass below, a lone figure stirred and resolved itself into the figure of a man. He lay in the sleet, surrounded by heaped bodies. Above him a chariot lay on its side and, gripping an over turned wheel, he pulled himself stiffly to his feet. Blood trickled down his face from a gash on his forehead and, slumping wearily against the carriage, he wrenched off a battered helmet and threw it from him. He barely looked as it bounced clattering down the mound of the slain. Nausea threatened to engulf him and he stood for a moment, head hung between mailed shoulders. When the sickness had passed, he bent down and grasped for the hilt of a sword. Tearing it out of a leather armoured corpse, he came erect again and fell back to the chariot, looking painfully into a blood red sky. His left hand gripped the upturned carriage for support and the sabre in his right hand was stained crimson to the hilt. His mail shirt hung in tatters. Yet, beneath the tangled shock of his yellow tousled hair, green eyes still blazed with life.

After a while, he limped down the bloody mound, looking aghast at the horror around him. Everywhere corpses were strewn in great sprawling heaps. Banners snapped forlornly in the wind; axes and lances stood driven into the hard earth. He stared blankly as a wind swept down from the mountains, driving sleet across the torn landscape. Wiping the back of a wrist over his brow, he shook his head.

He heard something approaching, a rapid drumming over the frozen ground and whirled, raising his sabre. A striped horned beast was coming towards him. A riderless zama! As it thundered past, he reached out and grabbed the reins. It reared, screaming into the sky. Bracing columned legs, he brought the beast's hooves crashing back to earth.

"Woah, nag! You're safe now," he said, grateful to see another living thing amidst all the desolation. It hung its head and stood panting in exhaustion. Calming it with soothing words, he saw that it was in good shape. Tied to the saddle was a full canteen of water.

"Wyrm's teeth!" exclaimed a gruff voice.

Turning, the battered warrior saw two figures coming his way. He saw that they were mutants, dressed in half armour. Their skins were slick with sweat, as if they had been running. Looped at the belt of the first was a long chain, the end of which had a viciously curved hook. The other, carrying a large casting net, stooped awkwardly, his long gangly arms nearly touching the ground. An axe was tied over the hunch of his disfigured back. Their pale skins were hairless, lending them the appearance of starving rats.

Looters! Every battlefield had its scavengers, both human and non-human.

"We thank you for intercepting our steed, friend," the first one spoke, showing rows of sharp pointed teeth. "Now, if you will just stand aside—"

The rangy armed warrior smiled but his eyes were cold and hard. "I think not—*friend*. But I will thank you for herding this mount my way. It's a long walk out of this valley. He'll help me greatly in navigating the mountains." So saying he slapped a hand on the zama's lean striped flank.

The mutant's smile vanished. "You don't understand," he said lowly, "this is our mount. Gek, here, is very particular about his steed."

The swordsman raised an eyebrow. "Is that so? Well, unless I am much mistaken, the saddle on this mount belongs to Commander Arun of Brannica who fell in battle this morn. Nor do I recall seeing either of you in the fighting this day."

"Aye, you are much mistaken!" snarled the mutant called Gek, pushing past his companion. His small pointed ears were laid back against the base of his skull and his red eyes blazed angrily. "Now move aside, sell-sword, and go your separate way."

"Or what, scavenger scum?" The warrior's blood was up now and, moving forward, he crouched low, raising his bloodied sabre. The mutant known as Gek cursed and swung his net. It fanned out like a great spider's web and the warrior barely had time to hurl himself aside as it hit the ground where he had just been. He rolled, coming to his feet in a single motion, his blade ripping upward. Gek fell back, reaching for the haft of the axe slung over his shoulder, but was too late. The impetus of the swordsman's rush drove them both to the ground, tangled in a knot of desperately thrashing limbs. There was a spasmic grunt and blood vomited from the mutant's wide yawning mouth as the sabre slashed up through his abdomen and exited through his back.

The first scavenger howled, reaching for the hilts of two serrated edged blades thrust through his belt. Cat like, the sell-sword was on his feet. He leaned back just as the mutant's first blade sliced through empty air, barely missing his throat. He twisted lithely as the other blade chopped down, ringing off what was left of the tattered mail on his right shoulder. Then, quick as a play of summer lightning, his own curved blade swept out. It slashed downward, splitting the mutant's skull to the teeth in a crunching welter of brains and gore. As the corpse sagged lifeless at his feet, the swordsman stepped back, wrenching his blade from the cloven skull.

Head lowered, his eyes scanned the battlefield. No other signs of life met his gaze—scavengers or otherwise. He turned wearily, shaking scarlet droplets from his blade. He took a step forward then halted, eyes narrowing. Something had caught his attention. A jewel had spilled from a pouch tied to the waist of the first mutant he had killed. It lay by an outstretched hand, glinting like a drop of frozen blood on the ground. Different colours gleamed from it—bizarre, eldritch colours, many of which he had no name for. Fascinated, he bent and picked it up. As his fingers touched it a strange thrill went through him and he blinked in astonishment. It was as if alien tendrils were groping deep inside his mind, plucking with invisible fingers at his thoughts and memories. The nape hairs rose stiffly on his neck and he leaped quickly to his feet, eyes widening in fear.

"Yod the Accursed!" he swore.

He was about to throw the thing from him when something checked his move. He hesitated, his left arm drawn back, the jewel ready to be hurled across the battlefield. For an instant he stood thus then, lowering his arm, stared again at the alien craftsmanship in his hand. A cold wind sighed down the pass, driving wisps of sleet over the dead. Had he imagined what had just happened? His eyes lingered on the beauty of the piece in his hand. It winked in the light like an unearthly flame trapped in a prism of ice. How much, he wondered, would such a jewel would fetch in the markets of Tarkaresh?

Muttering an oath, he bent and tucked the jewel into the top of his leather boot. When he did, he put into motion events that would set him on a path more perilous and strange than any he had ever known.

But it is not for men to know their destiny.

Moving to the zama, he slammed his sword back into its scabbard before lifting the waterskin and drinking deep. Then, wiping the back of a studded wrist band across his lips, he swung into the saddle. He sat there for a while, the wind whipping wildly through his unshorn mane. To one side a solid wall reared jaggedly into the sky. Looming in the distance, the Brannica mountains cut off the horizon. He leaned down and patted the beast's neck. "There are streams and grass somewhere on the other side of this valley, mount. All you have to do is get us there."

Picking up the reins, he turned the zama westward. They headed up the gorge, picking their way through rows of the slain before coming to a fissure in the valley wall. Behind them, the two mutants lay stiffly in the sleet. Carrion birds came down, drawn by the scent of blood on the wind.

-2-

Runes.

The sun was a golden smear when the rider finally came to a cluster of hills lying far west of the valley. He had ridden all morning up a narrow trail that wound through long tufted grass. The cloak of a dead soldier hung from his mailed shoulders now and it streamed out behind him on scarlet tattered wings. His face was haggard and the eyes that stared down the trail were bloodshot, but there was a determination in the grim set of his jaw that showed the resilience of his breed. He looked up and, seeing clouds gathering on the horizon, cursed at the prospect of rain. Even as he stared, his attention was drawn to something etched against the skyline.

On top of one of the low lying hills, he could see a menhir thrusting up out of the loam. It reared like a jagged finger, pointing accusingly into the morning sky. But it was not this that had roused his interest. Rather, it was the figure of the man standing beside it. He could make out that the man was tall with long grey locks that stirred in the breeze. In one hand he held a staff and there was something stoic in the way he leaned into the bite of the cold northern wind. Perhaps he was a druid. After all, this land was ancient beyond imagining. Who knew what rites were practised in the shadows of these darkened hills? Even as he thought these things, the rider's hand strayed to the pommel of his sword. He rode slowly on up the trail, every sense alert for signs of ambush. Presently, he drew up beside the menhir and the old man stepped onto the pathway to meet him. A worn grey robe covered a once powerful frame, a frame well endured to the bite of cold, northern winds. Belted around his middle was a belt from which hung a pouch and a knife in an ornate wooden sheath. The thick staff he carried was carved with inscriptions. The warrior had no doubt now that he was the druid of some pagan god. He raised a hand in greeting. The old man nodded, his eyes meeting his own. "You look weary."

"Aye. Know you of a settlement where I can get food and rest?"

The old man regarded him shrewdly before looking back down the trail. "Maybe. How are you called?"

"Gunthar."

There was silence for a moment. The old man's eyes blue eyes blazed with an enigmatic light.

"There is blood on the wind, Gunthar. Aye! Even your name speaks of the death that follows you..." His voice trailed off into a hoarse whisper. As suddenly as it appeared, the fire died from his eyes and he shook his head. "Hah! I forget myself. Men call me Runatyr."

The sell-sword shrugged at his strange manner. "Well met, Runatyr. Until this morning, I was a mercenary in the employ of Brannica. There was fighting in the pass. You probably heard the clash of steel as my company and the men of Caerdruhn got hacked to pieces. We fought hard but were no match for Xomith's forces. I would say that, by now, the city is under siege."

The old man looked into the sky, as if staring into places only he could see. Then, suddenly, he spat. "Xomith!" The name rang out like a curse and he grasped his staff in a white knuckled grip. "May his soul be thrice damned! But nay, I speak not of that vile necromancer. There are others that have seen you. And they desire something you possess."

"What's this?" growled Gunthar, one hand snatching for his hilt. His eyes swept the terrain. He remembered the mutants he had fought, the zama he had taken, and the gem hidden in the fold of his boot. Had this old timer somehow been watching him? Were enemies, even now, stalking through the long grass intent on taking his life?

"Easy, lad," the druid murmured, holding up a placating hand. "I have the far sight. I see things that are beyond the ken of normal folk. It is a gift but not an easy thing for men such as yourself to understand. Here, let me show you."

Opening the draw strings of his pouch, the old man fumbled inside. Gunthar stared curiously as the druid knelt on the ground. In his hand were some flat stones, each etched with its own unique white symbol.

"Do you know what these are?"

"Runes," the sell-sword replied.

The old druid nodded.

"Watch, then, and I will show you magic as old as the hills, aye, as old as the very mountains themselves..."

He shook them in his hand and let them fall with a clack onto the frozen ground. Mumbling, he stared intently while passing a hand over them in concentric circles. "The strands of Freyja weave through you, there is no denying that. The very threads of destiny... ahhh!" He sucked in a breath, as if seeing something written in the markings. "War is your trade yet you are being pulled to something far greater. I see a woman with midnight hair... an army at your back... aye, and nomads who drink from the skulls of dead kings." He looked up. "Xomith's army. You are not done with them yet, my friend. Beware the Kalzhak! The harbingers of doom. Beware the fiends who drink human blood!"

"What mummery is this?" Gunthar spoke gruffly, lifting his lip in a sneer. Yet, despite himself, he felt an icy finger touch his spine.

The druid stared up at him. "No mummery. You believe. I see it in your eyes. You are a man of the west, for all that you wear accoutrements of the steppe."

It was true. All the pagan fears and superstitions of this land were close to his heart. He leaned back in the saddle, smiling faintly. "You paint a vivid picture, druid. But words won't fill my belly or strengthen my sword arm. I need food and rest."

Palming the runes, the druid shrugged. "You are welcome to share what food and shelter I have, but I fear it is not much." Gunthar nodded. "Then lead on. Anything is better than being stuck in this saddle another hour."

- 3 -

Dreams in fire.

Stars were gleaming frostily in the night sky when the pair finally settled around a make shift fire. Sitting in the clearing of a copse with his back to a fallen tree, Gunthar sighed as he sucked from his fingers the last morsels of meat he had just devoured. Runatyr watched him. He had set a trap earlier in the day and had been rewarded with something small. He had insisted that his guest take it. He chewed thoughtfully on a stash of nuts taken from his pouch, eyeing his grime stained companion over the flames.

"Where do you think you will go?"

Gunthar took a swig of water from his canteen before settling back against the trunk. His cloak was drawn out under him and he stretched his limbs with a grunt that spoke of aching joints.

"Most likely to the sea ports and the coastal cities."

The old man nodded thoughtfully. "When I said that destiny

had marked you, I did not lie," he said softly.

Gunthar rolled his shoulders. "If you say so, old man."

There was silence, interspersed by the crackling fire.

Runatyr said nothing more but sat staring into the flames. The warrior laid out his sword and drew his cloak over him. Soon snores filled the copse and the old man, gathering sticks, leant forward to tend the flames. His eyes gleamed as he mumbled under his breath. After a while, he drew a pinch of dust from his pouch and sprinkled it over the fire. It hissed and popped and a white mist rose briefly to be lost in the dark. Inhaling of its narcotic aroma, he leaned back and closed his eyes, a secret smile curving his lips.

Gunthar slept. And, in that sleep, he dreamed.

He stood looking into a valley with high walls that reared beneath stars and constellations he did not recognize. At the centre of the valley, inside a great ring of stones, stood Runatyr. Like a pagan deity, he reached up with arms outstretched, his staff held high in a gnarled fist. His head was thrust back and his grey locks streamed in the wind as he stared up at the bone white moon. His lips moved, speaking aloud the words of a vanished race. Gunthar stood transfixed. Then Runatyr whirled and stared directly at him. It was as if those enigmatic blue eyes pierced his very soul. He raised his staff and, as he did, flames shot up in a ring of fire about the stones. The druid's words echoed across the valley and roared deep inside his skull—*"You carry with you the power to defeat the lord of the Black Throne! Beware the Kalzhak! Beware!"*

Gargantuan laughter filled the pass and the stars wheeled in the sky, dripping blood. The face of the moon turned to an ebon shard and shattered like a vast mirror. The very earth began to crumble beneath his feet, turning the ground into rushing water. At last, Gunthar turned to flee but, too late, was dragged into the whirlpool.

He came up from where he lay, gasping and snatching for the hilt of his sabre. The blade was half drawn before he realized that he had been dreaming. He shook his head and blinked into the light of the sun rising over the treetops. Snapping the blade back into its sheath, he rose stiffly to his feet. A little way off, his zama was pawing at the ground. Runatyr was gone. He looked at the remnants of the fire then quickly around the grove. Of course there was no valley beyond the bare boughs of the trees, no standing ring of menhirs.

And yet—

He frowned then, shrugging the thought aside, bent to his belongings. Donning his mail-shirt, he swept the red cloak over his shoulders and, untethering the zama, swung up into the saddle. He dipped his hand into the fold of his boot and felt the smooth contours of the gem warm against his fingers. Satisfied, he straightened and heeled his mount through a narrow archway of trees. High up in the branches, a grey carrion bird regarded him before flapping lazily into the sky. Gunthar noted that its eyes were a startling blue. Bending his lips in a tight line, he hunched over the saddle and continued on his way, heading west.

- 4 -

Daughters of the moon.

Brannica was a land of sky rearing crags and deeply shadowed valleys. Further south, broken cliffs gave way to hills before merging into the low lands. It was here that Gunthar now found himself, his zama's hooves trudging through the mire of the fens. Reining to a halt, he stood in the stirrups and, shielding his gaze, stared out over the horizon. As far as the eye could see, the land stretched; broken only by lagoons and the long grass that rustled in the wind. Startled at the sight of him, giant birds took flight from the marshes. Long beaked with crimson bodies, they glided effortlessly, a splash of colour daubed against the skyline. He sat down heavily in the saddle again. If sunset found him in the fens, he was in for an uncomfortable night. Heeling his mount, they splashed on through the reeds. The wind was a dreary accompaniment and, as he wrapped his cloak closer about him, the sell-sword's thoughts turned to brighter times. He remembered the company of rogues and vagabonds, bawdy ballads sung and casks of wine upended as he rode the nameless roads of adventure. Too, he remembered the many dancing-girls of the cities; gasps of pleasure from a hundred lips in a dozen golden climes, their bodies slick with sweat as they gyrated to the sound of flute and drum.

He grinned. Life was for the living! Aye, and, as soon as he reached the sea ports at Tarkaresh, he would sell the gem in his possession and live it up for a few months. Who knows? Maybe he would even buy himself a ship.

They waded out into the quagmire, disturbing small rodents, until the beast's flanks and his boots were splashed with mud. The long day wore on until, at last, the pale sun sank below the hills.

As darkness fell, he found a clump of trees on a knoll rising from the marsh. Making camp in such dismal conditions was not easy but he had been reared on the harsh steppes of Tatukura. As a stripling, he had learned to make fire on wind swept hillsides and frozen escarpments. Soon flames were licking at the gathered wood, crackling and sputtering into life. He sat wrapped in his cloak, his sword stood driven into the soft loam as flames chased away the shadows with life giving warmth. His belly growled its hunger and he regretted not picking up a bow from the battlefield. After a while, he dozed but his sleep was light. Every so often he would open a wary eye. Above him, branches made strange waving shadows.

He did not know how long he slept but he came to suddenly, snapped into full wakefulness by some uncanny sixth sense. The night was still. No sound disturbed the clearing and the fire was little more than a pile of smouldering ashes. For a moment, he thought he had woken from a dream. Then he heard it. Something came whispering through the trees, a murmur that stirred the branches and breathed a cold wind down his spine. Silently, he reached for the hilt of his sword. He rose from beneath his cloak and, donning his mail-shirt, shrugged it down over his shoulders. Something was whispering out there in the darkness. He felt the words like a caress, the soft murmur of a kiss. He crouched and raised his sabre, the steel gleaming like a crescent of white fire in his fist. Before he knew it, he was moving through the trees, following the source of those strangely spoken words. One hand parted the branches and he emerged, looking out over the marsh. The land was bathed in a soft silver glow. An ecstatic sigh reached out of the fens, bending the rushes toward him. Suddenly, a scream cut the night and ivory bodies rushed him from the mists, springing to life from the very reeds. He threw back his mane, baring his teeth. "Witchery!" He spat the word.

  Behind, his zama snorted in fear as it pulled frantically from its tether. It bolted through the trees and the sound of pounding hooves could be heard as it fled into the distance. Gunthar cursed. They had lured him from his mount and the protection of his fire. He whirled, groping back through the trees toward the small copse. No sooner had he burst through the clearing then a pale shadow loomed up before him.

  By the light slanting through the branches, he saw a naked woman. But no such woman born of man had ever walked the earth in the full light of day. Her skin was moon white, her hair a tide of foaming midnight, cascading in a wave of darkness over her naked figure. She was lithe and powerfully built, with full budding breasts and wide curving hips. He looked into her eyes and knew a thrill of terror. They were black and soulless as the pits of hell. Her hands were webbed, ending in flesh rending talons. She lowered her head and hissed, showing sharp, needle like teeth. Before Gunthar could move, she lashed out, dealing him a powerful back handed blow that sent him crashing through the trees. He rolled in the mire, half stunned. Shaking his head, he groped with one hand at a tree bole and sought to rise. Then they were all around him, swarming over him. He reeled up, his blade a flashing silver arc as he fell back from the talons raking at his flesh. A severed head spun in the starlight, fountaining blood and, ramming his pommel into a fanged face, he tore free from the talons snapping at the links of his mail. With a desperate lunge, he broke from their embrace and sprang through the trees down toward the fens. His boots sank in the mire as the ghostly women gave chase. Ahead, he could see a granite monolith rearing out of the marsh. It was covered in some green phosphorus slime that glowed with a sickly light. Nonetheless, he made for it, determined to make a stand against these foul creatures. He splashed through the bracken, one hand grasping at the reeds as he hauled himself along. Wading through an open space of knee high water, he came at last to the menhir. At its base was a plinth and, setting a foot on it, he pulled himself up. He turned there to fall back against the eerily glowing stone. One hand holding the monolith for support, he leaned forward, raising his reddened steel. Gasping in great lungfuls of air, his eyes swept the reeds.

Then he saw them.

Whether they were demons, witches, or mutants twisted by contamination of the marsh-land, he only knew that they hungered for flesh and blood. Whatever semblance of humanity they wore was an illusion. Like phantoms, they weaved sinuously toward him and, in the pale light of the moon, he saw no life reflected in their eyes, only the black obsession of death. He remembered his dream from the night before. *The moon had turned to an ebon shard that had shattered and drowned him.* Was this, then, an omen of his fate? To drown here in the mire beneath an ominous moon, his life drained as he stared helplessly into eyes of darkness? His own eyes narrowed to slits. If death were to be his fate this night, he would not go down the long path alone.

Then they were upon him. Screaming his war-cry, his blade whistled in the starlight, weaving a scarlet web as the things were hurled back from him into the night. He ducked from the sweep of taloned claws and dealt a back handed slash that sent a pale body spinning through the air in a showering trail of blood. Another flung itself at him from his left, burying needle fangs into his up flung wrist guard. Bracing his back against the monolith, he launched out with a kick that sent the she-demon catapulting into the path of her sisters. His blade swept out, shearing through the ribcage of another. His laughter was short and fierce. In that moment he became more daemonic than they and they hesitated, falling back from the edge of his deadly dripping steel. He spat. "Come on, you hell-sluts!"

Where his mail was torn, scratches crisscrossed his limbs and his chest heaved from exertion. He tensed to spring among them, dealing death as best he might when an unexpected cry interrupted the tableau.

"Back!" It was a woman's voice that cried out, slashing through the darkness like the cut of a knife. Gunthar had no time to wonder at its source. An arc of lightning flashed across the fens, hitting the water with a searing hiss. The moon women fell back, screeching their displeasure to the stars. Another bolt of flame lit the dark, this time enveloping one of the she-demons in a crackling web of blue fire. There was a stench of burning flesh as she collapsed into the fens, a charred and smoking corpse.

"*Yod!*"... the name fell from the sell-sword's lips like a curse.

In wild desperation, the moon women fled, weaving through the reeds, hissing in panic. They scattered in all directions, leaving the clearing free but for the moonlight. The faces of their dead floated like lilies in the murky water. Falling back to the monolith, Gunthar drew a wrist over his brow and turned his head. At the edge of the reeds he saw a cluster of slabs. In the long ago, it had been a dolmen, an ancient tomb. Figures stood there now; vague, hulking shapes, ghoulish in the moonlight.

Before them, on the highest slab, was a strikingly beautiful woman. Clad only in brass breast plates and a long red silk kirtle, she held above her an ebon rod in both hands. At the end of it pulsed a crimson jewel with an eerie dripping light. As the moon women slithered into the darkness, the jewel's brightness ebbed and the woman lowered her enigmatic weapon. Gunthar knew it was from this that the lightning fire came. Her hair was black, square cut above the shoulders, framing an elfin face. Encircling her brows was a gold band cut with runic symbols. She exuded a brazen courage and Gunthar knew that he gazed upon a queen. A queen that commanded legions and loyalty, even unto death. Behind the slabs in the reeds he saw the dark figures of men and the long shapes of canoes.

"We've found him," grunted a voice and the woman lifted her chin, smiling.

"He looks dangerous," cautioned a small form crouched at her side. She raised her head. "Man! Come to us, quickly!"

Licking dry lips, Gunthar gazed out over the fens. Then, shrugging, he stepped down from the monolith and waded knee deep through the open water toward them. He still clasped his bloodied sabre in his right hand and, as he came up to stand below the collapsed stones on which they stood, he wiped the befouled blade on a tuft of torn reeds and slammed it back into his scabbard. Arms folded over his breast, he regarded the woman and her entourage.

"It's been a hell of a day. Even my mount has deserted me. If you have wine and a soft bed, lead on."

The small man crouched at the woman's side regarded him through beady eyes. "He is uncouth and insolent, your highness! Could it be that we have made a mistake?" The woman smiled thinly and shook her head. "No, Kereth. He is the one."

Small dark hunched figures came up, pushing a long canoe through the reeds. With a gesture they bid Gunthar enter. He paused for a moment, looking at the faces around him, before hitching up his sword-belt and swinging a long leg over the side. Sat braced in the middle, he was then surrounded by swarthy figures who took up paddles. Last to enter was the woman and her close clinging servant. She sat opposite him in the high end of the prow. Beside her, the little man regarded the sell-sword suspiciously. Drawing a purple cloak around her, the woman nodded to the mailed warriors on the rocks and they set off, pushed by a dark man dressed in salvaged scraps of leather and armour.

The paddles swept quietly, barely making a sound as they dipped in and out of the water. Behind them trailed another canoe. Surrounded by these dark, silent men Gunthar felt little at ease. They wore nothing but short leather kilts and high strapped sandals. At their sides were curved knives. Knotted muscles rolled under their swarthy skins. But it was not these things that made him uneasy. It was their eyes. They were unearthly—curiously slanted with small golden pupils. He realized that these men had been born and raised in the wet-lands. He looked across and regarded the woman in the prow. Although of the same race, she was clearly unlike them. She was brown skinned, curvaceous, of average height with a slim, athletic build. He drank in the rich curves of her figure, barely concealed by her attire. Her chiseled cheekbones and heart shaped face gave her an aristocratic cast. Beneath the circlet over her brows, her eyes were curiously shadowed. There was a measured maturity about her that made her age hard to determine.

"Who are you?" he asked after a while.

She raised her head. "I am Julinna, queen of Brough-Tyr."

"Brough-Tyr!" he grunted. "No myth, then. Is that where we are headed?"

"Yes. We have waited for you."

Digesting this cryptic information, Gunthar said nothing for a moment. Then; "What were those things I slew?"

Her next words were spoken with trepidation. "They are the daughters of the moon that worship Yeb-Shuggath."

She said nothing more and they lapsed into silence. Gunthar leaned back, staring up at the stars, his arms resting on either side of the canoe. The only sound was the creak of the boat, the soft slither of reeds as they scraped against the hull. Then, shortly before dawn, a structure rose up in the distance, rearing its bulk against the dimming stars.

"Brough-Tyr," said the queen lazily. He sat up, staring at the jagged spires and the bulwark of that once mighty city, trying to imagine what it had looked like in eons past. It was a sunken ruin now, half buried in the mire. Its towers were in decay and its once mighty walls sagged from centuries of erosion. The paddles dipped silently as they glided down a drowned avenue that flowed past crumbling ramparts. Warriors stood along the walls, watching them pass from beneath dark rimmed helms. Eventually, they drew up against a wide set of marbled steps and, as they did, a trumpet blew a mournful fanfare. Two dark men leaped out, drawing the canoe up and tying it to mooring pins driven into the marble. Barging up beside them, the second canoe did the same. Once they had disembarked, both parties came up the stairway. At the top were a double set of iron riveted doors set in a high thick wall. Before they reached the final step, those doors drew inward with a rumbling groan.

Thus came Gunthar to the city of Brough-Tyr.

- 5 -

Shadows and spires.

The pale glow of the morning sun did nothing to illumine the shadowed halls of Brough-Tyr. A vast fortress of shattered domes and worn spires, it crouched like the broken back of some vast behemoth, rearing stark and foreboding from the wet-lands.

On the highest parapet of the city stood three figures. The wind plucked at their garments and, as light drops of rain began to fall, the smallest of them looked up into the steel grey sky. He was furtive faced with a large bulbous nose and close set black eyes. Huddled in his threadbare cloak, he looked at the proud regal figure of his queen as she stood facing out over the fens. The wind fingered her purple cloak and stirred her hair, but she seemed hardly to notice. Sniffing, the little man wiped his nose. The other figure was a man of hulking proportions. His thick corded arms, beneath the scraps of his leathern armour, marked him as a warrior. He stood regarding his queen with one hand resting on the hilt of a blunt iron sword at his side.

"Tell me what you see, Kereth. Do the mists rise across the fens? I hear the cry of the *maraston* birds and can feel the tremor of the reeds rippling in the wind."

The small man turned. Putting a hand on the parapet, he gazed out over miles of wet-land. In the distance, through the rising mists, could be glimpsed the brooding shapes of the Brannica mountains. "Aye, your majesty. It is as you say. The mists are rising. Dark clouds roll in from the east."

She nodded slowly. "There is much work to be done. Caerdruhn has either fallen or is still under siege. Either way, Xomith's attention will be focused there for some time."

The hulking warrior squared his shoulders. "Then now is the time to strike! With one blow we can crush his infernal city and reclaim these lands back for the glory of Brough-Tyr."

Julinna smiled. "Patience, Galan. Each player has a designated place on the board. Our time will come."

Galan frowned and said nothing but his eyes fairly burned at the prospect of war. Looking at his scarred face, Kereth scratched a thumb over his chin.

"The yellow haired mercenary is not even of this land. Perhaps Dukkan can still lead us. He—"

Julinna stiffened. "Dukkan has the sickness," she snapped. As if in shame, Kereth lowered his gaze. Even Galan looked taken aback by the mention of Brough-Tyr's once great champion.

"Your minstrel forgets his place," he grunted. "A good cuffing is enough to keep such waywardness in check, I find." He glared meaningfully at Kereth and flexed the fingers of his right hand. The small man cowered back.

Julinna lowered her head. "Enough! Now is not the time for dissention. A time of change is upon us. Every man and woman within these walls will be voicing similar thoughts. You two are my most trusted. Your council in matters of state and war are invaluable to me." She turned, her voice softening. "What I must ask of you upon the morrow will not be easy but you must trust to my judgment."

For a moment no words were spoken. There was only the wind, whistling over the rooftops. Suddenly, Galan stepped forward. He knelt down, his right arm propped on his knee. "Should you command it, I would storm Xomith's dark keep myself! Gladly would I lay down my life, if it meant his power were removed from our lands." His eyes spoke for the sincerity of his words and Julinna laid a hand on his brawny shoulder. Kereth straightened. "From your heart to my lips, my queen. I shall see your orders obeyed," he said.

*

Laughter rang throughout the long chamber. Tapestries stirred from unseen drafts and a fire crackled in the small hearth. At a much worn table, Gunthar sat hunched over a platter of food. Two slim, dark girls moved around him, laying out his repast. The sellsword was a different man now from the grime stained farer that had first entered the walls of Brough-Tyr. In his eyes shone a new vitality. His hair was swept and bound back at the nape by a copper band. Washed and groomed, he wore a light silk tunic, dark leggings and leather boots that came up to just below the knees. He made a jest now and the laughter of the two girls pealed like tiny silver bells. Aware of a ravishing hunger, he turned his attention to the plate before him. The smell of roasted marsh boar made his mouth water. There were steaming potatoes, vegetables and bread. He ate greedily, tearing at the meat with the implements provided and then with his bare hands when the going got harder. Juices dribbled down his chin as he crunched the thick bones and sucked at the marrow. He gulped down the water, wishing it was a cold draught of Uhremon wine instead. Then he sat back and smacked his lips. A hand reached out deftly for the bare haunch of a girl leaning in to pour more water. She danced nimbly away, the water missing the goblet and spilling onto the table. Gunthar's roar of mirth set the two girls off into squeals of excitement. Their gold flecked eyes flashed coyly at him and their half smiles promised more willing service than they were already providing. The sell-sword's pulse hammered in his veins and he leaned across, taking the slim wrist of a girl in his rough hand. She gasped and made to pull back but something held her frozen, one hand rising to her breast, her eyes shining. He held her there for a moment, looking into her eyes, a half smile playing on his lips. Then, at the other end of the room, the doors flew open and the girl jerked back from his grip. Both women looked at the figures framed in the doorway and, bending their heads, went mechanically about their duties. Clearing up the platter and the half eaten bread, they scurried from the chamber. Still leaning across the table with his outstretched hand, Gunthar frowned then sat back, flinging his arm over the back of his chair. He regarded the small group coming toward him and, snatching up his goblet, drained the contents with a grimace.

"I trust you have been well looked after?" Julinna's voice was soft as the play of a harp. His eyes followed her movements as she swept toward him. Noticing the easy grace with which she carried herself, he grinned and set the goblet down.

"Had you arrived a moment later, you may have seen more service that you bargained for."

If the queen of Brough-Tyr understood his meaning, she affected not to notice.

"Kereth is right," growled Galan. "He is insolent and uncouth."

Standing directly behind her, the wide shouldered dark man glared at him through stone hard eyes.

Slowly and deliberately, Gunthar swung his booted feet up on the table. Cocking his head, he picked at his teeth with a sliver of bone. "So far the hospitality has been excellent. Though, I notice, I'm not out of sight of a man with a sword for very long."

Julinna smiled. "You're probably wondering why you're here."

The warrior snorted. "You need me for something. What is it? You need a throat slitting? A jewel filched?"

The queen stood silent for a moment. Behind her, Galan shifted uncomfortably, the fingers of his left hand fondling the hilt of his sword. To the other side of her, Kereth stood wrapped in his dark cloak, one hand idly stroking his chin as he gazed from under lowered brows at the outland swordsman. His dark eyes betrayed nothing. The queen raised her head. "It was imperative that we brought you here. However, lest you judge me too harshly, I did save your life."

"You did at that," said Gunthar, smiling wolfishly. "You're not what I expected. I heard in the courts of kings that Brough-Tyr is a city of despair. A seat of mourning. No one comes here, lest they contract the sickness of its people."

"Heathen!" exploded Galan. "Brough-Tyr was the seat and heart of *all* Brannica."

"Aye, *was*," said Gunthar, raising a cynical eyebrow.

"My queen, we are wasting our time with this upstart."

Julinna lowered her head, her fingers brushing a red jewel that gleamed in the golden circlet above her brows. "We are a shadow people, living shadowed lives... in a shadowed land." Her tone was without inflection, devoid of self pity or remorse.

The two men behind her glanced at one another. There was resentment in those glances, born of stung pride. Gunthar noticed this.

"But I get ahead of myself. I have not asked your name."

"Gunthar."

The queen nodded wearily. "You are right, Gunthar. There is something that I need you for. Indeed, that the whole of Brough-Tyr and the heartland of Brannica needs you for. And there is gold, much gold, if you will accept my offer."

Gunthar snapped the thin bone he was chewing between his teeth and leaned back in his chair. He shook his head. "My sword is not for hire. Not three days ago, I lost a whole company of men to a bunch of savages we should have easily annihilated. I've had my fill of this land and slaughter. The sea ports of Tarkaresh are calling me."

"You have no mount, no gold and no food."

The warrior shrugged. "I'll survive."

Julinna cast him an enigmatic look. "If you're thinking of selling that jewel you found once you get to Tarkaresh, I would think again."

A chill ran down the sell-sword's spine at these words. How—? His eyes flickered to the boot top where he had secretly stashed the jewel when handed new garments. Then his gaze shifted to Julinna. He saw the secretive smile that curved her lips and snatched at his boot with a curse. The jewel was still there. He almost laughed with relief. Then his brow furrowed in puzzlement. It felt somehow, *different*. Leaning forward, and swinging his boots off the table, he opened his hand to stare disbelievingly at what lay in his palm. It was a dull, featureless object of glass. Unremarkable in every way but for its odd shape. Disbelief was replaced with anger. Galan's laughter was a low mutter that echoed throughout the chamber. With a snarl, Gunthar hurled the object across the room.

"What trickery is this?" he growled, slamming a fist down on the table so forcefully that the water jug jumped. He half rose to his feet. Instinctively, Galan snatched for his sword hilt.

"Draw that blade against me, cur, and I'll feed it to you point first," snarled Gunthar. His fists were clenched, his eyes blazing murderously. For a long moment the two men glared at each other.

Then Julinna upheld her hand. "Enough! Galan!"

Grumbling, the squat warrior snapped his half drawn blade back into its scabbard. Turning her attention to Gunthar, the queen chose her next words carefully.

"What you thought was a jewel is a tool. Designed to hold communion between people over large distances. A mind stone. It's how I found you."

"You speak in riddles, woman."

"Some weeks ago, a man of mine was sent out from these walls to observe the march of Xomith's hordes. With him was a device with which he could communicate with me. Through it I could see, feel and observe everything he did. Our minds were attached. He was ambushed and killed by two mutant scavengers. They stole the mind stone, thinking, as you did, that it was a gem. Did you not feel something strange when you first picked it up?"

He remembered back to that uncanny sensation on the battlefield of something touching his thoughts and frowned. "Aye."

"It was in that moment that I locked my psyche with yours. I read your memories. Your thoughts were open to me... like the pages of a book. I knew then that you were the one we need."

Gunthar glared at her from under lowered brows.

"What do you want from me, witch?"

"To lead my army against Xomith and destroy the Black Throne."

For a moment, Gunthar stood like a statue. Then, as his lips twitched into a smile, he threw back his head and roared with laughter. The sound of it ran along the tapestried walls.

"Madness!"

Seeing the seriousness of their expressions, his face grew somber and he shook his head, folding his arms over his chest.

"I marched a hundred of my finest mercenaries into these hills for Commander Arun. We drilled his warriors mercilessly. Caerdruhn was our last line of defense. We had the high ground, yet those hairy savages crashed through us as if we were children.

Of the hundred that followed me, only I survived. I lost them all. Your finest soldiers have been routed and your cities are falling. What makes you think you can stand against them, let alone Xomith's necromancy?"

"We are not afraid to face him in battle," growled Galan.

"Remember that bravery when the wolves are gnawing on your bones. Don't throw your lives away. Xomith doesn't want you, he wants the strongholds of the north."

"For now." It was Kereth who spoke and he let the implication of his words hang heavily. Gunthar snorted. "You think he'll waste his time trudging through the fens just to take your half sunken ruin?"

"There is a reason we must fight him," said Julinna, stretching herself up to her full height.

Galan's eyes flickered to her. "My queen..."

Gunthar straightened. "Go on."

"Brough-Tyr is the reason Xomith is here," she declared. "It is not the strongholds of the Northern Reaches he wants. He has come searching for science and weapons of the times before the Great Dawn. We have them. Beneath us, in the catacombs of this very city. For untold generations we have sat upon the miracles of the ages— afraid, lest they fall into the wrong hands. We used them in the past but have sworn never to do so again. Now that oath must be broken. Before Xomith has a chance to unleash his own hellish weapons against us. We must fight fire with fire."

Gunthar blinked and shook his head. "This is beyond a swordsman's pay. All I ask is food and a good cloak for my journey. I'll be gone on the morrow."

"Listen to me, Gunthar," the queen said. Something in her tone gave the sell-sword pause. Her eyes... shadowed, enchanting... he had never seen anything quite like them. They were innocent, like the eyes of a child. Yet, staring into them, he thought to see the secrets of a thousand lifetimes etched there.

"Let me show you the treasures in our vaults," she said. "If I cannot sway your mind, perhaps they can. Then... if you still wish to decline my offer, we will do as you ask and you can leave. I promise."

Gunthar stared hard at her for a moment then frowned. "How long have you been blind?" he asked bluntly.

"Since the day of my birth. Now... shall we go?"

*

Flanked by small dusky warriors, the small party began to thread their way through the ancient halls of Brough-Tyr. Julinna walked ahead with Gunthar, Galan and Kereth behind her. The warrior's eyes were drawn to the sway of the queen's hips and he noted again a certain brazenness in the way she carried herself. But for his taciturn companions, he would have grinned appreciatively at the view. Shafts of sunlight slanted down through broken parts of the roof high above. Through cracks in the bulwarks, dreary winds shuddered. The people went about their business furtively, talking in sibilant whispers. As the party passed on through the great halls, some moved out of their way whilst others stopped to bow their heads reverently to their queen.

Gunthar felt the silence of the city's abandoned halls as an almost sentient thing. With every step, he felt the dust of the centuries stir beneath his feet. He stared up at the shattered domes and felt the sleet on his face from the sky beyond. He imagined he had died on the battlefield and was, even now, wandering through the twilight lands of the dead, following a queen of the slain, searching for the banqueting hall of the chosen. It could almost be but for the fact that these small dusky folk were more like goblins than the mighty heroes he had read of in the sagas.

At last, they came to a more dilapidated part of the city. Cobwebs hung in ghostly strands from sagging columns and they passed broken statues before coming to a set of stairs that led into darkness below. Here, Julinna turned and said something to one of the guards. That guard handed Galan a torch. While the rest of them stood back, the small party began to descend. Galan led the way with Julinna beside him. He held onto her elbow as the torched flamed above them. Gunthar and Kereth followed. The stairs were ancient and worn. Presently they reached the end to find themselves standing in a musty corridor. Before the flickering brand, they could make out the scroll work on a massive iron door.

"Here," breathed Julinna, "lies the treasure of Brough-Tyr."

Gunthar saw the imprint of a hand stamped into the metal on the door. As Julinna moved toward it, she pressed her own inside, fitting it perfectly into the shape. For a moment there was silence and then the outline of the handprint began to glow a deep throbbing red under her fingers. There was a hum and the sound of locks snapping back. With a sepulchral groan, the door moved away before sliding into the wall. Light sprang up from some hidden source and Gunthar grunted at what he beheld.

Bracketing the torch on the corridor wall, Galan looked at him. "Well, outlander?"

Julinna moved into the chamber, a gigantic stronghold housing heaps of gold and precious gems. The glare of it dazzled the warrior's eyes and, for a moment, he stood staring in amazement. There were shields of gold, encrusted with rubies and amethysts. Iron chests lay open to reveal a dazzling array of coins. He stepped into the vault as Julinna turned slowly toward him. Both Galan and Kereth came in behind. For a moment, none spoke as they watched the mercenary swordsman take in his surroundings. At the sight of so much treasure, all the avarice and ambition of the sell-sword rose up within Gunthar and he swallowed thickly.

As if sensing his thoughts, the queen spread her arms wide. "All this can be yours. We will even send an armed caravan with you to Tarkaresh."

Gunthar murmured. "You would pay me the treasury of your kingdom?"

"What use gold and jewels without freedom? Take them and

save Brough-Tyr. Save Brannica from the hands of savages and necromancy." She came to stand before him. Her face tilted up to his and, although she could not see him, he felt as if she were staring into his soul. Her voice lowered to a whisper. "Become commander of my army and destroy the Black Throne."

His head swam at the nearness of her. Could he do it? Could he lead the warriors of this city against Xomith? His arm reached out and, encircling Julinna's waist, he pulled her in close. She gasped, eyes wide. He bent his head, crushing her lips with his own. Behind him, he heard Galan's choked curse, the rasp of steel as it left leather. Twisting, Gunthar's sabre leaped into his hand. The dark man flinched, his eyes bulging at the sight of the glistening steel laid across his jugular. His own sword had not yet cleared its scabbard.

One arm still encircling the queen's waist, Gunthar smiled. "I slew the chieftain of one of the most powerful clans of Tatukura with this blade, Galan. Aye, and that before I had seen seventeen winters. If you want Brough-Tyr saved and Xomith destroyed, you will obey my orders and not question my authority. Is that clear?"

Galan's eyes flickered to his queen. He saw the easy way in which the mercenary held her in his corded arm and lowered his head resignedly. Sweeping the steel away from his throat, Gunthar slammed the blade back into his scabbard with a flourish. "Good! Now... where's the wine in this damned city?"

- 6 -

The Sons of the Fallen.

A tall, lean figure crouched knee deep in brackish water. Around him tall reeds shivered, waving like a tumultuous sea in the wind. Above, grey leaden clouds rolled, blotting out the sun. Hugging his furs closer about him, he bent the reeds aside with one hand to squint down the way. His hatchet face was gaunt, his eyes little more than tired, sunken holes. Over his back was a two handed war-sword.

"See anything?" a voice grunted.

Without looking round, the tall, gaunt man shook his head. He bit his lip as he craned his neck to see through the swaying rushes. No life disturbed the vista for as far as the eye could see. There was only grass and the marsh, the grey brackish water below and the grey rolling clouds above. In the distance, the brooding shapes of the Brannica mountains reared through the mists. Suddenly, his eyes narrowed. He caught glimpse of a lean shadowed shape moving toward them. In one hand it held a bow and, jutting over one shoulder, a quiver of near depleted arrows. As the figure came splashing through the bracken, it revealed itself into a woman. She drew closer and the tall man stood upright. Seeing him, she came wading across. As she did, two figures rose slowly behind him. At their inquisitive glances, she nodded grimly.

"Three scouts dead," she said, snapping the string of her bow.

A big man in plate armour nodded. "Good work."

"What now?" the tall one with the hatchet face asked. He stood with hands on hips, glancing round at his companions. The man stood nearest him in the begrimed plate armour was a hulking figure, big and black bearded with a bald tattooed head. In one hand he held a war-mace. Behind him was a short pot bellied man with a flaming red beard. He wore scale mail and a dented helmet. Over his back was a double bladed war-axe.

The big man shrugged, looking out over the miles of marsh land. "We keep heading south. The further we get the less likely we are to run into Xomith's dogs. Who knows?" he grunted, swinging his mace up onto his shoulder. "If we find a settlement maybe we'll be able to procure mounts and supplies. There must be something in the forsaken place."

The woman with the bow nodded. She was bedraggled, her light mail torn from the rent of spear and sword. Beneath a red scarf wound over her brows, a long golden braid lifted in the wind. "South it is. I've got three arrows left. If we're lucky, we'll find some game."

So began the long arduous trek through the marsh. The wind bit at them and they shivered, hunching over as they forged through the reeds and stagnant water. Not one of them believed they would live to see civilization again but they were soldiers, hard bitten and well used to the bitter casts of the dice that fate rolled for them. They waded through the fens and the only sound was their ragged breathing. A light rain began to fall, fine and drizzling.

Toward the end of the day, something big and hairy stepped out in front of them. It turned with a squeal and scampered away, bending the reeds in its paniced flight. With a wild shout the woman unslung her bow and raced in pursuit. She cursed as the stiff bladed grass slapped at her naked limbs. Even as she ran, she reached up over her shoulder for an arrow. She caught sight of something black and bristly moving ahead of her and fell to one knee, fitting the arrow to her string. The bow creaked as she drew back on the tough cord. The beast reached a clearing and, for a moment, she had a clear shot. Even as the arrow feathers brushed her cheek, the beast suddenly gave a bellow. It squealed and floundered before crashing into the water.

It lay unmoving.

Incredulous, she rose slowly to her feet and, creeping forward with bow half drawn, saw the blood laying slick on the surface around it. Even as she gazed at the black shaft of the arrow protruding from its neck, she was aware of the silent forms that surrounded her. Like phantoms, they emerged from the mist and the reeds. The sight of their dark figures and curious golden eyes sent a cold tremor down her spine. She spied their weapons, their short horned bows, the curved knives at their sides and almost breathed a sigh of relief to see that they were at least human. One of them spoke; "You will come with us."

She heard curses as more figures surrounded her companions.

Reluctantly, she lowered her bow.

*

They were brought in with the dawn. There was no welcoming fanfare as they were led up the steps to stand before the massive basalt walls of the city. Only the inscrutable gazes of the guards on the ramparts greeted them. The big man with the black beard and tattooed head swept those ramparts with a cool gaze. Their weapons had been seized, their arms bound to their sides by tough, woven grasses. Then the great doors drew inward to reveal the city of Brough-Tyr. Prodded by flint tipped spears, they walked into the deep shadowed depths of its dusky halls. From the darkness of crumbled archways, whispers followed them and they shivered, wondering what horrors awaited them in this cobwebbed kingdom.

At length, they were brought to a great throne room. The doors were pushed open and they squinted against the glare of torches held in niches along the walls. At the far end were a set of onyx steps and a high throne of white marble. As they drew closer they saw that the throne was richly detailed and carved of a single piece. But it was the figure that reclined upon it that drew their attention. She was a woman, dressed in the barbaric splendour of her race, the purple cloak draped over her shoulders barely concealing the lithe beauty beneath.

Clad in brass breast plates and a diaphanous red silk kirtle, Julinna leaned propped on one hip, chin resting idly on the heel of her palm. Her supple body reclined gracefully and one bare slender leg was stretched out across the dais. As the prisoners were brought in, she raised her head. The jewel in the circlet over her brows gleamed like a crimson stain in the torchlight.

Stood to one side of the throne, Kereth whispered; "They look to be mercenaries, majesty. Survivors, possibly, of the recent battle at Caerdruhn."

In his slim fingers he held a lyre of white bone. The instrument had muted when the great doors of the throne room first opened.

The dark men leading the prisoners came and knelt before the dais. They lowered their heads, laying their spears on the ground before their queen. The prisoners did not bow but stood silently scanning their surroundings. No fear was written on their faces, only a burning curiosity. Mercy was something they neither expected nor gave. Julinna sat up.

"My advisor tells me that you are strangers. Who are you and what do you do here?"

The prisoners exchanged glances. The big bearded man grunted. "We're lost farmers."

Behind them, the hall doors crashed open. "Murderers and thieves, more like! By Yod, crucifixion is too good for these rogues," a voice bellowed.

The four jerked their heads to stare down the length of the great hall. Leaning in the doorway behind them, they saw a tall, rangy muscled figure dressed in a white silk shirt and black breeches. One thumb was thrust casually through his sword belt. In his right hand he held a bone of beef which he was busily tearing at with strong white teeth.

"By the gods!" whispered the tall, hatchet faced man. The gold haired woman blinked. Even the red haired dwarf gave a deep throated laugh.

"Gunthar! The war monger from the steppes!" the man with the tattooed head blurted.

"Aye, none other. You dogs made it, then."

The woman with the golden braid spoke. "Men saw you die in the pass before Caerdruhn." Her voice was tinged with awe.

Gunthar shrugged. "I'll admit, it was a close thing. Those hairy dogs swarmed over me and I took a few dints to the helm. When I came to, the battle had rolled over and I awoke to a field of corpses." As he spoke, he swaggered into the hall, tossing the bone to a retainer who fumbled in his attempts to catch it. Wiping the back of a hand over his lips, Gunthar grinned and slapped a hand on the shoulder of the short, rotund, red bearded warrior in the scale mail. "Var! I trust you whetted your axe well in the blood of those savages?"

"Aye, captain. But it was a lost cause. It shames my heart, but we saw little sense in throwing our lives away. Commander Arun was too eager to push the Kalzhak into the pass. We knew it was a trap but he wouldn't listen." He shrugged massive shoulders and shook his head.

Gunthar nodded. He turned and stepped toward the throne where Julinna sat listening attentively. "Queen Julinna, these are my men." He jerked a thumb. "Or what's left of 'em. Those who have reason to curse them call them, 'the sons of the fallen'. A more vicious band of rogues you'll never meet."

"I heard a woman's voice."

"Zandia. As proud a son of the fallen as any man," Gunthar said. He jammed his thumbs through his sword belt and moved down the line of the prisoners, appraising them as if they were on parade. He looked to the broad, heavy set warrior with the black beard and tattooed shaven head. "The man you spoke to is Jal of Tharl. Wanted for murder and cattle rustling in a dozen different lands." He turned to the tall, gaunt looking man. "Next to him stands Turgun. A disgraced squire. As a youth, he stabbed a knight at the gaming tables and has been wanted for that crime ever since." Turgun lowered his head. Moving on, he looked to Zandia.

"Zandia. Brigand and wayfarer. Her pretty face adorns wanted posters along all the roads from Shumzun to Kulamir." She pouted mockingly. "And, finally, Var of Brokir. In a land of drunken berserkers, he's been considered too dangerous, even for them! He ranged far and wide before entering the gates of Kulamir to find a home among the sons of the fallen." The dwarfish figure in the mail shrugged, his eyes glinting like chips of blue ice.

"Then, if these are your friends, they must be freed at once," said Julinna, waving an arm. A dark man rose to his feet. Padding over, he slashed at their bonds with an obsidian knife. As the cords fell away, the mercenaries rubbed at chaffed wrists and arms. The big man, Jal, flexed his hands. "So what's the deal, black wolf?"

A smile touched Gunthar's lips. "All in good time. For now, let's get you dogs cleaned up and a decent meal in your bellies."

- 7 -

When the dead speak.

Flames licked the evening sky to sweep unchecked through the streets of Caerdruhn. Acrid smoke drifted across the rooftops and ash fell in a searing rain to choke the throats of the dying. Savages staggered down her once proud avenues, bloody scimitars trailing in the dust, their axes stained red with the blood of the innocent. All around, shadows, thrown by the flames onto the city walls, painted ghastly scenes of rapine and slaughter.

Through the glow of those lurid fires, a hulking shape came riding. Although he too was a savage, he showed little interest in the looting and massacre around him. He was Tremuk, chieftain of the Kalzhak. His scimitar hung at his side and his great horn bow was in his hand, the quiver strapped over his spiked leathern mail. With his top knot, drooping mustachios and bleak eyes, he was a fearsome sight- one to strike terror into the hearts of even the bravest of men. He rode up to the council hall that overlooked the central plaza and dismounting before its steps, gave his reins to a warrior in waiting. Across the way, a rooftop collapsed, drowning for a moment the screams of butchered men and ravished women. He paid the sounds little heed. Coming up the steps, he reached the great wooden doors and, pushing the remnants aside with both hands, paused on the threshold, savouring the smell of freshly spilt blood. Hitching up his sword belt, he padded into the great hall. All around, the bodies of mailed men lay in mangled, gory heaps. Tapestries were torn from the walls and the effigies of pagan gods lay smashed on the floor. He smiled. Sights such as these were like a fine wine to Tremuk. Ordinarily, he would have glutted himself in the orgy of violence outside. But, for now, his mind was on other things.

   He came striding into the council chambers. Before a high carved wooden seat, as his warriors had said, was a corpse in golden mail, the remnants of a shattered two handed war-sword still gripped in a gauntleted fist. This, then, was the chief councillor of Caerdruhn. He was a hacked corpse but he had not gone down without a fight. About him on the floor were the twisted figures of his Kalzhak warriors, their bodies rent by heavy sword blows. Stepping among the corpses, he looked around before reaching into a satchel at his side. Withdrawing something, he knelt beside the man in the golden mail. In his palm was a small silver beetle. Opening the dead man's jaws, he let the wriggling creature slide down his throat. Clamping the mouth shut, he rose quickly to his feet. Then, from his belt he took a small pouch and shook out the contents in a line of grey and silver dust. When the pouch was empty, he flung it aside. Next he breathed silent words that slithered around the hall to penetrate into the surrounding gloom. Those words were not of any known language, yet each syllable and twist of phrase resounded with power. At his feet, the grey dust began to shimmer and stir. He glanced quickly behind him. Woe to any man that would dare defy his orders and enter now! The very torchlight seemed to waver and dim as if all light were being sucked into an ebon inkiness. The sounds of slaughter faded, becoming little more than far off echoes. In the spectral silence that followed, the only sound was the war-chief's heart thudding in his chest. Suddenly, a groaning sigh, as of a thousand tombs being opened, resounded and Tremuk's hand fell to his sword hilt. His eyes were drawn to the dust shimmering before him now in the air.

   "I am here. What is your will?"

   Despite himself, the war-chief started. Something had reared up from the floor to stand before him in the darkness. It was the man in the golden mail, his broken blade still dangling in his hand. Tremuk twitched his shoulders. Taking an involuntary step back, he raised his head and hissed at the mangled remains of the corpse, making passes in the air as he did so with his left hand.

"I hold you to the pact that the dead must observe for the living. Tell me, where are the weapons of the old ages hidden?"

The corpse swayed uncertainly. A great gash in its head oozed with black blood and grey brain matter. The whites of its eyes were turned glassily upward, staring into spaces only the dead could see. For a moment the mouth hung slack like a gaping wound. A rattle sounded from its throat that could have been laughter.

"Caerdruhn does not hold that which you seek."

Tremuk clenched his fist in frustration. Every city sacked and burned had yielded the same answer.

"Then where?" he snarled impatiently.

The corpse groaned in tortured torment, reaching up to its own face and clawing at its eyes with a taloned hand. *"Death! Death! Come for me! I cannot live! I am dead! I must die!"*

The war-chief cursed. He must not lose this one. He must know!

"Answer me!" he snapped. "Where are the treasures of the Great Dawn? Tell me, and I shall release your soul back to the land of shades. I swear by the Great Wolf."

The council chief's arm slumped back to its side. A moment's silence filled the hall. Then, slowly, the mouth of the corpse began to move. As if dragged up from the bowels of hell, the lips writhed and formed words.

"Seek the city of Brough-Tyr. There, beneath the ancient throne lie the secrets of the old ages... the treasures of the Great Dawn."

Tremuk grunted. "Where shall I find this place?"

Slowly, the cadaver lifted an arm and pointed. *"To the west, in the lands of the fens. There you will find Brough-Tyr... Now, release me for I am thrall to the night."*

The war-chief uttered a phrase in that strange language and the corpse fell crashing to the floor. As it did, torches flared up again, berating the darkness. Tremuk breathed a deep sigh. Dealing with Xomith was an alliance forged of mutual understanding. But if his men knew that he too was trafficking in the powers of blackest sorcery... He tugged at his mustachios. The necromancer had instructed him well in the dark arts. Thus far, those arts had proved very useful. But at what eventual cost?

With a shrug, he turned on his heel and marched quickly to the hall doors. Coming out onto the steps he looked up at the red flames eating the sky then down at the warrior stood in the courtyard with his mount. "War-chief?" the warrior queried as he came swaggering down the steps.

Tremuk grunted. "We talk with Xomith." Taking the reins, he swung up into the saddle.

He looked up, feeling the heat of the burning buildings on his face. He closed his eyes, savouring the screams of the dying, the smells of scorched and burning flesh. *With every great victory comes sacrifice*, he thought and smiled.

- 8 -

Into the Crypt.

For Gunthar, the days passed in wearying monotony. He passed the time walking the lengthy halls of Brough-Tyr, observing the comings and goings of its inhabitants. He noted that they lived by strict ritual. Robed men pored over tomes in dusty libraries, reading ponderously to half naked inhabitants who sat cross legged on the floor, clinging to every word.

The people themselves moved as in a dream where there was no future, only the bleak predicament of the present. The past for them was a horror; dim with the scented musk of antiquity whilst fear lay upon them with a heavy hand, deciding their every waking action. They lived their lives in the vast shell that was their city, shunning the outside with its contaminations, whilst their elders, reading from crumbling parchments, clung to the rituals of a dead world. He wondered if the people ever dreamed of a time when they were free to rove under the sun—to wage war and love fiercely with the hot passion of life. For without dreams they were nothing. To Gunthar they were a fading race slipping quietly into the dusk of oblivion.

He was still in the grip of this strange melancholy when a royal aid informed that he was wanted in the throne room. Shrugging off his mood, he came into the hall and was surprised to see that he alone had been summoned. Apart form a handful of guards, there was only himself, Julinna and the ever present Kereth, lurking behind the throne with his lyre of white bone.

"Word has come from my scouts that Caerdruhn has fallen," said Julinna, wasting no time in preamble. "The time has come for action. I would have each of your men instruct and lead separate divisions of my warriors. I want them skilled in the use of bow, sword, shield and in strategic warfare, such as you learned in the southern lands."

Gunthar nodded. "These are my thoughts. Your men are used to striking from the shadows. The Kalzhak can fight in hilly terrain and on the flats, much like my own adopted peoples, the Tatukurans. Would that I could teach your men how to ride and shoot like them. But you don't use zamas to ride into war."

For a moment, Julinna pondered. "In past times, our ancestors used war-chariots, pulled by *herthrung*. We have such beasts. Is it possible to build chariots and ride into battle in such a way?"

Gunthar shrugged. "Aye. In fighting on the plains, a chariot division is an asset. Especially against the Kalzhak. But it would take time to maneuver an invading force out to where they can be used to best advantage. If you have a place in mind—"

Kereth spoke; "I know of such a plain and valley. It is not the biggest, or the best, but it might aid us."

Gunthar nodded. "I would have to see it to get an estimation of how many men and chariots we'll need."

Julinna gripped both arms of the throne. "Good! There is something else you must see. Something that will aid us greatly in the upcoming battle against Xomith and his forces."

*

The sun was a bloody shield hanging low on the horizon. All around, mists rose to become lost in the slowly darkening sky. Through the fens a long boat came silently drifting. The oars of the small dark men moved in quick unison and they bent to their task without looking up. Stood at the high curving prow were three figures—Julinna, Gunthar and Galan. On a bench sat Kereth wrapped in his dark cloak, occasionally plucking a melancholy chord on his lyre and mumbling a phrase. The queen rested one hand on the carved lines of the boat, lifting her face into the wind as it stirred her dark hair. They had been rowing for some time when the reeds thinned and they came out onto a lagoon.

"There," said the surly dark captain, straightening and pointing with a corded arm. In the distance, framed against the low hanging sun, was a curved building. Squinting, Gunthar could not see it clearly at first but, as the boat swept closer, he could make out heavy blocks of stone rearing from a graveled shoreline. As they neared, the dark men drew in their oars and they drifted up to the shore where they beached with a thump. Gunthar was first out, leaping quickly to the gravel. Turning, he held up his hand to Julinna. Her own hand felt for his and he moved forward, encircling her hips before lifting her over the side. Galan and Kereth noticed but said nothing. As he swung her over and her sandals touched the gravel, the queen moved off up the gentle incline toward the structure. The boat was drawn up onto the shore where the dark men stood waiting, their golden eyes expressionless in the waning light.

The building was an imposing sight, carved of great blocks of stone, rearing out of the fens like a blackened skull. A yawning archway was set in the front of the edifice and, as the small party trudged toward it, Gunthar noticed inscriptions cut above the lintel. As they passed within, the sell-sword caught the scent of centuries of rot and decay. Parts of the roof had crumbled in, allowing shafts of what little sunlight remained to filter into the building. Debris littered the ground, fallen blocks of masonry, splintered wood and the bones of dead fowl.

"Dukkan!" Julinna cried and that cry echoed softly around the walls. She came into the centre of the dome, her face lifted, her body taut, as if every sense was awake now and attuned to her surroundings. As the last of the echoes faded, something slithered at the far end of the building. Gunthar jerked his head. He had a fleeting glimpse of something gigantic crawling up the far wall before it disappeared through a rent in the stone. He caught only a momentary glimpse but his skin crawled in revulsion. It was armour shelled and had long feelers. His hand fell to his sword hilt. He was about to speak when a voice came whispering out of the darkness.

"Julinna..."

"Yes, Dukkan, it is I. Come to us." There was a strange inflection in her voice.

Something moved out of the shadows. Something big that dragged itself forward until it came to stand revealed in a shaft of dying sunlight. Gunthar's words died in his throat as he stared at the being before him. His feelings were a mixture of fear, abhorrence and awe. He stood frozen, not daring to move, watching this strange tableau unfold before him. He knew instinctively that the Queen of Brough-Tyr and this bizarre creature of a man were bound together by some extraordinary secret past.

"It is good to see you, my queen. You bring others. My mind... I remember them, I think. But not this gold haired one. He is not one of us."

"No, Dukkan. He has come to aid us. His name is Gunthar, a warrior from the south. We need him to help fight the hordes that have invaded our lands."

Even though he was hunched over, the man still dwarfed the slim figure of the queen. A misshapen head swivelled in Gunthar's direction before a huge bulging eye focused on him. The other eye was of normal size but did not move. His skin was of a greyish hue and his arms, long and gnarly, nearly touched the ground. His body, whilst huge and hulking, was deformed to tragic proportions. About his hips he wore a scrap of leather but that was all. Occasionally, drool formed at the corner of his mouth and he would wipe it away with the back of a hand. Into that huge eye came a light of recognition and, for a moment, some long forgotten flame burned in Dukkan's mind as he stared at the sell-sword stood behind his queen. He threw back his head. "War!" He clenched his fists and the word boomed throughout the dome. "Swords and death! Blood and screams! Victory for the conqueror!" The slash of his mouth curved into a twisted smile and he tittered, leaping away into the shadows in a capering dance, whirling and landing on his feet in a crouch, swinging his great arms about him as if at imaginary foes. Suddenly, he stopped and stood frozen. He swivelled his head, glaring back at his visitors, his one good eye burning with passion and fury. His huge hands flexed as if feeling the hafts of weapons between them. He lifted an arm and pointed. "Once I led the armies of Brough-Tyr to glory. Ahh... I remember! The clash of steel as we drove back those that sought to take from us our halls and treasures." He slammed a fist into an open palm and it sounded like a clap of thunder in the gloom. His eye misted as he became lost in remembering glories of the past.

Timidly, Julinna took a step toward him. Placing a hand on his huge shoulder and stretching to her full height, she whispered. "We need you still, Dukkan. We need the science and the weapons hidden in the crypts. To defeat the necromancy that threatens us."

Slowly, the huge head bent down and the great eye blinked. The fiery passion that had been there moments before faded now to be replaced with something else and he nuzzled her tenderly.

"Come, take us to the crypts!" she said excitedly.

A huge grin split Dukkan's face. "Yes! The crypts!" Turning, he began loping back into the darkness. With a glance behind, Julinna motioned for her companions to follow. Frowning uneasily, Gunthar looked at Galan and Kereth. Catching his eye, Galan whispered; "Once Dukkan was as strong and clean limbed as yourself."

"What happened?"

Galan and Kereth both exchanged glances. Wrapping his cloak closer about him, the small minstrel shivered. "Come. We don't have much time before the light fails us. I would be back in the warm halls of the city." So saying, he moved after his queen, the bones of small rodents crunching beneath his feet. Lowering his gaze, Galan followed. They did not go far. Capering with excitement, Dukkan suddenly crouched down. In the dust was a slab set at odds with the rest of the stone. The malformed man looked up at the small party as they approached. Between his feet was a rusted iron ring. With a grin that showed broken tusk like teeth, he gripped it in both hands. Slowly, he stood up and there was a hollow protesting groan as the slab came up with him. He hurled it aside and it crashed with a heavy boom that sent dust rising in a great blooming cloud. Beneath was a set of stone steps. Without waiting, Dukkan leaped down them in bounding strides. For a moment he disappeared in the darkness then there was a dull booming noise followed by a crackling hiss as light illuminated the stairway from below. With Galan guiding Julinna, Gunthar and Kereth followed down the worn steps. Once again, the mercenary found himself being led into mystery below ground. The stairs wound interminably, far below where he expected and, as they did, the walls became slimy and damp. A clammy chill pervaded the air and the worn stone beneath their feet became slippery with mould. At length they reached a stone corridor that stretched like a burrowed out tomb both in front and behind. Gunthar marvelled at this feat of engineering, for he realized that the tunnels must stretch far beneath the fens and, possibly, all the way back to Brough-Tyr. Water dripped in places from the ceiling to form small fungal patches on the ground. There was an eerie silence, broken only by the ever present static hum of the light source, and he wondered what strange things lurked in these forgotten catacombs, tunnelled in eons past by unknown hands.

"Dukkan, show us where the armour of the Old Ages is kept," said Julinna touching the giant softly on the arm. He grunted then loped off, beckoning them to follow. Branches led into other tunnels. Even Gunthar, who prided himself on his keen sense of direction, quickly became disorientated in this underground labyrinth. He wondered if the giant was playing some twisted game and was getting them deliberately lost. His hand rested on the hilt of his sabre and, as they walked, he stared down the hollow burrows of silent tunnels that they passed to both left and right. Just as the sell-sword began to wonder if his fears were true, they came to a large open chamber. A small set of curving steps led down into what appeared to be a miniature amphitheatre. They came down, looking in silent awe at the paraphernalia that greeted them. Huge thick glass vats filled with brown liquid connected to a series of wires and pumps stood lined the walls. Whatever was once in those vats had long since gone. In the centre of the chamber was an ebon slab rising up from the floor. Upon it, decked out in careful arrangement, was a suit of black armour. Beside it lay the dark curve of a single bladed axe with a long tapered handle, fashioned of the same black metal. Facing out at them at the end of the slab was a huge hexagonal shield. At the sight of this armament, Dukkan let out a deep moaning sigh. He crouched on the floor, staring with his one good eye and moving his head slowly from side to side. Julinna moved forward, feeling softly of the ebon slab, before running her fingertips over the hexagonal edges of the great dark shield. She shivered at its touch and wet her lips. Lifting her head, she seemed to be gazing with sightless eyes into somewhere deep within her own mind.

"With these weapons you will destroy Xomith," she whispered.

Gunthar moved forward to join her. Craning his head, he eyed the suit of armour. So intricate was it that it seemed carved all of one piece, from the breastplate down to the greaves. There was something vaguely disturbing in its design as if it were not made by human hands at all. The shoulder pieces were overlapping ridges of thin flexible metal. He leaned forward and, running a hand over those ridges, was not surprised that it felt like no metal he had ever touched. The helmet was an alien and frightening affair, vaguely insect like with slitted glass eyes. Forged and carved of a single piece, there was no visor, so that it covered the entire face of the wearer. The metal swept back from the head at either side into twin sharp streamlined wings.

"Take the thing and let's go!" hissed Kereth. Gunthar turned. The minstrel was huddled in his dark cloak, his face wan in the flickering light. Even Galan looked uneasy, his head hunkered into his shoulders and a frown of uncertainty on his face. Gunthar turned back to the dais. His hand reached out to take the axe. The curve of its handle seemed designed for his hand alone and was surprisingly light. He bent and hefted the great shield with its strange hexagonal design. He turned and indicated with his head. "Galan. You will have to carry the rest."

The dark captain rolled his shoulders and took a hesitant step forward. Grumbling, he began gathering the pieces together as the others looked on. The light flickered then came on again. Kereth was already turning, heading up the steps and out toward the tunnel arch. The others followed. They waited while Dukkan took the lead and, after what seemed an age, they climbed the slippery stairway and emerged back out into the domed hall. Kereth shivered as if to shake off the damp depths of those tunnels and, with Galan close on his heels, they headed back toward the entrance and the shore. Framed beyond the doorway, the men stood waiting with the boat, their torches flickering orange tongues of flame against the night that had fallen without.

Dukkan stood looking forlorn. A change had come over him since he had taken them into the crypt and shown them the armour of the Old Ages. He was silent and uneasy. He squatted in the dust now, looking at the retreating figures of the two men. Julinna stroked his head. "Thank you, Dukkan. I will return. In the days to come." He looked up at her then and bowed his head, rocking back and forth on his heels. The queen moved off and began walking toward the entrance. Gunthar came beside her, the dark axe in his hand, the great shield at his side. When they had reached the doorway and the night beyond, Gunthar spoke suddenly; "Wait."

Without further word he turned on his heel and trudged back through the shattered dome. Soft bars of moonlight fell across the floor as he came crunching up to where Dukkan crouched. The deformed man looked up with his one good eye as the yellow haired mercenary came to stand before him.

"I thought you were a mutant. But you're not, you were a warrior like myself. You wore the armour and wielded these weapons into battle in times past." He lifted the axe and the great dark shield. Gazing on them as with a great hurt, Dukkan nodded wearily. "I fought the armies of Yeb-Shuggath. The old god himself fled before the fury of that axe." He spoke softly, pointing at the great edge of the blade. "It is forged from a metal by a race long forgotten. But the power of the armour comes with a price. Do not succumb to its seduction as I did. Resist, if you can... " He coughed, a dry, hacking sound then spat an unwholesome colour into the dust. His shoulders racked with pain and he wheezed. "Once I was the champion of Brough-Tyr. Now I live in these ruins among the vermin and the spiders. Remember that, yellow hair."

Straightening, Gunthar nodded grimly, feeling a sudden

revulsion for the weapons he held in his hands and a great pity for the creature before him. For a moment his fist tightened on the haft of the dark axe. He saw its gleaming black curve. With one striking blow he could end this pitiful monster's suffering for good. As if sensing his thoughts, Dukan bowed his great head. Swallowing thickly, Gunthar's hand trembled.

"Goodbye, Dukkan," he said and his voice shook. He turned and walked back. Then he stopped and, turning slowly, looked on the strange thing crouched there in the dust.

"You and the queen were lovers, weren't you?"

Dukkan lifted his face. In the pale light of the moon, his features were full of sorrow. Looking away, Gunthar tramped back through the debris and the offal to the entrance way and the boat waiting beyond.

*

The moon was a huge bright shard, staring down among wisps of tattered cloud. The men bent to their oars, rowing in silent unison. Galan held a torch in one hand and, as they swept across the body of water, howls rose and shuddered the night. Men jerked their heads, looking nervously around. Kereth shrank into his cloak and even Galan gritted his teeth, sweeping the flame of the torch this way and that. Close and near by, something huge splashed in the water then was gone, leaving ripples in its wake.

"Faster, dogs!" the dark captain hissed, brandishing the torch above the backs of the rowers. Sweat beaded his brow. Gunthar scowled, his hand clamping on the hilt of his sabre. Wrapped in her purple cloak, Julinna pressed closer to him.

"Denizens of the dark," she whispered. "They know and remember the weapons of the Old Ages and are afraid." He slid his left arm around her and looked to the armour and the axe wedged at the bottom of the boat. The eyes of the helmet gleamed with a nefarious light from the torch Galan held and, for a moment, it seemed as if it were a living demon ready to rise up and wage war. Gunthar's heart leapt as he gazed on that helmet and the gleaming curve of the axe beside it. He did not fear the night and its terrors. An urge to raise that black curved weapon seized him. He wanted to brandish it aloft and scream out into the night and make the darkness shudder with fear. The stars glared down and, as they made the reeds, men dropped their oars and began poling the boat through the mire. The bulwarks of Brough-Tyr reared up but it was as if they moved at a crawl despite the efforts of the near naked men straining at the poles. Looking out into the darkness, Kereth thought to see dozens of flaming eyes staring at them from the reeds. Then, as the long-boat drew up to the stone walls, they vanished as if they had never been.

- 9 -

Shades and reflections.

In a chamber in one of Brough-Tyr's highest towers, Queen Julinna stretched herself languorously on a fur trimmed couch. Elaborate hangings covered the walls and occasionally they would ripple from some unseen draft. She sighed and, rolling over onto her stomach, turned to face the fire crackling in the hearth. She heard the restless scuff of the boots of the man sat on the stall opposite. Although she could not see him, she imagined his youthful sun darkened face drawn into a frown of impatience. A smile tugged at her lips as she reached for a silver goblet on the stand beside her. "Your men train my warriors without mercy," she said, before taking a sip and placing the goblet down again.

The broad shoulders of the man shrugged. "Mercy isn't something you get from those who live for war."

Julinna smiled. She heard the rustle of a sheaf of paper as he bent over the table before him, running a finger over the parchment of an ancient map. His brow furrowed. "Kereth speaks of a plain with a valley. If they find the ancient road way, Xomith's men will have to come up through it but it's not so easy for us to reach through the fens."

"The marshes have taken over everything," she sighed. "It's what has kept us so insular. That and those that dwell out in those fens."

Gunthar looked up. "You speak of those things that howled for our blood last night."

The queen nodded. "Yes. There are things out there that we know little about. Shadowed things that wear the shapes of men, but are not men. Our ancestors did not build this city. Brough-Tyr has been here from the time before the great devastation. We only reclaimed it from the mutants that our ancestors found sheltering here. That was in the days of the long night after the necromantic wars. Together, the true men banded from the ashes to reclaim what is rightfully theirs."

Gunthar listened, his chin resting on his fist. He imagined the years of conflict between the contaminated mutants and the new men, the bleak struggle for existence to forge a new kingdom in this twilight land. "For years we had prosperity and harmony," she continued, "before we found that the land was poisoned. Things stalked unseen, attacking under the cover of dusk. With the weapons of the elder world, we fought back, driving them into the marsh. They retreated but they still lurk out there. Old things, slaves to darkness and senile gods."

Gunthar looked thoughtful. "The plain that Kereth speaks of is two days ride from here. To reach it we must traverse the marshlands and bogs. I propose that we take the *herthrung* with us and build the chariots on site. As Xomith's forces must come up through the valley to reach the plain we could take them by surprise. It won't be easy, and we'll suffer some losses, but I wager we can win the day."

Julinna sat in silence for a moment. "What of Xomith? So long as he lives, we win nothing."

Leaning back with a sigh, Gunthar ran a hand through his hair. He reached for a wooden goblet on the table and gripped it. "After the battle at Caerdruhn," he said, "I met a man. A druid, who told me to 'beware the Kalzhak.' He said that I would meet a woman with midnight hair and that I would have an army at my back. I thought him mad. Later, in a dream, he told me that I carried with me the power to destroy the Black Throne."

Julinna stiffened. "Who was this man?" she asked, a fist clenching in the furs beneath her.

"He called himself Runatyr."

"Runatyr!" she whispered. For a moment a cold draught prowled through the room.

"You know him?"

"Aye! They call him the rune caster. The changer of fates. Well do the folk of Brough-Tyr know Runatyr. Listen, Gunthar," she said and she leaned forward, brushing his cheek. "Destiny has put a mark on you. I know who you are, Black Wolf, where you come from and how you came by that name. I know that life has not been kind and I know that—" she broke off, as if she had said too much.

"Know what?" Gunthar growled, leaning forward and grasping her wrist. "What else do you know of me?"

"You dare lay hands on me?" Her voice shook with outrage. "Blind, I may be. But I am not without sight. Yes, I know who you are," she said and, as her sightless eyes turned toward him, Gunthar felt a chilling premonition. "Exiled prince of Deirmuch! Aye, I know your secret. Or do you forget that when the mind stone touched you I read your memories? And I know your real name, Eri—"

With a curse, he threw her across the furs. He stood, his legs braced and his fists clenched. His voice was a low warning. "Have a care, woman. Do not speak that name," he rumbled.

There was silence for a moment. Then she spoke softly; "I know what happened to you as a child. I felt it, as I feel my own heart beating now." She lay where he had thrown her. There was something in her voice. Not pity, remorse or grief, but something else... *understanding*. Gunthar looked down on her, his face a mask of conflicted emotions. He clamped down on his thoughts, blocking out the memories of a time long dead. But deep in his mind he still heard the screams... the roar of the flames... the savage laughter.

The queen of Brough-Tyr rose slowly to her feet and, coming toward him, moved her hand up to his face. "The pain and the guilt. They are not yours to keep. Release them." She spoke simply. At her touch, the thoughts fled and he stood in the room once more, gazing into the sightless eyes of a young queen wise beyond the length of her years. Who was she? A witch? A sorceress? He shook his head.

She kissed him then and he reached up, taking her in his arms. He met her kiss with a passion that surprised him and, as his hands closed on her soft flesh, she moaned with a great longing. For a moment they were locked in a hot embrace before he had lifted her up and carried her over to the couch.

*

The drilling of the warriors of Brough-Tyr was grueling, for both the fighters and the mercenaries training them. At last as, the sun sank in the west and night fell, the weary took themselves off to their chambers whilst the five mercenaries gathered together in the great feasting hall. Deep in their cups they sat, mulling over the day's events and the upcoming battle.

"What made you sign us up to fight in the cheerless land, anyway, cap'n?" It was Jal who spoke, his face flushed from the barley beer that slopped down his jerkin. Gripping the edge of the table with one hand, he sat swaying on his stool.

Gunthar looked at him.

"My sword arm wearied of slinging dice instead of well honed steel," he said, raising a wooden goblet to his lips, "When an agent from Caerdruhn came to Kulamir offering gold to fight in the northern reaches, I couldn't resist."

"Ahh, Kulamir," sighed Var, a faraway gleam in his eye. "That temptress! A whore, luring with promises of gold and glory. Yet, for many, payment is only death and a lonely grave."

"Especially should they meet *you* on a dark and lonely night," rumbled Jal. Turgun laughed. Var slapped Jal a playful blow on the back that sent the bigger man reeling.

"Enough," sighed Zandia. "We've seen the treasure. When do we get to fight?"

"We wait word from Queen Julinna's scouts," said Gunthar. "There's no reason to suspect Xomith knows the technology of the old ages is hidden here. But if he gleans information from those in Caerdruhn, it could be a matter of weeks, days even."

Var shook his head. He lit a pipe from a taper then, sitting back, thrust it between his teeth, the foul smelling aroma wafting across the table.

"That don't bode well for us, if you don't mind me sayin'. We haven't had time to prepare. Much as them boys like to fight, they ain't no Khumralan regiment."

"Aye," said Turgun, his long arms resting over the table, his head bowed between bony shoulders, "and we have to build chariots on site then train them in their use. We don't have time."

Gunthar bent his head and stared at them from under lowered brows. "We'll make time. We've fought overwhelming odds in desperate situations before. That's why we were hired. By Yod, there's no one I would rather have with me in a fight than you four. You've fought and survived where others have died. We'll make this work."

The others nodded. All but Jal. He shook his head. Slamming his goblet down on the table, he reeled unsteadily to his feet. "I think you play a reckless game with our lives, captain. That there queen and the sight of so much loot has blinded you to what we face." He looked at the goblet on the table as if seeing it for the first time and reached for it again. Realizing it was empty, he stared at it in disgust before flinging it across the hall. "Hah! Well, I'm to bed. Those boys need more shield work in the morning if they don't want to be target practise for Kalzhak arrows." With that he staggered off down the hall. There was silence for a moment then, with a sigh, Var got to his feet. Thrusting his thumbs through his belt, he took a deep puff on his pipe. "Aye, I'll be off as well. There's work to be done on the morrow and us Brokir are early risers. Good night all."

The others murmured their goodnights and the dwarf trundled off down the hall, mail clanking. The three sat back to brooding at the table. Zandia was first to speak.

"Jal's a trouble maker, captain."

Gunthar snorted. "I'll handle him. What of you Turgun? If you have doubts, I'd hear them now."

Leaning back, the tall mercenary placed his hands behind his head. He was youngest of the four, barely twenty summers. "I see the desperation in your plan, I don't deny it. But you're a good leader. If you say it'll work then my blade is yours."

Gunthar nodded. Zandia looked to him, her sky blue eyes clear. She had drunk little that night. "The same for me. You know I've always been the first to pledge my name to whatever mad scheme you concocted, even before you became our leader."

Smiling, the outlaw swordsman from the wild plains of Tatukura raised his goblet in salute. It had been little over a year since he had first ridden through the gates of Kulamir. It was there, in that infamous sprawl of iniquity known as the city of swords, that he had fallen in with the band of mercenaries known as 'the sons of the fallen.' Proving himself a keen strategist and an even keener swordsman, he had quickly worked his way up to rank of leader. Word got around of the prowess of this fighting band and it was not long before they were offered a kingly sum to fight in the northern reaches. They had left Kulamir for Brannica; a company of a hundred men, offering their services to Commander Arun in exchange for as much gold as they could carry. Of that hundred, only Gunthar and the four at his side now counted themselves among the living. It was a bitter toast he proposed to the two sat before him but he was never a man to show weakness or uncertainty.

"Best you both turn in," he said, "there will be more challenges on the morrow and we need to be ready to move at a moment's notice."

The two mercenaries nodded. They rose to depart, leaving their captain brooding alone in the great hall. And brood he did. He remembered again the runes cast by Runatyr and his prattle of a dark haired woman intertwined with his destiny.

That night he had spent with the queen had revitalized him. Somehow, he felt as if a healing had taken place within him. A healing that he had not realized he needed. The years spent between his childhood until the moment he had been found alone, starved and half frozen to death on the plains of Tatukura were a blur of painful memories. Those that had fled his ravaged kingdom with him into those hills had been slain by bandits. Hidden by his bodyguards, he had crawled away to die. The marauders had not seen him. They had looted their caravan then left. Seeing the smoking fires, others came and found him. They were tribesmen, outriders of the Yugur clan. On a whim, they took him in and gave him refuge. Under their tutelage he had learned to ride and fight from the saddle, to hunt the mighty *herthrung* of the plains. Among them he had become a man.

Then, after years spent on the steppes of Tatukura, riding under wild skies, he left to find fortune in civilized lands. He, who had been born and raised a prince in one of the most powerful untamed realms of the west, was now a penniless adventurer. But that other life was a distant memory now, scattered like ashes on the wind of his burnt ancestral home. Even his real name was forgotten by those that presumed him dead. Perhaps, secretly, he yearned for a peaceful life. Maybe the storm of the wild riders was not in his blood after all. He wondered what Batbayar, his adoptive father of the Yugur clan, would have made of that. He lifted the wooden cup in salute. Ha! He was Gunthar! The Black Wolf of Tatukura! He drained the cup and set it down again, smiling thinly. If this woman was interlinked with his destiny, he would know soon enough.

"To whom do you toast?" The sound of the voice startled him, bringing him out of his reveries. It was Kereth. Emerging out of the shadows, he came to stand at the foot of the table, wrapped in his dark cloak.

Sweeping up a bottle from the table, Gunthar frowned. "To the ghosts of dead friends, minstrel. If you've come to play a song for me, you're too late. You've found me in a sombre mood."

Kereth inclined his head. "No, my lord. I did not come to play. I came to speak."

Gunthar raised his head. "Then do so, freely."

Their eyes met and locked over the table. Kereth's eyes were like hard black stones over the beak of his arched nose. "Galan is a loyal man. He is a bully but he is also a fighter and will honour an agreement to the death. He will serve you well."

Gunthar nodded. "Aye, much as I thought. And you?"

The minstrel drew himself up. His face was taut and his eyes narrowed wickedly. When he spoke his voice was a low venomous hiss. "My loyalties are to the wellbeing of this kingdom and its queen. Have a care how you tread, mercenary. The halls of Brough-Tyr can be very treacherous for the unwary."

"A threat?" Gunthar arched an eyebrow.

From his robes, Kereth whipped out a sliver of steel that glinted in the candle light. "If you hurt her, you will die."

Gunthar picked up his goblet and drained it. Setting it down slowly again, he smiled. "Keep that instrument finely tuned, Kereth. There are many verses to be made of the upcoming battle.

I wouldn't want you to miss your opportunity for glory."

Replacing the poniard back under his cloak, Kereth turned and withdrew silently from the hall. Gunthar smiled and, reaching for the half empty bottle on the table again, poured into his goblet.

So it was that the long, weary night passed.

- 10 -

When the war horn sounds.

"The Kalzhak are on the move!"

The voice ripped into the mind stone that Julinna wore in her circlet crown. She bolted upright in her bed and saw, through the imprints on her mind's eye, the steel legions of Xomith's hordes marching through the early morning mists. She knew they came along the ancient crumbled roadway that wound through the fens toward Brough-Tyr. She saw the battered naked man that was their guide tethered by a neck halter to the rear of the war-chieftain's saddle who rode out in front. He stumbled along on naked bleeding feet this man and his teeth were bared in a grimace of pain. Behind them, she saw the army silhouetted in the mists, imposing in the dawn light, dew glistening on their weapons, leathers and furs. Their flat, slant eyed faces were resolute, their eyes bleak. Then she saw a huge golden chariot pulled by two strange beasts. Hybrids, with flaming eyes and black hairless skins, they snapped and snarled, foam flecking their gleaming fangs. The man in that chariot commanded attention and she realized that she gazed on Xomith, necromancer of Vorlishka. Wrapped in a scarlet cloak, his features were obscured by a black featureless helmet in which only the eyes glowed with points of hellish flame. He held the reins in a black gauntleted fist. The riders of the Kalzhak gave that carriage a wide berth and, as its wheels trundled over the crumbled pave, the muscular beasts that pulled it prowled close to the ground like gigantic agitated dogs. The sorcerer stood straight, his eyes fixed on the way ahead. Knowing the ultimate object of his desire, a chill ran down Julinna's spine. Reaching up to her brow, she touched the red jewel and at once the vision faded. Darkness fell like a curtain and she slumped back to the silken sheets of her bed. She lay there gasping for a moment, her naked body clammy with sweat. The touch of the mind stone always brought with it crippling head pains and she waited until the nausea passed. She must have cried out for the door to her chamber crashed open and Galan entered, sword in hand. He stood poised in the doorway, staring into the gloom. "My queen!"

    She rose slowly, one hand at her throat. "Muster the men and awake Captain Gunthar. Xomith comes."

*

Through the heart of the wet-lands, a long column of men marched in ragged formation. That line wound snake like beneath the eye of the red sun, from the foreboding walls of Brough-Tyr out into the dreary marsh. The men were dark and silent for the most part, slight and furtive looking, wearing scraps of metal and leathern armour. They carried their bronze shields over their left arms and gripped their dark spears in knotted fists. From under steel caped helms, golden eyes looked grim with purpose. These were the warriors of Brough-Tyr and, at their head, rode five outlanders. Spread out at the side of the column were a straggle of other riders mounted on zamas. Half way down the line moved the lumbering *herthrung*, great shaggy beasts of burden, groaning and complaining. Hairy mountains of muscle, they carried equipment essential to the army, forged metals that would later be used to assemble chariots crucial to their plan. Hidden deep in the heart of the column, Queen Julinna rode her mount and, beside her came Kereth, the minstrel. Up at its head rode Gunthar. He wore a simple leather jerkin with his red cloak slung from his shoulders. They marched on through the day with hardly a word spoken until the sun slid down the sky and their breaths came out in ragged mists. Shortly before dusk, they spied the humped hills of the valley pass and knew they had reached the plain they sought. The Brannica mountains loomed in the distance. The mercenaries fixed their eyes there, knowing that Xomith's legions would be fast approaching from the north along the ancient roadway that led into the valley. Turning in his saddle, Gunthar bade Galan give the order to slow pace. The captain bawled to the long serpentine column of leather and metal behind him; a forest of spears rising black against the slowly dipping sun. They made the valley before nightfall. Throwing themselves down on the hard ground of the plain before it, the warriors prepared to rest. Though no fires were lit, they were at least grateful to be out of the fens. Beyond the bulk of the Brannica mountains stars blinked out like tiny, glittering jewels.

   Gunthar sat on a rock with his bronze shield leaning beside him. Surrounded by his mercenaries, he ran a whetstone over the curve of his Tatukuran sabre. Julinna came walking up the incline to where he sat. Beside her was Kereth. The queen was wrapped against the night chill in a thick furred cloak. At their approach, Galan rose quickly to his feet and bowed. The four mercenaries looked up with interest. Gunthar stopped honing. Flicking the sword from his lap, he rose and sheathed it with a fluid motion. "Queen Julinna," he said gruffly, inclining his head. There was a note of awkwardness in his tone but he smiled and his emerald eyes were warm. He bade her sit, guiding her by the elbow to the large boulder he had just vacated. Kereth stood silently, his eyes unreadable in the gloom.

   As Julinna sat, she nodded and two men came from behind the minstrel, laying the armour of the old ages along with the axe and great hexagonal shield down on the ground.

   "The time has come for you to try on the armour," she said.

Thumbs through his sword belt, Gunthar stood frowning down at the pile of black gleaming metal. There was a breathless sense of expectancy as everyone stared. Shrugging, he bent down and lifted the pieces. Turgun got to his feet and helped Gunthar struggle into the greaves and breastplate. As the shoulder pieces came on, he felt as if the metal were shrinking to fit the contours of his body, almost as if it were molding itself to his movements. Last to go on were the gauntlets and, as he flexed his hands, he grunted incredulously. So precise and tight fitting were they that they may have been designed for him alone. He looked around, seeing the expressions of his companions. There were murmurings from the men of Brough-Tyr. Only Kereth stood looking without any display of emotion. Lastly, Turgun handed him the helmet and, bending his head, he put it on. He looked up through the slitted eyes and, as he did, he thought he felt a fierce joy surge through him. It was almost as if the armour were synthetically alive and glad to be grafted once more to a human body. Bending down, he picked up the dark axe in one hand and lifted the shield with the other. The eyes that beheld him at that moment gazed on him with awe. Gunthar felt an involuntary thrill. Somehow, he felt invincible—able to crush whole armies into dust! Julinna rose to her feet and coming up to him, placed a hand on the dark breastplate. The eyes of the helmet burned with vaporous fires as Gunthar bent his head. She lifted her face to his. "The more you wear the armour, the quicker you will bond," she said and her voice was quiet. Was there a hint of bitter regret at the edge of her words?

"The symbiosis between the artificial intelligence embedded in the helmet and your own mind will allow you to act faster and stronger. But be careful. As beneficial as the technology of the old ages is to us, it is also harmful and poisonous."

Gunthar only half understood her. He lifted the axe, feeling the rippling leaves of the armour as his arm flexed. Through the eyes of the helmet he could see clearer. Shadows in the cliffs took on bold shapes where only before were insubstantial smudges.

"No sword or sorcery shall harm you as long as you wear this armour," Julinna said, stepping back.

From where he crouched, Jal of Tharl chewed thoughtfully on a dry meat ration taken from his pouch. "A demon walks among us," he said.

Putting down the axe and shield, Gunthar reached up to the helmet. Twisting it once to the right and jerking it up, released it from the shoulder plates. He stood there holding the object in his hands. "I hope you have more than this to aid us on the morrow, Julinna. Yod knows, I fear to stand against no man in battle, but against Xomith's necromancy..."

The queen drew her furs closer about her. "Once we have drawn his army out into the valley, we'll spring the real surprise." Nodding to her guards, who slipped silently away, she added; "I have a plan."

*

All through the long morning, the men of Brough-Tyr crouched hidden among the rocks. They gripped their bows, staring silently down the broken trail that wound into the gorge. At the edge of the valley, men lay flattened in the long grasses, swords and axes ready. No movement betrayed their presence. They were still as the granite walls that reared above them. Sweeping up from the valley floor, among the boulders and stunted trees, at the far end of that pass, twelve chariots waited on the plain. The *herthrung* grazed contentedly now as the warriors waited patiently, honing their weapons and tightening their shield straps. There were no jests traded among these men only a taciturn silence. A cold wind blew, bringing with it vagrant drifts of sleet. Above, the sky was a dull metallic grey and the sun was a pale shield, barely glimpsed.

Running a hand through his tangled mane, Gunthar swept the crags below with a practiced eye. No hint of movement betrayed the archers waiting there. They were as silent and patient as the hills themselves.

Suddenly, a lean figure stood up among those rocks and waved an arm before sinking down again. Gripping his shield, Gunthar loped down the incline and clambered up the cliff face. Reaching the summit, he crouched at the side of an archer who pointed silently. Narrowing his eyes, the sell-sword stared down across the fens to the ancient road way far below. A steel tide was moving there. Dust rose in great pluming clouds and, although no noise reached them, he could imagine the iron jingle of harnesses, the tramp of a thousand determined feet. Staring at that army, he breathed a silent curse. He set his jaw and, turning, made his way back down to where the men stood with the chariots.

"A thousand men to our six hundred but we have the element of surprise and a few tricks of our own."

He stared solemnly into their faces. Jal of Tharl was suited in his plate armour, his mace resting up on his shoulder. Turgun's face was tense. He fondled the hilt of his long-sword in anticipation. In her tight fitting mail, Zandia stood with hands on hips. Her bow and quiver were slung over her back and a short-sword hung from her waist. Only Var of Brokir sat seemingly uncaring on a rock, thumbing the edge of his great double bladed war-axe and humming a dirge to himself. Clenched between his teeth was his pipe. Almost lost in the foam of his beard, the smoke curled into the wind.

"You know your positions. Take up your points. I have nothing else to say except fight well and lead your men to victory."

Each mercenary nodded then split to join their assigned division. Whilst Zandia joined the archers on the rocks at the side of the valley, Turgun made his way down to the infantry hidden in the reeds at the foot of the pass. Together, Jal and Var waited with their captain. The two mercenaries would lead a separate flank of foot soldiers each that would swarm down the pass and close the trap. Then would come the Black Wolf himself, leading the chariots to sweep away the remnants of the Kalzhak forces and crush Xomith and his war-chief. Holding his shield and staring down into the valley, Gunthar felt a sudden apprehension. Never had he planned such a strategic maneuver as this! A fighting-man and a captain he was, aye, but not a general. He glanced over at Zandia as she picked her way up the cliff face then across at Turgun as he made his way down the valley. The men at either side of him were silent. Lifting his great axe, Var rose to his feet and stretched himself onto the tips of his toes. There was an audible crack and he winced, putting a hand to his buttocks.

"Oleif's beard, getting old is no fun."

Jal frowned. "Just how old are you, dwarf? I can't tell through that beard."

Var took his pipe from between his teeth and looked thoughtful for a moment. He lifted a ringed hand and began counting on his fingers. "A hundret? Hundret and fifteen?" He shrugged. Jamming the pipe back into his beard, he planted both hands on his lower back and groaned loudly. "Too bloody old for this, anyway."

Behind them, crouched at either side of the small plain, among the stunted trees and boulders, a force of two hundred warriors knelt on the frozen earth. These men wore the most armour. They held bronze shields and carried axes, swords and long spears. Beyond them, hidden back in the reeds, were the twelve chariots with their drivers. Queen Julinna herself was assigned one and would ride armoured into battle with Galan as her driver. Gunthar was uneasy about the addition of her own plan but he pushed the thought aside, trusting to the main might of his own strategy to carry the battle through.

Morning turned to afternoon and the wind picked up, howling bitterly down the pass. With it came flurries of snow, making the rocks slippery and wet. They could hear the rumble and clank of arms now, the creak of wooden carriages as the army drew nearer. Soon they would be forced into the narrow end of the pass but Gunthar knew that before that there would be outriders, picking the way ahead, searching for any traps. Sure enough, before long, two mounted Kalzhak warriors came riding up the way. They picked their way through the long grass shivering in the wind and stared about them through slanted eyes. Sat motionless in the valley, they scanned their surroundings, sweeping the rocks above them on either side and fingering their short horn bows as sleet swirled about them. One leaned over his saddlebow and spat. Guttural words passed between them and they turned their mounts, cantering easily back down the road again. Not one man hidden in that valley did not breathe a sigh of relief as they did. If they were discovered before the trap was sprung, the element of surprise would be lost. But now, in their arrogance, the steel legions of the Kalzhak came marching to their fate.

The great cloud of dust drew nearer and it seemed the crags shook from the tramp of feet on the ancient pave. Then the head of the column entered the gorge. Most were mounted but many were on foot. Waiting at the summit of the pass, Gunthar felt the weight of six hundred pairs of eyes turned his way as they awaited his signal to strike. Slowly, he closed his fist as, through narrowed eyes, he watched the horde pour into the gorge below. Xomith had no reason to suspect the people of Brough-Tyr knew he was coming for their city. The Kalzhak came on unsuspecting and, as the first of the great column reached half way across the valley floor, Gunthar reared up, his bronze shield flashing in the light of the pale sun that had broken through the clouds. Beside him, Var lifted a two handed war horn and gave a deep throated blast that echoed thunderously from the valley walls.

Then—chaos!

There was a deafening roar as the cliffs came alive. Shadowy figures reared up and boulders tumbled down on men and zama alike, burying them in an avalanche of rock and dust. Arrows sang and each feathered shaft drove into a Kalzhak mark. They fell in droves. Some wheeled their mounts, seeking to fight their way back through the press but a thousand marching feet moving forward drove those mounts screaming back into the slaughter. From the reeds at the foot of the pass, a hundred men sprang up, their long spears taking a terrible toll on the zamas and their riders. Those that fell from the saddle were hacked to bloody pieces by the axes and swords of those hidden on the opposite side. The wind tore down the valley and all was a confused mêlée of dust and rock and blood and screams.

   Grimly, Gunthar nodded to the two remaining mercenaries stood on either side of him and they turned away. Behind them, two columns of warriors stood up from the rocks.

"To glory or death!" roared Var, wheeling his great axe over his head in a circle and indicating down the pass. Foam flew from his lips and his ice blue eyes blazed. Jal cursed, looking to his own warriors. Swinging up his mace, he shouted; "By the gods, don't let the dwarf steal all the glory! Onward!"

   As one, the two columns sprang into life. Down the slope they came, a hundred men to either side and, at the head of each, a blood crazed mercenary swinging steel. They crashed into the disorganized Kalzhak line like a thunderbolt. Men and zamas went down screaming as spears and axes splintered in the press. Looking at the battle, Gunthar's heart pounded beneath his mail. It was with effort he suppressed hurling himself headlong down into the fray. Stood alone watching his men, he bit off a curse and turned to face the chariots that had wheeled forward onto the plain behind him. He saw Julinna, resplendent in a glittering dress of mail. She gripped the rail of her chariot with her right hand and a huge round silver shield was slung over her left arm. As Galan drove the carriage forward, the other chariots reined up behind them in a phalanx. The queen stood imperiously straight, her eyes shadowed as if she stared into unfathomable spaces. The gem in her circlet crown was a deep and bloody crimson and he wondered if she were in communion with a mind stone somewhere deep in the heart of the battle below. Gunthar came striding up to her. He knew that time was of the essence. When his men were signaled aside, there would be only a brief window of opportunity for the chariots to strike. If the Kalzhak organized themselves before then, the battle would be irrevocably lost.

"Julinna," he said.

The queen reached a trembling hand up to the circlet on her brow then swayed for a moment, both hands on the rail. Galan steadied her and she shook her head. "Gunthar," she gasped, "we must wait. Xomith has entered the pass. But he is protected by his warlords."

"There isn't time," growled the sell-sword, "we must strike soon or they'll recoup and overwhelm us."

Julinna nodded wearily. "I understand. But if we strike now, Xomith will have us all in the gorge and we will be prey for his necromancy. Do not underestimate what is at stake here. We fight with more than just swords this day. Climb into your chariot and don the armour of the Old ages. It will inspire the men."

Gunthar scowled. "The men need to be inspired by you. Not by an accursed thing worn by a fallen champion. Order Galan to sound the war-horn and let's sweep these dogs back to whatever hell they crawled from."

Julinna shook her head. "I cannot. We wait."

For a moment the sell-sword from the wild plains of Tatukura stood silent. Then he turned on his heel, walking back to the slope overlooking the pass. Already he could see the tide turning as struggling knots of his warriors were forced back by the deadly flickering scimitars of the Kalzhak. The marauders had grouped together, forming a deep wedge at the centre of the valley. They pushed forward and the warriors below staggered against the fury of their onslaught. Gunthar grit his teeth. He wheeled, tramping back over to the chariots. "The Kalzhak are rallying. Men are dying. Your men! By Yod, sound the charge." He looked into her face and saw only a grim resolution. Galan looked awkwardly at his queen. He reached down, fingering the great war-horn at the side of the carriage. His face was pale. "Perhaps, my queen, we should—"

"No, Galan. I have spoken. The time is not yet."

Gunthar's eyes blazed. He saw it all now—the pomp and charade of kings and queens, the disregard for men's lives as so much dust beneath their feet. He threw back his head and laughed. Ripping out his sword, he raised it to his lips and kissed the cold steel between the hilt and the blade in mocking salute. He swung away and, with blade in hand, came down into the gorge after his men.

- 11 -

Against the horde.

On one side of the valley, high up on the cliffs, where the fighting had not touched, a lone figure stooped. He watched the lightning flicker of blades and the crashing storm of shields below with avid interest. At times, he murmured to himself, shaking his head from side to side. Other times he would wheeze and cough as if suffering some deadly illness. Although he wore nothing but a scrap of leather about his hips, he seemed not to feel the bitter chill of the wind. If not for his distorted and twisted appearance, he would have been considered a giant among men. One hand gripped the stump of a blasted tree now and he leaned forward, clenching his fist as if imagining himself deep in the heart of the battle below.

"What do you do here, Dukkan, champion of Brough-Tyr?" said a voice in deep, rich tones. "I thought your fighting days behind you. Or do you still yearn for the clash and clamour of swords?"

The malformed man wheeled, surprisingly quick for one of his bulk. He grunted in surprise. He saw a tall, brown robed man standing there, his cloak streaming raggedly in the wind. In one hand he held a thick staff carved with inscriptions. Long grey hair fell about his shoulders and, in the crag of a weather beaten face, blue eyes gazed with deep and unfathomed wisdom.

"Runatyr!"

"Aye. You did not expect to see me again, did you?"

"No."

"Then, perhaps, you should have stayed on your island and not come here where the fate of a nation hangs in the balance."

"You knew?"

"Oh, I knew you'd come. Despite what the poison of the old technologies has done to your mind and body, you shall always be the champion of Brough-Tyr."

Runatyr moved forward to join him at the lip of the broken cliff and together they stared at the battle below.

"Have you cast the runes?" Dukkan asked. Runatyr nodded. He pointed to the chariots waiting on the plain. "Your queen fears Xomith's sorcery, and with good reason. But her champion has taken matters into his own hands it seems." They looked down at the struggling mass of fighting and saw a golden maned warrior with a flashing curve of steel rallying the men. They pushed into the Kalzhak forces, splitting them apart though they were still out numbered.

"Impetuous! He does not wear the protection of the armour. Xomith's sorcery—"

Runatyr laughed. "Watch! Not for nothing was this man chosen by the fates."

As if in a dream, Dukkan watched the events of the battle unfolding below. As he stood staring enrapt at that moving panorama, it was as if all time ceased to exist. Then, when at last, the fate of the battle had been decided and the sun bled out its life in a stream of bloody fire across the western mountains, Dukkan turned with a great sigh to the figure of the man standing beside him. A strange look was on his misshapen face. Under the cold white glare of the distant stars, he stood motionless as a statue, deep in thought. Then; "If man can take destiny into his own hands, can he make a difference, despite the will of the gods?"

The old man drew himself up to stare at Dukkan thoughtfully.

His gaze was icy as the waves of the cold northern sea. Under that stare, Dukkan shivered.

"Why are you here?"

Dukkan crouched. At his feet lay an object wrapped in linen. Carefully unwrapping it, he lifted it in both hands. It was a gleaming silver sphere, the size of a boy's head. Runatyr drew back. His eyes looked into those of the champion of Brough-Tyr.

"Is this what you want?"

Dukkan nodded. The old man's face was immobile as a wintry crag. "Then come. The fates have been written and the runes have been cast. Let us honour the champion of Brough-Tyr one last time."

Holding the silver sphere in the crook of his arm, Dukkan looked apprehensively at the old man and then into the vale below. He looked up, blinking his huge great eye into the softly falling snow. Then Runatyr laughed, a great booming laugh. Sweeping his grey cloak wide, there was a howling rush of winds and then the cliff face stood bare and empty.

*

The sun was sinking in a muddy haze. In the wind swept valley below, men bled out their lives. A struggling band of warriors fell back from the press now, overwhelmed by the advance of the invaders. Among those digging their heels into the hard ground were Jal of distant Tharl and Var of Brokir. Mercenaries, owing allegiance to none beyond their last earned coin, they yet fought side by side, hacking and slashing as if that ground was their own. Occasionally, one of the warriors beside them would fall to the blood slick earth and it would be up to the others to cover them with wild swinging strokes before they regained their footing. Faces came and went in the fray, blunt, coarse faces, snarling in unbridled rage. Still the blades of the mercenaries rose and fell as they struggled to hold the line. The battle was becoming a rout.

The tides of fortune had turned swiftly. Whilst the men of Brough-Tyr were not lacking in courage, their lack of experience against their war-like adversaries was proving to be their undoing.

Jal, fending off the thrusts of a dozen blades, turned his shaven head to squint into the lowering sun. "Damn that witch! Where are the chariots?" he roared. Then, indicating with his heavy mace; "Make back for the plain!" As he spoke a scimitar swung for him and he countered with a back sweep of his own weapon, crushing the attacker's head in a scarlet mist of blood and brains.

"Stand fast, you worthless dogs, and hold the line!" a voice bellowed. Jal turned. Silhouetted in the lowering sun, he saw the Black Wolf of Tatukura. His blue mesh mail was rent and torn. The shield slung over his left arm was shattered and his sabre was a crimson blur. His lips were set in a maniacal snarl and, beneath his yellow mane, his eyes blazed like hot coals. Men fell before him and blades shattered beneath the fury of his strokes. He pressed on, swinging his rent shield like a weapon, smashing helmets and slashing throats with the torn edge. Ripping through sinew and bone, the curved Tatukuran steel in his right hand howled its blood lust.

"Haidul's shade!" gaped Var, pushing back his dented helmet. "It's Captain Gunthar! He's gone mad."

Even Jal's blood ran cold when he saw the crazed look in his captain's eyes. He turned back, swinging the great mace. "Well, a short life and a merry one it is, then," he growled. Crusted from head to foot in gore, the dwarf laughed as he swung up his double bladed war-axe. "Aye, lad, let screams and steel be music to your ears!"

So saying, he drove forward, his axe crushing through armour and shields alike. Half a dozen savages lay around him and his mailed feet spurned their corpses. They knew the day was lost. But Gunthar's battle madness was infectious. The warriors of Brough-Tyr surged forward, their spears driving into furs and mail, their short swords hacking into flesh and bone. For a moment they were as frenzied as their foes, driven by primal passions as old as time. Even Jal lifted his head to laugh at the jest of it all.

Just then a wailing shriek cut in over the wind. The men of Brough-Tyr started, looking up from behind their harassed shields. There was nothing human in that cry. It grated in their ears and sent shivers down their spines. As it faded, the warriors of the Kalzhak fell back, taking up defensive positions as they began moving swiftly back down the pass.

It seemed then as if a great silence had fallen over the valley. Only the wind, the sleet against their numbed faces, seemed real in a landscape marred by violence and death.

Jal let his mace thud to the ground. He leaned panting on the blood slick haft as the remainder of the company came trudging toward them. Zandia, with her troops who had charged down the cliffs after laying the first ambush, and Turgun, with his men who had hewed their way up the pass. Battered, begrimed and weary from the day's fighting, they came to stand around Gunthar and, as they did, a fierce grin touched the captain's lips.

"What now? Where the hell are those blasted chariots?" growled Jal.

Gunthar glowered from under his sweat tangled mane. "We wait."

The big mercenary bit off a curse. Turgun looked around him. His hauberk and mail was covered in dust and gore. Hefting a sword over his shoulder, he shrugged; "As well make a stand here than die with an arrow in the back."

Weariness was evident in the lines of all their faces. But there was a defiance in their eyes, a defiance that spoke of a determination not to go down without a fight.

Yet the battle had taken its toll. They knew it would not be long before the whole army was driven back and they were swept away by the madness of the slaughter.

Lifting his sword, Gunthar pointed at the retreating Kalzhak. "Whatever they're planning, make formation and hold best you can," he growled. "If a man falls, close ranks and hold the line. Take two lives in return."

Beside him, Zandia gripped his arm, indicating a crag of rocks standing high up on the western ridge.

On that crag stood a small group of men. Prominent among them was a tall figure, his head encased in a sinister black iron mask. In a gauntleted fist was a black orb cut with runic symbols. It throbbed and burned as with a dark flame. The sorcerer lifted that orb now and, as he did, he leaned into the wind, his long scarlet robes swirling about him. The eyes of the mask burned as they looked directly into the valley below.

"Xomith!" breathed Zandia, her eyes widening in awe.

Gunthar scowled. "What deviltry is he up to?"

Suddenly, a warrior cried out, pointing with his spear down into the gorge. Every face turned to where he indicated.

Sheltered from the lowering sun, the foot of the pass was swathed in shadow. Somewhere deep in that darkness, grim figures came shambling up out of the gloom. As if through the haze of nightmare, the warriors watched the tattered, decaying corpses of men lurch and shuffle to the head of Xomith's army. They stood there motionless, swaying in the wind; lifeless husks, dressed in tattered mail, carrying notched swords and axes. Beneath iron helms, pale faces stared glassily into the distance.

"The war dead of Caerdruhn!" a soldier gasped, "See the insignia on their shields? Xomith raises the dead and sets our own blood brethren against us! We cannot fight them."

Gunthar glared past those silent ranks at the Kalzhak. The squat, slant eyed warriors were forming into a line. He saw the bending of short horned bows and, with a curse, looked to his men.

"Shields up! Look alive, dogs!" he roared just as a hundred bowstrings snapped and a hissing storm filled the sky. He barely had time to fall to one knee and raise his own mangled buckler before the arrows began to descend. He felt the impact, the wicked barbed heads penetrating through the battered bronze held above him. Beside him, he heard screams as the shafts struck home. Relentlessly, they drove into mud, armour and flesh alike. All around, men were falling, their cries cut short by the sting of black driven shafts. In droves, the army of Brough-Tyr were cut down like chaff before the scythe.

Suddenly, that deadly rain ceased. A deathly silence followed and, lowering his bristling shield, Gunthar came erect to survey the carnage. His lips bent in a grim line. The four mercenaries rose and stood staring with him. Scores of men lay in rows, their bodies sprouting arrows.

At the opposite end of the pass the Kalzhak horde... *waited.*

That strange skirling cry sounded again and, on top of the ridge, Xomith raised the dark glowing orb in his hand.

With a tortured groan, the line of living dead began to move...

- 12 -

Night of the living death.

"So this is how it ends," murmured a soldier. He raised the cross guard of his short-sword to his forehead, invoking the name of Tyr twice. All around, other warriors were doing the same, muttering the sacred oath of their kingdom. Gunthar tore his eyes from the army of advancing corpses to look at the faces of the men around him. He knew a sudden fierce pride for this fading race standing up against the dark of oblivion.

Zandia fingered the hilt of her sword. The red scarf wound over her brows was grimed in dust. Narrowing her eyes, she indicated up at the ridge. Xomith had gone. Only the darkening sky met their gaze. Then there was a skirling of pipes and a dull boom as of swords beating against wooden shields. Looking into the pass, they saw the necromancer in his war-chariot moving behind the slowly advancing warriors of the undead. A gauntleted fist held the reins and the eyes of his black helmet burned with yellow fires. The mutant hybrid dogs that pulled his carriage strained and slavered as if hungry for human flesh.

Gunthar's eyes blazed. *Oh, to be within sword's reach of that dog!* Casting aside his ruined shield, he rolled his shoulders.

The shambling horde of the dead were half way up the pass now, their axes and swords hanging in their hands. They moved awkwardly, their heads lolling to one side. They could see the gaping slackness of their dark mouths now, the hollow blankness of their eyes... Then, from behind them, Xomith raised the black orb. Spidery flickers of dark lightning played out from it, caressing the heads of the walking cadavers in front of him. When those flickers faded, their heads raised, the weapons in their hands lifting in a sharp etched display. Open mouths gave vent to a hellish scream and, as one, the undead began to charge headlong up the pass toward the living!

The line would have broken then if not for Gunthar. "Alright, men!" he roared, "let's skewer this carrion meat and send them to the hall of shades where they rightly belong. Present spears!"

The first line dropped to one knee. Ramming the butts of their pikes into the ground, they angled the tips. The undead horde came rushing in, seemingly oblivious to the forest of steel that awaited them. Gunthar stood with sabre in hand.

Suddenly, a loud horn blast rent the sky followed by a deep rumbling sound that shuddered the very roots of the mountains. Jal cursed, turning to see the gleaming chariots of Brough-Tyr descending down the slope behind them. The mighty *herthrung* snorted and bellowed as they came, the chariots thundering in bronze wheeled rage. Two abreast they rode.

"Break!" shouted Gunthar and, as pre-planned, the line split in the middle to allow the chariots to come through. In thunder and dust, they swept down past the warriors to open out in a ragged line. They crashed headlong into the advancing undead horde, crunching bone and smashing armour beneath the hooves of the great beasts and the bronze wheels of the carriages. Corpses rolled, only to jerk spasmodically and reel up onto their feet again. But, as the chariots came, Gunthar saw that each driver held clasped in their hand a long black rod with a smoking red jewel at its tip. He saw Julinna, her silver shield slung over her left arm, her midnight hair streaming out behind her, the jewel in the circlet on her brows throbbing a bloody crimson. In her glittering dress of mail, she looked like a war-maiden from some forgotten legend of her peoples. Hunched over the reins was Galan, lashing frantically like some mad fiend from the abyss. Held in the queen's hand was a lightning rod and, from it now, blue flame arced out to strike an undead warrior in the chest. He disintegrated in a burst of cryptic fire. Only the melting steel of his armour and weapons remained. Again and again, those lightning rods flickered. The chariots swept through the ranks of the undead and, where each flame found its mark, an ensorcelled cadaver burst into flame to melt in a puddle of sloughing flesh and steel.

Gunthar threw back his head. "Well? What are you waiting for?" he roared, thrusting his curved steel into the darkening sky, *"For Brough-Tyr!"* His words were greeted with a tumultuous yell. As one, the dark warriors lifted their shields and began surging forward. Those of the undead that stumbled up and made it past the chariots were met by the spears of the foot soldiers. Impaled on their lances, they were driven back and hacked into bloody pieces by crazed warriors wielding axe and sword. Jal pulped the head of one with his mace but the faceless corpse kept on coming, swinging steel in wide circles until he was brought down by a dozen thrusting spear points and his limbs were hewn from his body. It was dirty, vicious work and even the big armoured mercenary from Tharl looked pale as he stepped back from the spattered mush on the ground.

Gunthar leaped past his spearmen to confront an undead warrior swinging an axe. Ducking beneath its whistling edge, he slashed out, the cold Tatukuran steel in his hand tearing through the legs and leaving bloodied, hanging stumps. The cadaver crashed to the earth and, rearing up, the sell-sword brought his sabre down in a flashing arc that severed the head in a bloodless, grinning mask. Despite this, the corpse still sought to lift itself from the ground. Gunthar grunted in amazement. Stalking over to one of the Kalzhak slain, he snatched up a spear and, returning, drove it down though the undead warrior's back, pinning him to the earth.

Just then a lone chariot came trundling down the valley slope. It reined up beside him, the *herthrung* snorting and pawing the earth. Seeing the driver, Gunthar set a foot on the writhing cadaver and folded bloodied arms over his spattered mail. "Kereth!" he said with a cheerful grin. "Are you lost? Your mistress is already deep in the heart of the fray."

The minstrel frowned. His jaw clenched and his dark eyes flamed. "I do not fear battle if that is your implication, mercenary. I have been instructed to find you."

Gunthar stared at the battle raging around them. Then, ramming his bloodied sword into his scabbard, he gripped the side of the chariot and swung himself in.

"Indeed, minstrel! And what for?"

"The queen desires that you wear the armour and join her in striking Xomith. The time is now."

Kereth pointed past the heaving knots of men fighting in the valley to the chariots below. Above them, in the darkening sky, the lightning of the black rods flickered and flamed. But Gunthar saw what the minstrel had missed. The Kalzhak were loathe to confront those bronze wheeled carriages. Yet Xomith's own war-chariot was charging forward now, cutting a devastating swath through the defender's ranks. The huge teeth of his mutant dogs snapped and snarled in rage. Men went down, crushed beneath those powerful jaws or else were hurled through the air, torn limb from limb. Behind his steel car came the Kalzhak to cut down the wounded, their scimitars whickering into flesh. Directly in the path of those mutant dogs and that steel carriage was Queen Julinna. Gunthar's blood froze and he ground out a curse. "Galan, you fool!"

Oblivious to the doom advancing towards them, the dark captain swerved the chariot in a wide semi-circle as the queen struck out with the black rod at more of the undead. Where that blue flame struck, flesh and steel melted into smoke.

Wrenching a bronze javelin from the side of the carriage, Gunthar hefted it grimly. "Get us down there, minstrel."

"The armour, axe and shield. She instructed me—"

Gunthar looked at the armour of the Old Ages, netted and tied at the foot of the carriage. He gestured impatiently. "There isn't time. Get me within spears cast of that dog is all I ask." The minstrel looked for a moment at the dour faced mercenary then turned back to the reins. He lashed the *herthrung* and, as if from a catapult, the chariot shot forward. Into the valley they came, sweeping over carpets of the dead and avoiding struggling knots of figures clashing on the battlefield. The lines were broken now as chariots swerved in and out of the conflict, striking down what was left of Xomith's reanimated army. But not all the battle was one sided. Kalzhak arrows hissed through the air. Drivers fell and rod wielding warriors went down, grasping at black shafts driven through their necks.

Under the cold etched stars their chariot swept, the bronze wheels spurning the ground. Kereth bent low, holding the reins in both hands. Beside him, Gunthar stood with legs wide braced, the javelin drawn back in his right hand for the killing cast. As Xomith's war-chariot swung toward that of the queen of Brough-Tyr, they swerved recklessly into its path. The wheels grated together for a moment before they crashed, side on. Metal ground on metal in a torturous screech and an axle splintered, crushing a wheel beneath the sorcerer's carriage. In a bound, Gunthar was out of the chariot, yelling a war-cry. The javelin drove down and Xomith turned, the eyes of the mask spitting flame. Straight across the face that bronze tip slid, gouging a furrow. But it was not enough. Although a powerful thrust, the sharp edged bronze barely made an indent in that sinister black mask. Xomith's gauntleted fist swung and Gunthar's head snapped sideways as he was flung back into the foot well of the sorcerer's chariot. Both carriages came to a shuddering stop.

Entangled in the traces, the two mutant dogs reared up snapping and snarling. Sinking their powerful jaws into the *herthrung*, the animal bellowed in pain, its thick neck snapping under those iron slavering fangs.

Gunthar rose, bracing himself groggily with both arms against the sides of the car. His teeth were bared, his nose a bloody ruin, as he faced the necromancer. He bent to one knee, his hand groping for the javelin on the carriage floor. Braced against the further rail, Xomith thrust back his red cloak and raised the black orb in a gauntleted hand. Dark fires crawled along its surface, dripping venomous sparks. Staring at it, Gunthar's flesh turned cold. He heard a low slithering laughter come from the depths of the sorcerer's mask. But the sell-sword was only dimly aware. The world swam in a murky haze now. He felt himself pulled down, a darkness dragging at his soul from the aura of that uncanny orb. It was as if his mind were being drawn into an unfathomable void...

"Gunthar!" He heard his name shouted, but it was as if over vast oceans of time. Then he felt pain sear across his right arm. He jerked it back, spitting a curse. Looking up, he saw Kereth leaning between the two smashed carriages, a poniard dripping darkly in his fist. He saw the slice across his forearm, the blood flowing in rivulets over his wrist guard. Drawn back, as if from a vast precipice, he shook his head. *"Hah!* Thanks, minstrel. This jest isn't lost on me."

Kereth raised an eyebrow. "Nor I, mercenary."

Gunthar reached down to his boot top and, coming up, flung out his hand. There was a flash of silver and the sorcerer caught the hurled knife in a gauntleted fist. Flinging it aside, he laughed hollowly. "Fool! For that I will have your mind broken. Your corpse will join the ranks of the living death. You will know terror before you die, warrior. Look deep into the heart of the dark flame of Avkhurl. Look and know fear!"

He raised the dark globe once more and it seemed to grow gigantically in his vision, filling the universe with cyclonic black winds. It blotted out the landscape, the valley, the very stars themselves. With a growl, Gunthar snatched for his sword hilt but that burst of dark flame had dazzled him. The ground dissolved beneath his feet and it was if he were falling into an endless chasm. He heard laughter, mocking and hollow. Buffeted by whirlwinds, it seemed as if he were being dragged into the depths of that dark globe, sucked into a maddening vortex in which nothing was real—*not even himself.* He screamed then but the sound was lost in the maelstrom of Xomith's unholy sorcery...

- 13 -

The black throne.

There was a moment of sickening vertigo in which the world was torn apart and then just as suddenly reassembled. After what seemed eons, the wildly spinning universe began to right itself. As sanity began to seep slowly back into his consciousness, Gunthar opened his eyes. He found himself crouched on the ground, his sabre in his hand. The din of battle was eerily silenced. Only a dreary wind sighed and, lifting his tangled mane, he looked around. Nothing met his gaze. There was only a wide sweeping plain of black volcanic rock, scarred and pitted. Dark columns reared here and there under the eyes of the stars. Before him, shouldering the moon, was an iron black citadel. Gunthar knew a strange sense of foreboding when he gazed upon it. Never before had he seen such a piece of architecture. Carved with strange hieroglyphs, it seemed incongruous in this far northern land. Behind the tower was the surface of a dark lake, its mirrored waters reflecting the constellations. He came slowly to his feet. His head pounded and he felt a momentary weakness. Hearing a soft groan to his left, he turned and saw Kereth holding his head in his hands. Aside from them, they were alone in this desolate place where only the winds moaned and ebon columns reared like obelisks beneath the moon.

"Where in the nine hells are we?" muttered the sell-sword.

The minstrel retched on the hard ground and Gunthar laid a hand on his shoulder. "Easy, minstrel."

Kereth shook his head. "Xomith's domain. He has brought us here. For what nefarious purpose, the gods alone know."

The ground beneath their feet was fused solid. Here and there, volcanic glass glinted in the moonlight. The ebon columns gave off a deep throbbing sound, humming with some strange archaic force. Before them, the black tower loomed, its aura pregnant with unknown danger. Kereth shuddered and drew his cloak closer about him. Then, glancing at his feet, he pointed; "Look!"

Huddled in a pile of netting was the armour of the old ages. "I remember falling to the floor in the chariot when Xomith's black globe started to spin. I must have clung onto it."

Gunthar's jaw clenched. He looked to the armour, saw the dark axe and the hexagonal shield, then back at the archway of the iron tower brooding in the distance. He sensed something evil beyond it and his skin crawled. Cursing, he bent down and raised his hand. "Give me your knife." When Kereth did as he was bade, he sliced through the cording and began slapping on the armour. Clamping the greaves on his arms and legs, Kereth helped him with the breastplate and shoulder pieces. Again, it seemed to meld itself to his body, enmeshing him as if it were a second skin. He lifted the streamlined winged helmet and placed it over his head. His own sabre, he slung over his back. A gauntleted hand grasped the axe and, lastly, he lifted the great shield. He turned, the eyes of the helmet glowing with a feral light. All around them, the ebon columns pulsed and throbbed.

"This a cursed place," murmured Kereth. "A land of madness and shadows. It is forbidden to our people. Little wonder Xomith decided to make his stronghold here."

Gunthar stared at the mouth of the citadel. He could feel vibrations emanating from it now, pouring out in a cold wave of evil toward them. He pointed with the axe. "Something waits and is watching us."

Kereth swallowed. His eyes hardened. "I fear death as much as any man, mercenary. But promise me this. Promise that you will take that dark axe and slay me when the necromancer comes to enslave our souls."

Gunthar glared at him through the eyes of the helmet. "If any should fear for their soul this day, minstrel, it should be that corpse raising dog."

"What do you intend?"

"To tear down his citadel."

Kereth's laugh was short and bitter. Suddenly, his eyes went wide. Gunthar swung round. Something was emerging from the mouth of the citadel. Two shapes that spurned the ground like sleek ebon shadows. As they drew closer, they saw that those shadows were beasts. The same sort of giant mutant hybrids that had pulled Xomith's chariot. They came loping toward them now; juggernauts of death, iron curved teeth slavering in the moonlight, growling with the lust to kill. Gunthar crouched, raising the hexagonal shield before him, his eyes burning with an empyreal light over its edge. He leaned back, the axe held low in a gauntleted fist. "Behind me," he said in a hollow booming voice.

No sooner had he spoken than the first hybrid was on him. It came in fast, snapping and snarling, red eyes blazing with feral lust. Bracing his feet, Gunthar sprang to meet its charge. The edge of the shield swung in, slamming the giant head aside. Foam flew from the beast's lips then he was borne backward by its rush. At the same time, the dark curve of his axe swept out and, as they hit the ground in a rolling heap, blood jetted from the gaping wound in the creature's neck where the blade had followed through. The creature's howl shuddered the stars and Gunthar rolled, staggering to his feet. He whirled, turning to meet the second beast. Its jaws were nearly on him and he swung the great shield blindly, the iron fangs crunching into the ebon metal. Again the dark axe swept out, the blade shearing through bone and matter. The giant skull disintegrated under that wheeling stroke in a spattering slush of brains and gore. Killed instantly, the body sagged to the ground and Gunthar staggered back, wrenching his shield from its jaws. The first dog was circling warily behind him now, whimpering and whining, crawling on its belly. Its red eyes burned at him even as the wound in its neck still spurted blood. Although close to death, the beasts overriding instinct was to rend and kill. The circle was narrowing now and Gunthar followed its movements, his shield ready and his axe raised. Close to his back, Kereth gripped his poniard. Suddenly it sprang in and, twisting to one side, he allowed the beast to pass. Its claws scrabbled frantically on the hard rock and, as they did, a back handed sweep severed the beast's hind leg in a single shearing blow. It screamed in rage and pain then collapsed. Once, twice, it tried to rise before Gunthar stepped up and slammed the dark blade down in a whistling stroke that crushed its skull.

Kereth looked on in stunned amazement. He saw the grim clad figure of the mercenary rise, the axe dripping darkly in his hand, the eyes of the helmet blazing.

Gunthar felt an involuntary thrill surge through him. It was as if the armour vibrated to the tune of his actions, fed him symbiotically with its power. He lifted his head. Across the way he saw the gloomy archway of the tower. He growled then, a low ominous sound from the depths of the helmet. "Now for Xomith," he heard himself say, but it was as if those words were not his own. Mechanically, he began marching forward, his head bent low, the axe and shield held out to either side of him.

"Wait! It could be a trap!" called Kereth.

If he heard, the sell-sword from the wild plains of Tatukura paid no heed. As he came striding up to the dark maw of the citadel, the ebon columns began to hum and crackle to a deafening pitch. Gunthar stopped, looking around. From column to column, blue flickers of flame passed then suddenly lashed out toward him. Instantaneously, he fell to one knee, raising the great hexagonal shield. The lightning struck its surface, spitting and crackling. For a moment it seemed as if he were bathed in a blue aura, so intense was the fury of that strike, coiling and crawling about him in frenetic waves. Then it stopped and he rose, his armour smoking, the great shield glowing white hot fire for a moment before fading into nothing. It was as if the shield had *absorbed* the energy cast at it. Dark laughter sounded from inside the helmet and Kereth's blood froze. For that laughter was not the laughter of Gunthar. It was not even the laughter of a man. He hung back, clenching his long-knife, wondering if the armour of the old ages had unleashed a demon more frightening than Xomith himself!

Gunthar stepped up to the tower. There, on the threshold, his eyes swept the gloomy interior. He found himself looking into a vast hall. The floor was of black polished glass. Down its length, mighty columns marched row upon row in single file, rearing up into midnight darkness. At the far end, upon a flight of carven onyx steps, stood a black throne. To either side of it braziers burned with a hellish green flame. That throne was intricately built, fashioned entirely of human skulls. Stained black by some arcane art, their hollow eyes flickered in the light cast by the lurid glows, their teeth bared in eternal deathly grins. Upon that seat sat a figure in a rich scarlet gown. The black featureless helmet faced him across the hall, its eyes slitted and glowing as if awaiting some final judgement.

So this was the lair of Xomith, the faceless one, the necromancer of Vorlishka. And here was his black throne—his unholy seat of power, from where he directed atrocities against the cities of Brannica. Gripping the haft of his axe, Gunthar stepped into the hall. His booted feet rang on the polished surface of the floor and, as he walked, his eyes scanned the shadows lapping around him. Xomith leaned forward, gripping the arms of the throne in gauntleted hands.

"You have overcome much, warrior. Who are you? The champion of those fading people? You are nothing! Only the armour serves you and once I have boiled you inside it I will rip it from your still steaming corpse. The technology of the ancients will be mine."

"What power could you want, you midnight dog, that you do not already possess?"

For a moment the figure on the throne sat silent. Then a hollow rasp echoed from the depths of the black mask. "It will matter little to you as you shall soon be dead. I am dying. For centuries I have kept this decrepit body alive by virtue of my mask. But it is not enough. My necromantic arts fail me and I rely more and more upon the technologies of the past. I have travelled here from the desert lands, rousing the Kalzhak from their Granite Wastes. I promised them weapons that would make them invincible in war. Their penchant for cruelty and torture pleases me. But my need is of a different kind. The ancients, you see. They unlocked the doors of life. I must have a serum I know exists somewhere beyond the walls of your city. The weapons, the technology, all these mean nothing to me. But life! Ahh, that means everything. That is why I must take the city you call Brough-Tyr and plunder its secrets. But now... now you stand in my way and I must destroy you."

As he spoke those final words, Xomith leaned forward intently. For a moment no words were spoken as the black armoured warrior and the sorcerer glared at each other across the hall.

Then something landed heavily on Gunthar's back and he was brought crashing to his knees. Something slimy and writhing grappled with him there in the darkness and he felt the things fetid breath close to his ear. He braced the edge of his great shield into the floor and, with straining effort, sought to rise. He heard tittering, insane laughter. Saliva dripped from a cavernous mouth that hissed and burned corrosively through his shoulder plate. It singed his flesh and he roared in pain, forcing himself back onto his feet, the thing still wrapped and clinging to him. The weight of it staggered him and he lunged back, swinging his shield wildly, seeking to crush it into the arch of the wall behind. Green mottled arms coiled about his throat in a vice like grip. He had a fleeting glimpse of large webbed hands and thin whipping tendrils. Dropping his axe with a ringing crash, he reached up and, grabbing a writhing appendage, bent forward. Carried by its own weight, his assailant flew over his head. Staggering back, Gunthar reached for the axe and, sweeping it up, brought it down on a brown mottled creature that was seeking to lift itself from the floor in a writhing mass. Dirty brown ichor spurted and the thing's frog like mouth opened in a silent yawning scream. Horribly human eyes blinked up at him. As if gripped in the throes of a nightmare, he heard words, strangled and rasping, issue from the thing's throat.

"Kill... me... please... "

Gigantic webbed hands grasped at the iron greaves of his boots.

"Kill... me... "

In disgust, Gunthar buried his axe deep in the thing's skull. Wrenching it out with a cry of revulsion, he staggered past its odorous corpse into the hall.

"You have just slain the king of Brannica. What a pity. I thought to have more fun with him. He was an amusing pet for a while."

Gunthar shuddered to think what depravities had turned that once stoic ruler into the vile creature he had just slain. He lifted his head, glaring at the figure of the necromancer down the hall, the eyes of his helmet burning white hot slits of flame.

Then, without warning, Gunthar flung his axe.

End over end it whirled, a sharp edged fang of death. By the time Xomith saw it coming, it was too late. He jerked back and the blade struck the front of his helmet, shattering the unearthly metal in twain. The sorcerer screamed. The sundered half of his mask fell to the dais steps with a resounding clang. The axe bounced away, spinning into the shadows. Lurching upright, Xomith raised a gauntlet to his face. He reeled, making desperate passes in the air and shadowed winds reared up, enveloping him in a dark embrace. When they had died, the black throne stood bare and empty.

Snarling an oath, Gunthar loped over to the foot of the throne, his shield raised.

The necromancer had vanished!

- 14 -

Of wolf and mask.

Thunderous laughter echoed throughout the tower, shaking the columns. Gunthar staggered as the floor beneath him trembled.

"I OFFER YOU LIFE, WARRIOR. LEAVE NOW AND NO HARM SHALL COME TO YOU. STAY AND YOU WILL KNOW TORMENT UNENDING."

The words reverberated throughout the citadel, shuddering the very walls. Throwing back his head, Gunthar roared; "It is you who will know torment, sorcerer! The torment of fear as I carve your bones. Face me! My blade yearns to kiss your decaying hide!" The challenge echoed throughout the citadel and, for a moment, there was silence. Then the green vaporous flames of the braziers died and the hall was plunged into gloom. As if by an invisible hand, from behind the throne a door opened, illuminating a silver stair that stretched up into darkness. Warily, Gunthar crouched down, reaching for the haft of his hurled axe. Rising with it in his hand, he padded past the throne and mounted the gleaming stairway. It wound around the great citadel in a curving arc. Inside the helmet, awareness was a super heightened reality. Clenching the dark axe and the ebon shield, he followed the steps. He took them two at a time now, aware that at any moment a trap could send him plummeting to his doom.

Phantasms whirled about him, plucking at his breastplate. He swung his shield and they evaporated before its sweep like ghostly cobwebs. Grimly, he pressed on. Now it seemed as if everything dissolved around him into soft emptiness until only the stair remained, suspended in space. Stars gleamed in the blank vastness of his surroundings as he followed that stairway into a fevered infinity.

"You cannot win," a voice whispered from around him in that vast canvas of night, *"Turn back and save your soul..."* In the void, gigantic flames of light burned and he saw the shattered mask of Xomith hanging above him. A monstrous gauntleted fist swept down, wrapping its great steely fingers about his torso. Lifting him from the stair, Gunthar struggled in that vice like grip, felt his ribs creak beneath the weight crushing his armour. The arm holding the axe was pinned to his side but his shield arm was free and he held it above him now as he was drawn ever closer to the ruin of the shattered mask and the flaming eye hanging above him. His face purpled with effort and he felt blackness fog his brain. Gargantuan laughter nearly burst his ear drums. Inexorably, he was drawn toward the white hot flame of Xomith's vengeful eye. He felt the heat, the dazzling glare, as it filled his vision. At the last moment, he wrenched his head away...

Then he was in the citadel once more, standing on the stairway. Laughter sounded, taunting and mocking. Despite himself, he felt fear. It gnawed at his innards, held him rooted to the spot. Above, he could see a faint light, the etching of a doorway. But his brain was numb, turned to ice by a terror such as he had never known. His legs trembled and his arms felt heavy, weighted down by axe and shield. He wanted to flee this terrible place, to run until his legs could carry him no more. Then a spark flitted in the deep recesses of his brain. He remembered a fearful child on the escarpments of the steppe, his mind filled with terror from the monster that had stalked his dreams with slavering fangs and baleful eyes. That monster he had once beheld manifest in the flesh, watching him from the high plateau of a ridge. He had run then, grazing his legs on the sharp edged rocks, his hunting spear and bow forgotten in his young hands.

"What was it you saw?" had asked Batbayar, his adoptive father, later that night.

"A black wolf, father," he had replied, edging closer to the dimming fire, "A giant wolf. He haunts my dreams, hunts me, and howls when he knows I am afraid. Now he is out there... waiting."

Batbuyar had stared at him over the flames. "No. He is you. He is your fear. To tame him, you must become him. You must become the black wolf."

The Black Wolf!

Something stirred deep inside the pit of Gunthar's stomach. That feeling spread quickly like wildfire through his veins until it consumed him. He remembered then what he was. Opening a gauntleted fist, he let the axe fall to the marble at his feet. In rage, he flung the shield from him and it bounced clattering down the stairway. Hands tore at breastplate and shoulder pieces and, as he wrenched them off, he cast them aside. Lastly, he tore off the black helmet. As he hurled it down the stair, he laughed; the snarling laugh of a blood mad wolf. In his tattered shirt of mail, Gunthar snatched up the wooden scabbard of his sabre and tied the sword belt about his waist. The blade sang into his hand and he rushed up the remainder of the stairway on naked feet, his face contorted with rage.

He came to a silk hanging and through it saw Xomith, dread necromancer of Vorlishka. Tearing the curtain aside, he faced the sorcerer.

Xomith stood waiting. Behind the shattered ruin of his helmet, his face was a mask of debauched evil. He tore it off now and dropped the remnants to the floor.

"So outlander," he hissed, looking directly at Gunthar through the hollowed pits of dead blank eyes, "...you would damn your soul for a witch slut and a ruined kingdom!"

Crouching low in the doorway, Gunthar raised his blade in one bronzed fist.

"Aye, dog! Now prepare to greet your own dark god—in hell!"

Falling back, the necromancer reached inside his robes. When his hand came out it held a long, thin metal tube, the open end of which he pointed at the warrior's chest.

Tensing his long legs under him, Gunthar sprang just as Xomith pressed a stud on the back of the cylindrical object. Gunthar felt his entire body wrapped in a web of crippling pain. His slashing stroke went awry, the blade hissing an inch away from the sorcerer's scalp. He crashed to the marble floor and, with a curse, reeled up. Blood started from his nostrils at the pressure from the invisible ray being exerted upon him. He struck out blindly but the ray held him back; made his blow weak and ineffectual.
Xomith leaned over him, his face lit by an unholy, fanatical joy.

"Fool! Did you think to defeat me? You, but an untutored savage untrained in the arts of thaumaturgy?"

He moved forward, increasing the intensity of the beam's ray until Gunthar, weak and dazed, could barely lift his steel.

As the sorcerer's face leered down in gloating triumph, the air behind him was disturbed by a vagrant gust of wind. Xomith whirled to see two figures standing there. At the sight of them, he recoiled in horror. The first was a man old as weathered stone. His grey hair fell about his shoulders and he wore a simple brown robe, belted at the waist. In his hand was a thick carved staff. Towering behind him was a monstrous figure, stooped and hunched with misshapen features wearing nothing but a scrap of cloth about his hips. In the crook of one arm he held something that resembled a gleaming silver sphere.

Released from the beam's rays, Gunthar gasped and rolled quickly to his feet. He staggered back, blinking in amazement at what he beheld.

"Xomith!" the man with the staff cried. "You have brought

about your doom."

The monstrous figure of the naked man lumbered forward. In his arms was wrapped the metallic sphere. A huge eye gleamed with secret triumph as he confronted the sorcerer. "I am the champion of Brough-Tyr. This is from the crypts of our city. My gift... to you."

He held out the gleaming sphere and twisted it in both hands. It came apart, the centre throbbing with a glowing red and yellow heat. A whining noise sounded, rising in pitch and volume. When he beheld it, Xomith fell back, whimpering like a child. Bathed in the sphere's glare, Dukkan's face was one of ecstatic joy. Runatyr looked to Gunthar and, raising his staff, indicated the long black window behind him. "Go, warrior. Go and know that your destiny has been fulfilled."

The hairs rose on the back of the warrior's neck when he beheld that shrieking silver sphere. He did not want to be around when that banshee wail reached its crescendo. With one glance behind him, he hesitated, staring at the long ebon window. Beyond it he saw the bloated face of the moon. Time ceased to exist in that moment as if, somehow, he had lived these moments before. He heard Runatyr's final word, shouted now over the deafening wail of the silver sphere. "Go!"

Whirling, Gunthar launched himself at the tall glass, his sabre slashing out before him. As it connected, he followed through, the moon shattering into great ebon shards. Then he was falling... falling down, in a wailing gust of wind as glass glittered all around him in gleaming fragments. He knew not what strange things were about to occur in the tower above but he knew that a clean death on the rocks below was preferable to whatever horrors awaited him there. Even as he thought these things he saw the mirror of the dark lake rise up beneath him and then he had struck the cold glacial waters. For a moment he knew nothing as he was swallowed down into its icy depths. Then, with a powerful kick of his legs, he broke the surface. Flinging back his hair, he gasped.

His body was numb from the impact but he was alive! Amazingly, he still gripped the hilt of his sword.

Just then, from the citadel, there sounded a dull booming noise. He turned his head. The whole tower began to collapse inward, sucked into a formless vacuum. There was no explosion. Inexplicably, it just began to disappear. The waters of the black lake began to seethe, following that rapidly vanishing citadel into an imploding void. Dragged down, Gunthar was helpless in the grip of the rushing waves as they pulled him toward the centre of a forming whirlpool. Fighting the tide, he kicked and struggled but to no avail. Powerless, he was borne along in its grip. The waters seethed and he was tossed high into the air by a crashing wave. At the bottom of that wave was a swirling hole and, as he slid down its sides, he felt the mud and detritus of the lake's bottom. Scraped along, he remembered the sword in his hand and reversing the grip, plunged the blade deep into the thick mud wall. He clung on grimly as the waters rushed by him and then all at once there was a back wash that flung him rolling across the drained lake bed. He lifted himself to his knees, coughing and retching in the thick sludge. Looking behind him, he saw a crater where the citadel had once stood. The high obsidian rocks of the lake's banks reared above him and he staggered wearily to the nearest side. Sheathing his sword, he began to climb. He had almost made it to the top when a hand reached down and clasped his forearm. With a heave and a strain on both sides, Gunthar came up onto dry land. Lying panting on the rocks, he looked to see Kereth lying and looking almost as exhausted as himself. "By the gods," the minstrel panted, "what manner of man are you? True to your word, you tore Xomith's citadel down."

Turning to look at the black crater where the citadel had stood, Gunthar grunted. "Not quite. I had some help."

Sitting up, Kereth pointed. "Someone comes."

Gunthar jerked to where he was looking. From the crater, a small figure was making its way toward them from across the fanged rocks. He carried a long staff and his grey hair streamed in the wind. As he came closer, he stopped to regard the two men. He lifted his head and stood gazing off into the distance. "The power of the black throne has been broken. Return to your homes and know that victory belongs to the people of Brough-Tyr. Brannica sleeps easy again."

"Who are you?" Gunthar asked, getting to his feet.

The old man regarded him through eyes cold as breaking ice. "I am the wind and the moon, the sun and the sky, I am the betrothed of the earth."

Reaching to his waist, beside his dagger in its ornate sheath, he pulled from his pouch the flat stones with the curious markings. "The runes will fall and the runes will speak. I am their servant and their master, as are we all. Now, I bid you go. Your work is done here and the threads of destiny are a-weaving once more." He dropped the runes with a clatter and, as they fell, it seemed the stars were extinguished from the sky and the moon was hidden. Then, as suddenly as they had vanished, they re-appeared. But the old man had gone. Kereth started. With a gasp, he laid a hand on his companion's shoulder. The stars were strewn once more in the firmament above them. But there was a difference. They were back on the battlefield in the valley.

- 15 -

Queen of the night.

The sun stared down from a featureless sky. Not a cloud disturbed the vastness for as far as the eye could see. Yet it was cold and the northern winds still shuddered and prowled throughout the halls of Brough-Tyr as was their want.

The city had seen much celebration over the last few days in an almost fevered abandonment. It was as if the people had woken from a cold winter and had warmed to the sun to embrace life in all its hot, stinging glory. But now the festivities were at an end and the people retired back to their lives behind the walls of their vast, ancient city. As they did, Gunthar felt a restless need for the warm climes of the south.

The battle of the valley pass had taken many lives, among them two of his own.

Jal of Tharl and Turgun would no longer ride with him under the hot sun, nor trade jests with him over the fires of dismal battlefield camps.

Jal had been brought down by a Kalzhak arrow. He had died with a curse on his lips, leading the men of Brough-Tyr in a final concerted rush against the horde.

Turgun met his end at the hand of Tremuk, war-chief of the Kalzhak. Defending the queen of Brough-Tyr, he had yet proved no match in sword play against the chieftain of those wild nomads and had died with the Kalzhak's scimitar through his heart. Disgraced in honour and made an outlaw in life, he had yet died protecting a queen. Not minutes later, the war-chief himself was brought down by a sword thrust from Zandia who, during a crush in the fighting, had rammed her own sword blade deep under his heart.

It was then that the deciding fate of the battle was cast and the Kalzhak fell apart to be destroyed by the fire rods of the chariot riders. In the rout, Galan had taken a sword blow to the shoulder. Severely wounded, he had driven the chariot until passing out from lack of blood. He still lived, tended to now by the city's finest physicians.

Var of Brokir had glutted his fill in the slaughter. He was beside Jal when a Kalzhak arrow took him down and was with him as he breathed his last. A berserk rage had fuelled the dwarf and his axe was stained crimson with the blood of many nomads. Those that made it back to the Granite Wastes would whisper fearful tales of the dwarves of the northlands and their supernatural abilities in battle.

Alone now, in a chamber in one of Brough-Tyr's highest forgotten towers, Gunthar faced Queen Julinna for the final time. The night they had spent together had been one of unrivalled passion. Now, in the crisp light of the early morn, the warrior from the wild steppes drew on his war-boots and threw about him his scarlet cloak. The queen rose and placed a hand on his shoulder. "I promised you the treasury of my kingdom in return for our freedom. I do not go back on my word."

Taking her hand, Gunthar grinned. "So much gold would only weigh us down. We've saddled up enough already, don't worry about that. Besides, you have given me more than you know, Queen of Brough-Tyr. There is a shadow in me less dark, because of you."

Julinna's lips curved into a smile. "For that, I am happy. Yet I am sad at so much death. Dukkan... "

"Died a man. A champion. If not for him, I do not know that we would have won."

The queen nodded and closed her eyes. "What will you tell the people of the southern cities of me?"

"That you are a proud and beautiful queen."

"That I am a witch?" she asked mockingly.

He grinned. "No. That you are a fighter and that you love your people."

She sighed. "My kingdom fades. We are passing into dusk and I am a queen leading them into the darkness."

He shrugged. "All things must pass."

Reaching into his pouch, he held something which he pressed against her fingers. An oddly shaped object of glass. "I will take this with me to Tarkaresh after all," he said gruffly, fondling the mind stone. "Who knows? If one day it starts gleaming I can show whoever is watching the wonders of the world."

Julinna smiled. "Goodbye, Gunthar, and good fortune."

He nodded and turned to the door.

*
—

A cold wind blew under the pale disc of the sun, sweeping out across the fens. Reining his zama, Gunthar looked to the two riders behind him, his cloak fluttering in the wind. In the distance the brooding walls of Brough-Tyr shouldered the morning sky. His eyes lingered there a moment before he turned his head and breathed deep of the crisp morning air. Puffing on his pipe, Var of Brokir hummed a vibrant song to himself, a marching song of the mountains. Zandia was quiet, her long golden hair streaming in the breeze. Each rider wore new clothing and their saddlebags bulged to bursting. Life was good and the road was clear.

"Where to now? Back to the city of swords?" asked the swordswoman.

Gunthar shrugged. "I say the coast. Three swords will make better coin in Tarkaresh."

Just then Var jerked back on his reins. His companions followed to where he was staring, their hands lowering to their sword hilts.

In the distance, beside the fallen arch of an ancient ruin, they saw a brown robed figure. Proud and tall he stood, leaning on a thick staff. For a moment it seemed he was watching them. Then a grey shadow passed over the sun and he was gone. The dwarf shifted the axe across his back. "By Haidul's shade, I saw him walking among the dead on the battlefield. I thought I had gone mad with the battle lust."

"I saw him, too," murmured Zandia. "Yet he only came among the slain of Brough-Tyr."

Gunthar leaned on the pommel of his saddle. "These hills are old! Older than our reckoning. There is magic in them. Aye, and in the blood of her people, too. Who knows what gods of the ancient times still dwell here?"

They rode in silence down to the sea.

Printed in Great Britain
by Amazon